D0765159

CALGARY PUBLIC LIBRARY

OCT - 2011

BLOOD AND
OTHER CRAVINGS

Also Edited by Ellen Datlow

Blood Is Not Enough

Alien Sex

A Whisper of Blood

Little Deaths

Off Limits

Twists of the Tale:
Cat Horror Stories

Lethal Kisses

Vanishing Acts*

The Dark*

Inferno*

The Del Rey Book of
Science Fiction and Fantasy

Poe:
19 New Tales Inspired by
Edgar Allan Poe

Lovecraft Unbound

Tails of Wonder and Imagination

Darkness:
Two Decades of Modern Horror

Digital Domains:
A Decade of Science Fiction
& Fantasy

Naked City:
Tales of Urban Fantasy

The Best Horror of the Year
Volumes 1–3

Supernatural Noir

With Terri Windling

Sirens and Other Daemon Lovers

A Wolf at the Door:
and Other Retold Fairy Tales

The Green Man:
Tales from the Mythic Forest

Swan Sister:
Fairy Tales Retold

The Faery Reel

Salon Fantastique

The Coyote Road:
Trickster Tales

Troll's Eye View:
A Book of Villainous Tales

Teeth:
Vampire Tales

The Year's Best
Fantasy and Horror
First through Sixteenth
Annual Collections

The Adult Fairy Tale Series

Snow White, Blood Red

Black Thorn, White Rose

Ruby Slippers, Golden Tears

Black Swan, White Raven

Silver Birch, Blood Moon

Black Heart, Ivory Bones

With Kelly Link
and Gavin J. Granvt

The Year's Best
Fantasy and Horror
Seventeenth through Twenty-first
Annual Collections

With Nick Mamatas

Haunted Legends*

*A Tor Book

BLOOD
AND OTHER
CRAVINGS

Edited by

Ellen Datlow

A Tom Doherty Associates Book
New York

This is a work of fiction. All of the characters, organizations, and events portrayed in these stories are either products of the authors' imaginations or are used fictitiously.

BLOOD AND OTHER CRAVINGS

Copyright © 2011 by Ellen Datlow

All rights reserved.

Tor Books Editor: James Frenkel

A Tor Book
Published by Tom Doherty Associates, LLC
175 Fifth Avenue
New York, NY 10010

www.tor-forge.com

Tor® is a registered trademark of Tom Doherty Associates, LLC.

Library of Congress Cataloging-in-Publication Data

Blood and other cravings / edited by Ellen Datlow.—1st ed.
    p. cm.
  ISBN 978-0-7653-2828-1
  1. Vampires—Fiction.   2. Horror tales, American.   I. Datlow, Ellen.
PS648.V35B54 2011
813'.08738—dc23

2011019917

First Edition: September 2011

Printed in the United States of America

0 9 8 7 6 5 4 3 2 1

Copyright Acknowledgments

"All You Can Do Is Breathe" copyright © 2011 by Kaaron Warren.

"Needles" copyright © 2011 by Elizabeth Bear.

"Baskerville's Midgets" copyright © 2009 by Reggie Oliver. Originally published in *Madder Mysteries*, Ex Occidente, 2009. Reprinted with permission of the author.

"Blood Yesterday, Blood Tomorrow" copyright © 2011 by Richard Bowes.

"X for Demetrious" copyright © 2011 by Steve Duffy.

"Keeping Corky" copyright © 2011 by Melanie Tem.

"Shelf-Life" copyright © 2011 by Lisa Tuttle.

"Caius" copyright © 2011 by Bill Pronzini and Barry N. Malzberg.

"Sweet Sorrow" copyright © 2011 by Barbara Roden.

"First Breath" copyright © 2011 by Nicole J. LeBoeuf.

"Toujours" copyright © 2011 by Kathe Koja.

"Miri" copyright © 2011 by Steve Rasnic Tem.

"Mrs. Jones" copyright © 1993 by Carol Emshwiller. Originally published in *OMNI* magazine, August 1993. Reprinted with permission of the author.

"Bread and Water" copyright © 2011 by Michael Cisco.

"Mulberry Boys" copyright © 2011 by Margo Lanagan.

"The Third Always Beside You" copyright © 2011 by John Langan.

"The Siphon" copyright © 2011 by Laird Barron.

I dedicate this book to Jim Frenkel,
and thank him for his continuing support
of my work over the years.

Contents

BLOOD AND
OTHER CRAVINGS

Introduction

Vampires have been with us for a very long time. If one wants to research the roots of vampire legends, there are folktales and myths from which our contemporary notions about vampires can be traced. And of course, Bram Stoker's classic *Dracula* is undeniably a work that has inspired countless subsequent vampire tales, both in print and on the screen.

But in the past few decades, vampires have become more than popular—they have become hot—in commercial terms and also, often, sexual ones. One might trace the rapid increase in the popularity of vampire tales to the 1976 publication of Anne Rice's breakout novel *Interview with the Vampire*, or perhaps to the 1977 Broadway production and subsequent 1979 film version of *Dracula* starring the young, handsome, sexy Frank Langella as the eponymous count.

Béla Lugosi as the count in the earlier stage and film versions of Dracula was a figure of menace and creepiness, with his heavily Hungarian–accented English, piercing gaze, and portentous delivery ("I never drink . . . wine," pronounced *vine*). Despite the fact that he tended to victimize young women, and there was an undeniable element of domination in the power he wielded over them, there was nothing like the sensuous, titillating appeal that oozed from Langella's landmark performance.

Since then, vampires have been a staple in books, stories, films, and on television, and in the past ten years or so, they have led the way to enormous popularity of a panoply of franchises based on one type of supernatural creature . . . and often a whole crew of creatures.

While Anne Rice's vampire series continues to sell, Stephenie Meyer's Twilight saga, Charlaine Harris's Southern Vampire series (with Sookie Stackhouse), and Laurell K. Hamilton's Anita Blake series have become popular phenomena far more successful than any of their type that came before. They're just the tip of the iceberg, though. There are others: Kim Newman's Anno Dracula series, L. A. Banks's Vampire Huntress series, Brian Lumley's Necroscope saga, Sherrilyn Kenyon's Dark-Hunter series, Chelsea Quinn Yarbro's Olivia series and Saint-Germain chronicles, the Vampyricon by Douglas Clegg, and other long-running series that just sell and sell and sell.

If you're looking for stories that focus on the sensuous side of vampires, you probably want to find another book. Some of the stories here have sensuous elements that will inflame readers' interest. But these tales are about much more. More than sex; more than blood.

Two anthologies I edited, *Blood Is Not Enough* (1989) and *A Whisper of Blood* (1991), were World Fantasy Award finalists. In each of those books, there were some traditional vampire tales, but also stories that went well beyond the idea of the traditional vampire as a bloodsucking creature of the night. Now, after two decades of increasing sophistication and invention in the realm of vampire fiction, writers have developed a greater range in their conception of what we might call a vampire.

The stories presented here ask you to consider a creature that can be in all ways human, and yet craves, for whatever reason—physical, psychological, or emotional—the satisfaction of feeding upon *something* from another. What the vampiric person drains from his or her victim might be blood, but it might also be the victim's energy, or the unfortunate's will to live, or perhaps even something else of the victim's substance.

Such themes were explored in the previous two anthologies, but I hope you will agree that the tales that follow offer new and thought-provoking approaches to traditional modes of the vampire story. There are two reprints and fifteen original stories by a roster

of authors who have distinguished themselves in many previous
works of fiction. They hail from the United States, England, Canada,
and Australia, sharing a bond of nothing but the theme described in
the title, *Blood and Other Cravings*. All the stories are contemporary,
some have actual vampires in them, but many deal, in a variety of
different, unique ways, with the "other cravings" part of the title.

To be more explicit would spoil the fun of discovery. So I will
leave you to the tender mercies of the authors and their inventions.
If you are ready for dark imaginings, I trust you will not be disappointed. There are some extremely dark tales ahead.

Good hunting.

—Ellen Datlow

ALL YOU CAN DO IS BREATHE

Kaaron Warren

Kaaron Warren's first short-story collection was the award winning *The Grinding House* (CSFG Publishing). Her second collection, *Dead Sea Fruit*, is published by Ticonderoga Publications and is shortlisted for two Ditmar Awards. Her first novel, *Slights*, (Angry Robot Books) won the Australian Shadows Award for fiction, the Ditmar Award, and the Canberra Critics' Award for Fiction. Angry Robot Books also published the novel *Walking the Tree*, (shortlisted for an Aurealis Award) and most recently, *Mistification*.

Warren lives in Canberra, Australia, with her family. Her website can be found at kaaronwarren.wordpress.com.

Stuart lay trapped underground for five days before the tall man appeared and stared into his eyes.

He thought he sensed movement. Flicked on his cap lamp—"Barry? Did you make it through the wall?"—but there was no one here.

There was something though, in his face, so close he pulled back and banged his head on the rock behind. He shouted, mouth open, squeezed his eyes shut. He'd never felt such terror, not even when his daughter had fallen into the pool and they didn't notice for god knows how long.

This was a man. Something like a man. Tall, elongated, the thing looked deep into his eyes. It reached out and almost took his chin with its bony fingers, keeping his head still, paralyzing him even though it wasn't actually touching him.

Stuart could smell sour cherries, something like that. It made him hungry, and that hunger somehow beat out the terror.

He pulled his head backward. The man nodded, stepped back, and was gone.

Within a minute or two, Stuart was sure he'd imagined it. Though he had words in his ear. "See you soon, Stuart." He was sure he'd heard those words.

It felt like the walls were getting closer, but he kept testing by stretching his arms and the distance was the same. The part of the mine he was working had collapsed so quickly, it seemed like time stopped and froze, and when it started up again, he was surrounded on all sides by rock.

Barry, his workmate, was on the other side, but he'd heard nothing from him for twelve hours now.

Thank god for the luminous hand on his watch. The kid gave it to him for Father's Day years ago, and even at the time he'd been thrilled. You don't always get that with Father's Day presents.

It wasn't what you'd call a worker's watch. It was full of gadgets, like the watches of the office men who drove to work each day, passing him as he stood, cold in the dark, at the bus stop with the other miners. Their cars blinked with gadgets.

This watch kept perfect time, and followed the date, and the hand provided a warm green glow in the pitch black. At home he had to keep it in his bedside drawer at night because the light kept his wife awake. But he could still see the thin green line across the top of the drawer where the light escaped.

Since the walls came down, he'd slept sporadically, waking a couple of times thinking he was home in bed because of the glow. He'd covered it up with his lunch box and only a small line escaped.

He had his cap lamp, but he really didn't want to use that. There'd been mine rescues lasting two weeks, and he wanted to know he could have bright light if he needed to. He knew they wouldn't give up. They never left a body underground, mostly because they didn't want it found much later.

He had his GPS so they knew where he was. He could see Barry's blip, too, but that didn't mean he was still going. Just his GPS.

Stuart stretched his legs and arms out and in, counting to a hundred. His wife was always on at him to do more exercise, so she'd be pleased to see him do this. His water and food had run out on the third day. He knew there was no sense keeping the food. It'd just go off and make him sick. Some gritty water dripped down the wall. Licking it made his tongue ache it was so cold, and there wasn't enough of it. He pissed into his water bottle and knew that drinking it wouldn't kill him. He pretended it was lime cordial, the sour stuff, not the sweet.

Foodwise he knew he could last without for a while, but it didn't help the hunger pains. Lucky his wife packed him heaps and there was Barry's lunch as well, on Stuart's side of the wall where Barry couldn't get to it.

He'd tried moving the rocks but it just caused more of a tumble no matter where he took the rocks from. He wanted to keep trying but his instincts told him just to leave it.

Bugs skittered about and he could eat them. The strap of his lunch box was leather and he chewed on that, making jokes that it was about as good as his sister-in-law's roast dinner. If he got out, he'd make that joke and people would write it up and his sister-in-law would be famous for her bad cooking.

Stuart tried to sleep when he figured it was nighttime outside, to keep a routine going. It was hard without a change of light and with an empty stomach, and he hadn't done anything to wear himself out. Usually he'd drop into bed after a shift and a feed exhausted. On a Saturday, if he hadn't been in the mine, he and his wife might have sex, but it wasn't something he thought about much.

He thought about it now.

He spent a lot of the time with his eyes closed, but he tried not to think about the dark. Instead, he went through football matches he remembered.

It was seven days before they found him. Nowhere near the record, but enough to have a media frenzy going on. As they were getting close they'd managed to get a tube through to him, and sent him notes from his wife and daughter, and bags of glucose. They dropped some biscuits down, too. "I was hoping for a meat pie," he called up the tube. He could talk with his mouth close to the tube, tell them shit he wanted his family to know. Tell them all the jokes he'd thought up while he was down there. Nothing worse than a joke without an audience. They called questions down, like, "Are you scared?"

"Naah, I'm not scared. I'm fearless! Nothing scares me!"

He asked them about Barry and they said they were working on it. Ever since the long man had visited him, Stuart had had a bad feeling about Barry. He thought perhaps that was Barry's ghost and he felt bad about screaming. He wished he'd said, "G'day, mate," whatever.

It was overcast when they pulled him out, but still far warmer than inside the mine. It meant he didn't have to squint because of the sun. His wife, Cheryl, was there, and his daughter, Sarah, and for a long time he couldn't talk, just held them and cried. He'd never actually cried before, not since he was a little kid, anyway, but this he couldn't help. He thought he'd never see them again and he loved them, loved them hard. Sarah looked so beautiful, so grown up for her thirteen years. Underground he'd imagined her future. In his darkest times, like the hours after the long man disappeared and he felt like giving up, he imagined her future. Who she'd be, what she'd do, who she'd marry. What her kids would look like. He dreamed it all in case he didn't get to see it, and now, there she was.

His rescuers were there, too. None of them keen to go home. Dirty faced, exhausted, he couldn't believe how happy they were to see him. He knew he'd have to live well, every day of his life, to justify what they'd done.

"Where's Barry? Did you get him out yet?" he asked once he'd had a warm drink. They loaded him into an ambulance although he said he felt fine.

"They haven't got Barry yet," Cheryl said, but her eyes were downcast and he knew she was fibbing. She didn't do it very often and he thought only to protect him. Like the time half the mine was shut down and the wives knew about it first. And the time Sarah had broken her arm because of the kid next door. Cheryl didn't want to tell him that because she knew how angry he'd be, but he didn't do anything about it. The kid was never allowed in their front door again, but that was it.

"I'd rather know than not know," he said.

There were news cameras, people with microphones and others with notepads.

"Why do you think you survived?" they shouted at him. "Why you and not Barry?"

The tears took again at that and Cheryl squeezed his hand hard. The ambulance crew shut the door and then it was a week in the hospital before he had to face the questions again.

They told him about Barry once they thought he was all good. Barry'd been trapped, his leg under the rocks. Stuart could imagine how bad that must have felt. So Barry tried to cut his way through, Jesus, cut his way through his own leg.

They said he bled to death.

"He wrote you something while he was down there," Cheryl said.

"He was always scribbling, that Barry. He'd write a letter to the Pope if he could get the address," Stuart said. It was an old joke, which made him tear up, thinking that Barry would have laughed at this one.

"He was hallucinating, they reckon. But still. You should read it."

I thought you'd got through the wall, Stu. I didn't hear you but heard a rock shift so thought you must be to my left. You wouldn't answer me so I cracked the shits. I couldn't turn my body but turned my face as far as I could, twisted my cap lamp around to catch you. I figured you wanted to kill and eat me, that's how stupid I was.

    Wasn't you.

    My light went right through this thing. I could see it, though. Looked almost like a man, but stretched out like a piece of bubble gum or something. Or when you press Blu-Tak onto newspaper and get some print and stretch it out. Like that. He had long fingers, twice as long as mine. Dunno if you heard me scream but this thing freaked me out. It came at me and I would have pissed myself if I wasn't already sitting in my own wet pants. It leaned forward and put its eyes real close to mine. Stared into me. I screamed my head off, no reason, just scared shitless. It came at me, touched my nose with its long finger, then it shook its head and drifted back.

    I thought, shit, it's going to Stu, and I screamed louder. I wanted to warn you. But what do you do? I didn't know what to tell you.

    I don't know if I'll last until they find me. Tell my mates they did me proud and if you can find my mother tell her I'm sorry.

"Do you know anything about this long man, Stuart? Did you hear anything, see anything?" his wife asked him.

Stuart nodded. He spoke quietly. "I saw a man like that. I thought I must have imagined it. But maybe it was a ghost. Maybe someone died in there and he was looking at us, going, 'You're not going to make it. No way. You're going to die.' Because he made me feel so bad I almost wanted to die."

"That's awful, Stuart. We're so lucky to have you back." He kissed her, as he did any chance he got.

"Maybe keep it just between us for now. About this long man. Other people won't understand it. Don't tell the media types. Okay?"

"You think I'm crazy."

"No, I don't. But I know you and they don't. Just keep it to the simple stuff, hey? Shouldn't be hard for you!"

He discovered he was good at talking. Cheryl thought it was funny. "You're a gabber now, Stuart. Couldn't get ten words a day out of you beforehand!" She fixed his hair, getting him ready for the next press conference.

"Yeah, well, they're always asking me for answers," he said. He didn't mind. It was always the same thing, so he didn't have to think too hard. This one, the room was packed. They knew he was fully recovered and had some others to talk, too. The mine owner, who Stuart had never met. One of his rescuers. And some doctor, a psychologist.

They had a good go at the mine owner for a while about responsibilities and compensation, then they turned to Stuart.

"Did you always think you'd be found?"

"I always expected to be found. I'm a bit like that. I expect I'm gonna get good luck. Just that kind of person. All credit to the rescuers, though. I can't believe those guys, still can't believe what they did. We'll be friends for life because of it."

The rescuer next to him clapped a hand on his shoulder.

"Was there any time you wanted to give up?"

He thought of the long gray man and the feelings of despair he'd left behind. They wouldn't believe him if he talked about that, think he was mad.

"Nah. I just thought of my wife's pot roast and that got me through."

"What is it you've got? Why did you survive and not Barry?"

"I can't answer that."

The psychologist stepped in. "There are many reasons why people survive. For Stuart, he had thoughts of his family to sustain him. Barry didn't have that and studies have shown it makes a difference. Also, Stuart was less dramatic in his actions. Maybe he thought ahead a bit more, and maybe Barry thought he could get out of it."

"You're saying it's Barry's fault he was trapped? His own fault he died?"

"No. Not at all. But the fact is that Stuart thought it through and trusted the rescuers."

"Do you think yourself lucky, Stuart?"

"Couldn't be luckier," Stuart said. "Luckiest man left alive."

"I'm sure your rescuers will be happy to hear that. Do you feel any sense of obligation to them? Do you owe them anything?"

"Yeah, look, they're all spread out around the place, but they can come to my place for a feed any time they like. And you know what I really owe them? I owe them a good life."

He and the rescuer shook hands, and the cheering of the audience went on for two minutes.

"What do you say to the idea that some people don't survive because they may have died helping others?"

"Yeah, well, if I coulda helped Barry survive I would have."

"What about his food? Is it true you ate his food?"

"Yeah, I ate his food. He couldn't get to it and it was only going off. That's not what killed him."

The psychologist said, "It is true that often it is the survivors don't help others. Especially in times of famine. Survivors are the ones who will take food from a child's mouth."

Stuart felt stunned. He wasn't sure how the conversation had turned against him and what a hero he was, but it seemed it had.

"All I did was survive," he said. "No one had to die for me to survive. I did it because I love my family, I love my life, and I wanted to get here on TV for the free beer I've heard about."

With that, he had the audience back.

Afterward, there was plenty of beer drunk. The crew took him out to the local pub and he was there long after they left. People had watched the interview and they all wanted to talk to him about it.

"If only we could bottle what you've got, there'd be no little kiddies dying of cancer," people said to him more often than he wanted to hear.

"If only we could bottle it, you'd be a rich man."

"If only we could bottle it, we'd save the world."

They thought he had some magic power, that it wasn't a willingness to drink your own piss and a great desire to have proper sex with your wife again, it was something else. Something they couldn't have.

He took a drink well but even he was feeling a bit woozy by around midnight. By 3 A.M., the pub was almost empty. He could no longer remember who he'd spoken to, so when a sad-faced man said hello, he nodded and went back to his beer.

"Hello, Stuart," the man said again. His voice was soft. It had an amused tone, as if he knew more than other people, found something amusing. Stuart no longer wondered how people knew his name. Plenty of them did. He rather liked the celebrity. He'd always enjoyed making connections with people all over.

Stuart looked at him this time. "Do I know you?" he asked.

His teeth were bright, white and even. Clearly false. His hair, pale blond, sat flat on his head. He smelled strongly of aftershave, the kind Stuart used to smell wafting out of the cars while he waited for the bus. His mouth drooped. *Sad man*, Stuart thought.

"How are you holding up?"

"I'm okay. Bit tired."

The man moved so that he looked directly into Stuart's eyes. Stuart froze. This is how the apparition in the cave had looked at him. With this intensity. He was used to people staring at him greedily, but this was different. The sad face, the long arms. Long, long fingers.

It was the apparition from the mine.

The man's hand went out and grabbed Stuart by the wrist with a powerful grip.

"Hold still, Stuart. This won't take long."

Stuart shivered, feeling as cold as he had underground. Chilled to the bone and dreaming of snow.

"Leggo, mate, wouldya?" he said. He tried to pull back, but he felt a deep lethargy, as if he'd been injected with golden syrup and his limbs couldn't move.

The man raised his other arm and brought it up to pinch the bridge of Stuart's nose. Stuart was paralyzed. He wanted one of the other drinkers to intervene, to hit the man, knock him away, but no one did. It was so quiet Stuart felt as if he were back in the mine and the idea of it made him choke.

No. It wasn't that. He had a nose bleed, blood pouring backward down his throat because the man held his sinuses so tight.

He let go and Stuart slumped forward, spitting blood. He felt movement return.

Turned his head away from the man.

The man bent and helped him up. "Nose bleed, nose bleed, make a bit of room, I'll take him and clean him up. Nose bleed, he'll be fine."

Stuart tried to pull his arm away. His mouth was full of blood.

"Come on, Stuart, it'll be all right."

He led Stuart into the men's toilets. Propped him against the wall.

Stuart heard a skittering sound, like cockroaches across the kitchen bench at midnight. He thought he caught a whiff of them, that slightly plasticky smell. A smell of sour cherries.

"It won't hurt," the man said.

Stuart felt the creatures and, by straining his eyes, could watch them walking up his arm. The scream in his head deafened him.

Up his forearm, his biceps, over his shoulders and onto his neck, where he could feel them latching on.

"It's not your blood they're taking," the man said. His voice was soft and almost too broad to listen to. "It's something else. You won't miss it. It'll be like it was never there. You won't know."

He clicked his tongue and Stuart thought the sucking stopped. He felt light-headed and nauseous. The man plucked a beetle off Stuart's shoulder and ate it. Crunched it like it was a nut and took the next. Two more, and he was smacking his lips. Stuart couldn't move. He felt so cold he felt like he'd been buried in snow. Or was back in the cave. But it was light in here. Very bright.

"Look at me." The man's cheeks were pink, his eyes bright. He looked younger. Happy.

"Thank you, Stuart. Have a good life."

He tapped Stuart on the head and Stuart slept.

He awoke on the filthy toilet floor. Someone had dropped a wad of shitty toilet paper and he could smell that.

He felt little compunction to rise, to lift himself. It was like this was the only moment and there was nothing beyond.

Another man came in and helped him up. "Home time for you, mate? Wait here while I take a piss and I'll get you to a taxi."

"Do I know you?" Stuart said. Things seemed blurred and he couldn't remember much.

"Nah, but you'll always help someone in trouble, right? Specially a survivor like you."

I am a survivor, Stuart thought as the stranger helped him to a taxi. *That's what I did.*

But he felt as if he could never do it again.

He woke up on his lounge room floor, his shirt stiff with dried blood.

"Big night, was it?" Cheryl said, poking him with her toe.

Sarah stood over him, ready for school, her shoes all shined, her white socks folded neatly.

He shivered, feeling cold. "The long man pinched my nose." His face felt swollen and he knew he must look awful.

"Get off the floor," Sarah said. "You're shivering."

"I will soon." He felt a deep sense of pure lethargy.

Cheryl helped him up onto the couch and brought him a cup of tea. "You're too old to drink like that anymore."

"Wasn't the drink. Well, I did give it a bit of a hiding, but it was this guy. This long gray guy who gave me a bloody nose and then did something to me. I'm tired. I'm so tired. And cold."

She brought him a fluffy pink blanket and covered his knees with it. "The TV producers sent over a copy of your interview. Sarah and I have already watched it twice! Want to have a look? You come across really well."

She didn't wait for his answer but played the DVD anyway.

He watched the interview over and over that day, wondering at the person talking. "Jeez, I'm a smart-arse, aren't I?" he said, smiling at his Cheryl. She kissed his forehead.

"You always were." The lightness of her tone warmed him slightly. She had suffered post-natal depression and he was terrified every day it would come on again. He saw it behind her eyes sometimes, in the droop of her mouth. A wash of sadness. Those were the times he tried harder to lift her up. Out of the corner of his eye he thought he saw a bug climbing the wall and he curled up, pulling his blanket up over his eyes. "We need to get the rentokill guys in here. Get rid of the cockroaches," he said.

She nodded. "Ants, too. All over the kitchen, rotten little things." She sat beside him, laying her head on his shoulder. "I still can't believe you're back," she said. His little bird, his sparrow, but a tower of strength at the same time.

Usually sitting beside her he felt something. Irritation, often, when she went on about small domestic details, none of which interested him. Boredom, talking about her family. Affection, when they sat together watching TV. Love, when they laughed together at a joke he'd made, when her eyes crinkled up and little tears formed. He loved those little tears.

She held his hand. He let it lie loose.

"Are you okay?" she said.

"I just can't really feel anything. It's all gone numb."

She stared at him. "We have to tell the doctor. Something's wrong. You shouldn't feel like that."

"I don't feel anything, love. That's the thing. Nothing at all. Just cold. Like I've got an ice block inside my stomach." He didn't tell her he meant emotionally as well, that looking at her left him cold.

To cover it up, he kissed her. Usually they'd do this stuff at night, with the door closed, but he kissed her with passion and moved his hands around her body, touching all his favorite bits.

The weeks passed. He ate meals he had no real desire to eat, had conversations and many, many interviews. Sponsorships brought money in. Newspaper reports listed everything he'd eaten underground and those people approached him. It was Vegemite, Tip Top bread, Milo chocolate bars, apples (the local fruit shop took on that one), and the local butcher had a go, too. The watch company put him on TV, talking about how he'd never need another watch, that one was so good. So at least he didn't have to work. People kept asking him if he was going back underground and he'd bluff at them, give them the real man answer, the hero stuff, but he wasn't going back.

He spent a lot of time reading the paper. He started cutting out stories of other survivors, especially the ones who talked about the cold, about the deep bone chill they felt after a few days.

"Dad, let me hook you up with an online forum. You can meet other survivors. Talk to them. Most of them are probably feeling what you're feeling," Sarah said. He sat at the computer for a while but it only made sense when she talked him through it, and he didn't want her to know it all.

She asked him about the long man. "The one you said pinched your nose. We should try to track him down and make sure he doesn't do it again. People can't go round pinching my dad's nose like that."

"Willy-nilly," he said. It was an old joke. "I don't know if we'll find him. I don't think he's at the pub much, or if he's got a job. I saw him when I was buried, you know. He sent his ghost in to find me."

Others had talked about seeing visions. Buried in the snow, or caught in a car for two days on a country road. They said, more than one of them, that a long man had visited them. "It's not just me," he told Sarah. "No one knows why he doesn't help. He just looks."

"Did he pinch their noses? This is the stuff we can find online, Dad."

"Yeah, maybe. Maybe. What about stuff about cockroaches? How to get rid of them? I saw a huge one in the bathroom. They say they'll survive nuclear war. That's what they reckon." He shivered. "I hate them."

He felt like a fraud. Life exhausted him, all the people wanting what he had. And Cheryl and Sarah got nothing but harassment. "Lucky your dad's alive, your husband," people said to them. "Imagine what life would have been like without him, how sad, how hard." Making them think about it. All those people wanting to talk to him, but they paid him, at least, and it kept them in beer and roast beef. Always the same questions.

"What is it you think you were kept alive for?" they asked, putting the onus on him to make something of his life. As if he'd been given a second chance and he'd be a fool to waste it.

"Dunno what I was kept alive for, but mostly I'm enjoying every extra minute with my daughter and my wife," was his stock answer.

But he no longer really cared.

They asked him, "Are you scared of anything? Seems like you're not." It was a stupid question, he thought. Who wasn't scared?

"Cockroaches. I really hate cockroaches." The interviewer sighed in agreement.

Another question they always asked him was, "Put in the same situation, would or could you do it again?"

"Well, I won't, mate, will I? Just not going to happen."

They always ended with, "If only you could bottle it." His standard joke was to hold out his wrists.

"Ya wanna take a liter or two? Go for it! I can spare it!"

It was all an act and he was good at it.

He was waiting in the queue to buy fish-and-chips ("Aren't you that guy? That miner guy?") when he smelled sour cherries. It took him straight back to the cave and the smell of the long man. He felt cold through his layers of clothing and did not want to turn around. He felt someone behind him, close, but people did that. They seemed to think if they got physically close to him they could absorb some of him, that they could be like him.

He took his package of food and left the shop, eyes down. Climbed into the car some sponsor had given him, sat there to eat it.

The long man opened the passenger door and climbed in.

Stuart dropped the food on his lap where it sat, greasy and hot. He barely felt it. He scrabbled for the door handle but the long man took his wrist. Pressed hard and Stuart couldn't move. Just like last time.

"You seem to be enjoying that fish, Stuart. You know what that tells me? That I didn't take it all. The fact that you want to eat tells me that."

Stuart tried to shake his head, to say, "I'm faking it, it's all fake, I can't feel a fucking thing," but the cockroaches were out, skittering and sucking, and if he thought he was cold before, *that* was nothing. His eyelids felt frozen open, his nostrils frozen shut, breathing was so painful he wanted to stop doing it.

"That's it now," the long man said, picking cockroach feelers out of his teeth. "You're done."

Stuart sat slumped in the seat for a while, then started the car. A tape was playing; one of his interviews. He liked listening to himself, hearing his own voice.

"I'll do anything to stay alive, anything to keep my family alive," he heard himself say. "You know I got stuck in a pipe once when I was a kid. Fat kid, I was. I sang songs from TV shows to keep me occupied." Listening from his car, chilled to the bone and tired, Stuart wondered if he'd seen the long man then. If the long man had waited, and waited, until he was good and strong.

He pulled out of the car park. It was only his sense of duty making him do it, long-instilled. He had to go to a school visit someone had organized for him. Some school where there was a survivor kid, a young girl recently rescued. It took him a while to get there: wrong turns, bad traffic. Angry traffic. He thought there was more road rage than usual but then wondered if it was his driving. If all that stuff about driving carefully did make sense, because he didn't care now, didn't care how he drove or what he hit.

"We'd like to welcome Stuart Parker to the school. He's taken time out of his busy day to talk to us and to talk to Claire, our own hero."

The children clapped quietly. Stuart guessed they were tired of hearing about Claire.

She'd been trapped in the basement of a building. A game of hide-and-seek gone wrong; no one knew she was playing. No one knew where she was. It took six days for them to find her.

"Tell us how you coped, Claire," the teacher said.

"I pretended I was at school doing boring work and that's why it was so boring. Sometimes I thought about this nice man from the mine. He said he kept thinking of nice things and that's what I did, too."

The children shuffled, started to talk, bored. Claire looked at them wide-eyed. "I ate bugs. Lots of bugs. Like he did. And I had some chips I took from the cupboard but I didn't want to tell Mum and Dad cos I didn't want to get in trouble."

She had their attention, but not completely. "And then there was the creepy guy."

"You were alone in the basement, Claire, weren't you?" the teacher said, passive-aggressive. "No one there."

"Who did you see?" Stuart said. He hadn't had a chance to speak before then. "What did he look like?"

The audience were rapt. They didn't often get to see adults this way, all het up and loud.

"I was all by myself but then this creepy long guy was there. I never seen him before but I thought he might help me to get out. But he didn't, he just stared at me. I told him he should go away but the only thing I think he said was, 'See you soon, Claire.' That's why I'm scared. I really don't want to see him again."

Stuart wanted to care. He wanted to save her but there was nothing left in him. Only the memory of the man who would have killed to save that girl. Would have ripped the arms off any man who tried to hurt her.

Just a memory, though.

"Stuart, we haven't heard from you. What can you tell the children?"

"That there is no purpose in life. We all die and rot and none of it is worth anything. You're only taking up space. And that the long man is real. You need to keep her safe from him because he'll destroy her."

The principal, stunned and speechless, took a moment to answer. The children were silent and he wondered if he'd laid seeds of sadness and emptiness in them all. He didn't mean to. But he was too tired and cold to lie anymore.

"But . . . but Mr. Parker, you're a role model. We asked you here to lift the children. Inspire them."

"I'm nothing. Nothing at all," he said.

Claire. Claire was in the news and so was he, with his awful statements, his cruelty to the children. He had the media at his door again but they hated him now for turning on the children; you don't do that to the kiddies, do you? He watched Claire; she didn't look chilled to the bone, so he thought perhaps the long man hadn't come to her yet.

His house was full of his sponsors' food and friends came over to eat it because he wouldn't. Some of the rescuers too, looking at him as if they'd wasted their time. Sitting there in front of the television, warm rug, warm slippers, all skinny and pale.

He couldn't even fake a smile anymore. His famous watch had slipped off his wrist and sat in the dust under the couch.

"We shoulda bottled it. We could give him a taste of his own self," one of the rescuers said. He knew they were disappointed in him, that he wasn't doing what they wanted him to do.

"Three days of my life, I gave to save him," he heard one say in the kitchen.

"Now look at him."

They left him alone.

And he didn't care.

NEEDLES

Elizabeth Bear

Elizabeth Bear was born on the same day as Frodo and Bilbo Baggins, and very nearly named after Peregrin Took. She is a recipient of the John W. Campbell, Sturgeon, Locus, and Hugo Awards. She has been nominated multiple times for British Science Fiction Association and Philip K. Dick Awards. She currently lives in southern New England with a famous cat. Her hobbies include murdering inoffensive potted plants, ruining dinner, and falling off rock faces.

Her most recent books are a space opera, *Chill*, from Bantam Spectra, and *By the Mountain Bound* and *The Sea Thy Mistress* from Tor.

The vampires rolled into Needles about three hours before dawn on a Tuesday in April, when the nights still chilled between each scorching day. They sat as far apart from each other as they could get, jammed up against the doors of a '67 Impala hardtop the color of dried blood, which made for *acres* of bench seat between them. Billy, immune to irony, rested his fingertips on the steering wheel, the other bad-boy arm draped out the open window. Mahasti let her right hand trail in the slipstream behind the passenger mirror, like a cherub's stunted wing.

Mahasti had driven until the sun set. After that, she'd let Billy out of the trunk and they had burned highway all night south from Vegas through Cal-Nev-Ari, over the California border until they passed from the Mojave Desert to the Mohave Valley. Somewhere in there the 95 blurred into cohabitation with Interstate 40, and then they found themselves cruising the Mother Road.

"Get your kicks," Billy said, "on Route 66."

Mahasti ignored him.

They had been able to smell the Colorado from miles out, the river and the broad green fields that wrapped the tiny desert town like a hippie skirt blown north by prevailing winds. Most of the agriculture clung along the Arizona side, the point of Nevada following the Colorado down until it ended in a chisel tip like a ninja sword pointed straight at the heart of Needles.

"Bad feng shui," Billy said, trying again. "Nevada's gonna stab California right in the balls."

"More like right in the water supply," Mahasti said, after a pause long enough to indicate that she'd thought about leaving him hanging but chosen, after due consideration, to take pity. Sometimes it was good to have somebody to kick around a little. She was mad at him, but he was still her partner.

She ran her left hand through her hair, finger-combing, but even at full arm's stretch, fingertips brushing the windshield, she didn't reach the end of the locks. "If they thought they could get away with it."

She curled in the seat to glance over her shoulder, as if something might be following. But the highway behind them was as empty as the desert had been. "We should have killed them."

"Aww," Billy said. "You kill every little vampire hunter who comes along, pretty soon no vampire hunters. And then what would we do for fun?"

She smiled in spite of herself. It had been a lot of lonely centuries before she found Billy. And Billy knew he wasn't in charge.

He feathered the gas; the big engine growled. He guided the Impala toward an off ramp. "Does this remind you of home?"

"Because every fucking desert looks alike? There's no yucca in Baghdad." She tucked a thick strand of mahogany-black hair behind one rose-petal ear. "Like I even know what Baghdad looks like anymore."

The door leaned into her arm as the car turned, pressing lines into the flesh. The dry desert wind stroked dry dead skin. As they rolled up to a traffic signal, she tilted her head back and scented it, curling her lip up delicately, like a dog checking for traces of another dog.

"They show it on TV," Billy said.

"They show it blown up on TV," she answered. "Who the fuck wants to look at that? Find me a fucking tattoo parlor."

"Like that'll change you." He reached across the vast emptiness of the bench seat and brushed her arm with the backs of his fingers. "Like anything will change you. You're dead, darlin'. The world doesn't touch you."

When you were one way for a long time, it got comfortable. But every so often, you had to try something new. "You never know until you try."

"Like it'll be open." The Impala ghosted forward with pantherine power, so smooth it seemed that the wheels had never quite stopped turning. "It's three in the morning. Even the bars are closed. You'll be lucky to find an all-night truck stop."

She looked out the window, turning away. The soft wind caught her voice and blew it back into the car with her hair. "You wanna try to make L.A. by sunup? It's all the same to me, but I know you don't like the trunk."

"Hey," Billy said. "There's a Denny's. Maybe one of the waitresses is knocked up. That'd be okay for both of us."

"They don't serve vampires." Mahasti pulled her arm back inside, turned to face front. With rhythmic push-pull motions, she cranked the window up. "Shut up already and drive."

Colorado River Florist. Spike's Bar-B-Que. Jack in the Box. Dimond and Sons Needles Mortuary. Spike's Saguaro Sunrise Breakfast. First Southern Baptist Church (Billy hissed at it on principle) and the Desert Mirage Inn. A Peanuts cartoon crudely copied on the sign over a tavern. Historic Route 66 ("The Mother Load Road," Billy muttered) didn't look much as it had when the Impala was young, but the motel signs were making an effort.

Of Needles itself, there wasn't much *there* there, which was a good thing for the vampires: they crisscrossed the whole downtown in the hollow dark before Billy pulled over to a curb and pointed, but it took them less than a hour.

Mahasti leaned over to follow the line of his finger. A gray corner-lot house with white trim and a yard overrun by Bermuda grass and mallow huddled in the darkness. It was doing a pretty good impression of a private residence, except for the turned-off neon OPEN sign in the window and the painted shingle hanging over the door.

"Spike's Tattoo," she said. "Pun unintended?"

As they exited the car, heavy swinging doors glossy in the street-lit darkness, Billy cupped his hands and lit a cigarette. It flared bright between streetlights. "Why is everything in this damned town named after some Spike guy?"

Mahasti tugged her brown baby-doll tee smooth from the hem. An octopus clutching a blue teddy bear stretched across her insignificant breasts. Billy liked Frye boots and black dusters. Mahasti kicked at a clod with fuchsia Crocs, the frayed hems of her jeans swaying around skinny ankles. "Because he lives in the desert near here."

Billy gave her a dour look over the ember of the cigarette. He took a drag. It frosted his face in orange.

"Peanuts?" she tried, but the blank look deepened. "Snoopy's brother? It's their claim to fame."

Billy didn't read the newspapers. It wasn't even worth a shrug. He flipped the cigarette into the road.

He was dead anyway. He hadn't been getting much good out of it.

"Come on." Gravel crunched on the dirty road as he strode forward. "Let's go ruin somebody's morning."

Mahasti steepled her fingers. "I'll be right back. I'm just going to walk around the block."

Spike's Tattoo bulwarked the boundary between the commercial and the residential neighborhoods. Mahasti turned her back on Billy and walked away, up a quiet side street lined on either side by low block houses with tar-shingled roofs that wouldn't last a third of a Minnesota winter.

They didn't have to.

Mahasti moved through the night as if she were following a scent, head tilted to one side or the other, nostrils flaring, the indrawn air hissing through her arched, constricted throat.

Billy came up behind her. "You smell anything?"

She shot him a look. "Your fucking menthol Camels."

He smiled. She jerked her chin at the gravel side drive that gave access to the gate into the backyard of Spike's. "I'm taking that one. You better go roll a wino or something."

"Bitch," he said without heat. "I'll wait at the front door, then."

He spun on the scarred ball of his cowboy boot. He was lean, not too tall, stalking down the street as if the ghosts of his spurs should be jingling. The black duster flared behind him like a mourning peacock's tail, but for once he hadn't shot the collar. A strip of brown skin with all the blood red dropped out showed between his coarse black hair and the plaid band of his cowboy shirt. Even as short as that, the hair was too straight to show any kind of curl.

She sighed and shook her head and turned away.

"Tucson was fucking prettier." Mahasti could bitch all she wanted. There was no one to hear.

The houses here had block walls around the back, water-fat stretches of grass in the front. The newer neighborhoods might be xeriscaped, but in the 1940s a nice lawn was a man's God-given American right, and no mere inconvenience like the hottest desert in North America was going to stop him from having one. She walked up a cement sidewalk between stubby California fan palms on the street side and fruitless mulberry in the yards, still pausing every few feet to cast left and right and sniff the air.

She finished her stroll around the block and found herself back at Spike's Tattoo. A sun-beat gray house, paint peeling on the south side, it wore its untrimmed pomegranate hedge like a madman's fishy beard. The side door was sunken, uninviting, between shaggy columns of leaves and branches. A rust-stained motorboat, vinyl canopy tattered, blocked the black steel gate that guarded the passage between the side drive and the backyard.

Mahasti, who'd been sticking to the outside sidewalks on the block she was walking, looked both ways down the street and crossed, fetching up in the streetlight shadow of one of those stubby palms. She eyed the house as she walked into the side yard. It eyed her back—rheumy, snaggled, discontented.

She looked away. Then she stepped out of her squishy plastic shoes ("What will they think of next?" Billy had said, when she'd pulled them from a dead girl's feet outside of Winnemucca) and lofted from ground to boat deck to balance atop the eight-foot gate in a fluid pair of leaps, pausing only for a moment to let her vulture shadow fall into the gravel of the yard.

She spread her arms and stepped down lightly, stony gravel silent under her brown bare foot, the canopy of her hair trailing like a comet tail before swinging forward heavily and cloaking her crouched body to the ankles. It could trap no warmth against her, but it whisked roughly on the denim of her jeans.

Hair, it turned out, actually *did* keep growing after you were dead.

She tilted her head back, sniffing again, eyes closed to savor. When she smiled, it showed white, even, perfectly human teeth. When she uncoiled and glided forward it was one motion, smooth as any dancer. "Everything we need."

There was a dog in the yard, stretched out slumbering on a pallet made of heaped carpet squares. The third security window—long, narrow, and a foot over her head—that she tried with her palms pressed flat against its glass slid open left to right. There were no screens.

Hands on the window ledge, she chinned herself. In a cloak of red-black hair robbed of color by the darkness, she slid inside.

It was a cold space of tile illuminated by a yellow nightlight: the bathroom. Mahasti's bare dead feet were too dry to stick to the linoleum, her movements too light to echo. The door to the hall stood ajar. She slipped sideways through it without touching and paused just outside. The rasp of human breathing, human heartbeat, was stentorian. Their scent saturated the place.

Three. Infant, woman, and man.

Mahasti slithered around the open bedroom door, past the crib, one more shadow among shadows. The little boy slept on his stomach, knees drawn up under him, butt a round crooked mountain under the cheap acrylic blanket.

When Mahasti picked him up, he woke confused and began to cry. The parents roused an instant after, their heat crystal-edged against the dimness, fumbling in the dark. "Your turn," the man said, and rolled over, while the woman slapped at her nightstand until her fingers brushed against her eyeglass frames.

"You probably have a gun in the nightstand." Mahasti hooked the hem of the octopus shirt and rucked it up over her gaunt, cold belly, revealing taut flesh and stretch marks. She slung the baby against her shoulder with her left hand. "I don't think you want to do that."

The woman froze; the man catapulted upright, revealing a torso streaked with convoluted lines of ink. *His* feet made a moist noise on the floor.

"Lady," the man said, "who the hell are you? No wetback fucking junkie is gonna come in my house. . . ."

"You shouldn't put a child to sleep on his stomach."

The baby's wails came peacock sharp, peacock painful. She

cupped him close, feeling the hammering of his tiny heart. She freed her breast one-handed and plugged him onto the nipple with the deftness of practice.

He made smacking sounds at first, then settled down contented as her milk let down. Warmth spread through her, or perhaps the chill drained from her dead flesh to his living.

The vampire didn't take her eyes off the man, and he didn't move toward the nightstand. The mother—a thick-shouldered woman bare-legged in an oversized shirt—stayed frozen, her hands clawed at her sides, her head cocked like a bird's. An angry mother falcon, contemplating which eye to go after first.

Mahasti moved. She closed, lifted the woman up one-handed, and tossed her across the room. Trivial, and done in the space of a blink; the mother had more hang-time than it took Mahasti to return to her original place by the door. The man jumped back, involuntarily, as the mother hit the wall beside him. "Shit," he said, crouching beside her. "Shit, shit, shit."

The woman pushed herself up the wall, blood smearing from a swollen lip, a cheek split over the bone.

"What's your son's name?" Mahasti said, threat implicit in her tone. The babe had not shifted.

The mother settled back on her heels, but the stretched tension in the tendons of her hands did not ease. "Alan." She gulped air. "Please don't hurt him. We have a little money. We don't have any drugs—"

Mahasti stood away from the door. "We're going out front," she said to the man. "And then you're going to open the front door."

It took thirty seconds and a glare from the woman before the man decided to comply. Once he had, though, he moved quickly around the bed and past Mahasti. He was lean as a vampire himself, faded tattoos winding down the ropy stretched-rubber architecture of his torso to vanish into striped cotton pajamas.

He paused in the doorway and glanced back once at the nightstand. Mahasti coughed.

He stepped into the hall. The woman made a noise low in the back of her throat, as involuntary as an abandoned dog.

"You, too." Mahasti snuggled the baby closer to her breast. "Go with him. Do what I say and you won't get hurt."

* * *

She made them precede her down the short hall to the front of the house, which had been converted into the two rooms of the tattoo parlor. A counter constructed of two-by-fours and paneling divided the living room. Cheaply framed flash covered every wall.

Bullet-headed as a polar bear, sparing Mahasti frequent testing glances, the man went to the door. He turned the lock and pulled it open, revealing Billy with his hat pulled low, on the other side of the security door. A muscle jumped in his jaw as the man opened that lock, too, and stepped back, as if he could make himself flip the lever but not—quite—turn the handle.

"Invite him in," Mahasti said.

She came from another land, where the rules were different. But unfair as it was, Billy was cursed to play the game of the invader.

"Miss—," the woman said, pleading. "Please. I'll give you anything we have."

"Invite," Mahasti said, "him in."

"Come in," the man said, in a low voice, but perfectly audible to a vampire's ears.

Billy's hat tilted up. In the shadow of the brim, his irises glittered violet with eyeshine.

He opened the security door—it creaked rustily—stepped over the threshold, and tossed Mahasti's Crocs at her feet. "Your shoes."

"Thanks."

He shut the security door behind him. The woman jerked in sympathy to the metallic scrape of the lock. An hour still lacked to dawn, but that didn't concern the rooster that crowed outside, greeting the first translucency of the indigo sky. Dawn would come soon, but for now all that light was good for was silhouetting the shark-tooth range of mountains that gave Needles its name.

The man drew back beside the woman, against the counter. "What do you want?"

The baby, cool and soft, had fallen asleep on Mahasti's warm breast. She gently disconnected him and tugged her shirt down. "I want you to change me. Change me forever. I want a tattoo."

She told him to freehand whatever he liked. He studied her face while she gave him her left arm. Billy held the kid for insurance, grumbling about the delay. The mother went around hanging blankets over the windows and turning on all the lights.

"What are you?" he asked.

"A 'wetback fucking junkie,'" she mimicked, cruelly accurate. "Do you think if you talk to me you'll build a connection, and it will keep you safe?"

He looked down at his tools, at the transfer paper on the book propped on his lap. "You don't have much accent for a wetback."

He glanced up at Billy and the baby, lips thin.

Mahasti held out her right hand. "Give me Alan, please. He needs to suckle."

"Ma'am." The woman pinned the last corner of a blanket and stepped back from the window. "Please. I'm his mother—"

Billy glared her still and silent, though even the force of his stare could not hush the sobs of her breath. He slid the baby into the crook of Mahasti's arm, supporting its head until the transfer was complete.

"When I learned what would become your language"—Mahasti spoke to the man as if none of the drama had occurred—"it was across a crusader's saddle. I was too young, and the child the bastard got on me killed me coming out." She smiled, liver-dark lips drawn fine. "And when I was dead I rose up and I returned the favor, to both of them."

He drew back from her needle teeth when she smiled. His hands shook badly enough that he lifted his pencil from the paper and pulled in a steadying breath. Without meeting her eyes, he went back to what he had been drawing once more.

At Mahasti's other breast, the child suckled. The touch still warmed her.

"Somebody will notice when we don't open," the woman said. "Someone will know there's something wrong."

"Maybe," Mahasti said. "In a week or two. You people never want to get involved in a goddamned thing. So shut up and let him fucking draw."

He drew, and he showed her. A lotus, petals like a crown, petals embracing the form of a newborn child. "White," he said. "Stained with pink at the heart."

"White ink." She held up her brown arm for inspection. "You can do that?"

He nodded.

If a child changed her once, maybe a child could change her again. She said, "You've got through the daylight to make me happy. When the sun goes down we're moving on."

He didn't ask "and?" Neither did the mother.

As if they had anyway, Billy said, "And there's two ways we can leave you when we go."

"I'll get clean needles," said the man.

Billy paced while the man worked on Mahasti's arm and the baby dozed off against her breast once more. Dimly, Mahasti heard the flutter of a heart. The woman finally sat down on the couch in the waiting area and pulled her knees up to her chest. The man kept wanting to talk. The dog barked forlornly in the yard.

After several conversational false starts, while the ink traced the arched outlines of petals across Mahasti's skin and the at first insistently ringing phone went both unanswered and more frequently quiet, he said, "So if she was a kidnapped Persian princess, what were you?"

Billy skipped a boot heel off the floor and turned, folding his arms. "Maybe I was Billy the Kid."

Mahasti snorted. "Billy the Kid wasn't an Indian."

"Yeah? You think anybody would have written it down if he was? What if I was an iron-fingered demon? I wouldn't need *you* to get me invited in."

With a cautious, sidelong glance at Mahasti, the man said, "What's an iron-fingered demon?"

"If I were an iron-fingered demon," Billy said, "I could eat livers, cause consumption, get on with my life. Unlife. But no, *you* get to be a *lamashtu*. And *I* had to catch the white man's bloodsucker disease."

Mahasti spoke without lifting her head, or her gaze from the man's meticulous work. The lotus taking shape on her skin was a thing of beauty. Depth and texture. No blood pricked from her skin to mar the colors, which were dense and rich. "You *could* be an iron-fingered demon. If you were a Cherokee. Which you aren't."

"Details," he said. "Details. First I'm too Indian, then I'm not the right kind of Indian? Fuck you very much."

"Billy," Mahasti said, "shut up and let the man work or we won't be ready to go when the sun sets."

She was a desert demon, the sun no concern. It was on Billy's behalf that they stalled.

The dog's barking had escalated to something regular and frantic. A twig cracked in the yard.

Mahasti looked at the man, at the cold baby curled sleeping in the corner of her arm. She lifted her chin and stared directly, unsettlingly, at the woman. "Mommy?"

The mother must have been crying silently, curled in her corner of the couch, because she stammered over a sob. "Yes?"

"You've been such a good girl, I'm going to give you Alan back. You and Billy can take him to the bedroom. I know you're not going to try anything silly."

The woman's hands came up, clutched at air, and settled again to clench on the sofa beside her bare legs. "No."

Mahasti looked at the man. "And you won't do anything dumb either, will you?"

He shook his head. Under the lights, his scrawny shoulders had broken out in a gloss of sweat. "That's good, Cathy," he said. The eye contact between him and the woman was full of unspoken communication. "You take Alan and put him to bed."

"Here," Mahasti said, offering him up, his heartbeat barely thrumming against her fingertips. She tingled, warm and full of life. "He's already sleeping."

Billy sat cross-legged on the unmade bed, his boot heels denting the mattress. The woman pulled all the toys and pillows from the crib and lay the baby on his back atop taut bedding. She moved tightly, elbows pinned to her rib cage, spine stiff. He slouched, relaxed.

Until the front door slammed open.

"Fucking vampire hunters." He was in the hall before the words finished leaving his mouth, the woman behind him bewildered by the fury of his passage. A spill of sunlight cut the floor ahead, but the corner of the wall kept it from flooding down the corridor.

Billy paused in the shadow of the hall.

* * *

Three men burst into the front room—one weedy, one meaty, and one perfectly average in every way except the scars. Mahasti moved from the chair, the disregarded needle blurring a line of white across her wrist, destroying the elegance of the artist's design. The artist threw himself into a corner behind the counter. By the time he got there and got his back against the wall, the fight was over.

The perfectly average man was fast enough to meet her there, in the sunlight, and twist her un-inked right arm up behind her in a bind. The silver knife in his left hand pricked her throat. An image of a Persian demon, inscribed on the blade, flashed sunlight into Mahasti's eyes.

"Well, fuck," she said.

The meaty one grabbed her free hand and slapped a silver cuff around it.

"Silence, *lamashtu*," the vampire hunter growled, shaking her by her twisted arm. "Call the other out, so I can burn him, too. You'll terrorize no more innocents."

She rolled her eyes. "He's not coming out when there's daylight in the room."

"Really?" he laughed. "Your protector thinks so little of you?"

"I'm my own protector, asshole," she said, and kicked back to break the bone of his thigh like a fried chicken wing.

She threw the meaty one down the hall to Billy, and ripped the throat out of the weedy one while the perfectly average one was still screaming his way to the floor.

She shut the door before she killed him. The noise was going to bring the neighbors around. Then she went to help Billy drag the third body up to the pile, and make sure the woman hadn't run out the back in the confusion.

She was still crouched by the crib. Mahasti left her there and met Billy in the hall. "See?" he said. "More fun if you don't use 'em up all at once."

Mahasti said, "He had a knife with an image of Pazazu etched on it. That could have been the end of *all* our fun."

"He got prepared before he followed us here." Billy grimaced. "They're getting smarter."

"Not smart enough to use it before asking questions, though."

Mahasti jerked her thumb over her shoulder, toward the rear of the house. The white lotus and babe, blurred on her wrist, shone in the dark. She felt different. Maybe. She thought she felt different now.

She said, "What about them? If there are any more hunters they will be able to answer questions."

"We could take them with us. Hostages. The Impala's got a six-body trunk. It's cozy, but it's doable."

"Fuck it," Mahasti said. "They'll be a load. It'll be a long fucking drive. Leave them."

"Fine," Billy said. "But you got what you needed from the kid. *I* still have to get a snack first."

He met her on the concrete stoop two minutes later, licking a split lip. Smoke curled from his fingers as he pulled his hat down hard, shading his face from the last crepuscular light of the sun. "Cutting it close."

"The car has tinted windows," she said. "Come on."

Traffic thinned as the night wore on, and the stark, starlit landscape grew more elaborately beautiful. Mahasti read a book by Steinbeck, the lotus flashing every time she turned a page. Billy drove and chewed his thumb.

When the sky was gray, without turning, she said, "Pity about the kid."

"What do you care? He was just gonna die anyway." He paused. "Just like we don't."

She sighed into the palm of her hand, feeling her own skin chilling like age-browned bone. There was no pain where the needles had worked her skin—but there *was* pain in her empty arms, in her breasts taut again with milk already. "Mommy's going to miss him."

Billy's shrug traveled the length of his arms from his shoulders to where his wrists draped the wheel. "Not for as long as I'd miss you."

They drove a while in silence. Without looking, she reached out to touch him.

A thin line of palest gold shivered along the edge of the world. Billy made a sound of discontent. Mahasti squinted at the incipient sunrise.

"Pull over. It's time for you to get in the trunk."

He obeyed wordlessly, and wordlessly got out, leaving the parking brake set and the door standing open. She popped the trunk lid. He lay back and settled himself on the carpet, arms folded behind his head. She closed the lid on him and settled back into the car.

Her unmarred brown left arm trailed out the window in the sun. Tonight, somewhere new, they'd do it all over again.

Once in a while, Billy was right. Nothing changed them. She could touch the world, but the world never touched her.

The Impala purred as she pulled off the shoulder and onto the road. Empty, and for another hour it would remain so.

BASKERVILLE'S MIDGETS

Reggie Oliver

Reggie Oliver has been a professional playwright, actor, and theater director since 1975. His biography of Stella Gibbons, *Out of the Woodshed*, was published by Bloomsbury (U.K.) in 1998. His other publications include four volumes of stories: *The Dreams of Cardinal Vittorini, The Complete Symphonies of Adolf Hitler, Masques of Satan,* and *Madder Mysteries.* An omnibus edition of his stories entitled *Dramas from the Depths* was published by Centipede as part of its Masters of the Weird Tale series. His stories have appeared in more than twenty-five anthologies, including successive volumes of *Best New Horror, The Best Horror of the Year,* and *The Black Book of Horror.* The year 2010 saw the first production of his play *Once Bitten* at the Orange Tree, Richmond (U.K.). His novel *The Scholar's Tale,* the first of the tetralogy The Dracula Papers, was published earlier this year by Chômu Press.

They say that the theatrical landlady is dead. Perhaps they are right, because even in the days when I regularly went on tour she was a dying breed. I am not much given to thespian nostalgia so I shed few tears at her departure, but there may be another reason for my lack of sentiment.

There was a time when almost anyone who was doing a week at the Queen's Theatre, Westport, would stay with Mrs. Ruby Baker at Stage Door, which is what she called her many-roomed boarding-house in Harbour Street. It was cheap, it was easygoing, you were only five minutes away from the theatre, and you could have your breakfast as late as ten in the morning.

When I first went there in the mid-1970s it was still a thriving concern, but one could tell that it had seen better days. The walls of the dining room were adorned with signed photographs in frames of the theatrical and vaudeville celebrities who had stayed there. But they were more than a decade old. These days the "stars" went to a hotel; it was only the also-rans like me who lodged at Stage Door.

Everyone used to say that Ruby was a character, one of those ambiguous terms which generally just means odd, sometimes self-consciously so. When I first knew Ruby, she was in her sixties, a big, blowsy bottle blonde with a cigarette end perpetually drooping from the corner of her mouth. I used to watch her anxiously as she carried in the plates of eggs and bacon—and baked beans, whether you liked them or not—into the dining room of a morning. The ash from her cigarette always threatened to fall onto our breakfasts, but somehow it never did. A fellow actor once informed me that she used to put a needle down the middle of her cigarette so that the ash would maintain its precarious hold, and thus tantalize her guests, but I suspect this was a myth. There were many tales about Ruby, most of which were also told of other theatre landladies, so probably had no truth in them; but the story of Ruby and the Baskerville Midgets is unique to her, and I can vouch for it.

My second visit to Stage Door was on a tour of *Dial M for Murder*, in which I was playing Captain Lesgate. It was mid-February and our company was only the second or third into the theatre after the pantomime, the subject of which had been *Snow White and the Seven Dwarfs*.

Since I had been at Stage Door over a year before, Ruby had become a widow. Her husband, Alf, a large, cheery man, had not seemed to me particularly moribund when I last stayed there, but a series of strokes had taken him. I was sorry because, to tell the truth, I liked Alf rather better than I had liked his wife. Nevertheless I felt it my duty when I checked into Stage Door on the Monday afternoon to commiserate with Ruby on her loss. She accepted my condolence listlessly, without letting the cigarette move from her lips. I suppose she had become used to similar speeches from near strangers and had wearied of them. We were standing in the hallway of Stage Door rather awkwardly, I still holding my suitcase while her dog Sheba, a large, shaggy collie-Labrador cross, panted and tail-wagged in the background. I noticed that the dog seemed to have aged since my last visit, had become less vigorously enthusiastic about new visitors.

"We had a good pantomime this year," said Ruby, changing the subject to something more congenial. "I had all the seven dwarfs here. Not children. Proper performers. Baskerville's Midgets, they were."

I had heard of them and said so.

"Of course, a dwarf is not a midget, you know." She looked at me solemnly as if demanding a response.

"I know."

"That's very important. The dwarfs and the midgets; they don't get on. A dwarf, you see—and I'm not being disrespectful—is out of proportion, with the big head and the bow legs, but a midget is what I call a proper little person. Everything in proportion, if you know what I mean. They're very polite, you see."

Her last sentence did not appear to follow logically from what had gone before, but I nodded again as if I had seen the connection.

"They don't get up to anything nasty like some of these dwarfs."

I did not argue with her. I felt, perhaps wrongly, that the eccentricity of her prejudice went some way toward excusing it.

"After Alf had gone I was feeling a bit low, as you might expect, but those midgets, they were a real tonic. Full of fun and games, but nice with it, you know. They're ever so talented. Each of them plays an instrument: that's their act. Xylophone, trumpet, tambourine, violin; and they play all the tunes: 'Charmayne,' 'Tea for Two,' 'We'll Gather Lilacs.' I used to call them 'my little gentlemen.' They liked that. They were always giving me presents. Chocs and flowers. It's nice to be pampered, isn't it?"

I did not quite know where this conversation was leading. "Baskerville?" I asked. "Is that their family name or something?"

"Baskerville is their manager. Mr. Leo Baskerville. He's not a midget. He's a big man: used to be in the army. Sergeant Major, I believe. He did come down to see them in the panto." I sensed a certain reserve, fear even, in Ruby's attitude toward Mr. Baskerville.

She followed me to my room and, while I unpacked, she continued to pursue the midget theme. I tolerated it because she obviously needed to talk about them. During the two months of the pantomime season they had become her life and now they were gone. It was a void she needed to fill with talk.

I eventually contrived to escape, saying that I had to get into the theatre for a line run, but before I did so Ruby insisted on leading me downstairs to show me something.

"I don't allow just anyone in here," she said, opening a door on the ground floor. "These are my private quarters." She offered no clue as to why she wanted me to see them, as she ushered me into a smallish back parlour. Sheba pattered in ahead of us and settled herself on the white sheepskin rug in front of the gas fire, whining slightly as she did so.

At first I noticed nothing out of order. It was an ordinary, cozy sitting room, of the kind I had seen in countless provincial boardinghouses all over the country. The pattern of the carpet was a violent clash of purples and oranges. There was a glass cabinet full of Coalport figurines and the walls were adorned with Constable reproductions in gaudy gilt frames. So far, so commonplace, but there was something odd about the furniture. It was the usual bulgy stuff, upholstered in a brownish velour, piped and tasseled in gold, but it looked as if it had sunk into the carpet. The seats of several armchairs and a sofa were barely a foot from the floor, and there were a couple of lacquered tables which were at knee height instead of coming up to the waist.

"I had my little lounge specially done up for them. I had all the legs cut off, you see."

I understood. The legs of the furniture had been removed or severed to suit the height of her favoured guests. Some of the amputations had been very crudely done.

I said: "I see." It was not a very profound response, but I was not quite sure how I was meant to react.

"I like it. I find it quite comfy myself. I said to them, 'Whenever you come to Westport, there'll always be a home for my little gentlemen.'"

There were two others from the *Dial M for Murder* company staying at Stage Door, and they also had to endure midget talk. When the following morning Ruby had finally left the breakfast room, one of them, Norman, the veteran actor C. Norman Wetherby who was our Inspector Hubbard, gave me a meaningful look and raised his eyes to the ceiling.

"I'm afraid this looks like a case of 'quoth the raven,' old boy," he said. That day we contrived to spend as little time at Stage Door as we possibly could.

On the Wednesday morning I had just come out of the breakfast room into the entrance hall when I heard the doorbell ring. Ruby emerged from the kitchen at a loping trot, a characteristic method of locomotion, closely followed by Sheba. She opened the front door.

On the very middle of the doorstep stood what I first thought was a six-year-old boy. After the few seconds it took me to accustom my eyes to the bleak February sunlight from outside, I saw that it was not a boy, but a tiny man, no more than four feet six in height.

"Hi ho!" said the man.

Ruby gave a scream of joy. "Rusty Dalgliesh, as I live and breathe!"

At that moment six other diminutive figures leapt out from behind Rusty.

"Hi ho!" they all said. I noticed that Sheba, having seen who her
guests were, turned tail and made off discreetly in the direction of
the kitchen.

"We've come back to see you, Ma," said Rusty, whom I knew
from Ruby's voluble explanations to be the unofficial leader of the
pack. He owed his name to the red hair, somewhat receding, that
he wore *en brosse*. There was a wisp of red goatee on his chin; his
eyes were prominent and staring.

Ruby ushered them all in with many expressions of delight and I
went up to my room as my exit from the house was temporarily
barred by the seven small men. I was not spared their company for
long, however, because within five minutes Ruby was knocking on
my door. When I answered it she was flushed and out of breath.

"I want you to meet my friends that I told you about."

So I was very formally introduced to them. There was Rusty
Dalgliesh, Percy Pink, Bob Dobley, and Billy Whiffin. I forget what
the others were called, but their names, without being outlandish,
were all mildly improbable. They showed enormous and rather embarrassing courtesy toward me, bowing as we shook hands. I, being
over six feet three in height, had to bow, too, but from necessity.

"What's it like up there?" said Rusty as he shook hands with me.
Everyone laughed.

To avoid having to find an amusing but inoffensive answer to this
I asked them what had brought them back to Westport—"apart from
seeing Ruby here," I added. Ruby beamed.

"We've just finished doing a week in Freddie Valentine's show at
Scarmouth," said Rusty. "We closed the first half, you know." Tradi-
tionally, the second most important act on a variety bill is the one
that comes directly before the interval. Rusty was obviously mind-
ful of status, so, after pausing slightly to allow this nuance to sink
in, he went on. "Well, we thought Ma Ruby's just up the coast,
we'll drop in and see our favourite landlady. We might even stay a
few days if it's agreeable."

"Could you squeeze us in a back room, Ruby?" said Percy Pink.

"If you've got the time!" said Rusty.

Ruby shrieked with delight. "Ooh! Rusty Dalgliesh, you are a one!"

"He's a caution and no mistake," said Percy, who had obviously appointed himself Rusty's straight man.

So it was arranged. There was room enough to accommodate all seven of Baskerville's Midgets, provided that I was prepared to move to a smaller room, my present one being large enough to hold two beds. Ruby was so delighted by their arrival that I could not protest, but perhaps the disruption they caused gave me from the outset a slightly jaundiced view of our new guests.

As I was moving my stuff to the new room, I was conscious of activity everywhere. There might have been twenty midgets, not seven, to judge from the noise they made. For such small people they were surprisingly heavy-footed, especially when using the stairs, which they seemed to do the whole time. And then their high, quacking voices were continually raised in laughter or argument. The whole house quivered with unrest.

I could not quite understand the purpose of the commotion, because the midgets were not really making themselves useful. It was Ruby who did all the fetching and carrying, and several times I heard Rusty giving her orders. He was particularly insistent that she make them tea: "Let's have a brew, Ma!" And a little later: "Come along now! Where's that brew, then?" Once I heard Ruby say: "Oooh! I'm rushed off my feet!"

The following day my two *Dial M* companions, Norman and Elspeth, the company stage manager, made their excuses and left Stage Door. I stayed on, partly from sheer inertia, partly out of a vague loyalty. Ruby had enlisted my sympathies from the outset and I found myself incapable of betraying her.

There had been talk and laughter and tramping about from the men far into the night. This was bad enough, but what settled it for Norman and Elspeth happened at breakfast the next morning. The three of us came in rather late to find Baskerville's Midgets already breakfasting, seated at their own special cut-down table, on cut-down chairs. They had finished with their eggs, bacon, and baked beans and were now calling for "a fresh brew" and extra rounds of toast.

Norman had a habit of beginning the *Telegraph* crossword on one day, then leaving it in the dining room to complete at breakfast the following morning. On this morning he picked up his paper to find that all the clues on the crossword had been filled in. "And the little buggers hadn't even come up with the right answers," he told me later, "they'd just put down any old rubbish."

Ruby entered with a fresh pot of tea for the midgets, followed, as usual, by Sheba. When she had left, Sheba lingered behind to lick a few crumbs off the carpet. This was noticed by Billy Whiffin, the fattest and, in some respects, the wildest of the troupe. He played the xylophone.

"Ah, diddums!" he said. "Isn't Ma Ruby feeding you enough?" He threw a half-eaten piece of toast at Sheba, which caught her on the ear. She yelped, more perhaps out of indignation than pain, and scurried from the room.

Norman threw down his vandalized *Telegraph* and got up from the table. "Right!" he said, "That's it! Come along, Elspeth!" Elspeth, a nondescript middle-aged woman who occasionally consented to sleep with Norman on the tour, followed obediently.

Later on I heard Norman coming to rather querulous terms with Ruby in the hall. As he passed me on his way out, he muttered: "'Quoth the raven,' old boy, 'quoth the raven.'" Norman never knowingly undersold his jokes.

I had reason to sympathize with Norman's attitude when I came back to my digs that afternoon to fetch a book. On entering I found Ruby standing in the middle of the hall with her hands over her eyes.

"Ninety-one, ninety-two, ninety-three . . . ," she was saying. At her feet sat Sheba, looking up at her. Perhaps it was my fancy, but to me the look on that dog's face was anxious, even pitying.

". . . Ninety-eight, ninety-nine, one hundred!" Ruby uncovered her eyes. "I'm coming!" Then she saw me and I detected a trace of embarrassment. "Just a little game of hide-and-seek," she said. "It's their favourite." She smiled brightly, but her eyes were weary.

As I went upstairs I heard mutterings and giggles from all corners of the house. From somewhere—I could not quite locate the sound—a voice whispered hoarsely, teasingly: "Roobee!" I heard Ruby climbing the stairs behind me.

"Now, where are my little gentlemen?" she said.

"Roobee!" it came again, this time with a hint of menace.

My unease did not diminish when I had entered my room and shut the door. I felt curiously self-conscious, in a way I had not felt when alone since adolescence. My ears had become sensitized to the smallest sound. I picked up the book from my bedside table, went to the window, and stood there leafing through it, all the time conscious of the artificiality of this act. It was like the feeling you get when you are on stage in front of an audience, but have nothing to say.

My ears picked up a small scuffling sound, coming from within my room. I turned from the window and looked about me, but the room appeared to be empty. Then there was another noise, this time louder: the sound of suppressed laughter. It was coming from under my bed. I looked, and there was Rusty. All I could see was his head with those poached-egg eyes staring at me. He grinned, but I could tell he was irritated by my presence.

I said: "I'm afraid you can't hide in here."

Rusty crawled out from under the bed and brushed his knees vigorously. "Just having a bit of fun," he said. "Ma Ruby likes her bit of fun."

I held the door open for him in silence and he left my room. I believe I am not a prejudiced man, but I have always distrusted anyone—male or female—who calls themselves "Rusty." All I can say in my defense is that to date this irrational instinct of mine has never been proved wrong.

After the show that night I went with the rest of the company to the Lord Nelson pub next to the theatre and stayed drinking with them till closing time. I was hoping that by the time I returned, Baskerville's Midgets would have exhausted themselves. I wanted to enter a quiet house.

It was nearly midnight when I let myself into my digs, feeling foolish from too much beer. I now regretted not having taken advantage of the opportunity of leaving Stage Door with Norman and Elspeth. The hall was dark, but the balustraded corridor that ran across the top of the stairs was lit. As I absorbed the reassuring silence I stared drunkenly at the dull maroon wallpaper bare of anything but its obscure early-seventies pattern.

There was a scratch of sound: it was the squeak of a fiddle tuning up. A tambourine was rattled, a few notes of a recorder were blown; now I was hearing the rasp of a muted trumpet and the squeeze of an accordion. All these formed themselves stumblingly into some sort of tune with a strong pulse from a tin drum and the tambourine.

Then I saw a procession emerge and pass across my line of vision along the passage at the top of the stairs. The seven Baskerville Midgets were slowly marching in line, swaying slightly to the rhythm of the music, each of them playing an instrument. They were stripped to the waist and barefooted, wearing either striped pajama bottoms or underpants. The only exception was Billy Whiffin, who was sitting astride Sheba, banging a tambourine, stark naked. Sheba, the unwilling participant in this rout, was being pulled along on a choke chain by Rusty, who, with his other hand, was holding a kazoo to his lips and blowing so hard that his cheeks were puffed out like a wind god on old map.

It was a grotesque bacchanal with Billy Whiffin as its miniature, swag-bellied Silenus. The bare flesh of stunted figures set against the dark red background suggested the painted frieze of a doomed Pompeian dining room. I watched the parade pass, banging, tinkling, and squawking as it went. The moment it had gone out of sight my paralysis left me. I let myself out of Stage Door and for the next hour or so I walked the empty streets of Westport under a freezing February moon.

The house was black and silent when I eventually returned. The passage light had been extinguished and I nearly fell over Sheba, lying exhausted across the threshold of my bedroom door.

As I had expected, the midgets were there before me in the breakfast room the next morning. Rusty sat at the head of their table. He was reading aloud to his colleagues from a local paper, *The Westport Echo*, and had chosen items of scandal with which to entertain them. I heard his rasping, self-important voice tell how a vicar's wife had been had up for speeding, a scoutmaster had been caught soliciting in a public lavatory, a local councillor had claimed for trips to Paris on his expenses. He turned a page and there was a pause.

"Well, I'm jiggered!" he said at last. "Listen to this, folks: the Tinytones are on the bill at the Pier Pavilion, Coldhaven, tomorrow night. That's just down the road from here." The murmur from the rest suggested both interest and unease. At that moment Ruby entered with the inevitable "fresh brew" for the midgets.

"Hey, listen to this, Roob," said Rusty, and he repeated the information he had just read out.

"And who are the Tinytones when they're at home?" asked Ruby.

"You know, Ma," said Percy Pink. "They're the ones we was telling you about. They do the same sort of act as us—"

"Only not so well," said Rusty.

"Only not nearly so well—"

"And they're dwarfs," said Rusty.

"And they're ruddy dwarfs, not proper midgets."

"Just because they once did a Royal Command at the Palladium, they think they're the bee's knees."

"And they were only on for about three seconds," said Percy Pink, determined to keep his end up.

"Blink and you'd miss them," said Rusty, capping him. Percy now withdrew defeated from the conversational field while Rusty expanded on the general inferiority of the Tinytones. "Still," he concluded, "we ought to pop down to Coldhaven. See what the competition is up to."

"Oh. Is that wise?" said Ruby.

"They might have pinched some of our act," said Percy Pink.

Rusty gave Pink a scornful, dismissive look. "We have to see them for professional purposes," he said. "We'll go incognito." I had to stop myself from asking how.

So it was decided. They persuaded Ruby to ring up the Pier Pavilion box office and reserve them seven seats in various parts of the house. She declined to accompany them on the expedition, and did her best to dissuade them from going. "There might be trouble," she said. "You know what these dwarfs are like." The midgets were deaf to her warnings, and I suspect that Rusty positively relished the idea of trouble.

The following day, the Saturday, I only saw the midgets briefly at breakfast. I had a matinee and evening performance while they had their appointment at Coldhaven, some ten miles down the coast from Westport. When I got back from the theatre that night, the midgets had not returned. Ruby was wandering about the hall in fluffy mules and her late husband's old tartan dressing gown, look-ing very worried.

"They should be back by now. It wasn't a late show or anything."

I had a cup of tea with her in the kitchen while Sheba frisked about, making herself very friendly, evidently buoyed up by the absence of her tormentors. Ruby lit another cigarette from the al-most extinct one on her lip and became calmer. I was thinking of leaving her and going up to bed when there was a banging at the front door. Ruby stood up; Sheba scuttled into her basket by the stove.

"Something awful has happened," said Ruby. "I know it."

We opened the door and Rusty staggered in, clutching his left side. He almost fell into Ruby's arms. I unzipped his little leather bomber jacket. The left side of his shirt from the waist up was red and wet with blood. Ruby became hysterical.

"I'll ring for an ambulance," I said.

"No! Don't bother. It's nothing," said Rusty.

"Get the ambulance!" shrieked Ruby.

When I had rung for an ambulance, we moved Rusty's surpris-ingly heavy bulk into Ruby's parlour and laid him out on the sofa. Ruby kept telling him to rest and not to talk, but Rusty would not obey her. He was determined to explain what had happened.

"They're a lousy act, them Tinytones. Unprofessional, that's what they are: no discipline, no timing. We was disgusted. They're giving our sort a bad name, I tell you. Well, after the show I was for making tracks, but Billy, he wanted a jar, so we go to the pub, the Turk's Head on the pier next to the Pavilion. Well, we was just sitting there, having a jar, minding our own business, when in comes the Tiny-tones, oh, very high and mighty. Very Royal Command, I must say; five pounds to look at them, not as you'd want to. Well, their leader, Bertie Banjo, his name is, was up the bar ordering his brandy and Babycham, when he sees us. And we're just quietly having this jar, minding our own business. And he comes over, and he says: 'Well, if it ain't the marvellous midgets.' All sneery-like, he was. 'What's that, to you, Bertie Banjo?' says Billy Whiffin. And Bertie goes: 'Don't think I didn't spot you lot in the theatre, clocking our act. What were you up to? Seeing how it's done properly, were you?' I goes: 'More like seeing how *not* to do it!' I was just joshing, like, see, trying to keep it light. By this time the other Tinytones are all gathered round with Bertie. And Bertie goes all hoity-toity: 'Don't you take that tone with me, Rusty Dalgliesh!' And I says: 'I'll take what tone I like, thank you very much.' And he goes: 'I don't care what tone you take, you little toe-rag.' Well, then, Percy Pink, who's been all quiet up till now, gets very shirty and says: 'Don't you call my friend here a toe-rag. You show some respect, you dirty dwarf.' And he throws his ginger beer shandy right in Bertie's ugly moosh. Well, by rights, maybe Percy shouldn't have done that, because that starts it. The Tinytones, they all pile in, and the next thing I know, there's a full-on ruckus between us and the Tinys. There's punches and kicks and beer bloody everywhere. And the whole rest of the pub is standing round, just watching us fight, laughing fit to bust, like it's a comedy act or something. Only it wasn't. They had knives, you see, the Tinys. Bob Dobley goes down, and then Billy Whiffin goes bloody bananas. He throws this broken beer glass right at Bertie Banjo and catches him a good 'un on the chin, and after that—my God, it was terrible. I got out quick but not before some little bastard of a Tiny stuck me in the ribs. Didn't think it was that bad at first so I gets a taxi here. I never saw the end of it, but Billy's a goner; I think Percy Pink's had it. Bob's probably a write-off. Mind you, we gave as good as we got. Effing dwarfs: they're nothing but trouble."

"Oh, Rusty!" was all Ruby could say. The ambulance arrived, but it was too late: Rusty was dead before he reached the hospital.

I had meant to leave on the Sunday morning and go back to my flat in London for twenty-four hours before traveling on to the next date of the tour, but Ruby was in a bad way, so I stayed on. The company's next port of call was Swansea, which I could easily make on the Monday. News of the fight at the Turk's Head pub came in during the day and it was bad: Billy Whiffin and Bob Dobley were dead; others had sustained horrific injuries. The Tinytones had come off rather better, but no one escaped unscathed.

In the afternoon Leo Baskerville, the midgets' manager, arrived, a big grim man with a black moustache who seemed to hold Ruby personally responsible for the tragedy. I tried to defend her but was brushed aside with a curt: "You keep out of this, young man." By the Monday morning there was nothing more that I could do for

Ruby, so I took my leave and traveled across country by a succession of trains and buses to Swansea. *Dial M for Murder* did particularly well that week.

I do not know what exactly happened to all the Tinytones and Baskerville's Midgets who survived the fight at the Turk's Head pub, but I am pretty sure that none of them ever worked again. There was a brief report of Percy Pink's suicide later that year in *The Stage*. For a long time afterward the whole idea of dwarfs or midgets on stage was anathema. If the pantomime subject was *Snow White and the Seven Dwarfs*, the little men were played by children from the local dancing school. Children are cheaper anyway.

It was another two years before I came again to the Queen's Theatre, Westport. This time, by way of contrast, I was playing Dr. Haydock in *Murder at the Vicarage*. I booked into Stage Door for the week. On the telephone Ruby had sounded a little faint and didn't at first seem quite sure who I was. I knew something was wrong almost as soon as I arrived at Stage Door on the Monday afternoon. Two minutes after I had rung the bell I began hear the faint sound of shuffling feet, and it was another full minute before the door was opened.

The cigarette was still there, hanging slackly from the corner of her mouth. She was more stooped, and her bottle blond had faded in patches to near white. What startled me most was that she appeared to be smaller in a way that could not be explained simply by the normal erosions of age and infirmity. Everything about her had shrunk. Sheba tottered up to her side. She too looked unkempt, and she had begun to smell.

"Where did you spring from?" asked Ruby.

I explained and she reluctantly let me in. She said: "When are the others coming?" I replied that there was no one but myself and asked which room I was in. She said I could choose and shuffled off into the kitchen.

I climbed the stairs and selected the room that smelled least of damp. It happened to be the one I had been moved to on my last visit. The bed was made up with clean linen, but a thin patina of dust lay over everything. In the corridor a tongue of the Pompeian red wallpaper hung down to reveal, on the wall behind, a miniature garden of green mildew.

I have been in such houses before and there the decay has been accompanied by a great absence, a deadness, but Stage Door was different. The place was full of small noises; nothing alarming, just a symphony of tiny clicks and creaks and sighs, as if the whole building were shifting in its last restless sleep. If this was decay, then it was active decay.

Ruby's voice called up to me: "I've made a brew. Would you like some?"

This encouraged me a little, so I went down to the kitchen where Ruby handed me the front door key as usual and a cup of tea. Her conversation occasionally made sense, but the thoughts she came up with were not connected with one another. Once she asked me if I knew when "the others" were coming; a little later she inquired: "Where are they hiding now?" I decided that I would stay that night and decide in the morning if it was still bearable.

Just before I left for the theatre that evening I thought I would look in on Ruby to tell her I was going, perhaps also to see if she was all right. The kitchen door was closed and I was about to knock when I heard her voice coming from within. It was hard to tell at first what she was saying; it was like some sort of chant. Then I recognized it.

". . . Ninety-eight, ninety-nine, one hundred!" A pause. "I'm coming!"

I walked quietly away from the kitchen door and left the house.

Usually when I was on tour I would call in to the theatre before going to my digs. This time I hadn't, and when I went into my dressing room I saw that the previous occupant had scrawled in lipstick across the mirror the words:

DON'T STAY AT STAGE DOOR

That Monday night the company went for a curry after the show so I was late into Stage Door. As I had expected there was no light on in the hall or anywhere in the house, and the darkness accentuated the presence of little noises everywhere. Most of the sounds could be explained by the terminal decline of the house with its creaking boards and hissing, rattling pipes, but some perhaps could not. I did not like to think about them.

I kept as many lights on as I could until I was safely in my room. If I was not mistaken the smell of damp and mildew, mingled with the faint odor of elderly and infirm dog, had become more pronounced. I opened a window, but it was too cold for that so I closed it again. To protect me from the dampness of the sheets I wore socks and a dressing gown when I got into bed.

I will definitely leave this place tomorrow, I said to myself. *I shouldn't have stayed tonight.* In the street outside the window a drunk was singing; I heard a smash of glass on the road. Then the house began to shake.

It was strange. I felt the shake before I heard the noise that presumably caused it. Someone or something was running heavy-footed up and down the passage outside my room. The whole house quaked at the sound. I got up, opened the door, and looked out into the passage. Through the gloom I saw the vague shape of Sheba limping unsteadily toward the stairs, but surely *she* could have not made the noise. I told myself that she could. I also told myself that there was nothing I could do for her. Ruby should have the dog put down. I closed the door and returned to bed.

There was silence for a few moments. Then someone under my bed whispered: "Roobee!"

I lay still, every muscle tensed. The room grew colder. Then it came again, this time more insistent, aggressive.

"Roobee!"

I knew the voice. It was the angry, hoarse whisper of Rusty as he lay bleeding on Ruby's sofa, telling us about the fight at the Turk's Head pub. I switched on the bedside light. I looked under the bed. Nothing. I dressed in a frenzy. I went out into the passage. Sheba lay at the top of the stairs. She looked as if she had been flattened, as if sat upon by something. She was surely dead. I ran down the stairs and out of the house.

I have no recollection of the next few minutes but I do remember the next five hours or so. I spent them on a bench in a shelter on Westport front, watching the reassuring lights of ferry boats as they glided in and out of the harbour. When dawn came up I returned to Ruby's house and transferred my bags to a café, where I had breakfast. Later that morning I found new digs. The landlady seemed perplexed at first by my unexpected arrival. When I said I was from the theatre, she grimaced and nodded as if this fact was a more than adequate explanation for my behaviour.

Some weeks later I saw this small paragraph in *The Stage*.

THEATRICAL LANDLADY FOUND DEAD

Mrs. Ruby Baker, the well-known theatrical landlady of Stage Door, no. 10 Harbour Street, Westport, was found dead yesterday in her own home. Neighbours raised the alarm after they had not seen her for several days and calls to her remained unanswered. Police broke into the house and conducted a search of the building.

She was eventually found in a linen cupboard, having somehow shut herself in there. Cause of death is thought to be asphyxiation from smoke caused by a cigarette end falling onto the bed linen in the cupboard and making it smoulder. It is thought that she was either too weak and malnourished or too confused to break out from her confinement. Neighbours say that in recent months her mental condition had deteriorated and that she had been heard talking of hiding from something or someone. Foul play is not suspected. Mrs. Baker was a widow and had no children.

Personally, I have always favoured dwarfs over midgets. We all have our prejudices, and our reasons for them.

BLOOD YESTERDAY, BLOOD TOMORROW

Richard Bowes

Richard Bowes has published five novels, two short fiction collections, and more than fifty short stories. He has won two World Fantasy Awards and the Lambda, International Horror Guild, and Million Writers Awards.

Recent and forthcoming stories appear in *The Magazine of Fantasy & Science Fiction* as well as in *Wilde Stories 2010, Nebula Awards Showcase 2011, The Beastly Bride, Haunted Legends, Digital Domains,* and *Naked City* anthologies. Several of these stories are chapters in his novel in progress, *Dust Devil: My Life in Speculative Fiction*.

His website can be found at http://rickbowes.com.

"Ai Ling, show Aunt Lilia and everyone else how you can play the Debussy 'Clair de lune,'" Larry said as his partner, Boyd, beamed at his side. Lilia Gaines was at the dinner party as a friend of one of the hosts, Larry Stepelli.

She had, in fact, been his roommate in the bad old days. Twenty-five years before she and Larry had entered Ichordone therapy as a couple and left it separately and stayed that way.

The exquisitely dressed Asian girl sat, tiny but fully at ease, at the piano. At one time Lilia had wondered if only well-to-do gay couples should be allowed to raise kids.

Behind Ai Ling the windows of the West Street duplex looked over the Hudson and the lights of New Jersey on a late June evening. And amazingly, almost like a beautifully rendered piece of automata, the child played the piece with scarcely a flaw.

Amidst the applause of the dozen guests and her fathers, Ai Ling curtseyed and went off with her Nana. Lilia, not for the first time, considered Larry's upward mobility. This dinner party was for some of Boyd's clients, a few people whom Larry sought to impress, and one or two like her whom he liked to taunt with his success.

A woman asked Boyd what preschool his daughter attended. One of his clients dropped the names of two senators and the President in a single sentence.

A young man who had been brought by an old and famous children's book illustrator talked about the novel he was writing: "It's

YA and horror lite on what at the moment is a very timely theme," he said.

Larry smiled and said to Lilia, "I walked past Reliquary yesterday and you were closed."

"Major redecoration," she replied. Their connection had once been so close that at times each could still read the other. So they both knew this wasn't so.

He tilted his handsome head with only a subtle touch of gray and raised his left eyebrow a fraction of an inch.

Lilia knew he was going to ask her something about her shop and how long it could survive. She didn't want to discuss the subject just then.

Larry's question went unasked. Right then the young author said, "It's a theme which sometimes gets overworked but never gets stale. The book I'm doing right now is titled *Never Blood Today*. You know, a variation on 'jam tomorrow and jam yesterday but never jam today' from *Alice in Wonderland*. In fact the book is Alice with vampires! Set in a well-to-do private high school!"

The writer looked at Larry with fascination as he spoke. Boyd frowned. The illustrator who had a show up in Larry's gallery rolled his eyes.

Larry smiled again, but just for a moment. For Lilia the writer's conversation was an unplanned bonus.

A woman in an enviable apricot silk dress with just a hint of sheath about it changed the subject to a reliably safe one: how nicely real estate prices had bottomed out.

Then Boyd suggested they all sit down to dinner. Boyd Lazlo was a corporate lawyer, solid, polite, nice looking, completely opaque. Lilia Gaines knew he didn't much trust her.

Lilia and Larry went back to the time when Warhol walked the earth, Manhattan was seamy and corroded, and an unending stream of young people came there to lose their identities and find newer, more exotic ones. Back then Boyd was still a college kid preparing to go to Yale Law.

These many summers later, Manhattan was gripped by nostalgia for old sordid days and Lilia had something to show Larry that would evoke them. But it was personal, private, and she hadn't found a moment alone with him.

At the end of the evening he stood at the door saying good-bye to the illustrator. The young writer looked wide-eyed at Larry and even at Lilia. The mystique of old evil: she understood it well.

As Larry wished him farewell, Lilia caught the half-wink her old companion gave the kid and was certain Larry was bored.

She remembered him in the Ichordone group therapy, standing in tears and swearing that when he walked out of there cured of his habit he would establish a stable relationship and raise children.

Boyd was down the hall at the elevator, kissing and shaking hands. Lilia and Larry were alone. Only then did he put his hands on her shoulders and say, "You have a secret; give it up."

"Something I just found," she said, reached into her bag, and handed him a folded linen napkin. You'd have had to know him as well as she did to catch the eyes widening by a millimeter. Stitched into the cloth was what, when Lilia first saw it years before, had looked like a small gold crown, a coronet. Curving below the coronet in script were the words MYRNA'S PLACE. The same words and emblem were above them upside down.

Before anything more could be said, Boyd came back looking a bit concerned and as if he needed to speak to Larry alone. So Lilia thanked both of them for dinner and took her leave. She noticed that Larry had made the napkin disappear.

Years ago when New York was a wilder, darker place, Larry and Lilia's apartment was on a marginal street on the Lower East Side, and they pursued careers while watching for their chance. He acted in underground films with Madonna before the name meant anything, and took photos; she sold dresses she'd designed to East Village boutiques.

Patti Smith and Robert Mapplethorpe were the model for all the young couples like them: the poker-faced serious girl with hair framing her face and the flashy bisexual guy. They were in the crowd at the Pyramid Club, Studio 54, and the Factory. Drugs and alcohol were their playthings. Love did enter into it, of course, and even sex when their stars crossed paths.

Since they needed money they also had an informal business selling antiques and weird collectibles at the flea market on Sixth Avenue in the Twenties.

In those days that stretch of Manhattan was a place of rundown five-story buildings and wide parking lots—fallow land waiting for a developer. On weekends first one parking lot, then a second, then a third, then more blossomed with tables set up in the open air, tents pitched before dawn.

It became a destination where New Yorkers spent their weekend afternoons sifting through the trash and the gems. Warhol, the pale prince, bought much of his fabled cookie jar collection there.

During the week Larry and Lilia haunted the auction rooms on Fourth Avenue and Broadway south of Union Square, swooping down on forlorn vases and candy dishes, old toys, unwanted lots of parasols and packets of photos of doughboys and chorus girls, turn-of-the-century nude swimming scenes, elephants wearing bonnets and top hats.

Since it kind of was their livelihood they both tried to be reasonably straight and sober at the moment Sunday morning stopped being Saturday night. While it was still dark they'd go up to Sixth Avenue with their treasures in shopping carts, rent a few square feet of space and a couple of tables, and set up their booth.

In the predawn, out-of-town antique dealers, edgy interior decorators, and compulsive collectors, all bearing flashlights, would circulate among the vans unloading furniture and the tables being carried to their places by the flea market porters.

Beams of light would scan the dark, and suddenly four, five, a dozen of them would circle a booth where strange, interesting, perhaps even valuable stuff was being set up. Lilia and Larry wanted that attention.

Then came the very drowsy weekday auction when they found a lot consisting of several cartons of distressed goods: everything from matchbooks and champagne flutes to mirrors and table cloths, all with the words MYRNA'S PLACE in an oval and the gold design that looked like a small crown, a coronet.

The name meant nothing to them. They guessed Myrna's was some kind of uptown operation—a speakeasy, a bordello, a bohemian salon—they didn't quite know.

Old, hard-bitten market dealers called themselves Fleas.

Larry said, "Fleas call the trash they sell Stuff."

"And this looks like Stuff," Lilia replied.

"And plenty of it," they said at the same moment, which happened with them back then. They bid their last fifty dollars and got the lot.

That Sunday morning they rented their usual space and a couple of tables. Other recent finds included a tackily furnished tin dollhouse, a set of blue-and-white china bowls, a few slightly decayed leather jackets, several antique corsets, a box of men's assorted arm garters, and a golf bag and clubs bought at an apartment sale. They had dysfunctional old cameras and a cracked glass jar full of marbles. Prominently displayed was a selection of Myrna's Place stuff.

The couple in the booth across from theirs seemed to loot a different place each week. This time it was an old hunting lodge. They had a moose head, skis, snow shoes and blunt, heavy ice skates, Adirondack chairs, and gun racks.

Larry and Lilia set up in the predawn dark as flashlights darted about the lot. Then one fell on them. A flat-faced woman with rimless glasses and eyes that showed nothing turned her beam on the golf clubs.

She shrugged when she saw them up close. But as she turned to walk away, her light caught a nicely draped tablecloth from Myrna's Place. "Thirty dollars for the lot," she said, indicating all the Myrna items.

Larry and Lilia hesitated. Thirty dollars would pay the day's rent for the stall. Then another light found the table. A middle-aged man with the thin, drawn look of a veteran of many Manhattan scenes was examining Myrna's wineglasses. "Five dollars each," Lilia told him, and he didn't back off.

To the woman who had offered thirty for the entire lot, Larry said, "Thirty for the tablecloth."

The woman ground them down to twenty. The thin, drawn man bought four wineglasses for fifteen dollars and continued examining the merchandise.

Lilia and Larry's booth attracted the predawn flashlights. It was like being attacked by giant fireflies. Nobody was interested in anything else. It was all Myrna's Place. Old Fleas paused and looked their way.

As dawn began to slide in between the buildings, the thin, drawn man found a small ivory box.

"Myrna Lavaliere, who and where are you now?" he asked, and opened the lid. It was full of business cards bearing the usual double Myrna's Place and coronet logo. Below that was an address on the Upper East Side, a Butterfield 8 telephone number, and the motto, "Halfway between Park Avenue and Heaven."

"More like far from Heaven and down the street from Hell," the man said. "You kids have any idea what you have here?"

Larry and Lilia shrugged. Other customers wanted their attention.

"Wickedness always sells," the man told them. "And after the war in the late 1940s, rumor had it this place was wicked. Myrna's was a town house where you went in human and came out quite otherwise."

A tall woman with a black lace kerchief tied around her long neck and wearing sunglasses in the dawn light had stopped examining a pair of Myrna's Place candlesticks and paused to listen.

She gave a short, contemptuous laugh and said in an unplaceable accent, "Oh please, spare these not terribly innocent children all the sour grapes stories spread by all the ones who couldn't get inside the front door of Myrna's. What happened there happened before and will happen again. If you know anything about these phenomena at all, you know that."

She faced him and raised the glasses off her eyes for a moment. Neither Larry nor Lilia could see her face. But apparently her stare was enough to cause the man to first back away, then scuttle off.

"Fifty gets you the candlesticks," Larry told her. They were getting bold.

"I just wanted to make sure these weren't as good as the pair I have. But I will let others know about you. I think the time is right."

Then the wizened pack rats and sleek interior decorators were all at the booth hissing at one another as they pawed through the items. Lilia and Larry tried to spot people they thought might actually have gone to Myrna's.

As morning sunlight began to hit the Sixth Avenue Market, club kids coming from Danceteria in fifties drag found Larry and Lilia's stall. Dolled-up boys in pompadours, girls in satin evening gowns who looked like inner tension was all that held them together, stopped on their way downtown. They seemed fascinated, whispered and giggled, but didn't buy much: a handkerchief, a cigarette holder.

But the stock of Myrna's Place items was almost cleaned out when a lone Death Punk girl, her eye shadow and black hair with green highlights looking sad in the growing light, appeared. She pawed through the remaining items, dug in her pockets, and gave Larry three dollars and seventeen cents, all she had with her, for a stained coaster.

Around then Lilia realized that if she held any of the items at a certain angle, the Myrna's Place design looked like an upper and lower lip and the coronet was sharp, gold teeth. Once she saw that and pointed it out to Larry, they couldn't see it any other way.

They weren't naive. In the demimonde they inhabited gossip lately concerned ones called the Nightwalkers. About then they began wondering about Myrna's Place.

2.

Thirty years later, on the morning after the dinner party, Larry called Lilia on her cell phone several times. But she was on an errand that took her uptown and onto the tram to Roosevelt Island. Though this situation hadn't occurred recently, Lilia remembered how to play Larry when she had something that he wanted.

Roosevelt Island lies in the East River between Manhattan and Queens. On that small spot in the midst of a great city is a little river town of apartment houses. Along the main street the buildings project out over the sidewalks, providing a covered way.

In one period of Lilia's life the sun was unbearable and had to be avoided. Now walking under cover she was glad the habit had remained and helped her avoid skin cancer.

Lilia remembered the others who took the cure when she and Larry did: the old man with wild white hair and gleaming eyes who required three times as much Ichordone as anyone else in the program and wore a muzzle like a dog because he tried to bite; the mousy woman who had been turned into a vampire when she saw Béla Lugosi as Dracula on TV twenty years before.

Generations ago Roosevelt Island was called Welfare Island. It was where hospitals for contagious diseases were located. Their ruins still dot the place. Hospitals are still located there, most of them quite ordinary.

But in one there is a ward for patients with polymorphous light eruption (allergy to the sun) and haemophagia (strange reactions to blood), and several other exotic diseases. Behind the hospital are cottages.

In one of those sat the person Lilia had come to see. She was in a wheelchair, wrapped in blankets and looking out the window at the sunlight and water. The woman had seemed ancient to Lilia that morning years before at the flea market when she examined the candlesticks and told the man to spare her his sour grapes stories. Now Myrna Lavaliere was a mummy—nothing more than skin and bones and a voice.

"When one is old the smell of rot—one is falling apart—is omnipresent. Men are the worst but none are immune. Each time you come here you are awestruck by my age and corruption. I don't blame you. I am well over a hundred. My addiction first to blood and then to Ichordone prolonged my life, but look at the result.

"Up in the hospital they'd have me in restraints with my head immobilized because they're afraid I'd bite them." She laughed noiselessly and showed Lilia her toothless gums.

"All I want," she said, "is to die in this room with a bit of privacy, not up in that cadaver warehouse." She indicated the main hospital building. "Like everything else in this country it requires money."

In earlier meetings she had told Lilia how much longer she had to live, how much that would cost, and how many treasures from Myrna's Place and other clubs she had stashed in storage lockers.

Lilia had told her of a plan she had. Today she told her what was required to implement it. "I need more bait for the market," she said.

Their eyes met and they understood each other. A nurse's aide was called and she brought Lilia a package of collectibles like the one she'd been given the week before.

3.

Lilia waited until she was back at her shop before answering one of Larry's calls.

Immediately he asked, "Where did you find it?" She heard voices echoing behind him in Stepelli, his large gallery space in West Chelsea.

She told him a tale of the Garage, that last sad remnant of the once sprawling Sixth Avenue flea markets and the napkin she found the Sunday before when she ducked in there to get out of the rain.

"Was there anything else from Myrna's Place?" he asked.

"This is all I found," she said. "But the dealer said there was quite a flurry when she opened. Young people, apparently."

"Where did she get it? Does she have any more?"

"Yes," Lilia told him, and gave no hint of her amusement. "She got it from a woman who got it from a man who may have more. I have a lead on her source." None of this was entirely true, but in his eagerness that escaped him.

It was Friday afternoon. They made plans to visit the Garage early Sunday morning.

Her shop, Reliquary: once so very trendy and notorious, later a charmingly creepy holdover, a bit of stylish nostalgia, now hung by a thread. The landlord, unable to find another tenant, had let Lilia slide on the rent from month to month. His patience was running out.

That afternoon as Lilia went on various errands, she remembered the Saturday night and Sunday morning after Larry and her first triumph.

The second week they brought all their good Myrna's Place stuff: the flasks, the scarves, the elephant foot umbrella stand. They were surrounded from the moment they set foot in the flea market. All the flashlights were around them. Customers from the previous week were back and others as well.

The dealers who looted a house each week had a day-care center's worth of children's chairs, toys. They paused to watch the commotion across the aisle.

Larry and Lilia discovered that the first Death Punk girl had been a harbinger. Out of the night, smelling of cigarettes and amyl nitrate, came club boys and girls in black from head to pointed toe shoes. There were the retro and extreme retro kids, dressed as twenties flappers, Edwardian roués and whores. One young man with a cravat and a face painted almost white carried a small, antique medical bag and was called Dr. Jekyll.

They bought small souvenirs—a tea cup or a doily. When asked what was so fascinating about Myrna's Place they shrugged and said this was Nightwalker stuff, the new thing.

Then, in the predawn, the club kids, awestruck, watched as half a dozen figures flitted toward them like bats, like shadows. Lilia heard the Flea across the way call out to someone, "Dracula and company just showed up!"

The newcomers all seemed tall, elongated. They wavered in the first light. Many of them actually wore capes. They were thin and their smiles were a brief flash of teeth.

As they moved through the kids around Larry and Lilia's tables, one of them reached over and, almost too fast to see, pulled down the collar of a girl's jacket and first kissed then nipped her neck. The club girl shivered with ecstasy.

Lilia was uneasy but Larry was starstruck. Here was true glamour, the very heart of the most exclusive club backrooms. The sky was getting light. The newcomers surveyed the booth, nodded, put on sunglasses, exchanged glances, and smiled. These people were impressed with him.

Raised cloaks hid what happened from the casual customers. In an eye-flash Larry's leather jacket and shirt were pulled off his shoulders. The smiles and fine sharp teeth looked like the ones on the Myrna's Place logo.

Larry's eyes went wide. A tiny trickle of blood ran down his chest. He stared after them as they left the market and didn't even notice Lilia pulling his clothes back in place.

Other customers appeared. Larry and Lilia were Flea celebrities and had a good day—even the dollhouse sold.

Larry was bedazzled. Lilia knew he always gravitated to the key clique and always managed to get himself accepted. Now he'd found a group so special it was legend, and they loved him.

That week Larry was distant and distracted. He got on her nerves. She got on his. The next Sunday morning they brought to market all the remaining Myrna's Place material and everything else they had for sale.

In the predawn the flashlights found them and so did the woman with the neck scarf and sunglasses. The club kids stared at her reverently. She glanced at Larry and almost smiled. She gave Lilia a slip of paper with some names.

"In one's old age, collections, however beloved, become a burden. These are ones who are ready to give up theirs."

As she turned to go, the young Nightwalkers appeared. They bowed their heads and parted for her.

"Myrna," Lilia heard them murmur, "Myrna Lavaliere." The woman nodded and disappeared into the last of the night.

When the Nightwalkers exposed Larry's neck, Lilia told them not to because it had made him stupid. But he pointed at her and capes were raised, Lilia's arms were pinned, her blouse opened. Before she could even cry out, she felt teeth and a nick on the side of her neck.

Lilia turned to see who had done this, but the effort made her head spin. Lilia knew a few things about drugs. None felt like this: it was like acid cut with heroin. She and Larry were in trances for the rest of that day and most of the next.

When they recovered, they took the list of names and telephone numbers the one the Nightwalkers called Myrna had given them. The people on the list were old and fragile, looking like they might break. But their eyes were sharp and sometimes their teeth. They all had memorabilia they were ready to get rid of. One or two liked to bite, but they were mostly harmless.

4.

Late on a summer night thirty years later, Lilia met Larry in front of Reliquary on West Broadway at the trashy end of SoHo. Tense, knowing things had to go just right; she noticed that he wore the napkin with the MYRNA'S PLACE logo displayed like a handkerchief in his jacket pocket. She did wonder where he had told Boyd he was going.

Cabs cruised and groups of young people searched for after-hours clubs. On weekends near the solstice, Saturday darkness comes later and Sunday morning is very early. There's almost no place left for the night.

Larry looked at the sign, the darkened windows and shabby aura of the store. "Some amazing times here," he remarked, and shook his head.

Once it had been different: "Cool Reliquary!" the ads in the *Village Voice* had said. "Not Your Mommy's Kind of Boutique—Not Your Daddy's Either" had been the title of the article in *New York* magazine just after the shop opened in the early eighties.

Suitable designer styles were offered: capes in a variety of lengths, parasols to keep the sun out of the eyes, shirts and blouses that displayed best half open and exposing the throat and neck.

Then there were the tchotchkes, relics from what turned out to have been an endless succession of mysterious clubs and salons. Fra Diablo just off Union Square had attracted rumor and curiosity in the 1870s, the Bat Bar flourished just after the turn of the century. Club Indigo in Harlem in the late twenties had introduced white patrons to an impeccable African-American staff and entertainment that could only be talked about in whispers.

"All those venues and every one of them produced artifacts," Larry said. "Certain individuals liked to have stuff like that around. Other people in the know would be aware of their interests without a word being spoken."

The two talked over old times as they walked toward Sixth Avenue while looking for a cab. They remembered the time the Nightwalkers first showed up at the Mudd Club, the way columnists in the *Village Voice* hinted at a craze that was not quite drugs or sex. The *New Yorker* had said, "Some call it a very old European tradition."

Everyone wanted artifacts to take back to Westchester, to Chicago, to Paris, to Rome, a sign they'd had at least a brush with the tingly and strange. Reliquary was where they got them.

"Daylight was something to be endured," Larry said. "We lived at night."

Lilia remembered those times like she'd seen them through the wrong end of binoculars. But she wasn't going to contradict him or mention the crash that followed the boom.

For her it began when her dentist noticed the way her teeth had grown and ordered her out of his office. Then on one of Lilia's rare visits to the Philadelphia suburbs her mother mentioned the pallor. "Are those hickeys?" she had asked, catching sight of the bite marks on Lilia's neck.

She remembered the day the newspaper and magazine articles

suddenly turned sour. "Blood Crazed!" the tabloids screamed. "Contagious Disease Disguised As Hip Cult," the magazines cried.

Rich kids' families pulled them into elite and expensive therapy. Everyone else ended up in city hospitals and day clinics. Ichordone, horrible and soul-deadening, was the methadone of vampirism. She wondered if Larry had managed to forget about that, guessing he had, and saw no reason to remind him.

At Sixth Avenue they found a cab and rode uptown through the Village and the old Ladies' Mile. Groups hung about the corners, stood in front of the desecrated church that had been a nightclub. For a moment, on a side street, Lilia thought she saw a figure in a cape. She felt Larry tense and knew he'd seen it, too.

"It's always been cycles, hasn't it," he murmured. She said nothing. "Every twenty-five, thirty years: one is overdue," he said, and she nodded.

The cab turned on Twenty-fifth Street and stopped at the Garage. This last stronghold of the flea market was set in the middle of the block and went right through to Twenty-fourth. The official opening was 8 A.M. but dealers were already setting up. Their vans rolled up and down the garage ramps and visitors were slipping in along with them.

A thin young woman and buff boy, both in black, went down the ramp to the lower level. Lilia let Larry take the lead and follow them down. She wondered if all this was going to work.

The place had none of the mystery of the predawn flea market. It smelled of exhaust and bad coffee and was lighted so there was no need for flashlights. Older buyers watched dealers unpack their stock.

The couple in black drifted toward the back of the selling floor and a little knot of young people in a far corner, just out of the bars and clubs.

Larry headed in that direction without looking to see if Lilia was with him. She was a step or two behind, following him back into a world they'd once known.

She knew what he was going to find: place cards with celebrity names—Cole Porter, Winston Guest, and Dorothy Parker—from Club Indigo. Delicate fans decorated with cats baring their teeth from the Golden Palace, which had flourished down in Chinatown once upon a time. And, of course, salted into the mix were a few items from Myrna's Place. This was the contents of the parcel Lilia had been given on Roosevelt Island a couple of days before.

She watched the way Larry took in not only the items for sale but the ones who had come to look at them. A few more kids stopped by. This was a gathering spot like their booth had been thirty years before.

They looked at Larry and his napkin with its crest of lips and teeth displayed. He asked the dealer where she had gotten the stuff and if she had any more.

The dealer was Eastern European and had trouble with English on certain occasions. She said a woman had sold them and hadn't left a name. No, she didn't have any more. She was good at this and didn't once glance Lilia's way.

The onlookers stirred. Lilia turned and saw figures in sunglasses moving in the shadows cast by pillars and vans. Nightwalkers had arrived. A new, less formal generation in shorts and flip-flops, though Lilia noticed that several still wore capes.

Other dealers and their customers paused and shook their heads. Lilia's spine crawled. She wondered if all this was worth it. Then she saw something which again confirmed that fate was with her.

The young writer of the Alice and the vampires book was borne along as a kind of trophy by the Nightwalkers. His eyes were wide and he looked dazed. His shirt was open and several small puncture wounds ringed his neck and throat.

Larry's eyes widened and Lilia knew he'd once again found his exclusive clique. Clearly it was open to the young and pretty but perhaps also to the well-to-do.

He reached for his wallet, asked the dealer how much she wanted for the lot of vampire tchotchkes. He didn't flinch at the gouger price Lilia had told her to charge. The crowd seemed disturbed by this interloper.

Lilia whispered, "I know the location of a treasure trove of similar stuff."

Larry nodded and distributed the items among the club kids and Nightwalkers alike. They became interested in this stranger. Then the young writer recognized Larry, got free of his handlers, hugged him, and nipped his neck a little.

Lilia handed out faded cards for Reliquary while promising, "Memorabilia *and* fashion. Come see us during the week."

As she did she thought about T-shirts—hip, enigmatic ones. She knew distressed fashions that could be turned over for very little money and she believed capes could be brought back one more time. Larry clearly was fascinated, so the money was there.

The crowd broke up, headed to the exits. Larry and Lilia followed them but when they reached the street all of them—club kids and Nightwalkers alike—had disappeared.

He seemed a little lost as they went toward a spot Lilia knew would be open at this hour. She wondered if he was remembering the Ichordone, the withdrawal, the dental clinics where teeth got filed down, the group therapy where a dozen other recovering vampires talked about their mothers.

"Don't worry, we'll get the audience back," Lilia said. There was a bit of blood on Larry's neck. When she pointed this out he dabbed it with the Myrna's Place napkin. And when she told Larry how much she'd need to get Reliquary up and going again, he nodded.

Lilia was certain she wasn't going to get hooked again. Larry probably would. For a moment she remembered his little adopted girl and hesitated.

Then she recalled the moment thirty years before in the flea market when she'd tried to keep the Nightwalkers away from him and he'd shut her up by siccing them on her.

So instead of little Ai Ling Lilia thought of Boyd, who might dump Larry but would make sure his daughter was well taken care of. She took Larry's arm and led him to the spot where they could discuss the money.

X FOR DEMETRIOUS

Steve Duffy

Steve Duffy's stories have appeared in numerous magazines and anthologies in Europe and North America. His third short-story collection, *Tragic Life Stories*, was launched at the World Horror Convention 2010 in Brighton, England, and is available now from Ash-Tree Press. In 2011, PS Publishing will release his fourth collection, *The Moment of Panic* (which includes the International Horror Guild Award–winning tale "The Rag-and-Bone Men"). Duffy lives in North Wales.

Author's Foreword

This much is a true story: in January 1973, police were called to a bed-sitter room at Number Three, The Villas, Stoke-on-Trent. The tenant, an elderly Polish immigrant named Demetrious Myiciura, had been found dead on his mattress, having apparently choked on a pickled onion. One of the policemen, John Pye, noted in his report that there seemed to be an unusual number of crucifixes in the room, and a quantity of salt had been sprinkled across the floor and the mattress on which the dead man had been found. His head was resting on a full bag of salt, and another lay between his legs. More salt, mixed with what seemed to be urine, had been placed in containers around the room, and there were also plates of excreta mixed with garlic on the windowsill. In the light of these circumstances, PC Pye suggested the coroner re-examine the circumstances of Myiciura's death, and it was subsequently ascertained that he had in fact choked to death on a bulb of garlic, which he seemed to have aspirated in his sleep.

These few details comprise nearly all that is known of the life and death of Demetrious Myiciura. What follows is not the story of his life, and should not be taken as biography. Instead, it is a story which takes its inspiration from his death, and works backward through nightmares in search of understanding.

* * *

For Myiciura, the mathematics is what clinches it. Sitting at a table in the Carnegie free library and laboriously filling a sheet of paper with penciled sums. Beginning with unity, the number one, simplest of concepts; unity first of all doubled, then redoubled, repeatedly, each night. One times one, times two, times four, times eight, times sixteen, thirty-two, sixty-four, a hundred and twenty-eight . . .

After a week it would already be a hundred and twenty-eight. In a fortnight, eight thousand one hundred and ninety-two. After three weeks, a million already. A hundred and thirty-four million, coming into the fourth week; once the calendar month was up, a billion. He draws a deep breath and sits back at the plain wooden table, appalled at the size of the number he has computed, a figure too vast for any man to comprehend. And all from the unity point, from perfect singularity to limitless multiplicity, all in the space of a month. Dear Jesus. No wonder these creatures are shunned and feared.

On the way back home, he sees a wooden sign outside a church, nailed to a stake driven deep into the grassless graveyard soil: *Our God is one, or rather very oneness, and meere unitie*. He frowns at the message while mouthing it to himself, as though its archaic language was chosen specifically to mock him. Our God is one. Not so, but three. See, there on the cross, Christ stretched beyond endurance, racked and slashed two thousand years. Around his head, the Holy Ghost; above him the Father, massive and implacable. One and one and one. And yet, these creatures . . . in the space of even one year, their number would be beyond all human computation.

This was in the summer, when he used to go out. Now, as winter sets in and the nights stretch unendurably from treacherous dusk to grudging dawn, his rented room becomes his fortress, his last redoubt. His single sagging armchair, his mattress on the floor, his wardrobe crammed with junk. The newspapers glanced at and never thrown away, the radio that has fallen silent. At nights he no longer dares to venture out into the common hallway, nor visit the shared bathroom at its end, not while the powers of night hold sway and footsteps he cannot recognize come creaking up the stairwell. Milk bottles, their curdled remnants emptied through the window, make good receptacles for liquid waste. Jam jars, scraped clean with a spoon. As for the rest of it, his digestive tract, starved of fodder, has come to an aching costive standstill. When the garlic makes him belch, underneath the pungent allium he tastes the sourness of his own substance. But he remains Myiciura. Myiciura in his stronghold.

The bottles and jars he arranges around the room, the cloudy piss mixed with salt for the virtue in it. The last time his bowels moved, he took the shriveled sordes and crushed them up with garlic, for the windowsill. See, here: this is Myiciura, and he is protected, yes, he knows wherein lies true magic and real influence. Baseness raised to power and made sound. *Oupire*, tread not in this house.

At night the flame of the paraffin heater glows cherry-red through the metal vents. He positions it close by the mattress, greedy for the pittance of warmth it gives to his corpselike form, lying wrapped in a blanket for a shroud. By its heat he is sustained; by its meager glow he sees all he needs to see. It is his savior till morning comes.

Years on night shift tending the big kilns have wrecked all the patterns of his sleep. Once the circadian rhythm is lost, it is not easily recovered. He has become accustomed to moving through darkness and inhabiting shadows, to sitting still and watching the flames through scratched and squeaking isinglass. He remembers the stove in his father's house, the village back home in Kashubia, how the whole family would huddle close to it while outside the horsemen went from street to street. His father would reassure him, they were only seeking out the *zhidim*, the Jews. They are vampires, he would explain, spitting with ritualistic heaviness on the bare boards of the floor. They suck the blood of Christian boys and mix it in their Passover bread. They prey on all good Christian souls. And this is why they are hated by all honest men, from *pan* to *chlop* to *Volksdeutsch*, even. Hated by all. Remember.

When his father leaned over him, broad face whey-pale and solid as a wheel of cheese, he could smell the garlic sausage on his breath. His father's eyes were intent and accusatory, polished black beads from a rosary. Like a crow's eyes, they were watching, always watching. He smiled infrequently, and his every word and action seemed freighted with a ponderous burden. When he was small, little Demetrious had been quite naturally scared of him: when his mother told him tales of the ogres that lived in the forest, they all had his father's face, those monsters glimpsed onrushing through the trees, thin branches splintering at their approach.

The massive stroke that dropped the old man at his workbench left him laid up for a fortnight before the end, as if death itself could find no easy way to pierce that massive bulk. Thirteen-year-old Demetrious had risen early in the chill hour before dawn, to set a copper of water to boil and see to the chores. A candle in his hand, shielded against the draft, disclosed the makeshift bed made up in the warmest kitchen corner for his father—no one could carry him up the steep and narrow stairs. He went over to see if he was awake, to see if he needed anything.

He held the candle high above the cot, saying, "Papa, it's morning, how are you." His father's eyes—black as raisins in the kneaded dough of his face—followed the light. "Papa," Demetrious said, "papa," and then he saw it, the fear deep down in those staring eyes. Incomprehensible, never before seen or dreamed of, yet now overmastering. How long had his father been lying there in the dark while the rest of the family slept, struggling with a terror that could not be held in check?

In this instant Demetrious learned a great lesson: that there is dread at the heart of all things, that fear comes to all men at the end and reclaims them for its own. Birthed in blood and chaos, we struggle a little while till inexorably we are undone, and horror waits panting at both ends of existence. He opened his mouth, wanting to ask his father what he saw in the wavering candle flame, but the words would not come. Instead he watched, fascinated and aghast at the same time, while the old man took one ragged sucking breath, and then another. He waited a long time for the next breath to come, and somewhere in that everlasting interval, he realized that his father was dead.

Soon afterward his mother died, too, and after that no one ever called Demetrious by his Christian name. Already he was Myiciura, only Myiciura; already he was in the cities, growing old before his time.

He left the land and went to Krakow, where he found work in the metal trade, operating a blast furnace night and day. He found a measure of comfort in the linked and logical processes, the feeding of ingredients in exact proportion, the skimming-off of slag, the knocking-out of the clay plugs when the kiln was ready for tapping. In the preparation of pig iron, the greatest ingredient by volume is air: the weight of the air used in the process exceeds the weight of all the other raw materials. They told this to Myiciura, and he nodded carefully, knowing that fire and air are at the heart of all good things, that a hunger for air is what separates the living from the dead. He himself would spend the hours between shifts lying back on a bed in his rooming house, windows closed against the clamor of the day, curtains tightly drawn against the obscure sooty sun, counting his own breaths and wondering at their stately regularity.

On Sundays he would go to church, because he had always gone there. The sound of the Latin soothed him without instructing him, and while hushed and sonorous prayers were sung by priest and congregation, he passed the time in eyeing the brutally crucified Savior who hung above the baldachin. Outside on the streets came revolution, then dictatorship, and soon afterward the Germans, and after them the Russians. Through it all, the production of iron remained sacrosanct, and Myiciura endured. The years of the Germans were filled with rumors; something, it was said, was happening in the forests. A dreadful thing. Death and horror, a hunger unappeasable, bodies uncountable, pits filled with the dead. Myiciura, a man of the cities now, remembered the ogres of his childhood and wondered. From preaching sermons against the vampire Jews and moneylenders, the priest turned his ire toward the vampire Bolshevists, blasphemers, atheist scum. Vampires again!

Myiciura marveled at the deceitfulness of it all. He'd been told many times by his father, by his mother, by everyone in his village, what crafty, scheming creatures were these. He understood how good Christian souls would not necessarily recognize them—this was commonly agreed, though each citizen was naturally unshakable in point of his own shrewdness—nor comprehend the evil they worked under cover of darkness.

Masters of deception, fathers of sin. Ah, then, how surely the virtue of true iron, pure and unalloyed, heated and refined by the breath of true life, must necessarily repel them! His work at the furnace assumed an almost religious significance; Myiciura would watch the fiery dribble of iron spill into its mold and cross himself, murmur the words of prayers whose meaning he was already forgetting.

But mark how they change their shape, he told himself, adding the information to his little hoard of knowledge, tucking it away like the last zloty of a miser. Mark well the cunning of these beasts. Be on your guard. Keep watch.

In the course of the war, nearly all the Jewish vampires disappeared, rounded up at dawn, when their powers were waning, and taken away by the soldiers. Myiciura watched in bleak satisfaction from his window as the trucks drove away in the thick mist of morning, leaving behind empty houses, suitcases scattered on the cobblestones, a vivid splash of lifeblood up against a wall. Taken to where? "Up the chimney," everyone said, then changed the subject, as if they feared being overheard. Again, this made sense to Myiciura: fire, you see, father of true iron, the sacred principle behind it all. The rushing force of God's breath drawn through the furnace, to rid the world of all contagion. For a while, Myiciura slept more easily.

Then the Germans were evacuating, and the Russians swept in on a tidal wave of bombs and guns and orgiastic bloodshed. And these were the Communist vampires, and from them there was no hiding place. Even the parish priest Father Usniewicz, Myiciura's primary source of information regarding the creatures of darkness: even he vanished one night, in the hours when their power was exalted. Next morning the church was boarded up, its windows smashed, its insides burned out. Myiciura endured it as long as he could, before a man told him about the people-smugglers who worked the cargo ships sailing out of Gdansk for the West.

And here in the West, in Stoke-on-Trent in the raw and misty November of 1972, Myiciura hurries home from the corner shop while it is still light. The shopkeeper is another refugee come to England in search of sanctuary, a Bangladeshi named Varendra Singh whom Myiciura regards with a furious mistrust. Can such as this be carriers? Myiciura gnaws the skin at the corners of his mouth, stymied again at the lack of such basic information, and no priest to ask, no father figure. Tomorrow the library, he decides. Or—

He is forced to an unexpected halt before the bus shelter. On the wall behind the shelter is a poster for the local cinema: big, primary colors, a splash of brightness in the claylike gloom of raw cold autumn. "DRACULA AD 1972," he spells out. With horror he beholds the familiar features of the beast, leering evil in his shroud of darkness. "The Count comes to swinging London," he reads, lips moving, "with a taste for . . . everything!" The address of the cinema is not far, a few blocks from his home. Myiciura recoils, appalled at the blatancy of the contagion. Even here; even now.

Mockery follows him down the twilight streets, children perched atop a wall like dirty scavenger birds who jeer as he limps past. *"Diabe jest twoim ojcem,"* he mutters. *The devil is your sire.* He shuffles on till he can no longer hear their laughter, till the roofs of the terrace block out the rising sickle moon, sharp tooth of the leering *oupire.* Safe in the shadow of the building, he glances up. A light shines in his uncurtained window. A light, where no light should be.

For a second Myiciura is speechless, motionless with dread, till he realizes what has happened. The electric light—he switched it on, did he not, to check the bread for mold before his trip to the shop? And forgot to switch it off. Foolish old man. Electric is not free. Soon the meter will need feeding, and so less for you to eat.

Slowly Myiciura nods. Relieved if hardly comforted, he lets himself in and hurries, alive to each creak of the staircase, each shadow he casts, up the unlit stairs to the refuge of his bed-sitter room. Barely through the door, he's already fumbling for the light switch. Ah, darkness. Shadows swallow up the room, and he slams the door to trap them safe inside. Then, by the light of the streetlamps outside, teetering on a high-backed chair like a man about to hang himself from the rafters, he unscrews the forty-watt bulbs, one after the other, one, two, three, from the chandelier fitting. He has seen how their light would give him away, would cast his fragile silhouette so clearly in the treacherous bright window. He will not reveal himself. He will not present so obvious a target.

And in the evening's long and lonely watches, as the light from the glowing heater gleams in the wardrobe's mirrored door, Myiciura stands before the smeared and dusty glass and examines himself. So thin now; so weak, so insubstantial. If one night he were to fade away and vanish, would he witness his own absence in the glass? Shaking his head, Myiciura returns to his nest of blankets and coats on the mattress, draws the rough wool up to his jutting chin. He does not expect to be warm, merely hidden, in this dark corner of a rented room. His sore jaws chomp with grim resolve on a cud of garlic clove.

Those things we once held to be necessary turn out, in the end, to be only a sort of habit. All through autumn, a slow process of subtraction refines Myiciura's existence, simplifies it—ennobles it, he tells himself. As the blast furnace banishes impurity from iron, so Myiciura is rendered pure down to his very essence. This is his conviction, even as his skinny body begins to give way. Already his organs, starved for months now of nutrition, have turned cannibal, begun to consume themselves for what little nourishment they contain. His few remaining teeth are loose in his shrinking gums; when he battens down upon a crust of bread, he sees blood around the bite mark. Blood shows scarlet in each morning's coughed-up sputum, and only garlic takes its taste away.

Bread, yes, because the Savior broke it, because it is His body. Kielbasa, for the comfort of the fat that coats his mouth. And clove after clove, bulb on bulb, of raw garlic, his safeguard and protection. Salt, though not for food: for distributing around the bed-sit, by way of defense. All this and a pint of milk—he requires nothing else. A weekly trip to the delicatessen and the corner shop meets all his needs. The rest of the time, he sits in his single room and reads his book, or walks the boards and waits till nightfall.

His book is stamped on its flyleaf with the words PROPERTY OF STOKE-ON-TRENT LIBRARY SERVICE. Myiciura saw it one day in the Carnegie library: his need was greater than anyone's could possibly be, so he simply tucked it under his overcoat and walked out, unchallenged. He dips into it at random, picking up the text at the top of the verso page, reading until his eyes ache, setting it aside with no marker. His finger follows each line, his lips mumble the words like mushed-up bread and milk as he reads aloud: "In all the darkest pages of the malign supernatural there is no more terrible tradition than that of the Vampire, a pariah even among demons. Foul are his ravages; gruesome and seemingly barbaric are the ancient and approved methods by which folk must rid themselves of this hideous pest." Seemingly barbaric, yes: Myiciura nods in appreciation, in his nest of filthy blankets, surrounded by his own waste in saucers and milk bottles. Safe, for the time being.

This is the passage which haunts Myiciura most of all: "Can the Devil endow a body with these qualities of subtilty, rarification, increase, and diminishing, so that it may pass through doors and windows? I answer that there is no doubt the Demon can do this, and to deny the proposition is hardly orthodox." Each time the book falls open at this page—page 174—he shudders, and looks to his defenses. Groaning with the effort, he struggles up from his rank cocoon, shuffles across the bare boards to the window, checks the containers and their contents. Once a week, stale is replaced with fresh, and in this way protection is assured. *Oupire*, see how I defy you.

And as the early evening settles over Stoke-on-Trent, as the orange streetlamps wink into life, Myiciura lights a candle and settles to his vigil. Outside, children run home through the streets, the rough music of their play a cheerful flourish in the dusk. Parents laden down with food from the supermarket arrive home, good neighbors calling good evenings to one another as they hurry up the garden path and let themselves in the front door. Soon, the blue light of television shines from sitting room windows up and down the terrace. Myiciura's window is dark, with curtains drawn tight closed. Inside, the flame of his single candle gutters and smokes; with a trembling hand, he pinches back the black and drooping wick. He has run out of paraffin for the heater, and so no heat: nonetheless, Myiciura will endure. At home in Poland there was no heat in the bedroom, but a candle, always. Light of a blessed candle, true shield against the *oupire*. Pray, that your immortal soul be spared this night.

And so by candlelight he waits for the life of the house to wane, for the lights in neighboring residences to go dark, the bell in the nearby steeple to toll twelve strokes, the short day's passing knell. Once the last door has creaked shut, the last TV fallen silent, all cisterns flushed and bedsprings settled in the rented rooms around him, there is just Myiciura and the night: its slow eternities of silence, its litany of secret sounds.

Since his youth he has been one accustomed to the darkness; he has learned to sit still in an empty room and watch the fire that keeps the shadow at bay, focus on it till all the world slips away around the edges, and there is just the flicker-dance of flame against nothingness. He has learned to listen to the sound of his own breathing, the air rushing in and out of his wheezing chest; and beneath it his heartbeat, frail and reedy. He has learned that Outside, the powers of darkness are always in wait—whirling through the air like flurries of black snow, seeking to enter where they may in a draft beneath the door, a crack in the window, a weak place in the heart. He must be strong. He must endure until the dawn.

The worst thing is the footsteps on the stairs. Each night now, each freezing winter midnight, he hears them. And knowing the footfall of every tenant, he still cannot say to whom they belong. To whom, or to what. He clutches the blankets at their approach, bites his chalky knuckle till he tastes his own blood.

They seem to Myiciura to proceed from the hallway up to the landing, where there is carpet and the thing may creep unheard. It is difficult to tell which way the *oupire* goes: he sees a skulking thing in his mind's eye, a tiptoeing thing that sneaks in shadows and never shows its face. A thing of little flesh. Cruel eyes that gleam palely in the dark. Sharp ears that would catch his breathing, be it ever so quiet and muffled by the blanket. See how Myiciura crams his bedding into his mouth in fear of being overheard, battening down on the rough woolen stuff of the blanket like the *oupire* that eats its own shroud!

For minutes on end he waits, hunched up with his back against the wall like a Mexican mummy, mattress dragged into the niche between the wardrobe and the corner of the room, for the footsteps to resume, for the doorknob to rattle, for anything to relieve the silence. At some indeterminate point in his vigil he realizes he has been sleeping, and has only just awoken. Outside the door, so far as he can tell, there is nothing. There is only his fear of what might have been there—of what might even be there still, for all he knows. When he pulls the sodden blanket from his mouth, he sees blood from his shrunken aching gums has stained the wool. Mechanically, he wipes his mouth with his sleeve, pops another clove of garlic into his mouth. Leaning back against the pillow, he settles once more to wait for dawn, and a chance of lasting sleep.

* * *

Christmas comes and goes, and the windows of the houses on Myiciura's street are brightly decorated, sparkling tinsel and fairy lights
wreathed against the darkness of the midwinter solstice. In Myiciura's room there shines no light, and the jam jars on the windowsill
filled with soil and waste are his only decoration. A terror has settled in on him, a gnawing at his very soul: he has seen the face of
the monster.

At midnight on the Redeemer's own day, the feast of the Savior's
birth, Myiciura dared set foot outside his room for the first time in
a whole season of evenings. As the church bells chimed a welcome
to the Christ-child, he slipped out into the corridor, heading for the
bathroom—the lady downstairs had given him a mince pie and a
glass of sherry that afternoon, and his bowels were churning abom-
inably. Accustomed to the dark, he did not turn on the light, even
in the bathroom. He sat perched on the pan, for all the world like
some rocking, praying rabbi, grunting slightly with the pain of the
whole business, the indignity, until he heard himself and abruptly
clenched shut his aching gums.

Hobbling back along the corridor, he came to the door of his room.
One hand on the knob, he paused. Downstairs, a fumbling at the
front door. A key in the lock. Myiciura, frozen stiff with fear, could
only listen.

A burst of laughter, quickly smothered, in the vestibule downstairs. Revelers. Myiciura recognized the voices: people of the house.
The fat lady from downstairs. *Do not let them see me.* Bewildered, ir-
resolute, he glanced back along the first floor landing. And then,
downstairs, a switch was flicked, and the landing light came on.

And in that instant he saw it, there in the pier glass at the landing's farther end. Thin, gray, caught with hand extended to the
door. The horror in its face; the horror. Myiciura had barely the
strength to scramble through his own doorway, slam it shut behind
him, and collapse, sobbing, on his mattress. His chest was so furious with pain, he could barely breathe. Though the pain receded,
the horror did not, not that night, nor for many nights to come.

And now, as New Year's chimes over the rainy rooftops of Stoke-
on-Trent, all hope is gone for Myiciura. Doubts and fears have eaten
away at him, and in the end have dragged him across the floor on
hands and knees to his own mirror, to face his destiny. There before

the glass, he searches in the gloom for his own reflection. What does he see? What does the candlelight catch, in the wreck of his bed-sitting room, in the miserable remains of his existence?

He sees what his father saw at the last, what fixed the old man rigid on his deathbed. There before him, revealed at last: the fearful *oupire*, the thing of night and horror, the beast now locked inside with him. His secret sharer, his dread twin. Creature of the dark. There the hunched thing crouches, rising from the shadows on the floor as if to lean over the bed in which he sleeps. A monster, gray and filthy as the grave, dead skin stretched across its long thin cemetery bones. Its mouth, its awful mouth: it gapes forever in a terrible soundless scream. And Myiciura, transfixed in horror, screams, too. Forever.

KEEPING CORKY

Melanie Tem

Melanie Tem's solo novels include her Bram Stoker Award–winning debut, *Prodigal*, and most recently *Slain in the Spirit* and *The Deceiver*. She has also collaborated with Nancy Holder on *Making Love* and *Witch-Light*, and with Steve Rasnic Tem on *Daughters* and *The Man on the Ceiling*. The earlier, novella version of *The Man on the Ceiling* won the 2001 Bram Stoker, International Horror Guild, and World Fantasy Awards. The Tems also collaborated on the award-winning multimedia CD-ROM *Imagination Box*.

Her short stories have been published in the collection *The Ice Downstream* on E-Reads and in numerous magazines, including *Colorado Review*, *Black Maria*, *Asimov's Science Fiction*, and *Cemetery Dance*, and in anthologies, including *Snow White, Blood Red; Acquainted with the Night; Poe; Portals;* and *Black Wings II*. She has also published nonfiction articles and poetry.

Tem is also a playwright and an oral storyteller. She lives with her husband, writer and editor Steve Rasnic Tem, in Denver, where she works as an adoption social worker. They have four children and four granddaughters.

On the clock was a 2 and a 5 and a 4. Janie squinted at the red numbers, puzzling. She was allowed to call at three o'clock. When would that be? The 4 turned to a 5, making her jump a little. Now there were two 5s. That was confusing.

She was only allowed to call one time because one day she called sixteen times, and then two more times to say sorry for leaving so many messages. The nice lady Hannah said she wasn't mad at her, just tired. Drained, she said, but Janie didn't get that. A lot of people said Janie made them tired.

So now Janie was only allowed to call one time every month. All those days and nights in between and all those clock numbers changing, she thought about what she would say in her letter to Corky. To her son. He was her son, and he was those other people's son, too, and she was allowed to write him a letter one time every month. She didn't write good, so she called up Hannah and said what she wanted in the letter and Hannah wrote it down on the computer, Janie could hear the clicks, and then Hannah always promised to mail the letter the very next day. Janie always wanted to call back and make sure she did, but she wasn't allowed to because Hannah was drained.

Janie didn't know how a letter got from one place to another place so she didn't know if Hannah really sent her letters to her little boy. Corky. Corky's other parents were supposed to write to her every year at Christmastime and on his birthday and send her pictures of him. They promised. They signed that paper. But they didn't do it. It was bad not to keep your promise. They were bad. Sometimes Janie thought and thought real hard and tried to get those letters and pictures out of them like she was sucking on a straw, but it didn't work very good.

Two times they sent her pictures, once when he was a baby and once when he was three. He was fifteen now. Janie counted. Fifteen years old.

The baby picture she had on the wall by her bed with a thumb tack. It was so cute. He had on a little suit with some words on it. Janie kissed it every day when she first woke up and every night before she went to sleep. She couldn't remember if that was what he looked like when she got to hold him in the hospital. She didn't get to hold him very long. She named him Corky. Corky was a nice name. She came up with it all by herself.

The three-year-old picture Ike stole. Maybe it wasn't really stealing, because Ike was Corky's daddy. She cried when he took it and she cried every time she thought about it because she didn't remember stuff good and she forgot what color his little shirt was, blue-and-white striped, she thought, and she forgot what he was holding. A truck? A bear? Janie cried every day when she forgot stuff about that picture of her son Corky a long time ago when he was three.

But she was happy Ike wanted it. He used to try to pretend sometimes he wasn't Corky's daddy, but he was. Janie knew that much. Janie knew where babies came from, and Ike was the only guy she ever did that with and ever would. After she thought really hard and all the air came out of his tires and made her tummy get all big and hurt until she could pass it, he quit saying he wasn't Corky's daddy. Maybe he knew she did that to his tires and maybe he didn't, she never told anybody what she could do because a long time ago her mom and dad used to hit her when she told them. You shouldn't hit kids. She would never hit her little boy Corky. Her mom used to say all the time that Janie just took everything out of her. Not everything. Not love. Janie loved her little boy Corky.

Then Ike stole the picture. She could visit it when she went to his place.

Janie could make him give it back. Or just take it back her own self. Sit in her chair and think really really hard and do something mean to him or slurp the picture down off his wall and into her. But she didn't want to hurt Ike and she didn't want to hurt the picture of her son Corky, and sometimes she hurt stuff when she didn't mean to.

Janie loved Ike. Janie loved Corky. She was a lucky girl to have two people to love so much. Some people didn't have any. Her mom and dad didn't. They didn't love anybody.

There was a 7 on the clock now. When she figured out she'd missed the 6 it scared her. Then she got scared it wasn't the right day and she had to go into the kitchen and look on the big calendar where the day she was allowed to call the nice lady Hannah every month had a big red circle around it that Ike put there for her. He could trick her. He could lie to her. Sometimes he lied to her. Sometimes he played tricks on her and he thought it was funny. That wasn't very nice. But Janie was pretty sure this was the right day. She poked it with her finger.

When she got back there was a 9 on the clock, and the minute she sat down by it all the numbers changed and it scared her and she wanted to run away and hide but she didn't because now it said 3:00. That meant three o'clock. That was the calling-Hannah time. Janie swallowed more beer and rubbed her hands together and got out her paper with all the numbers and poked them one by one by one.

She did it right the first time. "Angels of the Heart Adoptions, this is Hannah, how may I help you?"

Janie bounced up and down and yelled, "Hi, Hannah!"

"Hi, Janie. You're right on time."

Janie beamed. "Am I right on time?"

"You are, Janie, you're right on time. My computer's all ready."

"Your computer's all ready?"

"Yes, it is."

Janie almost said, "It is?" But she stopped herself and closed her eyes and tipped her head back and took a big breath and poured all the beer left in the bottle right down her throat. The feeling when something went down her throat like that was a happy feeling, a full feeling.

"Janie? Are you ready to write your letter?"

She tried to say yes but she still had beer in her mouth and she spit it out all over the place and then she couldn't stop laughing because it was so funny. Sometimes Ike and her would spit beer at each other and laugh and laugh and it was so fun.

When Hannah from Angels of the Heart Adoptions said her name, "Janie!" Janie knew she was in trouble. "Janie, are you drinking?"

"No, ma'am," Janie said, all serious, and then she started laughing again and she couldn't stop. Her belly hurt.

"Janie, what did we say about drinking while we're writing to Corky?"

Now Janie was really scared. Her belly hurt. "Don't," she said. "Don't drink when we write to my son Corky."

"That's right," the nice lady Hannah said, but Janie could tell she wasn't gonna be nice this time, she was gonna be mean. "We agreed that if you were drinking we couldn't write the letter to Corky. Do you remember that, Janie?"

Janie squinted at her paper with all the stuff she had to tell her son Corky, "I love you." "We love you." "Your birthparents love you, Ike and Janie." Birthparents was the word Hannah taught her. Janie liked it. It sounded so grown up. *Birthparents.* "I love you" about a hundred million times. She knew she didn't spell any of it right and her words got slanty, but that was okay, that was why Hannah put it on the computer for her. "Please," she said.

"I'm sorry, Janie, but we had an agreement. I've turned off my computer now. We'll try again next month. When you're sober."

"Tomorrow." She was shaking and she was going to throw up.

Hannah said, "No, I'm afraid I'm busy tomorrow. You call me one month from today, July 10, at three o'clock. Look on your calendar. We'll try again then, okay?"

Janie was crying. She needed a beer. She got up and started to the kitchen with the phone in her hand, telling herself not to put it down somewhere and forget where she put it, like in the fridge or something. "But I love him," she whispered to Angels of the Heart Hannah.

"I have to go now," Hannah said. "I'm going to hang up now, Janie. Good-bye. Make it a good day."

All of a sudden she had a really good idea that would make Hannah like her again so she'd write her letter to her son Corky for her and get those people Corky's other parents to send her pictures of him and a letter back. They promised. They signed that paper that her and Ike signed, too. Janie had that paper. Where was it?

It was such a good idea Janie bounced up and down and screamed into the phone, "He's the angel of my heart! He is! You put that in there!" Then she listened hard, holding on to a chair because she was kind of dizzy. But Hannah didn't say anything. After a while Janie heard that funny music and that other lady's voice and she knew that meant Hannah had hung up on her.

She fell down on the floor, hollering and pounding her fists and kicking her feet. If she threw the phone across the room it'd probably break and then she couldn't call Ike or call out for pizza or call Hannah at Angels of the Heart one month from today, July 10, at three o'clock. You could buy new ones but she didn't know how to do that and Ike would have to take her because he could drive and he could do money. It would cost a lot of money. She knew that much.

So very carefully she hung up the phone. She turned on Dr. Phil. But he was talking to some dumb girl about some dumb problem Janie didn't even get. Dr. Phil was saying sometimes we get what we wish for but we have to make it happen. The girl was ugly, too, and she was not very nice.

Janie got another beer and went back into the living room and reached to turn Dr. Phil off. Then Dr. Phil was talking about some people drain you and use you up and take everything you've got for themselves.

"You just suck the life right outta me, child!" Somebody used to say that to her a lot, Janie didn't remember who. Some nice old lady.

Then she remembered in one of those big buildings where she'd lived with all those kids, she used to get in trouble for drinking out of other people's cups, but she was thirsty, even when she drank a bunch of milk and pop and juice and water and even coffee from the grown-ups' cups and then she had to go pee or she'd wet her pants—even then she was always thirsty.

Then she started bouncing up and down in her chair with the beer bottle hitting her teeth because she remembered Ike used to want her to do stuff to him that was like that, like sucking and swallowing stuff out of him for her own self, and she'd feel dirty and sticky but she was a good girl, a strong girl, because she knew how to make Ike happy and what to promise him to get him to do what she wanted. Now he didn't even want her to kiss him. Janie cried and sniffed and wiped her nose.

On the TV Dr. Phil kept talking and the ugly sad girl kept crying and Janie remembered she didn't always have to be touching anybody or anything. There was that time in the ninth grade when that Paula kept teasing her and teasing her and wouldn't stop and Janie knew from gym class that Paula had great big boobies and Janie just stared at them and thought about them oozing pink pus right out of them and they did, you could see the pink on that Paula's yellow blouse and that Paula had to go to the hospital. After that Janie's boobies were bigger than that Paula's, so there.

What could she do to Hannah for being mean to her? What did she know about Angels of the Heart Hannah that she could use? But she couldn't keep her mind on it.

So she went to Ike's. He was playing Space Invaders and he got mad at her for talking loud, but she had to because Space Invaders was so loud. He didn't care about Hannah being mean. He didn't care about the letter to her son Corky. To their son Corky. He didn't care that Corky's other parents broke their promise. All he cared about was his stupid computer game, and that wasn't even real. Corky was real. Janie knew that much.

But now she didn't see the picture at Ike's. "Where's that picture?"

Ike didn't pay any attention to her. He yelled at the computer.

She pounded him on the back. "Where's that picture you stole? Corky when he was three years old?"

"What picture you talking about, girl? I'm busy here. Get away from me!"

"That picture of my son Corky when he was three years old? He had that blue-and-white-striped shirt and that bear?"

"In there, I guess." He jerked his head.

She didn't see the picture in the bedroom where he said. It was gone, it was gone, her picture of her son was gone, she couldn't write him a letter, she lost him, she gave him away, he didn't love her, Ike didn't love her, nobody loved her, she didn't have anybody to love. Janie started pounding her head on the wall and wailing.

"Goddammit!" Ike stomped in and put his arms around her from behind. It wasn't a real hug, Janie knew that much. It was to make her stop. He pulled her away from the wall so she couldn't bang her head but she didn't stop, she kicked and twisted her body and tried to bite him. "Stop it, Janie, goddamn, cut it out! The picture's right here. And it's a rabbit. He's got a rabbit. See? And his shirt is red-and-white striped, not blue. See? You don't even remember it right. Stop it! Calm down and I'll give back the picture, okay?"

Janie put her arms around his neck and cried. Ike held her and told her it would be all right. She kept crying a little longer than she really needed to so he'd keep holding her. But finally she couldn't anymore because now she was happy, she had the picture of Corky and Ike was holding her and July 10 was only one month from now and that wasn't all that long and it was on her calendar. She gave Ike a big mushy kiss and told him he was sexy and wouldn't he like her to do something special? But he went back to Space Invaders and she went home to think about Corky and to think about Angels of the Heart Hannah.

For five days she thought about Hannah. Thursday, Friday, Saturday, Sunday, Monday. She put an X through every day when it was used up.

What did she know about Hannah? Nothing. Not her last name—she always just asked for Hannah. Not if she was married or had kids. Not how old she was or where she lived or what she looked like or if she liked pizza or whatever. All Janie knew about Hannah was that she worked at Angels of the Heart Adoptions and her phone number, all those numbers on that paper

—where was it? Did she lose it? There it was on the chair. She put it away in her desk where it was supposed to be. If she lost it she couldn't call Hannah on July 10 at three o'clock. She put the paper with the numbers on it in her mind and thought about it as hard as she could to make it stay put, but she didn't know if that would work. Janie's mind didn't always work. She wasn't very smart. She knew that much.

She sat in her big chair anyway and drank beer and put her mind on Hannah for five days. It was hard for her to think about something for very long but she could do it when she had to. She used to go for a walk when she had to think but then one time she got lost.

One time she tried to think when she was taking a shower and she got the water too hot and almost burned herself. The only way she could do it was sit in her chair and rock back and forth and think hard, and even still it didn't work all the time but it was all she could do.

So that's what she did. For five days. She thought about Hannah and what she could do to her so she'd let her call her and write her letter to Corky. What she could take out of her. Her mouth kept getting all yucky-tasting so she couldn't do it for very long at a time but lots of short times all day and all night.

Then somebody else not Hannah called her from Angels of the Heart Adoptions. "Hi, Janie, this is—" Some other name.

"Hi. Where's Hannah? What's wrong with Hannah?" Janie was scared. Did she do something really really bad this time? Was Hannah's blood all gone and she was white and empty like a plastic bag? Janie was sorry, she didn't mean to.

"Hannah's not in today. This is—" That other name. "Hannah asked me to give you a call. How are you doing, Janie?"

"Is Hannah okay? Is she sick? I hope she's not real sick, I hope nothing really bad happened to her, I hope she's okay, I hope she's not—" Janie remembered her manners. "I'm fine, thank you. How are you?"

"I'm fine, thank you."

"How's Hannah? Is Hannah okay? She told me I'm supposed to call her on July—"

"Hannah's got a bad case of the flu, she's feeling pretty weak and drained, but she'll be okay.

"The flu like the runs and puking and stuff like that?" Janie giggled but then she got that yucky taste in her mouth again and she squinched up her face and stuck out her tongue and went "Bleaugh!" Then she put her hand over the receiver so the lady wouldn't hear her take a big swallow of beer and give a great big burp.

"Hannah asked me to call you to tell you that Matthew's parents sent us a letter."

"Who? Whose parents?"

"Your son's adoptive parents?"

"His name's Corky!" Janie tried not to yell. But his name was *Corky*.

"Oh, yes, I see now that his birth name was Corky."

"His name's Corky! That's what I named him. That's what his daddy and me named him! Did they send pictures? They promised—"

"Janie, Corky's parents don't want you to write him any more letters."

Janie sat there.

"Janie?"

"What?"

"Did you hear what I said, honey?"

"No."

"I know this is hard to hear. Corky's adoptive parents have asked us to stop all communication with you. I'm really sorry."

"But they promised. They signed that paper. Me and Ike signed it, too. Ike's Corky's daddy."

"Those are only good-faith agreements. They aren't legally binding. They aren't enforceable."

"But they promised. What's good faith mean?"

"It means—they promised." The lady laughed a little. It wasn't funny. "But nobody can make them keep that promise."

"The judge can make them." Janie remembered the judge and the big high table.

"No, the judge can't make them. It's not a legal contract. They've requested that we not send them any more letters from you. I'm so sorry, honey."

"Why?"

"Oh, I'm sorry because I know how much this means to you. Hannah has told me—"

Janie was bouncing up and down. Her head felt funny and her heart hurt. "No, no, no—" Sometimes she got stuck on a word and just kept on saying it and saying it and saying it. She thought really hard so she could stop saying no. It gave her a headache. "Why do they say I can't send letters no more?"

"They say Matt— Corky is kind of having a hard time right now, you know, being a teenager, what is he, fourteen?"

"Fifteen," Janie said. "He's fifteen years old."

"Fifteen, yes, here's his DOB. Well, that can be a hard age, you know. They think it would make things harder for him, confuse him, if you keep sending letters."

"What about presents? We already got his Christmas present. I already wrapped it." This wasn't true, but it seemed like it was and maybe it would make the lady take back what she said. "Wanna know what it is? It's a secret but I can tell you. It's a big fire truck with a siren and everything. Me and Ike played with it for a little while before I wrapped it up, and it works good."

"They are asking for no further contact."

"What about presents?"

"No presents, Janie. No pictures, no letters. I'm so sorry."

"When'll Hannah be back? I wanna talk to Hannah."

"I don't know. She's pretty sick."

"What's your name?" The lady said the other name again but Janie forgot it. Then the lady said good-bye.

They couldn't have him. She would take him back. She would keep him. They could've shared him, she would've shared him with them, but they couldn't have him all themselves, they couldn't take him away from her. He was her son. She gave him to them because her and Ike couldn't raise him right, they weren't smart enough to raise him, Janie knew that much. But the deal was, she got to keep him, too, because of letters and pictures and presents and letters and presents. They promised, and they went back on it, and so the deal was off.

Janie sat in her chair and drank every beer she had and cried and fell asleep and woke up and thought as hard as she could about those people. They used to be her son Corky's other parents but she wasn't going to let them be that anymore because they were mean and they went back on their promise and his name was Corky not that other name, that Matthew. She wasn't going to let them. She was going to take him back and keep him for herself and Ike.

But every time she tried to think about them, she was thinking about Corky instead. That was because she didn't know nothing about them. Nothing, nothing, nothing. And she did know stuff about Corky. She knew he grew inside her and she got big and fat but it was beautiful. She knew she didn't drink any beer as soon as she found out she was pregnant because she was his mommy and it was her job to take care of him while he was in her tummy, and that was hard to do but she did it. She knew what it felt like when he moved around inside her and kicked her and had the hiccups. The doctor said she was connected to her baby and blood and food and stuff went back and forth between them like through a straw. She knew it hurt a lot getting him born. It hurt a *lot*. He was so teeny tiny when he came out, so how come it hurt so much? And he was so warm in her arms when they let her hold him and Ike touched his cheek with one big finger, and he was crying screaming little red face and he scared her and she gave him to the nurse. She knew what he looked like in her two pictures, now she put them one on each knee where she could look at them and touch them with her finger, the one where he was a baby smiling and the one where he was three years old and he had on a red-and-white-striped shirt and he was holding a big stuffed rabbit, or was it a bear? She was pretty sure it was a bear no matter what Ike said, Ike was not right every single time, Ike was not the boss of her.

She knew a lot about her son Corky. Not fifteen-year-old Corky but baby Corky and three-year-old Corky.

So it was Corky she tried to think about really, really hard so she could get him back and keep him this time. About him coming out of her and making her bleed and that string thing they had to cut to get him away from her. About how he had her nose and Ike's hair, you could see it in that picture—well, she couldn't see it but that's what Ike said and Ike could drive and do money so he knew things. About how when he was inside her she used to feel his teeny tiny little heart when she put her hands over her own heart. About how Angels of the Heart Hannah said Corky would always be in Janie's heart and she'd always be in his heart, and Janie didn't really get that but it sounded nice being in each other's heart, each other's blood in each other's body.

It made her sick, all that thinking, and she went to bed and went to sleep. When she had to go to the bathroom it was dark outside. When she had to go to the bathroom again it was sunshiny. When she had to go to the bathroom again it was dark again. The phone woke her up. "Hello, Janie? This is Hannah from Angels of the Heart Adoptions. Did I wake you up?"

Janie pushed herself up against the wall. Her head ached. "Oh, Hannah, I'm sorry, is it July 10 at three o'clock? I'm sorry. Did I forget? I've been sick, I'm sorry, please—"

"Janie, Janie, no. It's not July 10 yet. Listen to me, Janie."

"Hannah? Are you okay? Did you get over the flu?"

"I'm fine. Listen, Janie. I have to tell you something hard. I have really bad news."

"I know, that other lady told me. I don't remember her name, I'm sorry. That other mean lady, I don't remember her name, she said I can't write to my little boy Corky anymore and I can't send him presents, oh but that's not true, is it? Hannah—"

"That's not the bad news I mean, Janie. Oh, God. Janie, listen."

Janie pulled her blanket up over her head and scrunched down and made herself as small and tight as she could. Into the phone she whispered, "Bad news? About my son Corky?"

"Yes. I'm afraid so. Janie, oh, honey. Corky died."

"Died?"

"His mom called me today. She said he had a hole in his heart. I guess it had been there for some time but nobody knew."

"I did." Angels of the Heart Hannah didn't hear her say that. Maybe she just thought it, or maybe she said it to her little boy Corky, it was their secret. "When did he? Die?"

"Night before last. He went to sleep and he—he just never woke up. He'd been bleeding internally—"

"I know what's wrong with his heart."

"I didn't see anything in the birth records or the social history you and the birthfather—"

"He's my angel of my heart. *My* angel. *My* heart. That's what." She nodded and bounced up and down as much as she could under the blanket. "We're part of each other."

Hannah said, "Oh, Janie." It sounded like she was crying.

Janie took the blanket off her head. Sunshine was coming through the window. Corky was a teeny tiny smiling baby. Corky was a little boy in a cute red-and-white-striped shirt. Her tummy was full of him, her throat burned, she was feeling a little sick.

She told Angels of the Heart Hannah, "I get to keep him now." And that was right. That was a true thing to say. Janie knew that much.

SHELF-LIFE

Lisa Tuttle

Lisa Tuttle was born in the United States but has lived in Britain for almost thirty years. She began writing while still at school, sold her first stories while still in college, and won the John W. Campbell Award for best new science fiction writer of the year in 1974. She is the author of eight novels (most recently the contemporary fantasy *The Silver Bough*) and around one hundred published short stories, in addition to several books for children and non-fiction works, including *Encyclopedia of Feminism*. In 1990, she edited an anthology of (mostly original) literary horror stories by women authors, *Skin of the Soul*. Her short story "Closet Dreams" won the International Horror Guild Award in 2007. Ash-Tree Press is publishing all her shorter work, beginning with *Stranger in the House: The Collected Ghost and Horror Stories, Volume 1*. She is currently working on a new novel.

Everyone should have a dream, of course. Yet I wonder if dreams shouldn't have a "best before" date woven into their fabric, a warning that they're just as perishable as the food that sustains us. Because you can sniff milk or meat, see the black or green spores of mold on bread or cheese that's been kept too long, but with a dream, it's harder to tell when time has turned it sour, or even toxic.

My own dream was nothing special; common enough to have inspired any number of TV series and magazines, it's probably the national obsession. We're all home owners now, or aspire to be, and although most of us live in cities there's a dream of the English countryside that's rooted deep in the soul.

My dream house was big and old, located on the edge of a small village, with a garden full of trees and flowers and space for children to play. I had grown up somewhere like that myself, but even if I hadn't, it was an image of home familiar from so many advertisements, novels, and films as to make it irresistibly alluring, the very representation of family happiness.

I wanted the house just as much as I wanted children, a loving husband, a comfortable life: in my mind it was a package deal, the future I expected. Only things didn't fall into place as readily as I'd imagined.

I met Matt when we were both past thirty, and although he was certainly the right man for me, worth waiting for, we got onto the property ladder a bit too late for comfort, and our first house was an overpriced, modern, two-bedroom semi-detached in a horrible suburb. Luckily, prices continued to soar, and we were able to trade up fairly quickly, but we were parents now, which meant most of my income (I was a social worker) went on child care, and having a good local primary school was a more important consideration than the size of the garden, and once again we paid more than we should have for a house we didn't love, and could only comfort ourselves with dreams of future profits.

But then house prices began to fall, there was the recession, Matt didn't lose his job, but he had to take a cut in pay. . . . Watching those programs on TV about people defying the odds to build their dream home and start a new life in the country became almost too painful to bear. Maybe our dream would never come true.

Then, in short order, several things happened. Matt's mother (who had been ill for some time) died, his father quickly followed, and when we put our house up for sale, just testing the market, we had an immediate firm offer from a buyer who was able to move immediately. Matt's inheritance meant we could look at houses in a higher price range, and we got a lead on a house in the country that was about to go for a song.

It was someone else's dream house: another couple like ourselves had bought a derelict barn in the middle of a field and poured money, time, and effort into turning it into a showpiece modern home until they were brought down by the recession. It was, all agreed, the most wonderful building, eco-friendly and energy efficient, and although it was more than two miles from the nearest village (which didn't even have a shop), it was a short drive to the motorway, within commuting distance of the city, and came with almost an acre of land.

Unfortunately, I didn't like it. My taste is old-fashioned, and to me the open-plan downstairs living area with vaulted "cathedral" ceilings looked more like a hotel/conference center than somebody's home. This was not the house I'd dreamed of someday owning. But it was the most tremendous bargain, we'd be crazy to pass it up. And although the major building work was finished, it was still something of an undecorated shell: choosing work surfaces and cabinets for the kitchen, deciding on color schemes for every room would be our way of personalizing the house, making it our own. We could afford to buy the Aga cooker I'd always wanted, didn't have to skimp on tiling the bathrooms, and, eventually, we'd turn the muddy field outside into an attractive garden.

Once Matt and I had made up our minds to be happy, the only problem, really, was the children.

They had reached an awkward, difficult age: Brandon already a teenager, Elle almost there. Neither wanted to leave their old stomping grounds, and complained loudly about being forced to change schools—even though Elle would have to move, anyway, into secondary, and Brandon hated his.

Their sullen resentment cast a pall over the move, and then my mother died, which was an enormous shock, as she was only seventy, and had seemed fit and healthy until the very end. She never even had a chance to visit us in our new home. Still, having so much to do was good for me, as it meant I was far too busy to mope around and brood over my loss.

Another shock came a few months later when my father phoned to tell me he had sold our family home. It was too big, too much work for him—even though he'd been paying a cleaner to come in twice a week—and he had his eye on a modern bungalow at the other end of the village.

Of course, the house was his to sell, and there was no reason why he should have consulted me or my brother about it beforehand, but I felt a childish wail of protest rising in my chest, and could not even speak for a few seconds as I swallowed the urge to cry. It had been my home, too, for more than fifteen years, and despite the passage of time, it was still the first place I thought of when I heard the word "home." It was what I was still trying, and still failing, to re-create for my own children, and for myself.

My father had phoned to ask if there was anything I wanted from the house before he had it cleared. There would not be as much room in the new bungalow, so he would have to get rid of most of the furniture, and all his collections.

"Your comics?" I was amazed, remembering his excitement whenever he'd found ancient copies of *Eagle* or *The Beano* in charity shops or at jumble sales.

"Oh, yes," he said, without emotion. "I've got a dealer coming to make me an offer on the lot. Should have done it ten years ago, really—people were paying silly money then, and they're not now. I know you and Paul aren't interested in them, or the models, but there may be other things you'd like to have. You should come soon."

And so, a few days later, I was down in Kent, with my brother, prowling through our childhood home as if it were a cross between a department store and a museum, knowing as we gazed at all these relics of our shared past that we must either integrate them into our adult lives, or let them go forever.

Paul lived in the same sort of small, semi-detached house that Matt and I had recently left, but his was near excellent schools and he could practically walk to work, so he did not plan to move. There wasn't any room for more furniture, but he said he would like a few of the paintings, two lamps, and the old apothecary chest. I coveted the chest, but since he was asking for so little, I didn't argue. Our new house had space for lots more furniture, and my parents had some lovely antiques. If my father didn't intend to keep them, I might as well have them all.

It took a long time to go through the house, the accumulation of more than one lifetime's worth of stuff, and I gained sympathy for my father's decision to make a clean sweep. As the day wore on, it was easier to shake my head and consign things I'd always liked to the auctioneer's block or the charity shop, and toward the end I was changing my mind about things I'd planned to take, removing the sticky pink notes indicating my claim. True, there was a lot of room in our new house, but that didn't mean I had to fill every empty space with furniture my mother had chosen.

Finally, we'd been through every room, and only the loft space remained unexplored. My father admitted he hadn't been up there for a while, but he thought it contained nothing but some old suit-cases, a box of Christmas ornaments, and a black-and-white televi-sion set ("It works perfectly, but nobody wants it"). Paul, impatient, wanted to forget it, but I insisted. If we'd been alone we would have been yelling at each other, but, out of consideration for our father, Paul simply said that he was going to put the kettle on, and I said I'd meet them in the kitchen in a few minutes.

I hadn't been into the loft in years. I remembered helping my mother take down my old high chair for Elle or Brandon, but the baby gear she'd saved from my infancy for her grandchildren was gone now. Poking my head up through the open hatch, shining the torch around, I saw exactly what my father had said I'd find, along with a few more cardboard boxes, their uninteresting contents indicated in large black letters: CURTAINS CUSHION PADS GLASSES & BOWLS. I might, at that point, have retreated back down the steps, but for a strange, stubborn determination.

I would just make sure, I thought, without knowing what I meant, and climbed up and through, straightening up too soon and cracking my head sharply against a beam.

Crying out, I shut my eyes and clenched my teeth against the pain, rubbing my head where I'd hit it. The pain was still pretty bad when I opened my eyes and shone the torch into the darker recesses, and it was through a blur of tears that the white paint first flashed out at me. Blinking, I moved the torch beam to see something I had never expected to see again.

It was a dollhouse, an old-fashioned wooden one that opened up at the front, designed in the classic manner of the houses children learn to draw—a rectangle topped by a triangle, with windows spaced evenly around a central door—and it had once been mine. But what was it doing there? My mother had sold it, or so she had said, more than thirty-five years ago.

Crouching lower still, I crept forward until I reached it, and then I pulled it open, to make sure it really was the same house. The rooms revealed when the hinged front opened were empty of furniture, but still familiar. There was the orange-and-brown-flecked shag pile carpeting in the sitting room (an off-cut of our own, gone like the seventies), the candy-striped wallpaper (starting to peel away at the top) in one bedroom, and the yellow walls of another, the square of mottled mirror-glass I'd glued to the bathroom wall, and the vinyl paper resembling black-and-white lino in the kitchen— staring at it in torch light as I crouched on the bare boards of the attic floor, the sight transported me back to the last year of my childhood, when I had spent so many hours fixing it up and furnishing it and then, not so much playing with it as inhabiting it in my imagination.

How could it be here? She had sold it— Suddenly my incomprehension turned to anger. My mother had lied to me. The fury that welled up then, anger at the mother I'd always loved and still mourned, was shocking, but I recognized that it came from the past, from the child I had been who resented her mother as if she were the very forces of nature making her grow up. I had come to understand, even before I had children of my own, that she had done her best for me, always acting in my best interests. Although it had felt like cruelty, to a girl clinging to the playthings of childhood, my mother had been quite right to take it away.

Far away in the house below me, I heard the sound of the electric kettle coming to a boil, or thought I did. They were waiting for me. I took one last look into each empty room, and then shut up the dollhouse. Its presence here suggested she had always meant to give it back someday, probably when she judged I was mature enough. But because it was something we never spoke about after its disappearance, she must have forgotten . . . or believed that I had.

I knew it would be awkward, lifting something so large and carrying it alone across the low-ceilinged space, but I would manage. Expecting no resistance, I didn't use enough force the first time, and absolutely nothing happened. Pulling at the dollhouse was like pulling at the house itself, as if I'd given one of the roof beams a casual tug to test its strength.

Frowning, I sank my weight into my legs, getting grounded, and pulled more firmly. It didn't budge. It felt so solidly a part of the wall that I wondered if it had been nailed in place, but a quick search by torch light revealed no evidence of that. I reasoned that with the passage of time the wood had expanded, or maybe the paint on the back of the dollhouse had melted slightly in the heat of a particularly fierce summer, and then solidified again, gluing it to the inside wall of the big house.

I began to pull again, at the same time trying to wiggle it back and forth, doing everything I could to pull it free. I pulled harder and harder, straining, until sweat broke out and I was grunting, almost growling with frustration. My head throbbed, and the spot where I'd bashed it felt like a knife in my brain. Something was going to burst, I thought, in an unwanted flashback to my long labor of giving birth to Elle: a blood vessel, a vein, something irreparable . . . but still I didn't stop; it was as if I couldn't, until with a horrible, tearing sound, the thing gave way, coming into my arms with a solid heft that nearly shook me off my feet.

Without pausing to inspect for damage, I shuffled across the attic floor, made awkward by the burden as well as the need to keep my head down. I didn't even consider going downstairs without it to ask for help. Somehow, I managed to get it through the hatch and down the hanging ladder all alone, without further harm.

My father and Paul stared as if at a ghost when I staggered in.

"What's that?"

"My old dollhouse." I set it down on the floor and then straightened up, trying to loosen the kinks in my shoulders and back. "Remember?"

"Can't say that I do," said my father. "You found that in the loft?"

"It was right at the back, tucked out of sight. Mum must have put it there ages ago." Although it seemed impossible to me that my father could have forgotten something so important, I knew events that loom large in the life of a child don't always register on adults. I looked at my brother. "You remember."

He shrugged and shook his head. "You could have had almost anything in that room of yours. 'No Boys Allowed; Especially Brothers!' Remember that?"

"Oh." I smiled sheepishly. "That's right." I picked up the house again. "Well—I'll just take this out to my car."

"That? Why?" My father looked almost comically surprised.

"Surely Elle is a bit old for dolls?" Paul put in, and won a glare from me. Who was he to pronounce on my daughter's maturity?

"Maybe I want it for myself," I said coolly.

"What on earth for?"

I turned back to my father. "That's an interesting question from a man who spent most of his adult life collecting old children's comics and models of cars and planes."

"Fair enough. But why not leave it with everything else until you can come back with a van?"

I had no answer that would not make me sound utterly paranoid, so I just shrugged and continued my journey toward the door, saying, "It'll fit in the hatchback. Anyway, I think Elle might like it. Always good to come back from a trip with something for the kids."

I don't remember how old I was or where I first saw one of those large, handcrafted, beautifully furnished dollhouses that are created more for adult pleasure than for the clumsy play of a child, but

I do recall how the wonder of it sank into my soul, and became an unspoken yearning. I never asked my parents for a dollhouse: I didn't have to be told that what I wanted was too expensive for a child's birthday present, and I didn't want a Barbie house or some other plastic disappointment. I dreamed, but never spoke of my dream, never expected it to come true.

Then one day wandering through a jumble sale held to raise money for the Girl Guides, I saw the house of my dreams lying beneath a table in the church hall. It was shabby and dirty, very much the worse for wear. Someone had scribbled on it with orange and purple crayons, the front door was heavily gouged, and the shutters had been broken off one of the windows. Inside—after I had crouched down and opened it up—I saw the formerly white walls of the empty rooms had been smeared with some dark brown substance that was more likely food than paint, judging by the rotten whiff that made me flinch away. It was not the beautiful house I'd dreamed of, but I knew that it could be. I stood up and addressed the two girls behind the table.

"How much?"

They looked at each other, then back at me. "You don't want that."

"Yes, I do."

"You can't afford it."

"How much?"

One girl looked down at her hands; the other looked at me and widened her eyes. "Two pounds."

That was an enormous sum of money. Jumble sales in those days were not like the car-boot and table-top sales that replaced them. Everything was sold cheap, even furniture, and toys, books, and clothes were priced in pennies. Even at the time it occurred to me that it had been priced so it would not sell—at least not to a child.

But I had two pounds of saved-up pocket money, and I'd brought it all with me, just in case, and I solemnly counted it out, and claimed the house for my own. The vicar's wife loaned me an old pram so I could wheel it home. There, I remember, my mother was appalled, although somewhat mollified to learn that the pram would be going back, and made me give "that filthy thing" a good scrubbing outside in the garden before I was allowed to bring it inside. Even then, when all the brown stains were gone from the inside and it smelled like our freshly washed kitchen floor, she was strangely unwilling for me to take it to my room.

"What did you want to buy that for? You're such a big girl now! You'll be going to the big school in September. I thought you'd stopped playing with dolls?"

That was true. "I don't want to play with it," I explained. "I just want to fix it up, make it look nice again, like a real house, you know?"

That seemed to make her feel easier. I didn't know myself if there was such a great distinction between playing with the house and fixing it up, but she accepted it as another summer project, like Egyptian hieroglyphics and working toward my lifesaving certificate at the swimming pool. She even helped, giving me off-cuts of carpet and fabric, tester pots of paint, and old magazines about interior decoration.

I enjoyed myself that summer, and remember it still as the happiest—as well as the last—of my childhood. By the end of the summer, my work on the house had left it looking fresh and smart enough to sell—something my mother had more than once suggested I might do. I didn't disagree, not openly, but I had no intention of letting it go to someone else. I had wanted a house like this for so long, now that I'd achieved my dream, why would I give it up?

Maybe if I'd settled in quickly at my new school I would have become involved in other activities and lost interest in the dollhouse. But that didn't happen. Cut adrift from my old routines, my former classmates scattered to other schools or simply lost as we grew in different directions, I needed something to cling to. I enjoyed the academic challenges, but there had to be something more to life than schoolwork. Since I made no new friends, there was nothing but the dollhouse to fill that gap, and it became an obsession. Although not for very long.

Like most adolescents, I suppose, I underestimated my mother, who noticed far more than I realized. She saw what was happening, and decided to intervene.

One day after school she met me with the news that she'd sold the dollhouse, and gave me fifty pounds to soothe the hurt. Fifty pounds! No wonder I never suspected she hadn't really sold it. Of course, even twice that much would not have been enough to make up for my loss—the wound I felt for a long time after—but although I sulked, I spent it, and gradually found other dreams.

It took more than four hours to get home—traffic was diabolical—and I was tense, tired, and hungry when I got in to find Matt asleep on the couch in front of the television. The house looked like a stranger's, cold and unwelcoming, too big for our little family, with the wrong sort of furniture and too little of it.

I hoped it would look better with my parents' carefully chosen, beloved antiques occupying all those empty spaces, but I wasn't sure. What if they made it look even more like a barn, one of those places off the main road selling cheap furniture and factory seconds?

I searched the kitchen for something to eat, but I hadn't had time to shop. There wasn't any bread, eggs, or cheese; not even a tin of baked beans. Evidence revealed that the children—Matt, too, most likely—had dined on pizza and the last of the microwave chips. I longed for the abundance of city life, to be able to phone out for my own pizza, or run down to the corner for sausage and chips, or Chinese takeaway. I gave my long-desired Aga a bitter glare. Why wasn't there the remains of a shepherd's pie, or vegetarian lasagna, being kept warm for me there? It wasn't Matt's fault. I was the one who'd insisted on that symbol of the old-fashioned good life; it wasn't *his* fault that I still hadn't properly got to grips with it, or that I never had time for the old-fashioned baking and cooking I loved. We'd both accepted that when we moved to the country Matt would have to commute to work, but somehow I'd imagined I'd find a job closer to home, making it easier to fit in all the household business. I should have realized that there were no jobs in the country unless you made them for yourself. Social workers—generally of a lower grade than my own—might visit people in rural areas, or attend meetings in village schools, but our offices, and most of our work, were in the city. Since I had no brilliant ideas for a business I could run out of my home, and I wasn't prepared to take a minimum-wage job at the local out-of-town superstore, I was stuck with a daily commute.

I spent so much time away from it, perhaps it was not surprising that I often felt like a stranger in this house.

When, the following day, I presented Elle with the treasure I'd recovered from her grandparents' attic, she greeted it with a typically adolescent eye roll. "What am I, six? Why would I want that? I don't play with dolls."

"Lots of people—adults—have them as a hobby," I said. Despite her disdain, Elle was interested enough to take a look inside.

"There's no furniture."

An obvious remark, but it gave me a strange pang, half-fearful, and I was almost breathless as I said, "Well, we could get some. If you like. I mean, it could be a hobby for you. . . . Anyway, I thought it would look nice in your room."

"Whatever."

She hadn't said no, so after I'd cleaned it up a little, and repainted the back with white gloss to cover the mottled scars where the old paint had ripped away when I pulled it out of its hiding place, I put it on the floor in her room. It did look nice. It looked at home there, and added an attractive touch of individuality to a bedroom that was still rather bland, waiting for Elle—who had given away most of her old childish things before we moved—to decide on a style.

Currently, she had adopted a sort of Goth look, wearing a lot of black with skull-themed accessories from Claire's, but I guessed this was provisional as she explored the possibilities on offer at the shopping mall. Despite fussing about the move, once she'd started school Elle had quickly settled in, and had no trouble making new friends, discovering new interests, or at least happily trying them on for size, as she joined in various after-school activities.

I was the one who missed her old friends—or at least their parents, the network I'd relied on for years. Nor had I really appreciated how much freedom I'd had when Elle's playmates lived within walking distance, and Brandon and she could take the bus. Now, they had to be driven everywhere, by one of us. Despite having grown up in the country, I had forgotten how difficult it was to get around.

Memories of the dollhouse often came to me, mostly when I was driving, or lying in bed at night, unable to fall asleep for making lists of things I had to do. Those empty rooms preyed on my mind. Although Elle had said nothing more to me about it, and I had no reason to believe she ever gave it more than the most casual, passing thought, it ought to be furnished. And probably it was for the best that I should do it, I thought, recalling not only how expensive well-made miniature furniture could be, but also the way that when I was Elle's age, furnishing the dollhouse had gone from a casual hobby to complete obsession, practically overnight.

As a girl, I'd known right from the start the sort of furniture the house must have, and it wasn't the mass-produced plastic tables and chairs in ridiculously garish colors sold in Woolworths. A bathroom set of that sort might be better than nothing, but I refused to furnish the whole house with such tat. At first, I had tried making things: a chest of drawers from four empty matchboxes, carefully covered in wood-effect lining paper; a bigger matchbox with lolly sticks and bits of fabric to make a four-poster bed; and so on. But they didn't look real enough. Expensive miniatures were the only things that satisfied me, and they were hard to come by. There was a shop in Canterbury that sold beautiful dollhouse furniture, but I didn't often have a chance to go there, and I had to save up several weeks of pocket money to afford one single piece, which came in a box reassuringly stamped THIS IS NOT A TOY.

I learned to keep my eyes open for novelties like the porcelain trinket box that looked like a lady's dressing table, or the pin cushion designed like a Victorian chaise longue in blue velvet, whether they turned up on a stall at a jumble sale, to be bought for ten pence, or in a neighbor's house, to be secretly pocketed.

Now, as an adult, with a credit card and Internet access, it was all so much easier. I wasn't forced to turn to crime to get what I wanted. I could have filled the little house from floor to ceiling with a hundred or more tiny treasures, all purchased in a single lunchtime.

The choice was staggeringly rich. Did I want to re-create a Victorian residence, or a home that was utterly contemporary, right down to a miniature computer workstation and flat-screen TV?

I decided on a retro look, attempting to re-create the early-seventies ambience of my own childhood. It was only after I'd made my choice that it occurred to me I should have consulted Elle. We could work on this together, and she could learn something about interior decoration. I decided I would order furniture only for the kitchen and the dining room, and leave the rest of the house up to her. Then, if my seventies style did not appeal, the damage would be limited.

I said nothing about it to Elle until my purchases arrived. When she came stumbling, sleepy-eyed, downstairs on Saturday, I set the parcels out before her on the table and offered to cook her breakfast while she opened them.

She gasped with surprise at the sight of the perfectly realistic red-and-black Aga cooker. "You bought this for the house? All this . . . is for the house?"

"Yes, of course. It needs furniture, don't you think?"

To my astonishment, Elle pushed back her chair and ran across to where I stood beside our real-life Aga, and grabbed me in a big hug. There was a catch in her voice as she murmured, "Thank you, Mummy!"

She hadn't called me that in ages, and it gave me a warm feeling. "So, you like it?"

She nodded enthusiastically. "It needs furniture," she said.

I followed her back to the table, as eager as she was. Miniature objects are so seductive, I found myself wondering if she would let me play with them—at least, I could help her arrange them in the house for the first time.

Although the boxes had looked so many, she soon turned to me, frowning. "Is that all?"

I felt as if I'd been slapped. "What happened to 'thank you, Mummy!'? I'd say that's quite a lot, and not even your birthday!"

That worried look was back on her face—a look, I realized, that had settled in over the past few weeks to become nearly permanent. "I know, but it's not enough. The kitchen will look totally awesome, but what about all the other rooms? They're still empty."

I shrugged. "Well, you'll just have to start saving your pocket money, won't you?" And yet I had so nearly bought enough to furnish the entire house. I don't know where my sudden meanness came from, why I felt it important to teach her a lesson: "You can make a list. It will give you something to work for."

Her face clenched; her hands, too. "I *can't* wait."

Her childish petulance only made me colder. "Oh, yes you can. I've just given you a very generous start. You can't expect to have everything handed you on a plate."

"Thanks a lot," she burst out angrily, jumping up from her chair. "Just thanks a whole hell of a lot, Mother dear, but you really shouldn't have bothered to buy me anything!" She ran out of the kitchen, and I heard her thudding up the stairs as I sighed, and gazed at a tiny sink unit with a wooden draining board, my throat hurting as I wondered how our little bonding session had gone so disastrously wrong.

I told myself there had to be limits. We'd never given the children everything they asked for, recognizing that some things are only appreciated when they must be worked and waited for. And although a part of me wished I'd gone ahead and furnished the whole house, I guessed that if I had, my daughter would have found something else to complain about, some other reason to hate me.

She probably couldn't help herself, torn between two contradictory desires, wanting to remain my loving little girl, and needing to push me away so she could grow up. I felt a bit that way myself.

I wondered what had happened to all the bits and pieces I'd used in my attempts at furnishing the dollhouse the first time around. Had my mother taken them away with the house, or left them behind, for me to dispose of? I simply couldn't remember. Had she realized how I'd acquired them? If so, she had never spoken of it to me, and I had never shoplifted or stolen anything again. Even when I saw things that I coveted far more than the wind-up rocking chair or miniature grandfather clock that I'd stolen, I had controlled myself. It had been different when it was something that the house needed. . . .

Looking at the furniture scattered across the table I felt a chill, and wondered if I'd just set something terrible in motion, if history was about to repeat itself.

Oh, Elle, I thought, despairing, *don't be a fool! Talk to me; tell me what's bothering you; we can work it out.*

Yet I didn't approach her. I couldn't begin this conversation; she would have to tell me if she wanted my help. I reminded myself that she got a decent allowance, and had money in the bank. She had managed to save enough last year to buy herself a Nintendo DS; dollhouse furniture was cheap by comparison.

The furniture vanished from the kitchen table later that day, and neither of us said any more about it. It was more than a week later when I happened one evening to walk past her bedroom door and heard her soft voice rising in an anguished plea:

"Isn't that enough? What do you *want* from me?"

I knew she was alone, but she might have been talking to anyone on her phone. Who would she address in that way? A boyfriend? A drug dealer, or a loan shark? My stomach roiled and I held my breath, restraining myself from bursting inside, waiting to hear more.

But there was no more, only silence, until I heard her sigh, in despair or resignation.

I rapped once on her door and went in.

She was standing in the middle of the room; must have turned at the sound of my knock, because she was staring right at me, dead-eyed with annoyance: she looked like a stranger, this dark-haired, pale-faced girl all in black, even her hair recently dyed to match. I missed the old pinks and purples.

"You're supposed to wait until I say come in."

"I thought . . . I thought I heard you say something." Both her hands were empty; I couldn't see her phone. Her room was not too untidy: the bed unmade, but only a few discarded clothes and her black schoolbag disturbing the creamy flow of carpet.

"No, you didn't; you didn't even wait, you didn't give me time to say anything."

"I'm sorry."

"What do you want?"

My mind was blank; I could think of nothing but those words I did not dare admit I'd overheard. "I'm going down to put on the kettle. Fancy a hot chocolate?"

"No thanks."

"Oh. Well . . . I'll be in the kitchen if you change your mind or . . . or fancy a natter."

She waited for me to leave.

By the time Matt got home—he and Brandon had been at their kick-boxing class—I'd decided against burdening him with my fears. The idea that my little girl knew a drug dealer, or had a boyfriend, was ridiculous. I knew where she was every hour of the day and night. She hadn't been on the phone. Most likely she was acting out some drama she'd seen on TV, practicing her part in an imaginary film.

Yet no matter how I tried to justify it to myself, the emotion in her voice had sounded so real, it set my maternal antennae quivering, so that the next morning, tired and rushed as I always was, I noticed something awkward in the way she carried her left hand, and grabbed it before she could stop me.

"Ow!"

There was a plaster pressed over a cut in her palm, still seeping blood. "What happened?"

"Nothing—a cut—it's all right!" Glaring, she pulled her hand away.

"How?"

"Just, y'know, cut myself."

"On what?"

She evaded my eyes. "Craft knife. I was, uh, it slipped, all right? An accident. That's all. It's not that bad, anyway; I washed it out, and it's stopped bleeding. It'll be fine."

If it had been Valentine's Day, maybe, but before breakfast, before school, running late as usual, for her to embark on some mysterious, unexplained project in her bedroom with a craft knife seemed unlikely.

I said nothing. I let her bolt her breakfast and hurry out the door in company with her yawning, tousled brother. I should have been rushing to get ready to go to work myself, but instead I finished a second cup of tea, waiting for the house to grow still and settled around me, waiting until there was no chance that either of them would come pounding back to report that they'd missed the bus, before I went up to Elle's room.

There was a faint, unpleasant smell there that I hadn't noticed before and could not identify. I saw the yellow plastic casing of the craft knife lying on the dresser, but no sign of anything she could have been using it on. Her wastepaper basket was piled with white tissues spotted bright red. I moved uncertainly around the room, pulling out drawers at random, no idea what I was looking for, but finding nothing—apart from the razor-bladed craft knife, which should have been downstairs in the toolbox—that seemed wrong or out of place.

Finally I went over to the dollhouse, standing like a solitary sentinel beside the door, crouched down, and opened it up.

And I was looking into a nightmare: white walls streaked with smears of dried blood; the body of a mouse deliquescing in the bathroom; another dead furry animal in the kitchen. That explained the smell.

I flinched, shut my eyes, and stopped breathing, although it was too late to avoid the foulness. I heard Elle's tragic voice again, demanding, "What do you want from me?" and knew that she'd been speaking to the house. When animal sacrifices were not enough, she'd turned the blade on herself.

That she would take it this way I had never imagined. But how could I? She was not me. She would take things her way, or not at all.

And now I had to do for her what my mother had done for me.

I phoned in sick and got to work cleaning up the mess. The rodents went into a plastic bag, then into the bin with the kitchen waste. I tried not to think of how she had killed them. My sentimental, squeamish little girl. There was a possibility she'd found a dead mouse somewhere, but the hamster must have been bought and smuggled into her room for the express purpose of being killed.

I wiped each piece of furniture and set it aside before washing the bloodstains from the walls. Then I washed all the walls, ceilings, and the floors as well, until the whole house looked and smelled perfectly clean.

Our loft space was much smaller than in my childhood home, and was more easily accessible. Instead of a ceiling hatch and a ladder, there was a door in the wall just at the head of the stairs. It was about half normal height, so you had to stoop to go in, and once inside even I had to be cautious about standing up straight. We'd been so ruthless about culling our possessions before paying someone to move them that we hadn't needed to use this space for storage. I moved the dollhouse in there, tucking it away to the side of the entrance so that even if someone happened to look inside they'd miss it.

Although I was prepared to lie, Elle never asked what had happened to the dollhouse. It was as if, once it had gone, she forgot all about it, and I think that was for the best.

As for me, I've continued to buy it furniture, but carefully, thoughtfully, searching out unusual things and making sure that each one is absolutely right. Gradually, room by room, it is becoming more and more like a real home.

At first, I only went into the loft when I was all alone in the house and could be certain I would not be disturbed. But such times are rare.

Now, I sneak in whenever I have a spare half-hour to myself, or everyone thinks I'm somewhere else, sometimes even late at night when Matt is so deeply asleep that I can slip out of bed without disturbing him.

I have my old exercise mat to sit on and a blanket to keep me warm, and one of those stick-up LED lights provides all the illumination necessary as I gaze into each tiny room, occasionally moving things around, imagining myself inside. At last, I feel at home.

Not blood, not sacrifice, never anything like that; even the furniture, I think, is not really necessary, but it pleases me to buy it, and helps to focus my thoughts. What the house wants, all that it needs, is me.

CAIUS

Bill Pronzini and Barry N. Malzberg

Writing solo and in collaboration with others, Bill Pronzini has published seventy novels, four nonfiction books, and twenty short-story collections. In 2008 he received the Mystery Writers of America Grand Master Award. He is also the recipient of the Private Eye Writers of America's Lifetime Achievement Award, three Shamus Awards, six Edgar nominations, and two "best novel" nominations from the International Crime Writers Association.

Barry N. Malzberg has been publishing science fiction and fantasy for over forty years. His volume of collected essays on science fiction, *Breakfast in the Ruins*, published by Baen Books in 2007, combines his 1982 classic *Engines of the Night* and many of the essays on science fiction published since. In 2008 the collection won the Locus Award (best related nonfiction) and narrowly lost the Hugo Award in the same category.

His collection *In the Stone House* was published in 2000; several of his 1970s science fiction novels have been reissued within the past half-decade.

aius watches the lights on the board, red, red, red, red, with eager eyes (not that he could be seen) and prestidigitating heart (not that he could be monitored). Elbows on the table, headphones tight against his ears. Throat cleared to allow his mellifluous voice to draw slowly, exquisitely, the pulp of his listeners' desires.

Jeremy, his engineer, picks one red light at random. No screening except for the FCC-mandated seven-second delay—Caius does not need to have his calls screened. There is no listener, no heckler, no type of problem or question that he cannot address with knowledge, wit, perfect aplomb.

This caller, as usual, is one of the faithful. Stan in Cheyenne. How're they screwing you, Stan, he asks, up there in the cold, cold Rockies? Stan mumbles, grumbles, spews harsh and bitter words into his ears. One and a half minutes of Stan is sufficient. Caius deftly cuts him short, waves to Jeremy to put on another caller.

Georgiana in Seattle. Yes, of course, he says to her, let's talk about the rule of the gun and the rule of law, not that there's any difference in these United States. He draws her out slowly, inexorably, tugging on and loosening the strangling rope of her consciousness.

"Now do you understand, Georgiana?" Caius says when her three minutes are up. "Do you know what must be done?"

"Oh, yes, Caius," she says. Her voice is breathless, as if his words have brought her to orgasm. "Oh, yes!"

In the glistening glass wall of the engineer's booth, he sees reflected the outlines of his own face. Strong jaw, ears like miniature radar scanners, eyes huge and glowing with testimony to his incontestable vision, his indomitable spirit. Caius, nomad of the Space Age airwaves. Caius, the man with the answers, the man with the power to strip away falsehoods and false fronts, to unburden and provide direction to so many in this age of inanition. Caius, the oracle of his times. How he has suffered for his art, his genius! How he suffers as confessor for these fools who know nothing of the gravity of his heart.

He feels their pain radiating through the headphones. He hears their murmuring voices, millions of voices, echoing through the corridors of his mind. He has come to give them what they need, not what they want, the difference accomplished through his own inextinguishable judgment.

We live in perilous times, he tells them again and again. Times in which the bad has been masked as good, in which destruction has been masked as compassion. Times which have taken from us what we might have had, what we should have received. Are they listening? Are *you* listening, Georgiana in Seattle, Stan in Cheyenne, Karl in Saginaw, Benjamin in Coeur d'Alene, all the rest of you?

Sometimes he thinks they ask too much of him, they ask more than he can give—he is, after all, only one man, one frail stanchion standing against the enormities of the present and the future. Sometimes he despises them, the puny, stupid ones unworthy of his benevolence. Sometimes he thinks it doesn't matter what he does, for his power, always, is in what he *could* do if he wanted to.

Jeremy signals that another caller is on the line. Caius waves him off, indicates that it is time to cut to the usual recorded commercial messages. Sighs, removes his headphones. Enough for now. Enough. He needs a few minutes to regenerate himself before he once again takes the fools through the inconstancy of this world and points them in the right direction. One day he might even lead them, all of them, all his faithful, into the promised land.

Dazzled by the images of himself reflected from the glass walls, he stands, stretches. Caius, cloned and magnified, larger than life.

The door to the control booth opens and Jeremy comes in. Caius favors him, as he does all his minions, with a beneficent smile. "Going well tonight," he says.

Jeremy nods. Jeremy nods at everything. A fawning youth, nothing like what Caius was at his age, no ambition for one thing, but he does his job and that is sufficient. If Caius needed more, he could have more. But he doesn't. Why should he? Jeremy is no different than Stan in Cheyenne or Gail in Indianapolis, but Caius is kind to him nonetheless. He is kind to all the members of his flock. One of the obligations of power.

"As always," Jeremy says. "You the man."

"Caius, nomadic interpreter of all their secrets."

"Absolutely right, that's what you are. Not even Limbaugh can keep them coming back the way you do."

"How many calls so far tonight?" Caius asks.

"Ninety-six."

"Grand total to date?"

"Nearly a million since you've been on the air."

"Six million listeners, one million calls."

"Amazing record," Jeremy says. "Amazing. It's an honor to work with a great man like you, a real honor."

An honor. That is what so many of them say when Caius releases them from the coffins of their unnecessary, irrelevant lives. What an honor to speak with you! What a thrill! Been listening to you for years, you taught me a lot, you make such good sense. Their praise, their unction coursing through him like the fever heat of his own blood.

"We need some sound bytes," he says to Jeremy. "You have them ready on the roll, of course?"

"Yes, sir. Always. Ready when you are."

"Numbers forty-two and fifty-seven," Caius says. "Those are the ones I want tonight. First the one where the Pope attacks me personally, by name, then my clip at the Correspondents' Dinner."

"Forty-two and fifty-seven. Right." Jeremy chuckles. "I remember that dinner clip. Pretty funny stuff."

"Yes, very amusing."

"You nailed the bastards in that one," Jeremy says. "Nailed 'em right up there on the cross, just like Jesus."

Just like Jesus.

And just like Jesus, Caius thinks, I have my disciples. My Caiusites. My Causations. My Causators. The groveling faithful that pour through all the tangled and whizzing lines of the nation directly into me, Caiusites drawing from the power which is mine.

In the early years he had traveled everywhere, spoke from the trenches and the front lines in all the gleaming, devastated parts of the nation, advancing to this destination in stages, in movements as careful and well planned as those on a chessboard. He has a history, he sometimes likes to remind his listeners, his disciples, he didn't get to this point without years of study, questing, humility, honor, suffering.

He heard their pleas then, the same ones he hears now: Tell us, Caius. Lead us, Caius. But he also heard, sometimes still hears, their bitterness and their spite. Why are you where you are, Caius, and we're trapped down here in the swamps of human existence? How did you get the power instead of us? When he is confronted with such apostasy he thinks of sucking out their brains, the gray and spongy material which surrounds their tiny thoughts, and draping them on a line to wave in the breeze before he puts the torch to them. Blinding fire against the sky. Caius remembers John Lennon. First they ask for an autograph and then they come back and kill you. That Spider's Kiss.

But Lennon's fate will not be his. No, never. He is above such an absurd end to his life and his life's work. He is destined to continue his mission for many more years to come. Caius, the invincible.

Jeremy gestures at the clock. "Almost airtime again," he says.

"Yes, I see."

The engineer leaves the booth quickly and quietly, and Caius sits again in his comfortable chair. Headphones on. Microphone on. Green light on. And here I am again, listeners, disciples, Caiusites, he thinks but doesn't say. Go ahead, Ronald in Little Rock, he says. What's on your mind this evening, Ronald? How can I help? How can I bring you the wisdom of Caius?

The board continues to light up with incoming calls, red, red, red, red, red. Jeremy makes his selection, Caius presses the button that opens the line. The voice of Elaine in Charleston drones in his ear. Tormented Elaine, until Caius's words elevate her to new heights of consciousness and perception.

Another green light. Marvin in San Antonio. Another. Big Dave in Biloxi. Another. Linda and Jolene, mother and daughter, suffering in Corpus Christi. Help us, Caius. Lead us, Caius. Save us, Caius.

One after another he takes the calls, listens to the voices of the faithful and, now and then, the unfaithful. So many voices. Night after night. And after a while they begin to blend and flow together, to rise to a roar that pours through the headphones, through his ears, into the center of him. The voices of admiration, of love and approbation, these are what he lives for.

And yet—

And yet, the voices grow decibel by painful decibel until they fill him, swell him to the bursting point. Frantically he signals to Jeremy to cut off the new caller—Darlene from Thousand Oaks? Andrew from Sheboygan?—but the engineer ignores him. Caius rips off the headphones, claps his hands over his ears. The roar of the million voices continues to increase, louder, louder, louder, until it reaches a thunderous crescendo.

Caius's vision dims when this happens, shifts, and the glass walls shimmer, Jeremy shimmers in the control booth, everything shimmers, blurs, fades, and then reemerges as something other than the familiar surroundings of the studio, as white cushioned walls, white cushioned floor, bare cot, screens and bars, Jeremy in a white uniform. The voices cease their babel; all at once he finds himself wrapped in a deep trembling silence. He cries out, but there is no one to hear him, he is alone. Alone. He understands then, the monstrous knowledge descends that he is no longer the feeder but the fed upon, and he screams, he screams—

—and the white room shifts, shimmers, fades, and then reemerges as the interior of his booth at the studio, where he is once again sprawled in his comfortable chair, headphones on, microphone on, his mind as clear as the glistening glass walls. He looks at the board, red, red, red, red. Sees Jeremy signal, then turn one flashing red to green. Smiles, winks, gives the thumbs-up. And safe, secure, supremely confident as always in the efficacy of his genius, he takes a call from Eric in Council Bluffs.

Caius, nomad of the Space Age airwaves. Caius, oracle of his times. Caius, the man with the answers, the man with the power, the man who will one day show them all the way into the light, finally and forever into the light.

SWEET SORROW

Barbara Roden

Born in Vancouver, British Columbia, in 1963, Barbara Roden is a World Fantasy Award–winning editor and publisher. Her short stories have appeared in numerous publications, including *The Year's Best Fantasy and Horror 2006: Nineteenth Annual Collection*, *Horror: Best of the Year 2005*, *Best New Horror 21*, *The Year's Best Dark Fantasy & Horror: 2010*, *Bound for Evil*, *Strange Tales 2*, *Gaslight Grimoire* and *Gaslight Grotesque*, *Apparitions*, and *Poe* (Solaris), as well as in several anthologies published by Ash-Tree Press. Her first collection, *Northwest Passages*, was published by Prime Books in October 2009; the title story was nominated for the Stoker, International Horror Guild, and World Fantasy Awards.

S he vanished on a spring evening soft with the promise of rain, which should have played out according to a well-rehearsed script. Rushed dinner, rounding up of children, out the door and down to the park. Children launching themselves from cars, excited shouts, organized chaos as players found their teammates and others congregated on the playground. Gathering everyone and everything, after, and home, leaving park and playground to the shadows. On this night, however, someone had made a change to the script that no one knew about until the Danforths, looking for their daughter—first with impatience, then with anger, finally with a gnawing, gut-wrenching panic that grew heavier and more clutching as hours passed—failed to find her. Despite weeks of searching, eleven-year-old Melissa Danforth was never found.

Melissa had been a gleaming, shimmering presence in Brian's life. She was the most beautiful creature he had ever seen, a graceful girl with white-blond hair that seemed made of spun silk and blue eyes in which laughter was never far from the surface. He had worshipped her since kindergarten and had, in his awkward, unsure way, tried to show her this, smiling an extra-big smile when she turned to pass something back to him in class. Not long before her disappearance, Brian had summoned up the courage to speak with Melissa outside the classroom, and she had seemed to enjoy being more or less alone with him for too-brief snatches of time. He knew that older kids went on "dates," and while Brian did not want to ask Melissa on a date, the idea of being properly alone with her, away from his watchful friends and her giggling companions, appealed to something in him that he could not name, could only vaguely begin to understand.

Then she was gone, punching a hole in Brian's life that threatened to suck everything else in at the edges. He heard little about the details of the disappearance and investigation, the leads followed up and gone cold, the rumors, theories, speculation. He knew when his parents were discussing it, because they stopped talking when he entered the room, and the newspaper was kept out of sight. His mother began walking with him on the short trip to and from school; if he went outside he was warned not to leave the yard; and in the evenings the streets were empty of children.

In the classroom Melissa's desk tormented him, drawing his eyes continually. The day after her disappearance it stayed in its accustomed place, her things still inside it: a pink pencil case with My Pretty Pony on it, two Hilroy notebooks, a battered novel from the library, a history textbook with a bookmark between pages 74 and 75 until, that first lunchtime, Brian pulled the textbook out of the desk and slipped the bookmark into his pocket. He recognized it as a project they had done in third grade, rough cloth with images—in Melissa's case butterflies and a rainbow—glued onto it. His own effort had long since been lost, but Melissa had clearly treasured hers, so Brian did, too.

He was just in time. At some point after school ended the desk was emptied of its contents—"By the *police*," Tommy Mitchell whispered the next day—and a few days later it was moved to the back of the classroom. Three weeks after Melissa's disappearance, it was removed altogether.

Long before that, however, flowers began appearing outside the Danforth house. Brian did not know who placed the first bright bouquet there, only noted it when he and his mother passed it on his way to school, two mornings after Melissa's disappearance. They looked like the ones Mr. Chan kept in buckets outside his corner store, and when Brian returned home several more had been added. He and his mother stopped, gazing at the splotches of color spilling across the gray sidewalk in front of the hedge that separated the Danforths' property from that of Mr. and Mrs. Gleason next door.

"People are so thoughtful, aren't they," said Brian's mother. "Paying tribute like this."

"Paying tribute?" It sounded like something Mr. Waters would say in church.

"Showing their respects," said a voice, and Brian jumped. Looking up, he saw Mrs. Gleason standing on her side of the hedge. "Showing poor Mr. and Mrs. Danforth how much people thought of Melissa, and how they feel for their loss."

"But . . ." Brian was confused. "We don't know what happened to Melissa," he said. "She could . . . she could be okay, just lost somewhere, or hurt. Maybe"—he groped for the word he'd read in a Hardy Boys mystery—"maybe she has amnesia, and she'll wake up and tell people who she is and . . . come home."

Melissa's face swam in front of his eyes, as he'd last seen her, turning around to pass something to him on the day she'd vanished. She couldn't be gone, she *couldn't* have vanished forever. Nothing bad could have happened to Melissa. Brian gave a cry and tried to blink away the tears that were suddenly in his eyes.

"Oh, sweetheart," said his mother, hugging him. "He's feeling it rather hard," she said to Mrs. Gleason. "He's known Melissa since they started kindergarten."

"Of course," said Mrs. Gleason. "You were in her class at school, weren't you. It must be a terrible blow. Such a lovely girl."

Brian could say nothing, do nothing other than cling more tightly to his mother. Mrs. Gleason's voice continued.

"Such a dreadful thing, something like this. She has so many people who love her, so many people who will be feeling for her parents."

Brian gave a stifled sob.

"And so much uncertainty." Mrs. Gleason's voice was relentless. "It's the not knowing that must be the hardest. I hope—we *all* must hope—that Melissa is found safe. But in the meantime, poor Cathy and Donald."

Brian's mother nodded. "I don't know how they bear it."

"I saw Cathy earlier today," said Mrs. Gleason. "She looks dreadful. I can't imagine she's had any sleep since Melissa disappeared.

My husband and I have come to know them fairly well since we moved here. Melissa was in and out of our house as if it were her own, and we . . . well, we thought of her as the granddaughter we never had, and never will." She dropped her voice. "It's not something we talk about, but we, too, lost a daughter—our only child—many years ago. Not under these circumstances, but we do know a little of what they must be going through. It never leaves you. I think the Danforths find it helpful, talking to someone who understands."

Later that evening Brian paused outside the living room door.

"Did you know that the Gleasons lost a child?" he heard his mother ask.

"No, I can't say I did," his father replied. "I've never really got to know them very well, though, apart from seeing them at church. I think he's got some health problems. The last time I saw him was . . . oh, well before Easter, and he looked terrible. Some sort of mouth or throat cancer, I think."

"She hasn't been very well, either," said his mother. "I was glad to see her looking better today, although there's no telling what effect all this will be having on them. They were very fond of Melissa."

"Everyone was," said Brian's father. He sighed. "I don't know what the world's coming to."

By Friday, four days after Melissa's disappearance, the flowers had accumulated to the point that they were heaped in a pile to avoid blocking the sidewalk. There were cards among the flowers, and even a stuffed animal: a white rabbit with a pink bow, much loved by someone, judging by its bedraggled fur and mismatched eyes. Brian stopped to look, while his mother continued along the sidewalk. When she noticed that Brian was no longer with her, she stopped and turned.

"Brian! Hurry up! I have to get the chicken ready for dinner."

"It's all right, Mrs. Henderson," said a voice by Brian's side. Once again he turned to see Mrs. Gleason standing beside the hedge, only today she was wearing a pair of gardening gloves. "If he wants to stay that's fine. I can watch him safely home."

"Are you sure?"

"Yes, of course. A little break will do me good. I've been out here for most of the day."

"I'm glad you're feeling well enough," said Brian's mother. "How is Mr. Gleason?"

"He's . . . better," said Mrs. Gleason. "We both get a bit tired and run-down, sometimes. Age, you know. But we always rally. My husband hopes to be well enough to come outside again soon. He dislikes having to stay cooped up in the house."

"He must do." Mrs. Henderson turned to Brian. "All right, you can stay for a little while, but come straight home. And don't tire Mrs. Gleason out."

Mrs. Gleason didn't look very tired, Brian thought; certainly much less so than when he had seen her on Wednesday. He tried to think of something to say, couldn't, and looked instead at the pile of flowers. The stuffed rabbit caught his eye.

"It's so very touching, don't you think," said Mrs. Gleason, as if reading his thoughts. "A little girl brought it earlier today. I was out here gardening, and saw. The poor thing was crying dreadfully. I think it was a favorite toy of hers, but she wanted to leave it for Melissa, she said. It was very sweet."

Mrs. Gleason was staring at the rabbit, a small smile on her face. Brian thought she looked pleased, but when she turned to him the smile was gone.

"Is there anything you'd like to leave for Melissa? You knew her for a long time, after all. Surely there's something."

Brian thought for a moment. "I could buy some flowers," he said at last. "From Mr. Chan's store."

"Yes, flowers would be . . . enough. But I was thinking of something more personal. Something you value."

"A toy? Like that rabbit?"

"Yes." Mrs. Gleason nodded. "Something that comes from you, that you otherwise wouldn't part with. It would have more meaning than flowers from a store."

Brian considered the idea. He didn't think Melissa would appreciate LEGO bricks or an action figure. Perhaps one of his stuffed animals. . . .

Then he remembered the bookmark. It was still in his pocket, and he pulled it out with a hand that trembled slightly. Mrs. Gleason's eyes narrowed.

"What's that? Something you made?"

"No. Melissa made it. When we were in third grade."

"And she gave it to you?"

"No." Brian closed his eyes. "I took it from her desk," he whispered. "I wanted to keep it. So I could remember her."

"You miss her so much, don't you." Mrs. Gleason's voice was soft, her *ess* sounds like those of a snake. "Miss her terribly. So lovely, so bright, always smiling and happy."

"Yes." Brian could barely say the word. "She was."

The tears were there again, pricking the back of his eyelids, and he felt as if something was stuck in his throat. He gave a cry.

"I want her to come back!" he wailed. "I want Melissa to come home again!"

Even through his cry he heard Mrs. Gleason draw in her breath. He looked up, blinking, and saw that she was smiling. No, grinning, her lips pulled back from her teeth, her eyes seeming to glow. The look was gone in a moment, however, and he wondered if he'd merely imagined that Mrs. Gleason had, for an instant, seemed happy.

"Of course you want Melissa to come back," Brian heard her say. "And if she does, then won't it be nice for her to see all this? Her bookmark would be there, too, and I'm sure she'd like to have it back."

"I could . . . I could just give it to her then."

"Yes, you could. But if you leave it here with the other tributes, it would show how much you cared about her."

Brian looked down. The hand that was holding the bookmark trembled. Before he could stop himself he had knelt down, placed the bookmark beside the white rabbit, and stood up again, gasping slightly as he did so.

"Good boy," he heard Mrs. Gleason say in a soft voice. "Such a good boy." Her hand in its slightly soiled gardening glove rested on his shoulder for a moment. It was hot, and Brian felt sick and dizzy. He shook himself like a dog coming out of water and Mrs. Gleason withdrew her hand.

He risked a glance up at her, and his eye was caught by movement in the large window at the front of the house, behind her. *Mr. Gleason*, he thought. His face was stark white and distended, as if pressed tight against the glass, and his mouth was open, as if he were trying to say something. His lips were a terrible blackish-red, and even at that distance Brian could glimpse the white of his teeth against them. With startling suddenness the lips snapped shut, and Mr. Gleason stepped back and vanished into the depths of the room.

"I-I have to go now," Brian stammered.

"Yes, yes, you go. Thank you for your tribute. It *is* appreciated," said Mrs. Gleason. Brian knew she was watching him all the way to his house, and he could not turn in at the gate quickly enough.

On Sunday there was church, and Brian was surprised when he saw the crowd: more than he ever remembered seeing at church, even at Christmas or Easter. Mr. and Mrs. Danforth were there, looking shrunken somehow, with a number of people Brian supposed were relatives, and the crowd parted before them, anxious murmurs and soft words accompanying their walk to the front of the church. The Gleasons were there, too, Mr. Gleason still pale but obviously in better health. Mrs. Gleason also looked considerably improved, even in the space of two days. "Amazing what Sunday best does for some people," Brian heard his mother whisper to his father.

Sunday school was cancelled for the day, and Brian sat with his parents through the whole service. The Danforths were mentioned in the prayers, and one sharp, stifled cry was heard from their pew. Mr. Waters paused and gazed over the congregation.

"In considering the terrible occurrence which has taken place in our community, I consider it fortuitous, in a way, that this is the fifth Sunday after Pentecost, and as such we have heard several readings which show the love and kindness of Our Lord, even in the midst of terrible grief. The story of Jairus's daughter raised from the dead is one such, and another is the passage from Lamentations which we have already heard: 'For the Lord will not cast off forever. But, though He cause grief, He will have compassion according to the abundance of His steadfast love. For He does not willingly afflict or grieve the children of men.' That is something we must all believe, at this time of sorrow: that the Lord will not willingly afflict or grieve us, and that His compassion abounds, and will be made manifest. Already we have seen evidence of this. Only yesterday I drove past the Danforth house and saw the beautiful and touching tributes that have been placed there. . . ."

Brian turned and glanced to where the Gleasons were sitting at the back of the church. Their bright eyes were roving over the congregation, darting here and there with an intensity that startled Brian. He turned round to face Mr. Waters, but it was not long before he was looking back again, as surreptitiously as he could. Still there was that intensity about the Gleasons, their eyes never still, their faces speaking of . . .

Suddenly Mrs. Gleason shifted her gaze slightly, so that she was looking directly at Brian. For a moment he froze, and something like the feeling of dizziness he had had two days before swept over him. He closed his eyes, and when he opened them again both the Gleasons were staring at him. Mr. Gleason was smiling, and Brian got a glimpse of bright white teeth behind dark lips.

He turned round to the front once more, and did not look back again.

After lunch his father suggested a walk to the park. As soon as they had turned out of their gate onto the sidewalk, Brian saw another father and child approaching from the opposite direction, and recognized Angela Morris, a year younger than Melissa but one of her best friends. As they drew closer Brian could see that Angela was clutching a battered stuffed bear, and that she was crying. She and her father stopped at the makeshift shrine, and Brian's stomach lurched as Mrs. Gleason moved into sight from behind the hedge and bent over Angela, saying a few words that made the girl cry even harder. Then Angela took a step forward, the hand holding the bear outstretched.

Brian gave a sharp cry. Then, half-screeching, half-yelling "No!" he barrelled down the sidewalk. Angela stopped, her arm suspended over the pile, and stared at Brian, who flung himself in front of her.

"No, Angela, don't do it. Keep your bear. Melissa doesn't want it."

Above him and to his left there was a sharp intake of breath. Mrs. Gleason was beside him and for a moment, while he looked at her face, he saw a deep, raging anger, as of a dog that lunges at something just beyond the reach of its chain. Brian looked back at Angela.

"Don't do it," he said again. "It's . . . it's not right."

Angela's lip trembled. "But she said I should," she half-whispered. "Mrs. Gleason. She said Melissa would like my bear."

"Melissa *won't* like your bear."

"But she did, she *did* like Whitey. She told me."

Brian took a deep breath. "Melissa's not coming back." Angela gasped, and pulled away from him. "She'll never see it. It'll just rot like the flowers and then someone'll throw it away. If Melissa liked Whitey then you keep him, and think of how much she liked him, and keep him safe. Melissa would be happy about that, wouldn't she? She'd like to know Whitey was safe with you."

Angela stared at him, and two fat tears leaked down her cheeks. Then she turned and flung herself at Mr. Morris, who gathered her up and, after throwing a half-puzzled, half-angry glare at Brian and his father, turned and marched away down the sidewalk, Angela still clutching Whitey.

Brian's heart was thumping in his chest, so loud that he thought it must be audible. It was not, however, loud enough to obscure his father's voice.

"Brian, what on *earth* was that . . . that outburst about?"

Brian looked down at the ground.

"I'd like an explanation. And an apology."

Brian continued to stare downward.

"Brian!" His father's voice was sharp. "I'm speaking to you. What do you have to say?"

Brian looked up: first at his father, whose face was red with anger, then at Mrs. Gleason. She was angry, too, but he noticed that the tiredness of a few days earlier was gone, and that while her face was red, it was the ruddy glow of health. He stared at her for a moment, then said in a flat, calm voice, "I'm sorry, Mrs. Gleason."

"I don't think it's Mrs. Gleason you should be apologizing to," he heard his father say, but Brian simply continued to stare. Finally Mrs. Gleason blinked.

"I've had enough of your insolence, young man," she said. "I thought you were a good, kind boy, but I see now that I was mistaken."

Brian saw, over her shoulder, the front door open, revealing Mr.

Gleason just inside. He looked as if he were going to come down the front walk, and for some reason that thought terrified Brian, so much so that he took an involuntary step backward. Mrs. Gleason did not turn around, but she must have sensed her husband there. She waved a hand behind her dismissively.

"Everything is fine. Brian and his father are just leaving. *Aren't you.*"

This was said directly to Brian, who was already turning and walking away, so quickly that he was halfway to the house before his father caught up and clamped a hand on Brian's shoulder, forcing him to stop.

"I'd like an explanation of what that was about, Brian." He didn't sound quite as angry as before. Brian stared along the empty sidewalk, then turned to his father.

"I don't know," he whispered. "I just didn't want Angela to do that."

"I gathered that, young man. We all did. What I want to know is why you spoke to Angela in that . . ."

His voice trailed off as he looked at Brian's face, which was white and sick. He knelt down and placed his hands on Brian's shoulders.

"It's okay," he said quietly. "You've gone through a lot. Probably more than we know, your mom and me. Why don't we just go home now, champ, and you can have a lie-down for a little while, all right?"

Brian nodded dumbly. As they set off down the sidewalk he reached out and took his father's hand for the first time in a long time, and felt in return a comforting squeeze that did little to comfort him.

Spring wound into summer, and there was no sign of Melissa. The news conferences and community meetings and appeals for information dwindled from a flood to a stream to a trickle. In mid-July police admitted that, despite their best efforts, no trace had been found of Melissa, no suspects had been identified, and the investigation would be halted completely, unless new evidence came to light. By the time school resumed in the fall, life had returned to—if not normal, then something approximating it. Brian was once more able to walk to and from school by himself, and he made sure he saw as little of the Gleasons as possible, crossing the road to avoid having to pass directly in front of their house. Even so, he could not help noticing that, after the swell of tributes gradually slowed and stopped and was cleared away, a small cross bedecked with flowers appeared beside the hedge, and over the following months attracted the occasional bouquet, particularly in February, when Melissa would have turned twelve.

In May, a year after Melissa's disappearance, there was another flurry of tributes, and it had hardly abated before the Danforths put their house on the market. It was as if, having held out for a year, they could do so no longer. There was no fresh news, and the prospect of another year in the house, marking the same sad round of strained holidays and cheerless anniversaries, must have struck them as something that could not be borne.

Not long after the Danforths moved, the Gleasons put their house up for sale. Brian saw the sign on their front lawn as he came home from school, and he heard his parents talking about it in the kitchen before supper, when he was supposed to be doing his homework at the dining room table.

"Glenda Mitchell told me this morning," said Brian's mother. "Mrs. Gleason came into the office and said they're moving back east, to be close to a dying relative of hers. A sister—or was it an aunt? I can't remember. A woman, anyway."

"Not her mother," said Brian's father with a short laugh. "She must be long dead."

"Oh, I don't know," Brian's mother replied. "I thought, at one point, that they were both quite old, the Gleasons, but they can't be more than—what, mid-sixties?"

"They both looked mid-eighties, some time back."

"Yes, but illness can make you look older. They've both recovered very well, considering . . . well, all that's gone on in the last year. I saw them both outside the other day, in the garden, and thought how healthy they looked."

The Gleasons moved, and Brian was not sorry to see them go. Life continued, superficially in much the same way as before, although Brian felt more an observer than a participant. He went to middle school, then high school, and got good enough grades to be accepted into a decent university. During his four years there he fell in and out of what passed for love at regular intervals, never really expecting much and never being disappointed. When he emerged with a Bachelor of Science degree he was mildly surprised to find himself offered a job in Vancouver by a large firm looking for bright young talent, and it was there that he eventually met Patty, a blue-eyed, blond-haired woman with a ready smile whom Brian thought—for the three years of their marriage, at least—was The One. The ostensible reason for their split was her wish to have children, and Brian's opposition to the idea; but that was only a part of the picture, as Patty informed him one (admittedly) booze-fuelled night just before she left.

"You never seem to be there," she sobbed and, when Brian asked where *there* was, replied, "Here! Anywhere! You're never"—she paused, looking for words—"it's like you're just going through the motions. Pretending. Your body's here, we talk, we do stuff together, but *you're* not really *here*. It's . . . like living with a ghost, only in reverse."

And so the next few years went by. His parents still lived in the same house he had grown up in, and he saw them at Christmas, and sometimes for a few days in summer. Occasionally there would be a mention of "the Danforth case" in the local paper, and his mother would clip the articles out and send them to Brian. There was never anything new in the pieces, but he would read them through several times, as if he could—if only he tried hard enough—decipher the clues, succeed where all others had failed.

Spring 2010, twenty-two years after Melissa's disappearance, and Brian found himself in an upscale hotel room in a good-sized city in southwestern Ontario, to participate in a training seminar. He arrived on Sunday, and by late Tuesday evening felt as if he had been there a week. He had politely refused an offer to go out for after-dinner drinks with some of the other trainers—"Jet lag," he'd murmured, wondering how long he could get away with that excuse—and was flipping through the television channels, finally settling on a local news program. He was leafing without much interest through a magazine, thinking he should turn in, when the words of the newscaster caught his ear.

". . . latest in the story of the disappearance of ten-year-old Kayley

Porter yesterday. Police have now issued an Amber Alert for Kayley, who vanished yesterday evening in the Westbury neighborhood. Her parents were alerted when Kayley, who had gone to the
park on Elgin Road to watch friends play soccer, failed to return
home. With more on this developing story, we go to reporter Debo-
rah Taylor."

Brian turned to the TV screen, where he saw a reporter standing
on a suburban street, in front of an unremarkable two-story brick
house. It took him a moment to concentrate on what she was saying.

". . . reeling after news of the disappearance of ten-year-old Kayley, who failed to return home last night after a visit to the local
park. Police have been conducting door-to-door inquiries, but so far
have very little to go on, and are appealing for help from anyone
who might have information on Kayley's whereabouts."

A picture of Kayley flashed up on-screen, and Brian saw a smiling girl with brown hair and braces and laughing eyes. When the
camera cut back to the reporter, she took a few steps to her left, and
a small group of people came into view, standing between the Porter house and its next-door neighbor. Brian's eyes roved across the
faces as the reporter continued.

"Residents of this quiet neighborhood are in shock this evening,
as at the moment there are more questions than answers. The Porter family has declined to comment, but a press conference is sched-
uled for tomorrow. In the meantime . . ."

Brian had, however, stopped listening. Even if he had wanted to
hear what the reporter had to say, it would have been drowned out
by the sudden roaring that filled his head. For there at the back of
the group, turning her head slightly to one side, was Mrs. Gleason.

Brian scrambled closer to the television, and for the few more
seconds that she was on screen he stared at the woman. Yes, it was
Mrs. Gleason, beyond any shadow of a doubt. But—Brian shook his
head, and mouthed the word *no*—it was Mrs. Gleason looking pre-
cisely as she had looked twenty-two years earlier.

He knew he was right, knew it was Mrs. Gleason, and not just
another woman who happened to look remarkably like her. *How is
that possible?* asked a voice inside his head. He sat for some time on
the edge of the bed, then opened the minibar, pulled out the first

bottle that came to hand, emptied it at a gulp, and picked up the phone.

"Hi, Mom, it's Brian."

"Brian!" She sounded surprised to hear his voice. "Is everything all right?"

"Yes, I'm fine." He spent a few moments reassuring her, answering questions, before he was able to get to the purpose of his call.

"Look, Mom, I need to ask you something. You remember Mr. and Mrs. Gleason, who used to live down the road? I know this is going back a few years, but do you remember where they came from? Where they lived before they moved onto our street?"

"Goodness, Brian, that's an odd question! It was such a long time ago. Let me think. . . ."

Brian tapped the desk with the pen he was holding.

"I'm not sure if I'm mixing them up with someone else, but I think they said they came from somewhere in British Columbia, and I remember it was a place where a school friend of mine had moved to. . . . No, not Vancouver, I'd remember that. Not Victoria, either. . . . Oh dear, my memory is dreadful these days. It began with a C, I think, or possibly a K. I'm sure I'd know it if I heard it."

"Clearwater? Castlegar? Kamloops? Kelowna?"

"That's it!" said his mother in triumph. "Kelowna! I remember now. Irene Patterson moved there, and I lost touch with her. A shame, really, as we'd been—"

Brian cut her off. "Do you remember how long they'd lived on our street, before . . . before Melissa disappeared?"

"Dear me, now that *is* a question, Brian. Not very long, I don't think. Two years, perhaps three? Yes, that sounds right. Three years, I believe. Why on earth do you want to know all this?"

Brian hardly knew that himself. He said something vague, half-listened for a few more minutes while his mother talked, and then, promising to call again soon, hung up. He powered up his laptop, Googled "Kelowna BC + disappearance + 1980s," and hit Enter.

A list of links appeared on screen, and he scanned down, eyes darting about the page. One name and date appeared over and over again: Sophie Dawson, 1984. Feeling sick, he clicked on www.miss ingpersonsofBC.com.

Two hours later, surrounded by empty bottles from the minibar and several sheets of paper covered in increasingly illegible hand-writing, Brian pushed himself away from the desk and stumbled into the bathroom, where he splashed cold water over his face and dried himself off. When he went back into the room he was dully surprised to note how dark it was. Rather than turn on a light, how-ever, he went and stood near the window, leaning his head against the cool glass, going over and over what he had learned.

The facts themselves were simple enough, and confirmed by site after site. Eleven-year-old Sophie Dawson had disappeared from her quiet Kelowna neighborhood in May 1984. She had been to a local park with her older brothers, who had gone off to play with friends and left Sophie in the company of a group of other children, all of whom Sophie knew. At some point Sophie had disappeared, and despite an exhaustive search and prolonged police investiga-tion, she had never been found. An article in the Kelowna *Daily Courier* from 2009 had revisited the case and looked at periodic attempts, over the years, to reopen the investigation and uncover fresh leads, but the author was forced to the conclusion that there was little chance, now, of discovering what had happened.

Brian sighed, and turned back to his laptop. Dropping heavily into the seat, he punched the Enter key and the screen obligingly powered back into life, revealing a page from a site called www.wherearetheynowBC.ca. There was a lengthy entry about Sophie Dawson, complete with photo gallery, which was now displayed. On it were pictures of Sophie, her family, the park from which she had disappeared, and the Dawson house. This last picture had been taken some days after Sophie's disappearance, and showed a make-shift shrine of flowers and other items which had been placed on the sidewalk in front of the house. "Neighbors gather to pay touch-ing tribute to the missing girl" read the caption underneath.

It was not the flowers that drew Brian's eyes, however. Instead, he focussed on the figures grouped to the right of the photo: a little girl placing a bouquet on the pile; a youngish man and woman (her parents?) slightly behind her; half a dozen other people ranged be-hind them. At the far edge of the photograph was an older woman, her face and body slightly blurred, as if she were trying to move out of range of the shot and had left it a second too late. Blurred as she was, however, Brian could still recognize the face of Mrs. Gleason.

He put his head in his hands. What should he do? *The police*, he thought. But what could he tell them that wouldn't sound like the raving of a madman? He had nothing concrete, only a crazy story he didn't fully understand himself. At best they'd laugh, tell him to go away and sleep it off; at worst they'd keep him in overnight for being drunk and disorderly. He needed proof.

He stumbled only slightly on his way to the minibar, fished out another bottle—vodka—grimaced slightly as it went down, then returned to the desk and stared at the screen again. One of the pictures showed people filing into a church. "Memorial service for Sophie Dawson" said the caption, and suddenly Brian was back in church with his parents on the Sunday after Melissa disappeared, turning to see the Gleasons hungrily surveying the congregation. What had Mr. Waters read out in the sermon? Unbidden, the word "Lamentations" came into Brian's head, and he fumbled in the desk drawer. Sure enough, it contained a Gideon Bible, and it did not take long to find the passage he was seeking, the one which Mr. Waters had read. He mouthed the words silently, the unfamiliar King James version sounding odd and yet soothing, somehow. He went back a few verses, and began reading again. Mr. Waters must have read those words out too, earlier in the service, but he had forgotten them:

It is good for a man that he bear the yoke in his youth.
He sitteth alone and keepeth silence, because he hath borne
    it upon him.
He putteth his mouth in the dust; if so be there may be hope.
He giveth his cheek to him that smiteth him: he is filled full
    with reproach.

Brian gave a long, shuddering sigh. He knew what he had to do. He would not reproach the Gleasons, oh no; he certainly didn't plan on seeing *them*. But proof—he could get proof, he was sure of it, and then the police would have to listen, have to make them stop, so there would never be another Kayley, another Sophie. Another Melissa. He would do this for Melissa.

It was past one o'clock, and pitch black outside. The darkness was good. He found a map of the city in a folder on the bedside table, and traced with an unsteady finger where he needed to go. Then he stuffed the map into his pocket, picked up his wallet and the keys to his rental car, and left the hotel.

He was in no condition to be driving, and even with the map it took him some time to find the right street. He did not know the address of the Porter house, but it was easy enough to spot, and his stomach lurched as he noted the small pile of flowers already on the sidewalk outside it. He pulled the car to a halt directly across the street from the house, fighting the sense that he had been here before, seen it already. Then, with a deep breath, he turned to his left and looked, not at the Porter residence, but the houses either side. They would be in one of those, he knew.

The house to the left of the Porters' was, like theirs, two stories high. There was a neatly tended garden in front, and a basketball hoop over the garage door. It could have been put there by a previous occupant, but there was a soccer ball on the front lawn, and he could see a bicycle on the front porch. *Not that one.* He switched his gaze to the house on the other side—a bungalow, tucked away from the road, all the windows dark. That had to be it.

He had had too much to drink to wonder if he was wrong, think about what he was doing, consider the consequences. He needed proof; that was all he knew. Melissa's face was in front of him, and he whimpered softly. It had been twenty-two years, but at last he knew what he had to do.

He drove on, parked two streets over, and made his way back to the Gleasons' house. When he reached it he turned in at the driveway and went around to the back door. It was locked, and Brian stood staring at it, as if he could will the door to open. He needed to get into the house, find some evidence that he could take to the police. It was the one thought consuming him, fighting its way through the alcohol-induced confusion inside his head. But how? He couldn't break a window; that would wake up anyone inside, and he did not want to risk encountering the house's occupants.

He stepped away from the back door, and saw a sliding glass door leading off a small patio to his left. He stumbled slightly as he

moved toward it, and when he reached it gave the handle an explor-
atory tug, expecting it to be locked. To his surprise, the door slid
open, and without stopping to think about what this could mean
Brian slipped inside, pulling the door shut behind him.

He paused, listening, but there was no sound. Now that he was
in the house he realized he had no idea where to look, or even what
he was looking for. His head was clearing somewhat, and the real-
ization that this wasn't a good idea was starting to nudge at him.
Still, he had come this far. He couldn't back out now.

He was in a dining room; to his right there was a door leading
into the kitchen, and a light above the stove gave enough illumination that he could see. The main floor seemed simple enough: dining room, living room, kitchen, a short hallway leading to what he
assumed would be bedrooms and a bathroom. A door in the kitchen
showed there was a basement, however, and Brian knew that what
he was looking for would be down there. He opened the door with
care, noted the location of the light switch on the other side, and
closed the door behind him before flicking the switch.

At the base of the stairs a long bare room stretched away to his
right. Brian turned left, down a short hallway with three doors. The
first was a bathroom, the second a laundry room. The third . . .

He paused after his fumbling hand found the light switch. Two
armchairs in the center of the room, their backs to the door, faced a
row of floor-to-ceiling shelves covering the far wall. On these were
several scrapbooks, each one clearly labelled with a name and date.
Framed pictures—most cut from newspapers—were positioned at
intervals, and between them sat an array of stuffed animals and
other tokens. His eyes roved up and down the shelves, seeking,
seeking—

And there they were, positioned side by each, beside a photograph of Melissa: a stuffed white rabbit with a pink ribbon round its
neck and mismatched eyes, and a cloth bookmark decorated with
butterflies and a rainbow. "Melissa," he whispered. He reached out
with a shaking hand and picked up the bookmark, only to have it
flutter to the ground at the sound of a voice behind him.

"Well, well. Brian Henderson, all grown up."

He turned. Mrs. Gleason was standing in the doorway, regarding
him with a look half-amused, half-angry. She shook her head in

exaggerated fashion and wagged a finger at him. "You *are* a naughty boy, aren't you? And thinking yourself so clever. I'm a very light sleeper. I heard your car pull up a few minutes ago, and when I looked out and saw who was driving it I said to myself, 'I'll be seeing him again soon.' And here you are. I left the patio door open, to make it easier for you."

"Mrs. Gleason." It was all he could think of to say. She shook her head again.

"Dear me, no. That was some time ago. Mrs. Bryant, now. It does become difficult, sometimes, to remember, but we have . . . adapted."

"Adapted?"

"In so many ways. Over time we've learned to hide a good many things. Who we are, for example. The police are very thorough in these matters, when they begin an investigation. Oh, you have no idea how thorough! It would never do for them to find out too much about our past, so we've become very good at covering our tracks, protecting ourselves." Her eyes flicked from Brian to the shelves behind him. "I see you've been admiring our collection. It *is* lovely, isn't it? Of course, it has taken rather a long time to put it together."

"What are they—why do you have them? I don't understand." Brian was sobering up fast, but not quite fast enough.

Mrs. Gleason, as he still thought of her, laughed, a sound entirely without merriment. "I think you do, really, or you wouldn't be here. Call them—keepsakes. Mementos, if you will. Whenever we begin to flag, we come down here. So many memories of grief; only shadows of the real thing, but sufficient to sustain us. For a time, at least."

"And then you do it again," said Brian slowly. "You move somewhere else and . . . *sustain* yourselves for a while, and then do it again."

"Exactly!" Mrs. Gleason clapped her hands together softly, like a teacher pleased by the correct answer from a backward pupil. "There is, you understand, so much grief when a child disappears. Especially a girl, although that must sound *very*—what's the phrase?—politically incorrect. Mind you, we do have to be careful." She waved an arm at the shelves. "For example, when we move, we pack these ourselves. It saves so many potentially awkward questions."

For one mad second Brian wanted to laugh. Instead, he took a deep breath and gathered himself up. "You won't get away with it anymore," he said, in a voice that he almost managed to keep from shaking. "I'll tell the police. They'll come here and find all this and they'll figure out who you are and what you've done. No one else is going to suffer. Do you hear me?"

"And you would tell the police what?"

"I . . . I don't know."

"Who are we, Brian? What exactly have we done?" He stayed silent, and she made a clucking noise with her tongue and shook her head. "You really haven't thought this through very well, have you."

"If I could piece it together in two hours from a bit of news footage and some websites, the police'll be able to. Once I tell them where to start looking. And then—well, we'll see what they find."

Mrs. Gleason sighed. "What are you going to do? Push me out of the way? Rush upstairs and out of the house?"

"If I have to, yes."

"You *could* do that," she said, her voice thoughtful. "You're a young, strong man, and I'm an old woman. Of course, I could lock you in here, call the police, and tell them there was an intruder, but you'd easily have the door down before they arrived. Even if you didn't, as soon as you started telling them your story there would be enough questions that . . . yes, we could be in quite considerable danger."

Brian took a deep breath. "I don't want to make this any more difficult than it already is. Just let me out, and you won't get hurt."

"You never forgot her, did you. Melissa. So sweet, so pretty. So *much* grief."

"Shut up."

"All these years, thinking about her, wondering what happened to her. Would you like to know?"

"Shut *up*! Just shut the fuck up!"

Mrs. Gleason looked disapproving. "Language, Brian. You always did have a temper. It cheated us out of a delicious morsel of grief that should have been ours. And you do want to know what happened to Melissa, what we did to her. Although it would be more accurate to say what my husband did to her." She saw the look of horror on Brian's face, and clucked impatiently. "No, it's not what you're thinking. Such a filthy mind you must have, Brian. The grief sustains us both, as does our little collection, but my husband needs something more . . . tangible? Is that the word? Yes, tangible will do. By the time he's finished there's very little left. So convenient, don't you think?"

Brian was trying not to throw up. "I'm going now," he managed to whisper. "Get out of my way."

"Tell me, Brian, did you let anyone know you were coming here tonight? Ah"—catching the look that flitted across his face—"no. You didn't. You're not only a naughty boy, you're a very foolish one. That makes things so much easier."

"What do you mean?"

"Tsk. You obviously weren't paying very much attention to what I said."

"About what?"

"My husband," she said simply, and stepped inside the room. She had been blocking the open door throughout their conversation, and Brian, intent on her, had seen no indication of movement in the hall. Now he saw what she had been obscuring, as the figure of Mr. Gleason filled the doorway. His face was the stark white of Brian's memories, the lips still blackish-red, but now they were drawn back, and Brian at last saw the rows and rows of tiny sharp teeth they concealed. His last thought, before the scream choked his throat and blackness descended, was that he had always thought Mrs. Gleason was the more frightening, and stronger, of the two.

How wrong he had been.

FIRST BREATH

Nicole J. LeBoeuf

Nicole J. LeBoeuf has been writing stories since she was six. She sold her first story when she was eighteen. She lives in Boulder, Colorado, with her husband and their two cats but was born in, raised near, and is homesick for New Orleans.

LeBoeuf is a graduate of the University of Washington and the science fiction and fantasy workshop Viable Paradise. Her story "The Day the Sidewalks Melted" appears online at *Ideomancer Speculative Fiction*.

You can find out more at www.nicolejleboeuf.com.

This is her first professional sale.

It was time I went in search of myself. Everyone has to do it once in their lives. Each of my parents had, years before, and now I felt the pull that said it was my turn. Time to make my own pilgrimage.

They saw me off, standing in front of the house to watch me drift down the road. "Remember what we taught you," my mother said. "One foot in front of the other. You'll do fine."

"Hurry home as soon as you can," said my father, a wry smile hiding the sadness of parting. "You'll want to be here when the baby arrives."

I could only nod, looking first from face to face then down at the place where my unborn sibling waited to be breathed into life. I wanted to take their hands. I wanted to hold them and never let go.

But I couldn't touch them. I could not even speak. Not yet.

I've stopped counting the Jell-O shots and I'm starting to lose the spaces between the seconds, if you know what I mean, when the girl shows up right in front of me. The strange one. I've been noticing her on and off throughout the evening, the only person in the bar I've never seen before. My guess is, she's just some dumb rich kid up from the flats on a cheap time-share week, finding out the hard way what all us locals know: there's nothing to do in mud season. Ski resorts are closed. Everyone's bored out of our skulls and broke.

When I first spotted her, I grabbed Mack and pointed. "Who's the chick in the gray hoodie? You know her?"

Mack just went, "Who?" like he couldn't see her. And he probably couldn't. I actually did count his Jell-O shots before I started on
mine. He likes the orange ones. Robbie makes them with 190-proof
Everclear.

He makes the red ones, my favorites, with pepper vodka, and I
guess I've downed at least ten, because I have to squint to focus
even though the girl's right here. First things I see are her legs, bare
right up to mid-thigh where the hoodie ends. I can't make out
much more of her than that, just the tip of her nose and her mouth.
She's smiling this weird sort of amazed smile, probably tripping
on acid or E or something. Which is why I'm annoyed but not really surprised when she grabs my hand and starts playing with my
fingers.

Naturally I try to yank my hand away. But she hangs on, so I end
up pulling her off balance and into my lap. Now she's got both her
hands on me, feeling her way up my arm like she's never seen an
arm before. I roll my eyes and put up with it until she grabs my left
boob, and then I've had enough. I slap her hand away. "What the
hell are you doing?"

She sits there in my lap, examining her wrist from every angle
like she's trying to see if I left a mark. If I weren't so drunk I'd have
dumped her on the floor by now; as it is I can't seem to get up the
momentum. She touches her own face, then mine, then—"What
the hell," she says. And kisses me.

For just an instant I'm thinking *Oh, God, another idiot who thinks*
she's bi when she's stoned. Then the thought dissolves away until
there's nothing left but *Oh, God.*

It's like something inside me, something I never knew existed
but I can't survive without, rises up and goes spinning out of me
and into her. When she pulls away, I can't stop myself. I grab hold
of her, pull her back down, make her kiss me again just to try to get
that piece of myself back.

It doesn't work. I'm even more lost than before. It takes every
shred of concentration just to ask her, "Who are you?" as she runs
her fingers through my hair, against my scalp. Something's weird
about that. I can feel my head resting against the back of the couch.
There's no room between my head and the orange velvet upholstery
for her hand to be there, stroking from my hairline to the nape of

my neck and making my arms explode in goose bumps. I try again. "What's your name?"

She leans in close, lays her cheek alongside mine. "What's *your* name?" Right in my ear. Licking it.

The smell of her hair is sweet and slightly bitter, like someplace far away I'll never see. I answer her on automatic, "Jen," and then *"God!"* leaps out of my mouth as her teeth pierce my earlobe. The pain clears my head for a moment. I'm conscious of the warm, wet blossom of blood that drips like melted wax onto my shoulder, and of the absurd and slightly scary fact that I'm pinned under the body of a stranger and she's hurt me. I push at her, whatever I can reach, but I'm too drunk to have much effect. In fact, I'm so drunk that her knee, what little I can see of it around her hair in my face, seems to be passing right through the couch cushion.

She licks up the blood in two slow swipes, and the sudden clarity is just as suddenly gone. I can't think. She kisses me again with my blood on her teeth. More of me vanishes into her; I open my mouth wider so she can take whatever she wants.

"Jen, you okay?" Mack's voice. "Jen? Christ, Robbie, how many shots you give her?"

"You should talk, Mack. You aren't driving home, are you?"

"Nah, walking. So's she, thank God." Someone—Mack—gives my shoulder a rough shake. "Jen, you okay? Can you hear me?"

"A little busy now," I mumble around the lips that are slowly killing me.

He doesn't seem to hear me. "Jen, sweetie, maybe you should go home. Can you walk okay?"

The girl climbs off me and holds out her hand. Her smile is beatific. "Yeah," I say to Mack, unable to take my eyes from the girl's lips. "Yeah. Going home." I let her lead me out of the bar and into the parking lot.

The fifteen minutes it would take to get to my place seems an unbearably long time to wait. On the far side of the parking lot, I try to step up onto the grass and somehow I miss the curb. The girl catches me as I stumble. She nearly falls herself. We sway together against the back of Robbie's camper-top pickup truck, and now there's no question of walking to my place or anywhere else. She's at me again like you'd attack your first meal after the rescue copters get you out of the avalanche, and your hunger is a prayer of thanks. She's pulling my tank top over my head, ripping at my bra. It's February, there's snow on the ground, but I don't stop her. I reach to help her out of that hoodie of hers only to find it's gone already, just disappeared. Bare skin under my hands. I open my eyes and look into her face at last.

Her face. It's *my* face.

She stares back at me with my own eyes, her cheek marred by that same patchy birthmark I've hated all my life, her ear still wearing a clotted bead of my blood. That smile—I only found it so weird on her because it was so familiar. I stare at the living mirror before me and my hands fall limp at my sides to rest helpless on the truck's tailgate. Only they don't. They pass right *through*.

A chill sweeps my body like I wouldn't wish on anyone. It turns my stomach and stops my breath. I sag and start to fall, and the back of Robbie's truck doesn't stop me. I move through its plastic and metal like a ghost.

So does she. She dives forward to catch me, pulls me out into the clear, kneels with me in the snow. I cling to her solidity and she rocks me in her arms. And then I try to scream because now *she's* fading, I can't touch her anymore, and I can't touch the air, either, so no sound comes out of my mouth after all.

No one had told me how much it would hurt. "Remember," they'd said, "don't get distracted. It's hard not to. Experiencing physical sensations for the first time, it can be dangerously fascinating." Fascinating? Earth underfoot, it was more than *fascinating*. Jen's skin on mine was meat and drink to me, it was Mothersong and burnt offerings at dusk. I wanted it never to end. But it did, it had to, I knew that it had to. My parents had told me what to expect. Jen faded in my arms, becoming insubstantial as mist. A spasm seized my throat, making me gasp, and I breathed her in. She was gone.

"Fascinating." "Distracted." Oh, yes. But no one had warned me that I would love her. When my parents had recounted their own pilgrimages, years gone by, they'd never told me that their first tangible breath had been to weep.

I don't know how long I knelt there, alone in the snow surrounded by Jen's abandoned clothes. Her socks seemed particularly forlorn, half in and half out of her shoes. Her name stuttered uncontrollably off my lips. Her lips. My name now, to remember her by. Her name was mine, and her voice to speak it with. Her clothes were now mine; I remembered I was supposed to put them on. "Leave nothing behind." Besides, it was cold out. I could feel the cold sinking its teeth into Jen's body, my body, inch by inch.

I could feel. I could pick up a handful of snow. I could wear real clothes of solid fabric, never again need the gray imaginings that habit of thought had dressed me in for years. I could touch. I could breathe.

My sobs stilled simply because they made me aware of the miracle that I *could* cry. Maybe that's why no one mentions the grief; it's gone so soon, replaced by joy. "Jen," I said again, and then spoke the first words I could call my own. "Thank you."

I couldn't quite manage the shoes. The knowledge of them had come into my head with everything else, but I had little experience thus far using fingers. The cold made them clumsier still, putting the puzzle of hooks and eyelets and laces out of my reach. I carried the shoes instead, and the pain of snow on stocking feet was the most precious thing to me during that long walk to Jen's apartment. Walking, at least, I'd practiced. One foot in front of the other. Gravity had become a surprisingly rough playmate, and the alcohol in Jen's system didn't help, but I made a good start. It got easier step by slow, careful step.

"You'll probably find your way back without trouble," they'd said. "Usually it's a matter of hours. It might take longer, but that's rare." Longer? How much longer? "But don't worry about that. Just live her life for however long it takes, until the way home opens for you." Days, months of Jen's life stretched out in my imagined future, each dyed in the colors of boredom, slowly sinking under the weight of years, trapped in the same two miles of tourists and ski slopes and the same people doing the same thing through the unrelenting sameness of endless seasons—

But my pilgrimage ended as ordinarily as I could have hoped. I got to Jen's apartment within the hour, fumbled it open with the key from her jeans pocket, and, simply as a dream, found myself walking into my parents' house.

They were in the bedroom, my parents, Daya upon the bed and hard into advanced labor. Avell knelt beside her, both his hands enclosing hers. It was dim in there, for Daya's comfort, but I could clearly see the sweat glistening in sheets upon her bark-brown face. The breath whistled thinly in and out of her, a terrifying sound.

Yet her gaze rose to meet mine. Alerted by her smile, Avell turned. Moments later I was in his arms.

At first he simply held me, and I felt the uneven rise and fall of his chest that told me he was crying. I was crying, too. Finally he held me out at arm's length and looked me over with grave, careful attention, as though seeing me for the first time. I suppose he was. What had I looked like to him, to either of them, all these years? A gray ghost, seen but never heard, communicating by blurred hand-signs they must have strained their eyes to read. No more. I could speak now.

But Avell gave me a stern look, and I remembered what my first words upon homecoming needed to be. "Avell my mother," I said, "behold your song made flesh."

He smiled. "It is a beautiful song," he said. Then he brought me to the bedside and addressed the woman laboring there. "Daya, father of our child, see the breath you breathed into me."

"It is a beautiful breath we breathed together." She said it strong despite her travail. "What name has our breath brought home?"

"Jen," I told them. Names are important. They're how we remember. "Her name was Jen."

"Is," Daya corrected me. "Her name *is* Jen. And it is a good name." Then she gasped, her smile sliding sharply out of sight. "Bone and blood! Oh, see indeed. 'The breath you breathed into me—'"

Avell caressed her brow. "Now, love, did I complain so when I lay there laboring with our Jen?"

"You did. You complained *more.*"

"Then it's a good thing we didn't conceive twins, isn't it?" Avell chuckled. "Imagine Jen coming home to *that* scene. Both of us lying there, complaining and cursing—"

"Earth forfend I deliver this child on a curse!" But it was only mock-horror. Daya had found strength to laugh again.

I was too dazed to join in the joke. Avell had used my name so easily, so naturally. I sank to my knees beside him, the things in my heart too big for my newfound words. I laid my hands upon Daya's belly where the unborn child moved like an extra breath between Daya's breaths.

Avell's hand closed upon my shoulder. "Jen," he said, carefully and clearly. "Tell me what troubles you."

Finally it burst out of me, and the words, when they came, were so simple. "I loved her. It hurt so much—"

"Oh, Jen," murmured Daya. She placed her hand over mine.

"But why didn't you warn me?" I found myself shouting, anger burning through my tears. "You both made it sound so—technical. So practical. Do this, don't do that. *Rules*. Why didn't you tell me it would break my heart?"

The sadness in Avell's eyes shamed me then. "What could I have said? What would you have done, had you known? Hardened your heart against her, become a predator devouring prey? Staged it as a tragedy in which you played the starring role? No." He squeezed my shoulder. "You both deserved love, and there's no preparing you for that. We could only have ruined it by trying."

"But what good is love, when it killed her?"

"No." Daya's voice, strained as it was, allowed no argument. "She is with you. In you. Always." She punctuated that with a fierce grip on my hand. "She will live in your children, and their children."

Avell touched my face, tracing the curve of my cheek. "I can see him so clearly in you," he said. In my imagination he doubled, stood face-to-face with himself, that other man who had held a life safe and waiting for him to claim. "How much I loved him—it makes me love you that much more."

A cry from the bed, sharp and surprised. Daya flung her head back against the pillows and drew a breath. And kept drawing it, on and on. It seemed she would never stop, not until she'd inhaled every bit of the Earth's atmosphere and become herself a planet with her own weather patterns, her own seas. Avell's hands and mine rose with the profound expansion of her belly. Then, at the crest of the wave, she held that great breath, creating a moment of stillness in which I held mine also. In silence she smiled at us, the smile of a goddess telling Her people, *Be not afraid*. I gripped Avell's hand tightly and watched Daya's lips.

She opened her mouth and breathed that great breath out, and my sister, insubstantial as a mist, was born.

TOUJOURS

Kathe Koja

In 1991, Kathe Koja's first novel, *The Cipher*, inaugurated the Dell Abyss line and won the Bram Stoker Award for best first novel. In 2008 her novel *Headlong* was featured in *The New Yorker*'s "Book Bench" roundtable. In between, her dozen novels include *Skin*, *The Blue Mirror*, and *Talk*, and a short fiction collection, *Extremities*. *Under the Poppy*, her first work of historical fiction, is her latest novel. Koja's books have been honored by the ASPCA, the International Reading Association, the Horror Writers Association, and with the Parents' Choice Award. *The Cipher* is in development for film, and *Under the Poppy* has been adapted for an immersive stage presentation.

H*ey, hey, is he in?* That's how they talk to me, these girls, girls with their knee boots and tiny little telephones, leaning against the elevator doors, tugging on their hair, lighting cigarettes— cigarettes! and right on the building wall the sign NO SMOKING. In Italian *and* English! *Hey, is he in?*

Foolish, I told my wife, my Lu. *These girls—twenty years I am with Señor, and not one of these girls will ever learn my name.*

She shrugged, she poured the coffee. Her hair, in the sun through the windows—gold and silver, like a painting, a Titian. *Ah,* she said, *they are infants. Can you be angry with an infant? Besides, Charles knows your name. . . . Maritsa called again this morning. The christening dinner—*

Señor may need me. Today the journalists come, and the man from the art school—I will try.

To give the toast, at least? He is your grandson. And Maritsa says—

I took her hand, her left hand with that tiny seed drop of a diamond; she deserves something grander, I have said this before. *I will try.*

And then I was on my way, from the table, the apartment with the sunny windows, the terrace where she grows her flowers, pots of white daisies, I used to call her Daisy, as if she were an American girl. The good smell of coffee in the hallway, the stone faces at each landing like the saints and gargoyles one sees at cemeteries: weighing, approving, denying— That journalist, that English fellow from

Le Pop!, said the same last month of me: *An aging but formidable factotum, forever looming like a gargoyle over the Ezterhas brand.* That is how this business is, if there is nothing to say still they must say something. This business, where the money flies and they take so many drugs, and the girls—"infants," yes, and younger all the time, but none too young to spread themselves for anyone, anywhere, at the shows, in the atelier, the things I have seen—!

See them now, this very morning in Gold Street: one busy with her little phone, the other scowling behind round black sunglasses, the Desmundo glasses they all wear this season, leaping up like greyhounds when I approach: "Listen, hey *listen*, Charles wants me, he called—" while the other one shoves forward, "Me, too—he wants me, too!" Breathless and rude all the way up in the elevator but I make them wait outside, Señor inside with a pair of gloves, blue leather, very nice goods. He pulls on the left, smiles at me, holds out his hand; I adjust the right.

"They sent two pairs," he says, "one red and one blue. Which do you prefer?"

"Red-handed," I say, "that's guilty, *non?*" and he smiles, white as the petals of a daisy. When I first met him, he never smiled at all.

"You think of everything, Gianfranco. All right, blue it is."

"Did you call for models, Señor? From Vita?" and when he nods I let them in: greedy they clamber up beside him, grab his blue hands, no thought between them to thank me who opened the door. But Señor nods as I take the empty glove case from the table, he nods and he smiles as I leave.

Later, I fish the Desmundo glasses from the *pissoir.* Crying, monotonous crying, from outside in the hall. The man from the art school is early, he brings another girl, another bony creature with pale hair and bright eyes, they stay for drinks, they stay for dinner. Señor has far too much wine. Maritsa sends me several angry messages. Lu is asleep when I come home.

He was half an infant himself when I met him in Paris, peasant boy with the loden jacket and the little colored pencils: serving me *café noisette*, swabbing the table, one shoulder tucked down as if something pained him: *Did you eat today?* I asked, and he shrugged, he was ashamed. Those crooked, pointed, wolfish teeth; he was ashamed of that, too, and ashamed to have been fired. *Three times in one month, from three different cafés. Because I was drawing.*

I looked at his pictures, his "girls." *You are not from the city,* I said, because already I knew him, I had been waiting for him, I knew exactly what I must do: speak to the café manager, speak to his uncle, some turd from the suburbs blustering, *He should be in school, Charles, not making silly pictures, "fashion," what do you want with my Charles?*

I want to feed him dinner, I said. To him I said, *Go get your things.*

I took him from Paris, from the rain and shit in the gutters, I brought him here to the sun. For the first six months he slept in the room off the terrace, helping Lu water the flowers, prowling the little shops and the galleries; he drew many more "girls." When I bought the apartment on Gold Street he worried that it was too big, too much, *All these rooms?* But *An atelier,* I said, *needs space.* The clothes followed the drawings, the first show sold all the clothes— and he came to me then, very early, still awake from the night before and *Willys,* he said, *wants the whole line. And* Vogue *wants to interview me—she called me a wizard.* He looked around the terrace, the pots of daisies, the sun just rising. *Jesus! You're the wizard, you gave me everything, I'd still be in that fucking café if—*

Don't curse, I told him. *This was all meant to be. Consider the lilies.*
What?

Señor, I said; he almost flinched, to hear me say it. *Señor, it is my will to serve you. Always.*

Since then I have served Señor in many ways: with the journalists and their editors; with the buyers, those sharks, and the stores, the licensing—now they want to put his name on condoms, Ezterhas Golden Fleece, how stupid and vulgar. . . . I have served Señor as well with the girls, the models, Señor has a sometimes regrettable taste in models but he is always very sorry afterward, and there is always a new girl, many new girls to choose from for a season or a night. At times he has seemed to prefer one over another, like last winter, that dark one from Vienna with the nervous laugh, when she went back to Vienna Lu sighed: *Ah, poor Charles, is he missing that little one? Why did she go, do you think?*

She went because I bought the ticket, because I called her booker, because I made it plain to her that *He deserves better;* I am wiser than his own heart in such matters, I do not bend to heat or caprice. . . . When it is time for Señor to settle down, I will make certain that his choice is the best one, not like the Viennese girl, or the pale thing last night—

—who is here again, blue slacks, blue blouse, almost demure though none of these girls ever bother with brassieres; in the sunlight her hair is white as bone. No Desmundos for her, her gaze comes squarely to mine as "Good morning, Gianfranco," and she hands me a little pink bag: *amaretti* from Sofia's, the ones I most prefer, a perfect blend of bitter and sweet. Behind me I hear Señor's approach, rapid, the Hermès loafers he wears slapping against the marble floor.

"Gitte," he says, with far too much pleasure. "You're just in time for breakfast."

She smiles, not at him, but to me. Her smile is very white.

"Please join us," she says.

From then on she is here every day, Gitte who smiles, who does not smoke, who speaks very little and never says where she is from, Gitte who brings *amaretti* for me until I tell her to stop, and yogurt and vitamins and machinery for Señor, today it is an ugly little steel contraption shaped like a pregnant tube: "Look," says Gitte, manipulating traps and levers until a stream of cloudy green bursts forth, sickening, a color like bile. "It's a juicer," she says to my stare. "Avocado juice."

"Ah. You are a waitress, then?"

She smiles, unperturbed. Señor drinks the bile: "Oh, delicious. You cured my hangover." As he kisses her, she looks at me.

She is not a waitress, not a model, not a journalist. She came with the man from the art school, but she is not an artist, or a student, either: *Gitte? No,* he says when I call, *she was in the photography program but that was a while ago. I guess you could call her my assistant, kind of, she did a little bit of everything—*

A factotum.

Sure, right. . . . She's amazing, isn't she? And a monster fan of Charles, you two have a lot in common, which is true, terribly so, she knew it first but I know it now as well. The juicer, then the bracelet to count his heartbeats, then the walking trip. "Just for the weekend," Señor says to me, as if the collection is already finished, as if there is not so much work left to do, a tremendous amount of work. "Gitte says we need some fresh air." I wave one hand at the windows. "I mean—like a getaway."

"Get away from what?"

Señor does not answer. His face looks leaner, its planes more pronounced, like hers; he wears blue now as she does, his hair has been cut very short. Such great changes in such a little time, the girl has been here barely three months; it is monstrous. He fiddles with the heartbeat bracelet, he shrugs, maddening, placating: "I'll work so much better if I have a chance to relax first, Gitte knows this fantastic walking trail around Sóller—"

"Spain! You don't like Spain, Señor, you have never liked—"

"—and I know—I mean, there's a little bit of friction between Gitte and you"—he says it that way, her name first—"but if you'd only spend some time with her— You've been after me for years to slow down on my drinking, right? Now I have. She's a very good influence on me, you can see that, can't you?" His voice is a plea, almost a whine. "And she respects you so much, she talks about you all the time, always asking questions—"

What sort of questions? but I do not ask because I know, the same way I know she will come to me next, and she does: dressed in blue so dark it is almost black, like the sea at night, her eyes are black as a barracuda's and "He'll work better," she says, "if he feels better. I can make him feel good. Why would you want to ruin that?" I do not trouble to answer. "You ought to come with us."

"To Spain?"

"To wherever we go."

I lean very close to her, so close I can smell her scent, bitter and sweet, yes: like *amaretti*, like almonds, like poison. "I have been with Señor since before you were born," I say into her ear. "I have seen girls like you come and go, many many girls who—"

"There are no girls like me," she says.

We gaze at one another, there in the hallway, a phone trilling from the office, Señor whistling in the *pissoir*. Gitte shrugs. "If you don't come with us," she says, "you'll be left behind." And she walks away, her loafers, Hermès loafers, slapping the floor as she goes: down the hall, off to Spain, deeper and deeper into his heart.

Does one believe in lamia, in succubae? Did Medusa ever smile? What sort of perfume, one wonders, did Messalina prefer?

I sit alone on the terrace, still in my dinner jacket; Señor did not attend the Fashion Association's formal dinner, the annual dinner, everyone was there. In his stead I accepted the award, the "True Visionary" award—visionary, and he now so blind! Lu steps past the doors, calling for me, but the moon is concealed in clouds, her pots of flowers—verbena, lady's slipper—become obstacles in the darkness. She stumbles, until my hand guides her, draws her to the bench, to my side and "Here," I say. "Sit down, I have something for you."

With my other hand I reach into my pocket for the jeweler's box, the bright canary diamond to replace the battered solitaire: I tug on her ring finger, tug until she gives a little wail, until the old ring pulls free at last. "For you, my Lu, my daisy. Take it into the light, see what I give you. . . . You're not crying?"

She is crying. "Beautiful," she says. "Only—my little ring."

"You deserve better."

We sit so, I clasping her hand, she wiping at her eyes. Finally "I forgot," she says, half-rising. "You have a visitor—that nice girl, Charles's girl," who waits for me on the landing, looking up at the gargoyles and the saints as "You come here," I say; my voice is too loud. "How dare you come here, to my home, after you kept him from the dinner, from the people who meant to honor him."

"He sent me," she says, "to tell you."

I take a step down, two steps. "Tell me what." Four steps, six. Now I am beside her, looking down at the upturned face, *forever looming like a gargoyle*, and she is really very small, this Gitte, small as a child in a new blue dress—one of his dresses, already he has said he will name this collection for her, "Toujours Gitte"—her child's hand rising, narrow fingers like twigs, if one squeezed them just a bit too hard the bones would snap in two—

"Look," she says: she wiggles her twig finger: a ring. A diamond ring. "That's where he was tonight, asking me to marry him." She smiles; she cannot help herself, foxy, satisfied, those little white teeth. "Don't you like it? I picked it out myself."

I do not answer, I cannot, my tongue feels thick and hot; the gargoyles seem to ring her, like Lilith and bad angels, her smile changes and "Why do you hate me so much?" she murmurs. "I'm a lot like you."

"You— Where do you come from? No one knows you, no one—"

"With him I can be a queen. Like you were the king for so long. Don't worry," softly, cruelly, "there'll always be a place for you in our lives. Unless you insist on being a prick."

Now Lu is here—how did Lu come to be here?—exclaiming, embracing, admiring the ring, "Why, that is wonderful, Gitte, too wonderful! Gianfranco, you knew? Of course you knew, Charles tells you everything. . . . Oh, we must have a celebration!"

"Charles will love that," says Gitte. Her smile is fearless.

There is a celebration, a large one, everyone wants to attend, from Milan and Madrid and Paris and New York; there is a wedding, even larger, even the long-ago uncle from the suburbs is invited. I host them both, I pay for everything, I give the toasts, I dance with the bride who wears a dress specially created by her new husband; he will design a whole new line, she says, a special collection for the modern bride. She might be a medieval queen, a Medici, in her headdress and sapphires, ice blue sapphires against her white curls; all the guests say that she looks radiant.

"You look radiant," I tell her. "You make him very happy, Señora."

"I'm glad you see that now," she says.

I give the dinner toast—"May your lives together be the stuff of dreams"—and all the tables applaud. Lu's eyes shine with tears, she kisses my cheek: "It's like being the papa, no? Though it tugs at your heart, I know it does, to have to let him go."

After dinner, he leads me aside, Señor, just past the arch of ivy and white roses: his eyes are shining, too. "What a day," he says; he wrings my hand, he is more than a little drunk. "Gitte, and you here, it's everything." He wrings my hand again. "Everything I ever wanted."

I hold him to me for a moment, just one moment; *like being the papa.* Sharper than a serpent's tooth, her white teeth: she watches from across the hall, from inside her circle of bridesmaids, of well wishers and sycophants, she cannot hear what we say. "I wish you all happiness, Señor, always."

"I know you didn't—you weren't sure about her, at first. But I'll tell you something," he mumbles. "A secret. She's going to have a baby. A little baby boy, we saw the image at the doctor's already. . . . She doesn't want me to tell anyone, but I'm telling you. Only you," and he wrings my hand again.

I draw him to me once more, I murmur in his ear. "Do this one thing for me." Radiant, yes: now I know why. A little baby boy. "One thing only. Say to me that you will name him Gianfranco."

A tear trickles down his cheek. "Jesus, sure, we will. We will."

She is leaving her magic circle, she is crossing the dance floor now. *You were the king for so long. Why do you hate me? Unless you insist on being a prick.* "Promise me, Charles, for all I have ever done for you, for your work, all the years, everything."

"I will, I swear I will."

Now she is between us, she links her arm with his, pretends surprise at his tears, turns to me a scolding, playful look that is truly neither: "Now what's all this? Did you make my husband cry?" And she dabs with her sleeve at his eyes and laughs, and he laughs with her, and I laugh, too, just a joking old man, a funny old friend of the family, a doting grandfather. . . . Half an infant when I met him, yes, but a *real* infant, a baby, baby Gianfranco, think of that. My name, my hand on the cradle, my voice the first voice he hears, singing, soothing, teaching— And Mamma busy at the atelier and the office, Mamma too busy cradling Papa, why, who better than funny old grandpapa to help Baby grow, to be everything his father was not, could not be, was too weak to be. Always there beside him, always my voice in his ear—

"He cries," I say, "for pure love of you, Señora." Charles beams. She does not know how to answer me. I beam as well. "Look, they're calling for you, see? Time to go and cut the wedding cake."

I shepherd them back across the floor to the cake and the bridesmaids, I take my seat again beside my Lu, the silver knife is lifted, the happy music starts. The cake is delicious, it tastes of almonds; its bitterness is sweet. *There'll always be a place for you in our lives*, oh my, yes; always, *toujours*, Señora, world—my world—without end.

MIRI

Steve Rasnic Tem

Steve Rasnic Tem has had recent stories in *Asimov's Science Fiction*, *Postscripts*, and the anthologies *Werewolves and Shape Shifters*, *Visitants*, *Mountain Magic*, and *Specters in Coal Dust*. A collection of all his story collaborations with his wife, Melanie Tem, *In Concert*, recently came out from Centipede Press. Also, Speaking Volumes (www.speakingvolumes.us) has brought out *Invisible*, a six-CD audio and downloadable MP3 collection of some of his relatively recent stories, most of which are previously uncollected.

They spread the blanket over the cool grass and took their places. The puppet stage was broad and brightly lit, with a colorful and elaborate jungle set. Rick framed his children inside the LCD screen on the back of his camera as they settled in front of him: Jay Jay, who was too old for this sort of thing but would enjoy it anyway, and seven-year-old Molly, worrisomely thin, completely entranced, her large eyes riveted on the stage as oversized heads with garishly painted faces danced, their mouths magnified into exaggerated smiles, frowns, and fiercely insistent madness.

The colors began to fade from the faces—the painted ones, and his children's—he took his eyes away from the camera and blinked. The world had become a dramatic arrangement of blacks and whites. Molly raised her stark face and stared at him, her eyes a smolder of shadow. *Where is she?* he thought, and looked around. He thought he caught a glimpse—there by a tree, a pale sliver of arm, a fall of black hair, lips a smear of charcoal. He could feel the breath go out of him. *Not here.* But he couldn't be sure. He closed his eyes, tried to stop the rising tide of apprehension, opened them, and found that all the colors had been restored to the world with sickening suddenness.

He quickly took a dozen or so more shots, his finger dancing on the shutter button. Elaine patted his hand and took the camera away. "Enough already," she whispered into his ear. He tried not to be annoyed, to no avail. She had no idea what she was talking about. It didn't matter how many pictures he took—it would never be enough.

Between the kids lay the pizza box with their ragged leftovers. Jay Jay would finish it if they let him. Molly would sneak a guilty glance but would not touch it. Rick had no idea what to do to help her; next week he would make more calls.

"You're a wonderful dad, and a really good person," Elaine whispered, and kissed that place above his ear where his hairline had dramatically begun to recede. Especially in this early evening light she was lovely—she still managed to put a hitch into his breath.

He smiled and mouthed *thanks*, even though such naked compliments embarrassed him. He'd finally learned it was bad form, and unattractive, to argue with them. So even though he was thinking he just had a few simple ideas, like always giving your kids something to look forward to, he said nothing. In any case it would be hypocritical. Because he also would not be confessing that he wasn't the good person she thought he was. Or telling her how often he wished he didn't have kids—it had never been his dream, and sometimes spending an entire day with them and their constant need left him drained, stupid, and angry. He was ashamed of himself—perhaps that was why he sometimes made himself so patient.

An unreal ceiling of stars hung low over the lake, the park, the puppet stage, and all these families sitting out on their assorted colorful blankets. Elaine pulled closer to him, mistakenly saying, "I love that you still love the stars."

But he didn't. These stars were a lie. This close to the center of the city you couldn't see the stars because of the electric lights. And the dark between them had a slightly streaked appearance, as if the brush strokes were showing. Somehow this sky had been faked—he just didn't know how. But he knew by whom.

Was he lying when he allowed Elaine to mistake his silence or his distraction for something sweet and good? If so he was a consistent and successful liar.

His gaze drifted. Off to his left an elderly couple standing on their blanket looked a bit too textured, too still. At the moment he decided they were cutouts the vague suggestion of a slim female form moved slowly in behind them, looking much the cutout herself, a black silhouette with a painted white face, a dancing paper doll. She turned her head toward him, graceful as a ballerina, presenting one dark eye painted against a background of china white, framed expressionistically by black strokes of hair, black crescent cheekbones, before she turned sideways and vanished.

"I'll be right back," he whispered to Elaine. "Bathroom." He climbed absently to his feet, feeling as if his world were being snatched out from under him. *If I could just get my hands on that greedy, hungry bitch.*

The kids didn't even notice him leave, their eyes full of the fakery on stage. He quickly averted his glance—the color in their faces, the patterns in their shirts, were beginning to fade.

He moved through the maze of blankets quickly, vaguely registering the perfectly outfitted manikin couples with rudimentary features, their arms and legs bent in broken approximations of humanity. Near the outer edge of the crowd he bumped into a stiff tree-coat of a figure with a gray beard glued to the lower part of its oval head. He pardoned himself as it crashed to the ground, scattering paper plates and plastic foods onto the silent shapes of a seated family.

He passed into the well-mannered trees, which grew in geometric patches around the park. He could see her fluttering rapidly ahead of him, alternating shadow side and sunny side like a leaf twirling in the breeze off the water. She peeked back over her shoulder, her cheek making a dark-edged blade. She laughed as sharply, with no happiness in it. Something was whipping his knees—he looked down and the flesh below his shorts had torn on underbrush that hadn't been here before, that had been allowed to grow and threaten. He started to run and the trees grayed and spread themselves into the patchy walls of an ill-kept hallway—inside the residential hotel he'd lived in his last few years of college. Dim sepia lighting made everything feel under pressure, as if the hall were a tube traveling through deep water.

Wearily he found his door and stepped into a room stinking of his own sweat. He slumped into a collapsed chair leaking stuffing. He thought to watch some television, but couldn't bring himself to get up and turn the set on. Gravity pushed him deeper into the cushion, adhering his hands to the chair's palm-stained arms.

The knock on the door was soft, more like a rubbing. "Ricky? Are you home?"

He twisted his head slightly, unable to lift it away from the thickly padded back. He watched as the doorknob rattled in its collar. He willed the latch to hold.

"Ricky, it's Miri," she said unnecessarily. "We don't have to do anything, I swear. We could just talk, okay?" Her voice was like a needy child's asking for help. How did she do that? "Ricky, I just need to be with somebody tonight. Please."

She knew he was there, but he didn't know how. He'd watched his building and the street outside long before he came in—she'd been nowhere in sight.

"Are you too tired, Ricky? Is that it? Is that why you can't come to the door?"

Of course he was tired. That had been the idea, hadn't it? Everything was so incessant about her—you couldn't listen without being sucked in. She wanted him too tired to walk away from her. He closed his eyes, could feel her rubbing against the door.

He woke up in his living room, the TV muted, the picture flickering in a jumpy, agitated way. It looked like one of those old black-and-white Val Lewton films, *Cat People* perhaps, the last thing he'd want to watch in his state of mind. He was desperate to go to bed, but he couldn't move his arms or legs. He stared at his right arm and insisted, but he might have been gazing at a stick for all the good it did. He blinked his grainy eyes because at least he could still move them. After a few moments he was able to jerk his head forward—and his body followed up and out of the chair. He almost fell over but righted himself, staggering drunkenly down to their bedroom.

He couldn't see Elaine in the greasy darkness, but she whispered from the bed. "I know it's the job, wearing you out, but the kids were asking about you. They were disappointed you didn't come say good night—they wanted to talk more about the puppet show. Go and check on them—at least tomorrow you can tell them you did that."

He felt like lashing out, or weeping in frustration. Instead he turned and stumbled back out into the hall. He could have lied to her, but he went down to Jay Jay's room.

The boy in the bed slept like a drunk, with one foot on the floor.

He looked like every boy, but he didn't look anything like his son. What his son actually looked like, Rick had no idea.

Molly had kicked all the covers off, and lay there like a sweaty, sick animal, her hair matted and stiff, her open mouth exposing a few teeth. She seemed too thin to be a child—he watched as her ribs made deep grooves in the thin membrane of her flesh with each ragged breath. How was he expected to save such a creature? He walked over and picked her sheet off the floor, tucked her in, and when she curled into a sigh, kissed her good night.

When he climbed into bed Elaine was asleep. He avoided looking at her, not wanting to see whatever it was he might see. He must have looked at his wife's face tens of thousands of times over the years of their marriage. If you added it all up—months, certainly—of distracted or irritated or loving or passion-addled gazes. And yet there were times, such as after the 3 A.M. half-asleep trudge to the bathroom, when he imagined that if he were to return to their bedroom and find Elaine dead, it wouldn't be long before he'd forget her lovely face entirely.

He sometimes loved his family like someone grieving, afraid he would forget what they'd looked like. An obsession with picture-taking helped keep the fear at bay, but only temporarily. As a graphic designer he worked with images every day. He knew what he was talking about. It didn't matter how many snapshots he kept—we don't remember people because of a single recognizable image. In his way, he'd conducted his own private study. We remember people because of a daily changing gestalt—because of their ability to constantly look different than themselves. The changing set of the mouth, the tone of the skin, the engagement of the eyes. The weight lost and the weight gained. The changing tides of joy and stress and fatigue. That's what keeps people alive in our imaginations. Interrupt that flow, and a light leaves them. That's what Miri had done, was doing, to him. She was draining the light that illumined his day. Sometime during the night he turned over and made the error of opening his eyes, and saw her face where Elaine's used to be.

"Rick, you're gonna have to redo these." Matthew stood over him, a sheaf of papers in hand, looking embarrassed. They'd started in college together, back when Rick had been the better artist. Now Matthew was the supervisor, and neither of them had ever been comfortable with it.

"Just tell me what I did wrong this time—I'll fix it."

"It's this new character, the Goth girl. The client will never approve this—it's the wrong demographic for a mainstream theater chain."

"I didn't—" But seeing the art, he realized he had. The female in each of the movie date scenes was dark-haired and hollow-eyed, depressed-looking. And starved.

"She looks like that woman you dated in college."

"We didn't date," Rick snapped.

"Okay, went out with."

"We never even went out. I'm not sure what you'd call what we did together."

"I just remember what a disaster she was for you, this freaky Goth chick—"

"Matt, I don't think they even had Goths back then. She was just this poor depressed, suicidal young woman."

He smirked. "That was always your type, if I recall. Broody, skinny chicks."

Now his old friend had him confused with someone else. There had never been enough women for Rick to have had a type. "Her *name* was Miriam, but she always went by Miri. And do you actually still use that word 'chick'? Do you understand how disrespectful that is?"

"Just when I'm talking about the old days. No offense."

"None taken. I'll have the new designs for you end of the week."

Rick spread the drawings out over his desk and adjusted his lamp for a better look. He never seemed to have enough light anymore. There was an Elvira-like quality to the figures, or like that woman in the old Charles Addams panel cartoons, but Miri had had small, flattened breasts. It embarrassed him that he should remember such a thing.

In college all he ever wanted to do was paint. But it had really been an obsession with color—brushing it, smearing it, finding its light and shape and what was revealed when two colors came against each other on the canvas. He'd come home after class and paint late into the night, sometimes eating with his brush in the other hand. Each day was pretty much the same, except Saturday, when he could paint all day. Then Sunday he'd sleep all day before restarting the cycle on Monday.

Women were not a part of that life. Not that he wasn't interested. If he wanted anything more than to be a good painter it was to have the companionship and devotion of a woman. He simply didn't know how to make that happen—he didn't even know how to imagine it. To ask a woman for a date was out of the question because that meant being judged and compared and having to worry if he would ever be good enough and unable to imagine being good enough. He'd had enough of that insanity growing up.

At least he was sensitive enough to recognize the dangers of wanting something so badly and believing it forever unobtainable. He wasn't about to let it make him resentful—he wasn't going to be one of those lonely guys who hated women. The problem was his, after all.

He was aware a female had moved into the residential hotel, because of conversations overheard and certain scents and things found in the shared bathroom or the trash. Then came the night he was at the window, painting, and just happened to glance down at the sidewalk as she was glancing up.

Her face was like that Ezra Pound poem: a petal on a wet black bough. Now detached from its nourishment, now destined for decay.

A few minutes later there was a faint, strengthless knocking on his door. At first he ignored it out of habit. Although it didn't get louder it remained insistent, so eventually he wiped the paint off his hands and went to answer.

Her slight figure was made more so by a subtle forward slump. She gazed up at him with large eyes. "I'm your neighbor," she said, "could I come inside for a few minutes?"

He was reluctant—in fact he glanced too obviously at his unfinished painting—but it never occurred to him to say no. She glided in, the scarf hanging from her neck imbued with a perfume he'd smelled before in the hall. Her dress was slip-like, and purple, and might have been silk, and was most definitely feminine. Ribbons of her dull black hair appeared in the cracks among multiple scarves covering her head. She sat down on a chair right by his easel, as if she expected him to paint her.

"You're an artist," she said.

"Well, I want to be. I don't think I'm good enough yet, but maybe I will be."

"I'll let you paint me sometime." He stumbled for a reply and couldn't find one. "I have no talents. For anything. But it makes me feel better to be around men who do."

She didn't say anything more for a while, and he just stood there, not knowing what to do. But he kept thinking about options, and finally said, "Can I get you something to eat?"

There was a slight shift in her expression, a strained quality in the skin around the mouth and nose. "I don't eat in front of other people," she finally said. "I can't—it doesn't matter how hungry I am. And I'm always hungry."

"I'm sorry—I was just trying to be a good host."

She looked at him with what he thought might be amusement, but the expression seemed uncomfortable on her lips. "I imagine you apologize a lot, don't you?"

His face warmed. "Yes. I guess I really do."

"I'd like to watch you paint, if that's okay."

"Well, I guess. It'll probably be a little boring. Sometimes I do a section, and then I just stare at the canvas for a while, feeling my way through the whole, making adjustments, or just being scared I'll mess it up."

"I'd like to watch. I'm not easily bored."

And so she sat a couple of hours as if frozen in place, watching him. He might have thought she was sleeping if not for the uncomfortably infrequent blinking. Now and then he would glance at her, and although she was looking at him, he wasn't sure somehow that she was seeing him. And his dual focus on her and on his painting was rapidly fatiguing him. He appreciated her silence, however—he might not have been able to work at all if she'd said anything. It occurred to him she smelled differently. Under the perfume was a kind of staleness—or gaminess, for lack of a better word. Like a fur brought out of storage and warming up quickly. Finally it was he who spoke.

"You're great company." It was the first time he'd ever said such a thing. "But I'm feeling so tired, I don't know why, but I think I might just fall over. I'm sorry—I usually can work a lot longer."

"You should lie down." She stood and led him to the bed in the other room of the small apartment. So quickly there hardly seemed a transition. Despite her slightness she forced him down into a re-clining position. And without a word lay down beside him, close against him like a child. But even if she had said something, even if she had asked, he would not have said no. And of course he didn't stop her when she first removed his clothes, then threw off her own. It was all such a stupid cliché, he would think later, and again and again, for the six months or so their relationship lasted, and for years afterward. All the bad jokes about how men could not really be seduced, because they were always ready to have sex with any-one, with anything—it was just part of their nature. They couldn't help themselves. It embarrassed him, he felt ashamed. He'd never thought it was true, and now look at how he was behaving.

For there was this other sad truth. Men who never expected to be loved, who'd never even felt much like men, had a hard time say-ing no when the opportunity arrived, because when would it ever come again?

At least he had never been able to fool himself into believing that she actually enjoyed what they were doing. Most of the time she lay there with her eyes closed, as if pretending to be asleep or in some drug-induced semi-consciousness. He was never quite sure if he was hurting her, the way her body rose off the bed as if slapped or stabbed, her back arching, breath coming out in explosions from her as-if-wounded lungs, eyes occasionally snapping open to stare from the bottom of some vast and empty place. Certainly there couldn't be any passion in her for it, as dry as she was, her pubic hair like a bit of thrown-out carpet, so that at some point every time they did it he lost his ability to maintain the illusion, so much it was like fucking a pile of garbage, artfully arranged layers of gristle and skin, tried to escape, but like that moment in the horror movies when the skeleton reaches up and embraces you, she always pulled her bony arms around him, squeezing so hard he could feel her flailing heart right through the fragile web of her rib cage, as they continued to rock and bump the tender hangings of their flesh until bruised and bloody.

* * *

"Daddy! I *said* I saw a monkey at the zoo today!" Across from him at the dinner table, Molly looked furious.

"I know, honey," he said. "I heard you."

"No you didn't! You weren't paying attention!"

He looked at Elaine, maybe for support, or maybe just for confirmation that he had screwed up. She offered neither, was carefully studying the food on her plate. "Honey, I'm sorry. Sometimes I don't sleep too well, and the next day I have a hard time focusing, so by the time I get home from work I'm really very tired. But I'm going to listen really closely to you, okay? Please tell me all about it."

Apparently she was willing, because she began again, telling a long story about monkeys, and thrown food, and how Brian got on the bus and started throwing pieces of his lunch like *he* was the monkey, and what the bus driver said, and what their teacher said, and how lunch was pretty sick-looking, so she couldn't eat anything again anyway, except for a little bit of a juice box, and some crackers. And the entire time she was telling this story a tiny pulse by her left eye kept beating, like the recording light on a video camera, but he still kept his eyes on her, and he made himself hear every tedious word, and he let the pictures of what she was telling him make a movie in his brain, so that he felt right there.

Even though at the corners of his eyes his view of the dining room, and his daughter speaking at the center of it, was breaking down into discordancy, into a swarm of tiny black and white pixels, and even though Miri's face was at one edge of the dining room window, peering in, before her silhouette coiled and fell away.

So that by the end of his daughter's little story he had closed his eyes by necessity, and spoke to her as if in prayer. "That's a really nice story, sweetheart, thanks so much for telling it. But you know you really must eat. Why, tonight you've hardly touched anything on your plate. That little piece of meat hung up in the edge of your mouth—I can't tell if it's even food. But you have to keep your strength up, you're really going to need every bit of strength you can find."

The rest of the evening was awkward, with Elaine pleading with him to see a doctor. "You're not here with me anymore," she was saying, or was that Miri, and that was the problem, wasn't it? He no longer knew when or with whom he was. It was all he could do to keep his eyes in the same day and place for more than a few minutes at a time.

By the end Rick had known Miriam for six months or so. He'd told Matt about her, but then had been reluctant to share more than a very few of the actual details. He just wanted someone to know, in case—but he didn't understand in case of what. Matt ran into them once, when Rick had tried to drive her to a restaurant. He'd been so stupid about it—he should have been driving her to a hospital instead. She'd lost enough fat in her face by then that when she reacted to anything he couldn't quite tell what the emotion was—everything looked like a grimace on her. When she walked she was constantly clicking her teeth together and there was a disturbing wobble in her gait. He knew she must eat—how could she not? But it could not be much, and she had to be doing it in secret because he'd never actually seen her put anything into her mouth except a little bit of water.

When she breathed sometimes it was as if she were attempting to devour the space around her—her entire frame shook with the effort. When he first experienced this he tried to touch her, pull her in to comfort a distress he simply could not understand. But soon he learned to keep his distance, after getting close enough he felt he might dissolve from the force of what was happening to her.

He hadn't told her they were going to a restaurant. He said he just wanted to get out of that building where they spent virtually all of their time. Finally she stumbled into his car and caved into the passenger seat. He drove slowly, telling her it was time they both tried new things.

"What, you're breaking up with me?" A thin crimson line of inflammation separated her eyes from their tightly wrinkled sockets.

"No, that's not what I meant at all. I mean try new things together, as a couple. Go places, do things."

"You have the only new thing I need, lover." Her leer ended with a crusted tongue swiped over cracked lips.

"It doesn't feel healthy staying in the way we do. Maybe it's okay for you, but it doesn't work for me."

He pulled up in front of a little Italian place. It wasn't very popular—the flavors were a bit coarse—but the food was always filling.

"No," she said, and closed her eyes. She was wearing so much eye makeup that it looked as if her eyelids had caved in.

"All I'm asking is that you give it a try. If you don't like it, okay. No problem. We'll just go home."

She slapped his face then, and it felt as if she'd hit him with a piece of wood. She continued hitting him with those hands of so little padding, spitting the word "lover!" at him, as if it were some kind of curse.

He had no idea what to do. He'd never been struck by a woman before. He couldn't remember the last time he'd been in a physical fight with anyone. And now she was screaming, the angular gape of her mouth like an attacking bird's.

"Hey! Hey!" The car door was open, and someone was pulling her away from him. Miri was beside herself, struggling, kicking. Rick was leaning back as far as possible to avoid her sharp-pointed shoes. Over her shoulder he saw Matt's face, grimly determined, as he jerked her out of the car.

She spat at both of them, walking back toward her apartment with one shoe missing, her clothes twisted around on her coat-hanger frame.

"I should go get her, try to coax her back into the car," Rick said, out of breath.

"Glad you finally introduced us." Matt was bent over, wheezing.

Of course she had apologized in her own way, showing up at Rick's door the next night, naked, crying and incoherent. He got her inside before anyone else could see. And then she would not leave for weeks, sleeping in his bed, watching him eat or stand before his easel unable to paint. Most of the time he slept on the floor, but sometimes he had to have something softer, and lay on the bed trying to ignore her mouth and hands all over him, in that fluttering way of hers, until she stopped and lay cold against him.

"I'm glad you were able to join us today." Matt stood at Rick's office door, looking unhappy. "Were you really sick, or did you get Elaine to call in and lie for you every day?"

Rick was unable to do anything but stare as Matt's words rushed by him. He'd been in the office for only five minutes or so and already he was feeling disoriented. Papers were stacked all over his desk, and message notes were attached around his monitor, even to his lamp base. He never left things like this.

Finally, he looked up at his old friend. "I have no idea what you're talking about."

"You haven't been here in four days! I can't keep coming up with excuses for you with the partners."

"Four days?"

Matt stared at him. It made him uncomfortable, so he started sifting through the piles of papers. But these were piles of print on paper, black on white, black and white. Before he could turn away he was seeing the shadows of her eyes, the angles of her mouth in the smile that wasn't a smile. "Maybe you *are* sick," Matt said behind him.

"You said Elaine called in every day?"

"Right after the office opened, once before I even got in."

"Elaine never lies. That's one of the best things about her. I don't think she even knows how," Rick said absently, looking around the office, finding more phone messages. Some appeared to be in his own handwriting.

"Well, I know. Of course. Look, I didn't mean—"

"Are you sure it wasn't someone who just *pretended* to be Elaine?"

But then someone was softly knocking, or rubbing, on the door outside. And Rick couldn't bring himself to speak anymore.

"Ricky?" she had said. "Are you home?"

But he couldn't get out of his so well cushioned chair. The doorknob rattled in its collar. He willed the latch to hold.

"Ricky, we don't have to do anything," she said in her child's voice, muffled by the door.

"Ricky, I just need—are you too tired, Ricky? I just need—"

After a few weeks she had stopped. Later he heard she'd killed herself, but he never saw a word about it in the papers. One afternoon a truck came and took away all the stuff in her apartment. A white-haired man came by, knocking on each door. But Rick hadn't answered when the old man knocked on his. Later one of the other tenants would tell Rick the white-haired man had claimed to be her uncle.

The next week was when the color-blindness had come over him like some sort of virus, intermittently, then all at once. One of the doctors he saw said it appeared to be a hysterical reaction of some sort. Whatever the source, or the reason, he stopped painting, and she mostly left him alone for a long time after that, reappearing now and then to monochrome the world for a while, or to take a day or two, or to eat one of his new memories and leave one of the tired old ones in its place.

And now it had looked as if he was going to be happy, or at least the possibility was there, and she couldn't just leave that be.

The bedroom was completely black, except for a few bright white reflections of window pane. And the side of Elaine's face, as she slept on her back. Lovely and glowing and ghostly.

The children were out there asleep in their own beds, or should be. At least he hadn't heard them in hours. He prayed they were. Sleeping.

But it was all so black, and white, and something was rubbing at the door.

MRS. JONES

Carol Emshwiller

Carol Emshwiller grew up in Michigan and in France and currently divides her time between New York and California. She is the winner of two Nebula Awards for her stories "Creature" and "I Live with You." She has also won the Life Achievement Award from the World Fantasy Convention.

She's been the recipient of a National Endowment for the Arts grant and two New York State grants. Her short fiction has been published in many literary and science fiction magazines, and her most recent books are the novels *Mister Boots* and *The Secret City*, and the collection *I Live with You*.

Cora is a morning person. Her sister, Janice, hardly feels conscious till late afternoon. Janice nibbles fruit and berries and complains of her stomach. Cora eats potatoes with butter and sour cream. She likes being fat. It makes her feel powerful and hides her wrinkles. Janice thinks being thin and willowy makes her look young, though she would admit that—and even though Cora spends more time outside doing the yard and farm work—Cora's skin does look smoother. Janice has a slight stutter. Normally she speaks rapidly and in a kind of shorthand so as not to take up anyone's precious time, but with her stutter, she can hold peoples' attention for a moment longer than she would otherwise dare. Cora, on the other hand, speaks slowly, and if she had ever stuttered, would have seen to it she learned not to.

Cora bought a genuine kilim rug to offset, she said, the bad taste of the flowery chintz covers Janice got for the couch and chairs. The rug and chairs look terrible in the same room, but Cora insisted that her rug be there. Janice retaliated by pawning Mother's silver candelabras. Cora had never liked them, but she made a fuss anyway, and she left Janice's favorite silver spoon in the mayonnaise jar until, polish as she would, Janice could never get rid of the blackish look. Janice punched a hole in each of Father's rubber boots. Cora wears them anyway. She hasn't said a single word about it, but she hangs her wet socks up conspicuously in the kitchen.

They wish they'd gotten married and moved away from their

parents' old farmhouse. They wish, desperately, that they'd had
children—or husbands, for that matter. As girls they worked hard
at domestic things: canning, baking bread and pies, sewing . . .
waiting to be good wives to almost anybody, but nobody came to
claim them.

Janice is the one who worries. She's worried right now because
she saw a light out in the far corner of the orchard—a tiny, flickering light. She can just barely make it out through the misty rain.
Cora says, "Nonsense." (She's angry because it's just the sort of thing
Janice would notice first.) Cora laughs as Janice goes around checking and rechecking all the windows and doors to see that they're
securely locked. When Janice has finished, and stands staring out at
the rain, she has a change of heart. "Whoever's out there must be
cold and wet. Maybe hungry."

"Nonsense," Cora says again. "Besides, whoever's out there probably deserves it."

Later, as Cora watches the light from her bedroom window, she
thinks whoever it is who's camping out down there is probably eating her apples and making a mess. Cora likes to sleep with the windows open a crack even in weather like this, and she prides herself
on her courage, but, quietly, so that Janice, in the next room, won't
hear, she eases her windows shut and locks them.

In the morning the rain has stopped, though it's foggy. Cora goes
out (with Father's walking stick, and wearing Father's boots and
battered canvas hat) to the far end of the orchard. Something has
certainly been there. It had pulled down perfectly good, live apple
branches to make a nest. Cora doesn't like the way it ate apples, either, one or two bites out of lots of them, and then it looks as if it
had made itself sick and threw up not far from the fire. Cora cleans
everything so it looks like no one has been there. She doesn't want
Janice to have the satisfaction of knowing anything about it.

That afternoon, when Cora has gone off to have their pickup
truck greased, Janice goes out to take a look. She also takes Father's
walking stick, but she wears Mother's floppy pink hat. She can see
where the fire's been by the black smudge, and she can tell somebody's been up in the tree. She notices things Cora hadn't: little
claw marks on a branch, a couple of apples that had been bitten into
still hanging on the tree near the nesting place. There's a tiny piece

of leathery stuff stuck to one sharp twig. It's incredibly soft and downy and has a wet-dog smell. Janice takes it, thinking it might be an important clue. Also she wants to have something to show that she's been down there and seen more than Cora has.

Cora comes back while Janice is upstairs taking her nap. She sits down in the front room and reads an article in the *Reader's Digest* about how to help your husband communicate. When she hears Janice come down the stairs, Cora goes up for her nap. While Cora naps, Janice sets out grapes and a tangerine, strawberries and one hard-boiled egg. As she eats her early supper, she reads the same article Cora has just read. She feels sorry for Cora, who seems to have nothing more exciting than this sort of thing to read (along with her one hundred great books), whereas Janice has been reading *How Famous Couples Get the Most Out of Their Sex Lives*. Just one of many such books that she keeps locked in her bedside cabinet. When she finishes eating, she cleans up the kitchen so it looks as if she hadn't been there.

Cora comes down when Janice is in the front parlor (sliding doors shut) listening to music. She has it turned so low Cora can hardly make it out. Might be Vivaldi. It's as if Janice doesn't want Cora to hear it in case she might enjoy it. At least that's how Cora takes it. Cora opens a can of spaghetti. For desert she takes a couple of apples from the "special" tree. She eats on the closed-in porch, watching the clouds. It looks as if it'll rain again tonight.

About eight thirty they each look out their different windows and see that the flickering light is there again. Cora says, "Damn it to hell," so loud that Janice hears from two rooms away. At that moment, Janice begins to like the little light. Thinks it looks inviting. Homey. She forgets that she found that funny piece of leather and those claw marks. Thinks most likely there's a young couple in love out there. Their parents disapprove and they have no place else to go but her orchard. Or perhaps it's a child running away. Teenager, maybe, cold and wet. She has a hard time sleeping, worrying and wondering about whoever it is, though she's still glad she locked the house up tight.

The next day begins almost exactly like the one before, with Cora going out to the orchard first and cleaning up—trying to—all the signs of anything having been there, and with Janice coming out later to pick up the clues that are left. Janice finds that the same branch is scratched up even more than it was before, and this time Cora has left the vomit (full of bits of apple peel) behind the tree. Perhaps she hadn't noticed it. Apples—or at least so many apples— aren't agreeing with the lovers. (In spite of the clues, Janice prefers to think that it's lovers.) She feels sorry about the all-night rain. There's no sign that they had a tent or shelter of any kind, poor things.

By the third night, though, the weather finally clears. Stars are out and a tiny moon. Cora and Janice stand in the front room, each at a different window, looking out toward where the light had been. An old seventy-eight record is on. Fritz Kreisler playing the Bach chaconne. Janice says, "You'd think, especially since it's not raining . . ."

Cora says, "Good riddance," though she, too, feels a sense of regret. At least something unusual had been happening. "Don't forget," Cora says, "the state prison's only ninety miles away."

Little light or no little light, they both check the windows and doors and then recheck the ones the other had already checked, or at least Cora rechecks all the ones Janice had seen to. Janice sees her do it, and Cora sees her noticing, so Cora says, "With what they're doing with genetic engineering, it could be anything at all out there. They make mistakes, and peculiar things escape. You don't hear about it because it's classified. People disapprove, so they don't let the news get out." Ever since she was five years old, Cora has been trying to scare her younger sister, though, as usual, she ends up scaring herself.

But then, just as they are about to give up and go off to bed, there's the light again. "Ah." Janice breathes out as though she had been holding her breath. "There it is."

"You've got a lot to learn," Cora says. She'd heard the relief in Janice's big sigh. "Anyway, I'm off to bed, and you'd better come soon, too, if you know what's good for you."

"I know what's good for me," Janice says. She would have stayed up too late just for spite, but now she has another, secret reason for doing it. She sits reading an article in *Cosmopolitan* about how to be more sexually attractive to your husband. Around midnight, even from downstairs, she can hear Cora snoring. Janice goes out to the kitchen. Moves around it like a little mouse. She's good at that. Gets out Mother's teakwood tray, takes slices of rye bread from Cora's stash, takes a can of Cora's tuna fish. (Janice knows she'll notice. Cora has them all counted.) Takes butter and mayonnaise from Cora's side of the refrigerator. Makes three tuna fish sandwiches. Places them on one of Mother's gold-rimmed plates along with some of her own celery, radishes, and grapes. Then she sits down and eats one sandwich herself. She hasn't let herself have a tuna fish sandwich, especially not one with mayonnaise and butter and rye bread, for a long time.

It's only when Janice is halfway out in the orchard that she remembers what Cora said about the prison and thinks maybe there's some sort of escaped criminal out there—a rapist or a murderer, and here she is, wearing only her bathrobe and nightgown, in her slippers, and without even Father's walking stick. (Though the walking stick would probably just have been a handy thing for the criminal to attack *her* with.) She stops, puts the tray down, then moves forward. She's had a lot of practice creeping. She's been creeping up on Cora ever since they were little. Used to yell, "Boo," but nowadays creeping up and standing very close and suddenly whispering right by her ear can make Cora jump as much as a loud noise. Janice sneaks along slowly. Has to step over where whoever it is has already thrown up. Something is huddling in front of the fire, wrapped in what at first seems to be an army blanket. Why, it is a child. Poor thing. She's known it all the time. But then the creature moves, stretches, makes a squeaky sound, and she sees it's either the largest bat or the smallest little old man she's ever seen. And with wings. She's wondering if this is what Cora meant by genetic engineering.

Then the creature stands up and Janice is shocked. He has such a large penis that Janice thinks back to the horses and bulls they used to have. It's a Pan-type penis, more or less permanently erect and hooked up tight against his stomach, though Janice doesn't know this about a Pan's penis, and anyway, this is definitely not some sort of Pan.

The article in *Cosmopolitan* comes instantly to her mind, plus the other, sexier books that she has locked in her bedside cabinet.

Isn't there, in all this, some way to permanently outdo Cora? Whether she ever finds out about it or not? Slowly, Janice backs up, turns, goes right past her tray (the gleam of silverware helps her know where it is). Goes to the house and down into the basement.

They'd always had dogs. Big ones for safety. But Mr. Jones (called Jonesy) had died a few months ago, and Cora is still grieving, or so she keeps saying. Since the dog had become blind, diabetic, and incontinent in his last years, Janice is relieved that he's gone. Besides, she had her heart set on something small and more tractable, some sort of terrier, but now she's glad Jonesy was large and difficult to manage. His metal choke collar and chain leash are still in the cellar. She wraps them in a cloth bag to keep them from clanking and heads back out, picking up the tray of food on the way.

As she comes close to the fire she begins to hum. This time she wants him to know she's coming. The creature sits in the lowest fork of the tree now and watches her with glinting red eyes. She puts the tray down and begins to talk softly as though she were trying to calm old Jonesy. She even calls the thing Mr. Jones. At first by mistake and then on purpose. He watches. Moves nothing but his eyes and big ears. His wings, dangling along his arms, are olive drab like that piece she found, but his body is a little lighter, especially along his stomach. She can tell that even in the moonlight.

Now that she's closer and less startled than before, she can see that there's something terribly wrong. One leathery wing is torn and twisted. He's helpless. Or almost. Probably in pain. Janice feels a little rush of joy.

She breaks off a bit of tuna fish sandwich and slowly, talking softly, she holds it toward his little clawed hand. Equally slowly, he reaches out to take it. She keeps this up until almost all of one sandwich is eaten. But suddenly the creature jumps out of the tree, turns away, and throws up.

Janice knows a vulnerable moment when she sees one. As he leans back on his heels between spasms, she fastens the choke collar around his neck and twists the other end of the chain leash around her wrist.

He only makes two attempts to escape: tries to flap himself into the air, but it's obviously painful for him; then he tries to run. His legs are bowed, his gait rocking and clumsy. After these two attempts, he seems to realize it's hopeless. Janice can see in his eyes that he's given up—too sick and tired to care. Janice thinks he must be happy to be captured and looked after at last.

She leads him back to the house and down into the basement. Her own quiet creeping makes him quiet, too. He seems to sense that he's to be a secret and that perhaps his life depends on it. It is hard for him to walk all the way across the orchard. He doesn't seem to be built for anything but flying.

There is an old coal room, not used since they got oil heat. Janice makes a bed for him there, first chaining him to one of the pipes. She gets him blankets, water, an empty pail with a lid. She makes him put on a pair of her underpants. She has to use a cord around his waist to make them stay up. She wonders what she should leave him to eat that would stay down. Then brings him chamomile tea, dry toast, one small potato. That's all. She doesn't want to be cleaning up a lot of vomit.

He's so tractable through all this that she loses all fear. Pats his head as if he were old Jonesy. Strokes the wonderful softness of his wings. Thinks: if those were cut off, he'd look like a small old man with long, hard fingernails—misshapen, but not much more so than some other people. And clothes can hide things. Without the dark wings, he'd look lighter. His body is that color that's always described as café au lait. She would have preferred it if he'd been clearly a white person, but, who knows, maybe a little while in the cellar will make him paler.

After a last rubbing of his head behind his too-large ears, Janice padlocks the coal room and goes up to her bedroom, but she's too excited to sleep. She reads a chapter in *Are You Happy with Your Sex Life?* The one on how to turn your man into a lusting animal. ("The feet of both sexes are exquisitely sensitive." And, "Let your eyes speak, but first make sure he's looking at you." "Surrender. When he thinks he's leading, your man feels strong in *every* way.") Janice thinks she will have to be the one to take the initiative, though she'll try to make him feel that he's the boss—even though he'll be wearing the choke collar.

For a change, Janice wakes up just as early as Cora does. Earlier, in fact, and she lies in bed making plans. She gets a lot of good ideas. She comes downstairs whistling Vivaldi—off-key as usual, but she's not doing it to make Cora angry this time. She really can't whistle on key. Cora knows that Janice knows Cora hates the way she whistles. Cora thinks that if Janice really tried, she could be just as in tune as Cora always is. Cora thinks Janice got up early just so she could spoil Cora's breakfast by sitting across from her looking just like Mother used to look when she disapproved of Father's table manners. And Cora notices, even before she makes her omelet, that one can of tuna fish is missing and her loaf of rye bread has gone down by several slices. She takes a quart of strawberries from Janice's side of the refrigerator and eats them all, not even bothering to wash them.

Janice doesn't say a word. She doesn't care, except that Jonesy might have wanted some. Janice is feeling magnanimous and powerful. She feels so good she even offers Cora some of her herb tea. Cora takes the offer as ironic, especially since she knows that Janice knows she never drinks herb tea. She retaliates by saying that, since they're both up so early, they should take advantage of it and go out to the beach to get more lakeweed for the garden.

Janice knows that Cora decided this just to make her pay for the tuna fish and bread, but she still feels magnanimous—kindly to the whole world. She doesn't even say that they'd already done that twice in the spring, and that what they needed now were hay bales to put around the foundations of the house for the winter. All she says is, "No."

It's never been their way to shirk their duties no matter how angry they might be with each other. When it comes to work, they've always made a good team. But now Janice is adamant. She says she has something important to do. She's not ever said this before, nor has she ever had something important to do. Cora has always been the one who did the important things. This time Cora can't persuade Janice to change her mind, nor can she persuade her that there's nothing important to be done—at least nothing more important than lakeweed.

Finally Cora gives up and goes off alone. She hadn't meant to go. She's never gone off to get lakeweed by herself, but she goes anyway, hoping to make Janice feel guilty. Cora knows something is going on. She's not sure what, but she's going to be on her guard.

As soon as Janice hears the old pickup crunch away on the gravel drive, she goes down in the basement, bringing along Father's old straight razor (freshly sharpened), rubbing alcohol, and bandages. Also, to make it easier on him, a bottle of sherry.

Cora comes back, tired and sandy, around six thirty. Her face is red and she has big, dried sweat marks on her blue farmer's shirt, across the back and under the arms. She smells fishy. She's so tired she staggers as she climbs the porch steps. Even before she gets inside, she knows odd things are going on. There's the smells . . . of beef stew or some such, onions, maybe mince pie, and there, on the hall table, a glass of sherry is set out for her. Or seems to be for her. Or looks like sherry. Though the day was hot, these fall evenings are cool, and Janice has laid a fire in the fireplace, and not badly done. Cora always knew Janice could do it properly if she set her mind to it. Cora takes the sherry and sits on the footstool of Father's big chair. It's one of the ones Janice had covered in a flowery pattern. Looks like pinkish-blue hydrangea. Cora looks at the fire. Thinks: All this has got to be because of something else. Or maybe it's going to be a practical joke. If she lets down her guard, she'll be in for big trouble. But even if it's a joke, might as well take advantage of it for as long as she can. The sherry relaxes her. She'll go up and shower—if, that is, Janice has left her any hot water.

For several days, Mr. Jones is in pain. Janice is glad of it. She knows how a wild thing—or even a not-so-wild thing—appreciates being nursed back to health. (As soon as he's better, she hopes to bond him to her in a different way.) She hopes Mr. Jones was too drunk to remember about the . . . amputation . . . whatever you call it. (Funny, he only has three fingers on each hand. She'd not noticed that at first.)

Cora is still suspicious, but doesn't know what to be suspicious about. The good food is going on and on. After supper, Janice cleans up and doesn't ask for help even though she's done all the cooking. And Janice disappears for hours at a time. Goes up to take her nap—or so she says—but Cora knows for a fact that she's not in her room. After the dishes are cleaned up in the evenings, Janice sews or knits. It's not hard to see that's she's knitting a child-sized sweater and sewing a child-sized pair of trousers. At the same time, she's working on a white dress, lacy and low-necked. Cora thinks much too low-necked for someone Janice's age. But perhaps it's not for

Janice. Maybe Janice has some news she's keeping from Cora. That would be just like her. Someone is getting married or coming for a visit. Or maybe both.

Mr. Jones is getting better. Eating soups, and nuts, and seeds, and keeping everything down, finally. Janice is happy to see that his skin has faded some. He might pass for a gnarled little Mexican or maybe a fairly light India Indian. And he's beginning to understand some words. She's been talking to him a lot, more or less as she used to talk to old Jonesy. He knows good boy and bad boy and sit, lie down, be quiet. . . . She thinks he even has the concept of "I love you." She's never said that to any other creature before, not even to the pony they'd had when they were little. She's been doing a lot of patting, back rubbing, scratching under the chin and behind the ears. Though he's always wearing a pair of her underpants tied up around his waist, and though she hasn't yet tried the stroking of the "exquisitely sensitive" feet, every now and then she notices his penis swelling up even larger than it already is.

One night, after rereading the chapter "How to Turn Your Man into a Lusting Animal," she puts on her flowery summer nightgown (even though the nights are colder than ever, and they haven't started up the furnace yet). She puts on lipstick, eye shadow, perfume, combs her hair out and lets it hang over her shoulders. . . . (She's only graying a little bit at the temples. Thank God, not like Cora, she's almost completely gray.) She goes down into the cellar with a glass of sherry for each of them. Not too much, though. She's read about alcohol and sex.

She tells him she loves him several times, kisses him on the cheeks and then on the neck, just below the choke collar. Finally she kisses his lips. They are thin and closed up tight, and she can feel the teeth behind them. Then she rolls her nightgown up to her chin. She hopes he likes what he sees even though she's not young anymore. (If anything, he mostly looks surprised.) But no sooner has she lain herself down beside him than it's over. She's even wondering, did it really happen? Except, yes, there's blood, and it did hurt. But this isn't at all like the books said it would be or should be. She's read about premature ejaculation. This must be it. Maybe later, when he knows more words, they can go for therapy. But— oops—there he goes again, and just as fast as before. After that he falls asleep. She not only didn't get any foreplay, but no afterplay, either. She's wondering, where's the romance in all this?

Well, at least she's a real woman now. She hasn't missed all of life. She may have missed a lot, but no one can say she's missed all, which is more than Cora can say. Janice thinks she is, and probably permanently—at least she hopes so—one up on Cora. She's joined the human race in a way Cora probably never will, poor thing. Janice will be kind.

Janice hardly ever drives. She has always left that to Cora. She knows how, but she's out of practice. Now she has several errands to do. She wants a nice pin-striped suit, though she wonders if they come in boys' sizes—a suit like her father would have worn. She wants a good suitcase, not one from the five-and-ten. Shiny shoes big enough for rough claws, though she's cut those claws as short as she could, using old Jonesy's nail clippers. Since Mr. Jones looks sort of Mexican, she'll get him a south-of-the-border Panama hat and dark glasses.

It only takes a couple of days for Janice to get her errands done, and then a couple more to get the guest room ready: aired out, curtains washed, bed made. (Good it's a double bed.) She whistles all the time and doesn't even remember that it bothers Cora.

Cora watches the preparation of the guest room but refuses to give Janice the satisfaction of asking any questions. It's easy to see that Janice wonders why Cora isn't asking. Once Janice started to tell her something but then turned red to her collarbone and shut up fast.

Janice has continued making good suppers of Cora's favorite foods. Cora is still waiting for the practical joke to come to its finale, but even . . . or especially if it doesn't end, she knows something's up. She hasn't let down her guard, and she's snooped around—even in the basement, but not in the coal room. Up in the attic she did find a large . . . very large piece of stiff leather, dried blood along its edges and so brittle she couldn't unfold it to see what it was. It gave her the shivers. Pained her to see it, though she couldn't say why. Perhaps it was the two toenails or claws that were attached to each corner. She's thought of throwing the dead-looking thing out in the garbage, but after she saw those claws that were part of it, she couldn't bring herself to touch it again.

Everything is ready, but Janice knows Jonesy needs a little more experience and training. She wants to pretend to go down and pick him up at the airport in Detroit. Cora, if she hears about it, will never let Janice go there by herself. But Cora mustn't be there. For lots of reasons, not the least of which is that Janice wants the trip to be like a honeymoon. They could sneak out in the middle of the night and they could take two or three or even more days coming back. Maybe a couple of days enjoying the sights of Detroit. Jonesy could learn a lot.

Janice has never dared to even think of going on a trip like this before, but with Jonesy she wouldn't be alone. She sees herself, dressed in her best, sitting across from him (he'll be wearing his pin-striped suit) in restaurants, going to motels, movies even. . . . She'd look right doing these things. Like all the other couples. They'd hold hands. They'd stroll in the evening after their long drive. Can he stroll? She'll get him a silver-handled walking stick in Detroit. Better than Father's cane. He may be a cripple, but he'll look like a gentleman, and the better he looks, the more jealous Cora will be.

Janice leaves a note for Cora mentioning the airport in Detroit.

And it started out being a wonderful honeymoon. Janice kept the choke collar under Jonesy's necktie and shirt, running the chain down inside his left sleeve so that when she held his hand she could also hold the chain just to make sure. She also found a way to hold the back of his shirt so she could give a little pull on it, but she seldom had to use any of these techniques. And how could he try to escape, hobbling as he does? Unless he learns to drive the pickup? But Janice wouldn't be a bit surprised if he could learn to drive it. Even before they get to Detroit, Jonesy is dressing himself, uses the right fork in fancy restaurants, can eat a lobster just as neatly as anyone can. (Though he throws it up afterward.)

Janice keeps a running conversation going, just as if they were communicating. She keeps saying, "Don't you think so, dear?" hoping nobody will notice that he doesn't even nod. Lots of husbands are like that. Even Father didn't answer Mother, lost as he was in his own thoughts all the time. But Mr. Jones doesn't look lost in his thoughts. And he doesn't look as if he feels hopeless anymore. He looks out at everything with such intelligence that Janice is considering calling him Doctor Jones.

In Detroit (they are staying at the Renaissance Center), Janice gets the good idea that they should get married right there in City Hall. Before she even tries to do it, she calls Cora up. "I got married," she says, even though it hasn't happened, and whether it ever does or not, Cora will never know the difference. "And isn't it funny, I'm Mrs. Jones, and I call him Jonesy just like old Jonesy."

Cora can't answer. She just sputters. She's been lonelier without Janice than she ever thought she would be. She has even wished the little light was still flickering in the orchard. She'd gone out there, hoping to find another nest. Partly she'd just been looking for company. She'd even left the doors unlocked and her window open. But then she'd put two and two together. She's had all these days to wonder and worry and wait, and she's been down in the basement where the coal-room door had been carelessly left open. She's seen the pallet on the floor, the bowl of dusty water, the remains of a last meal (Mother's china, wineglasses), three pairs of Janice's underpants, badly soiled. And she remembers that piece of folded leather with the dried blood on it, and she gets the shivers all over again. Cora knows she's been outmaneuvered, which she never thought could ever come about, but she suddenly realizes that she doesn't care about that anymore.

She sputters into the phone, and then, for the first time—at least that Janice ever knew about—Cora bursts into tears. Janice can tell, even though Cora is trying to hide it. All of a sudden Janice wants to say something that will make Cora happy, but she doesn't know what. "You'll like him," she says. "I know you will. You'll *love* him, and he'll love you, too. I know him well enough to know he will. He *will*."

Cora keeps on trying to hide that she's crying, but she doesn't hang up. She's glad, at last, to be connected to Janice, however tenuously.

"I'll bring you something nice from Detroit," Janice says.

Cora still doesn't say anything, though Janice can hear her ragged breathing.

"I'll be back real soon." Janice doesn't want to break the connection, either, but she can't think of anything else to say. "I'll see you in two days."

It takes four. Janice comes home alone by taxi after a series of buses. (The pickup is going to be found two weeks later up in Canada, north of Thunder Bay. Men's clothes will be found in it, including a Panama hat, dark glasses, and a silver-handled cane. The radio will have been stolen. There will be maps and a big dictionary that had never belonged either to Cora or Janice.)

As Janice staggers up the porch steps, Cora rushes down, her arms held out, but Janice flinches away. Janice is wearing a wedding ring and a large, phony diamond engagement ring. She has on a new dress. Even though it's wrinkled and is stained with sweat across the back, Cora can see it was expensive. Janice's hair is coming loose from its Psyche knot, and now she's the one who's crying and trying to pretend she's not.

Cora tries to help Janice up the steps. Even though Janice stumbles, she won't let her help, but she does let Cora push her on into the living room. Janice collapses onto the couch, tells Cora, "Don't hover." Hovering is something Cora never did before. It's more like something Janice would do.

Even after Cora brings Janice a strong cup of coffee, Janice won't say a single word about anything. Cora says she'll feel better if she talks about it, but she won't. She looks tired and sullen. "You'd like to know everything, wouldn't you just," she says. (What other way to stay one up than not to tell . . . than to have secrets?)

Cora almost says, "Not really," but she doesn't want to be, anymore, what she used to be. Janice hasn't had the experience of being in the house all alone for several days. There's a different secret now that Janice doesn't know about. Maybe never will unless Cora goes off someplace. But why would she go anyplace? And where? Besides, being one up, or getting even, doesn't matter to Cora anymore. She doesn't care if Janice understands or not. She just wants to take care of her and have her stay. Maybe, after a while, Janice will come to see that things have changed.

Cora goes to the kitchen to make a salad that she thinks Janice will like. She sets the dining room table the way she thinks Janice would approve of, with Mother's best dishes, and with the knives and forks in all the right places and both water glasses and wineglasses, but Janice says she'll eat later in the kitchen and alone and on paper plates. Meanwhile she'll take a bath.

After Cora eats and is cleaning up the last of her dishes, Janice comes in wearing her nightgown and Mother's bathrobe. As she leans to get a pan from a lower shelf, the bathrobe falls away. When she straightens up again, she sees Cora staring at her. "What are you ogling?" she says, holding the frying pan like a weapon.

"Nothing," Cora says, knowing better than to make a comment. She's seen more than she wants to see. There are big red choke collar marks all around Janice's neck.

But something *must* be said. Cora wonders what Father would have done. She usually knows exactly what he'd do and does it without even thinking about it. Now she can't imagine Father ever having to deal with something like this. She can't say anything. She can't move. Finally she thinks: No secrets. She says, "Sister." And then . . . but it's too hard. (Father never would have said it.) She starts. Again, she almost says it. "Sister, I love . . ."

At first it looks as if Janice *will* hit her with the frying pan, but then she drops it and just stares.

BREAD AND WATER

Michael Cisco

Michael Cisco is the author of four published novels: *The Divinity Student, The Tyrant, The San Veneficio Canon*, and *The Traitor*, as well as a collection of stories entitled *Secret Hours*. His short fiction has appeared in *The Book of Eibon, The Thackery T. Lambshead Pocket Guide to Eccentric & Discredited Diseases, Leviathan 3, Leviathan 4, Album Zutique, Phantom, Black Wings, Last Drink Bird Head, The Tindalos Cycle*, and *Cinnabar's Gnosis: A Homage to Gustav Meyrink*. Centipede Press is preparing a compendium of much of his published work to date, and two new novels, *The Wretch of the Sun* (Ex Occidente Press) and *The Narrator* (Civil Coping Mechanisms), are forthcoming. His story "The Genius of Assassins: Three Dreams of Murder in the First Person" will appear in the upcoming Corvus Books anthology *The Weird*. He is the recipient of the International Horror Writers Guild Award for best first novel of 1999.

Michael Cisco currently lives and teaches in New York. His website can be found at www.prostheticlibido.org.

I am gazing in fascination at the whiteness of a glass full of trembling milk that I've stolen from the kitchen. It's too perfectly white and cold to have come from an animal. It's so cold, I can't smell it at all. Cylinder of softly luminous whiteness, standing on a white counter. I close both my reedy hands around it slowly, then lift it up to my mouth. Holding that open, I tilt the glass and let in a trickle, flashing with cold. Now I press the glass to my lower lip and allow the upper to spread itself along the plastic surface of the milk, forming a seal. I drink. I take long pulls. I drink steadily. The glass lightens. The milk is so substantial. A single mass that drops down into my stomach and fills it. Barely any taste. I put the filmed glass down again carefully. Empty bubbles slide down toward the bottom. My hands press my abdomen; the milk sucks in heat from my feverish body, and I shiver. I love drinking. Drinking anything. Above all other pleasures I know. I want to drink infinitely cold drinks from an infinite glass. My stomach feels heavy and inert. I move over to the sink.

With a sigh, I tilt forward like a pitcher and eject the milk, the heave coming from well below in the body and rolling up into me like a boulder; the milk bounds from my lips and into the sink in a long jet with a fold in the middle. Puking is nowhere near as tiring as it used to be; my throat muscles seem to do as much work in either direction these days, and stretching my jaw open is like giving a pump handle a good long drag. My eyes don't water and my nose doesn't run, because there's no more bile. If it wasn't for the fact that it pools in the sink, mixing with standing drain water and spatters of washed-up food, the milk I vomit would look the same as it did in the glass: the time-out it took in my stomach hasn't altered it at all, hasn't even discolored it—in fact, it seems whiter than ever, it might have even gotten whiter in my stomach. And there's no trace of odor; if it weren't for an unreasoning aversion to vomit, I might drink it again. How could an animal make something as white as that? It should just have appeared inside the white refrigerator, like nectar inside a flower.

I could have sneaked it back to my bed, but the draft that chills my bare legs is making itself a part of the excitement of breaking a rule in plain view. So much the better, that the rule was established for my benefit. This way, I take back my benefit for a moment.

A groan escapes me. I sway against the edge of the sink and hold on with both hands. Some more vitality leaves me. I feel its absence in no particular place, just all over. Perhaps more in the lightness it leaves in my head. Wiping my lips with my hand, I turn and scuff back toward bed. It's only after I've toppled over backward onto the mattress that I realize I forgot to run the taps. She'll probably notice the milk in there, and realize what I've done. It doesn't look spilled; it's been obviously flourished around the sink. Another patient lecture is waiting for me, as if this weren't bad enough. The frown. I can feel the illness frisking. It likes to kick up its heels, and I shudder. It drags me down into a stale bed and then won't let me sleep, torments me with thirst and won't let me keep anything but blood in my stomach. I begged and begged; I suspect they began allowing it because they were getting the same thing from the others as well. It's not a kind of exception anyone would make for one person. The flavor was so revolting I wanted to gag then, but my body was all too glad to have it. Certainly, it assuaged my thirst, but no better than anything else would have—no, I'm wrong. Thin water is still the best. Thin thin thin. It can't get too thin for me; it goes down thin and it comes back up good and thin. Thinning blood doesn't work, it comes back up again and I have to taste it twice. Better this, though, than the IV. I came near going out of my mind with that thing stuck in me, there was no getting used to it; a feeling as if every cell I had was straining away from it, and them transfusing me again and again.

They were sure I had a hemorrhage. My scans baffled them. Despite the risks, the chance I might bleed completely dry, they cut

me open and examined my insides, and then I had to lie there, wondering if my sutures were going to give, and my body split apart,
while consultations took place and so on, my body split apart and
a steel needle buried, tenaciously buried in my arm. Nobody knew
anything. The doctors pursed their lips and looked judicious. The
blood went in and vanished. My flesh vanished. My sleep vanished.
Then other cases turned up and it was a syndrome. With a fanciful name. Looking back, I realize now I must have contracted it
from a bizarrely distinct mosquito bite. I was bitten in March,
when the weather was still cold. Only one bite, up above the elbow,
in my sleep. Then days of exhaustion. Then I rallied, and even grew
lively. I think I alarmed people. Giddy and emphatic, staring. Glassy.
Laughing at everything; my mouth opening, but not smiling, and
the diaphragm puffing, a spasm. Startle me then and I'd have jumped
across the room, and gone on jumping, out the window, from rooftop to rooftop, if I could. Then, in less than an hour, one afternoon,
it all fumed away, as if I'd gone through my entire ration of vitality,
and from then on I've been as weak as a plume of smoke. I watched
my flesh melt away, the heavy, meaty, big-dicked body I'd been
unwittingly so vain about, just sticks, shallowly breathing. Hairy,
knobbed, plucked stork. Huge driftwood hands. Raw eyed. Brittle
and rubbery at once. They're right about the aversion to mirrors, and
they're wrong about vanity being a sin . . . it's a punishment, I don't
lie when I say the anguish I went through over my appearance—a
man who habitually referred to himself as ugly when he was well—
was as bad as any of the rest of it. Of the four of us here, I'm the
worst.

We were installed six weeks ago, all at once. This is the third of a
series of dedicated clinics. Evidently our numbers are growing. Since I
have the honor of being among the first this disease has selected, I am
housed here at state expense. They want to watch and study and hide
us. It is after all an easily contracted disease, once you're exposed.
Does anyone visit? No one visits me. My family lives on the other side
of the country; they inform me they will visit as soon as they can. But
everyone else here was born and raised locally, and they don't seem to
receive many visitors. And fewer and fewer, as time goes on.

They propped us up in a pitiful little circle, what a bad idea that
was, like a collection of mummies taken down for a routine dust-

ing, and we introduced ourselves because we were going to be such great friends. Lifelong. There were six of us: myself, Jihan, Weldon, Carla, so-and-so who died the first week, and Tonya. I can't even manage to recall the face of the one who died—his voice, though, his cries. Some sort of attack. The sound came from down the hall. You can go on withering forever, or perhaps not; we are kept in the dark. But as a rule, from what I hear, death will probably be sudden, an attack without warning. Apart from turning into a parched and bloodthirsty mummy, that is. Carla saw someone die in the bed next to her in the hospital before she was transferred here, and she says this person burst out of a sound sleep with a piercing scream and went rigid, shaking violently, but conscious, crying out for help through her teeth. Carla was and still is a sturdy black woman, and she stirred herself as best she could for the performance, showing her teeth, shaking her arms out in front of her, flicking her long ornamental nails, raising her weary voice.

Jihan was a soft-spoken Hispanic man with African features. His air of thoughtfulness, which could still be distinguished from the vacant quiet of being sick, struck me. A graying mustache blurred the gauntness of his face, half obscuring his mouth, and his sleepy eyes were always downcast and apparently unseeing. He'd been present when the other one, the one I'd been introduced to that day, died. The nurses tried to keep our morale up by gathering us together periodically, and I heard about it the last day they propped us up in front of the television in the dayroom. We noticed that we were only five; the nurses evidently had planned to keep this from us, telling us only that so-and-so was a bit too sick to join us. Jihan, however, had been visiting this person when he went. Jihan struggled to make himself heard over *Garfield Goes Hawaiian*. With haunted eyes, he kept pressing his hands to his throat, and his lips trembled as he spoke. The remote was missing, and none of us could get up. Jihan's voice failed, but he continued to whisper to himself until the nurses came. Not more than a few days after that he hanged himself with the shower curtain from the back bathroom.

It's here.

I know exactly what's going to happen and there's nothing I can do about it. My body is paralyzed, my eyes riveted on the door.

It slides under, partially. The end lifts. It bobs up and down, like a dog sniffing the air. I'm what it sniffs. The rest slides through eagerly, coming directly toward me over the chessboard floor. It's a transparent, living platter with clear, gelatin organs; the membrane is furry with the dust it has picked up gliding over the floor.

It slithers beneath the horizon of the bed.

Now I feel the tug on the bedclothes as it climbs.

My bare leg is lying on top of the blankets, and there's a thick bandage there on one side of the calf. The bandage is sloppily made up, like a bundle of toilet paper. The thing rushes avidly to it and pushes at the bandage roughly, tugging it aside.

It will expose the open wound. It will push its way under the bandage. It will get inside me.

Perfect black. With a slender ring of gold lace. A gleaming crescent at the far edge. Apparitions of steam. That's only from an oblique angle. Looking directly down into the mug involves seeing myself, so I don't do it. Shifting my eyes askance, it looks like night seen through the pale sheen of lamp light on a windowpane, if the window were steaming. The mug is ivory off-white, thick and sturdy. I lift it, opening my mouth; the heat and the odor are overpowering. I can already sense the bitterness. Blood is opaque in just the same way. I never drink it hot—too much flavor. I like it so cold I can barely taste it. I haven't had anything this hot in I don't know how long; I haven't felt much like hot drink. But today I'm cold, so I ventured as far as the nurses' lounge and swiped a mug of coffee, and now I'm about to drink it in the safety of my bed. With a pan next to me.

I try again. Once again, the heat and the bitterness set me back. Now! The acrid heat cuts my mouth and throat. Down into my inert stomach. I can feel it blacken. I hear a gasp as alien warmth spreads into me from my stomach. Any minute now it will flip back up again; I lie still, propped up, forcing myself to breathe evenly and hold out for as long as possible. There's pressure in my head. I'm more awake and alert, hearing footsteps in the hall. The nurse is here and sees everything. Even before her hand can find the mug I'm pitching coffee into the pan.

"Oh for goodness' sake," she snips in disgust. "There, you see?"

Another gout into the pan, heat in my throat, my head racing.

"Why do you put yourself through this, Mr. Emory?"

I'm too busy to reply just now, nurse. The coffee is surprisingly still. Steam still escapes from it, here and there.

"All finished?" she asks finally, her mouth closing like a trap.

I nod and let my head fall back. She wipes my lips and takes the pan from me.

"At least you don't have to wipe my shit!" I call at her as she goes, but I don't think she can hear me.

The nurse passes Carla out in the corridor. She takes a prescribed walk every day, her right hand on the wall.

"Could I come in a moment?" she asks. Her emphatic way of speaking is at odds with the weakness of her voice.

I nod.

Sliding one foot at a time, holding on to whatever is in reach and, where she must cross open space, keeping her hands raised like a child, Carla comes over to me and settles gradually into the chair that creaks by my bed.

"Oh, gunness! Gunness!" she says under her breath. "Oh, my God!"

Once she's more or less in place, she sinks her head into her hands a moment. Now she draws a breath through her nose and raises her head again, out of her hands.

"How are you feeling today?" she asks.

"Weird."

She nods and compresses her mouth.

"That's a very good word for it."

Her shoulders rise and fall, and she sighs, showing her lower row of teeth. I smell blood as her breath washes past my face.

"I'm tired. Oh my God."

Why have this conversation?

"Listen," she says. "I wanted to ask you something."

"Sure."

She sighs again. Leaning forward, elbows on her knees, and lowering her voice, she shakes her hands to emphasize each word.

"Do you think," she asks, "that . . . if, God forbid, something should happen to me. Do you think they will take my blood and give it to you? To the other patients?"

Later, when Carla has tottered back to her room, trailing her sighs and her muffled ejaculations of distress, shedding size like the rest of us, I make an expedition to the little reception area, which has barred windows overlooking the street. The clinic was a private home once, sandwiched between big apartment buildings now. Through the bars, doggedly hanging on to the sill so I can stand, I watch the busy passings outside. Phantoms. Even without this window, there would be something dividing us. It would be, it is total, and life, not death. I don't know what that means but I know I mean it.

I'm lying in bed. It's my old bedroom, from years ago. The windows are open. It isn't exactly night outside. The house is dark, and there's a feeling of oblivion settled on it. I get the same feeling from the steely, bruise-colored glow that seems to paint everything it touches with powdered lead. I'm frightened. I lie on my back, naked, paralyzed, on a bare mattress. The glow from outside hurts the bones of my face, and there's a bitter flavor in the back of my throat fuming up into my sinuses and behind my eyes. Dread rivets my eyes to the windows, because I know something is going to come into the room through those windows.

Mosquitoes are landing on my legs. I see them all too distinctly, silhouetted in the glow. They're landing all over me now, on my legs, my chest, arms, my penis, toes, hands, my lips and cheeks. Welts rise like shallow nipples all over my swelling body; with a light, frisking sensation the mosquitoes are taking turns at my wounds. I feel each whisker as it is removed, as another is inserted in its place. I weaken steadily. My sight dims. My blood flies away from me in tiny atoms and swarms fill the room with an almost inaudible whining.

The day is formless and empty without eating. Drinking blood three times a day is more like taking medication: I don't savor it; I want to get it over with. Like anyone else, we can only tolerate human blood transfusion; we can, however, drink any kind of blood. Human blood being scarce, we drink. Rabbit, I think. Each one alone. None of us can stand to see each other drink, or being seen, which is worse. It comes in sets of three shallow plastic cups, like custard cups, sealed with foil. We all take it cold, I think; I puncture the foil and gag the stuff down, with the fingers of my free hand clamping my nostrils shut. Breathing out again, though, can't be postponed forever. I lie back with the red pool in me. Blood as still as a pool in a cave. There's no digestion. Instead, you feel there's gradually less and less. There's no hunger, either. The entrails are numb. There's thirst, but this doesn't affect that. I wash my mouth after I drink, with mouthwash. The mint mixes disgustingly with the blood, but I don't feel nausea, either, just mouth repugnance. As bad as it is, the mixed taste is less offensive to me because it's my revenge, and I rinse until mint gets the upper hand. One of us—I guess Tonya—always keeps a hard candy in her mouth, for the same reason. Candy clicks against her teeth whenever she talks. Carla chews gum. We have to lick salt.

Weldon stays in bed, writing. When I go a-roving, I have to pass his room. He is either facedown over a notebook or staring at the wall. His mouth and eyes have a determined setness; I think he's trying to write or reason the illness into submission. I go back down the hall in the gloom of the very early morning, and see his dark, bare arms spread out before him like two twigs, resting his aching forearms. His head lies on his arms; there are his almost luminous white teeth, so bright they almost seem to illuminate his inner lips. That's as much curiosity as I have strength for. I have preoccupations of my own.

I barely sleep. Two hours a night or so, and that's just to accommodate my nightmares. Even though I feebly paw my way out from under their suffocation with the same desperation as always, never jolting awake as I used to do, they are the most brilliantly intense moments of my day. In my nightmares I regain the vitality I've lost in my waking life.

Pull down my lower lip and look in the little shaving mirror. Little enough so that I can't really see more than a bit of me at a time. I still shave. Another symptom—tiny, cloud-colored blisters all in a row, embedded in the soft purple flesh inside the lip. Cool brine fills each one, as popping them reveals. They appear and disappear, a sign that the life of my body has joined itself to decay, whose processes are now my metabolism. These are my eyes, without a single red thread. White, and green, like cheese. My sallow skin . . . Put the thing away. Back in its little case. Outside my window I can see the huge air-conditioning unit down there. A puddle of rain water has gathered in a depression on the top of the box; the wind is high, and the clouds, lit from below, speed across the blackness. The puddle reflects the blackness except at the edges, and where the wind riffles the surface, where the sour color of the sodium lights is reflected like gold parentheses against the black water. I stare thirstily at that water, yearning to drink it and the gold and the wind and clouds and reflected blackness along with it in one clear draught.

Ada the nurse. One of them. She's in her forties somewhere, non-descript short hair, prefers formless, cheap, easily washed clothes. Puff shoes. A mouth. Some kind of a mouth.

"How are you doing today?"

". . . Hm?"

"I say, how are you doing?"

"Fine."

"Are you sleeping?"

". . . Fine."

"How many hours did you sleep last night?"

". . . Don't know. . . . Two, maybe."

"Would you like some more tablets?"

Wave my hand.

"Well, think about it anyway."

Checks my eyes.

"Still seeing okay?"

Nod.

"And hearing, other feeling okay?"

Nod.

"Are you cold?"

Shake my head.

Touches my soles.

"Feel me?"

Nod.

"This'll only be a minute more."

Nod.

March 7: Lip nodules. No fever. Groggy, but not sleeping. Emaciation. Weakness. Hair thinning. Night terror.

March 10: Unchanged. Unresponsive. ["Minimally" written in by hand and a caret to indicate insertion before "unresponsive."] Still feeding.

March 15: Unchanged. Unresponsive. Got up only twice since 3/10.

- - - T. Rei seizure, 10:10 PM, transferred to Emergency.

March 17: T. Rei deceased, 7:16 AM. No cause given.

March 20: Unchanged. Totally unresponsive. Stays in bed.

March 22: Nodules on outside of lips. No fever. Emaciation advanced. Hair loss advanced. Not sleeping. Night terror. No perspiration. Still feeding.

March 25: Unchanged from previous.

March 26: Unchanged.

March 27: Emaciation extreme, below 90 lbs. Same conditions. Paralysis. Still conscious. Feeds normally.

March 28: Unchanged.

March 29: Unchanged.

March 30: Unchanged.

March 31: Unchanged.

April 1: Unchanged. Red spots on cheeks.

April 2: Unchanged.

April 3: Unchanged. Overall less sallow.

April 4: Unchanged. Sleeping.

April 5: Slackening of skin [crossed out, and written above it in cramped space, "putting on flesh beginning"], sleeping more. Movement. Nodules gone, inside and out. Otherwise same.

April 6: Same.

April 7: Same.

April 8: Slept six hours.

April 9: Slept eight hours. Emaciation seems less. New hair growth. Almost normal color.

April 10: Same.

April 11: Same.

April 12: Same.

April 13: Same. Joked about date.

April 14: Slept over ten hours. Sleep increasing. Night terrors.

April 15: Same. Patient walked.

The family won't reveal evidence. Main Street full of old department stores. I didn't like being out in the open—life doesn't mean a thing here.

The room is dark; Ada enters. Without turning on the light she hurries to my bedside and presses the cool bladder into my hand, disappears. The stiff plastic crackles as I raise it to look at. A bulging, clear bag of purple shadow, with a dimly fluorescing white label. The label reads: "T. Rei. Posthumous exsanguinate."

No straw. I'm not hungry. Is there a label? Does it really say that? Or am I dreaming again? While I am thirsty, I know this isn't going to fix me. It will vanish into me in a spasm of disgust, and the failure of anything to change will be the only sign. If it is hers, perhaps it will do more, though. "Drink your blood, Beaumanoir," de Rais said. Why didn't I remember that one a long time ago? I slip the bag carefully under my pillow.

Chuck back the covers and pause a moment to take stock. I'm meating up again, even though she isn't feeding me all that much extra. Not like it used to be, the flesh is firm but springy, a little like the bag. Beautiful egg of muscle on each calf again. Slab thighs, very firm, almost like before. I yank the gown off over my head, which would have cost me so much painful effort just a month ago, and study my naked body in the gloom. I can't see my ribs anymore. My whole body is upholstered in a fine, spongy brawn, my dick fills the crease of my thigh like a roll of dough. It has stopped playing games with me; warm, heavy, and useless, now it just grows, steadily, without hardening, never shrinking, like a sprouting twin highminded Ada has designs on. Not that she would admit that. The hair has grown back on my scalp, thicker than before if anything, and finer, drier. I rub my chin and I can hear it.

I leap up onto my feet and land on the moon. The air slides over my skin like water, and that reminds me. I have cleverly secreted a bottle of water—a glass bottle—in the useless vegetable crisper of the refrigerator. Now I have it. The light retreats into the box and I twist off the metal cap. The glass smells a little fruity, and dabs of rust are on its lips. Clear trembling. I tilt it into my mouth, the rapture of drinking. I don't pour it in. It slides in on purpose, I capture it for a moment and then pull languidly, and a delicious evening out of levels and surfaces occurs. The cold becomes piercing and I have to stop two thirds of the way into my orgy, gasping. Whiskers of cold in my temples, and down into my numb interior. I want to get it all down before. I won't bother hiding the bottle. I brazenly relish the stony coolness of the water, and when it gushes from my mouth into the sink again a moment later, it's every bit as cold and refreshing as it was going down. That's the last of it. Now my insides are cold clean and silvered.

All of the others, they are all looking more and more drawn and feeble. I suppose all that vitality has drained away into me. If it has, I don't feel it, I'm not aware of having been made to feel more lively as an effect of Ada's secret withdrawals from them. If I am getting up more often, and becoming more active, it might be because I feel obligated to show that I'm putting my feed to good use. Ada stands in the doorway, gazing at me with an expression I can't name. The power has been out for most of the day, and the hall is dim. One of her hands grips the frame. I can hear her breathing. She's been bleeding herself for me, too. I suppose she feels this makes her a part of me. She's wrong about that, but how can I explain? Her devotions will admit nothing from me. There doesn't seem to be any limit, apart from my own disgust, to the amount I can bib down. I've explained that I don't need it, any of it, apart from the daily ration. This new vigor comes from some other source. I'm positive of that. The daily ration keeps me within its availability, I mean the vigor's, but there's no correlation of quantities. Blood imbibed. Vigor regained. I see no correlation.

"It makes you stronger," she says, staring. "You must never become that weak again. I couldn't stand it!"

"What are you talking about? You brought me the first extra a whole week after I began to improve."

Ada doesn't seem to hear. After a moment or two, she gets up, sways, and resumes her rounds. The gifts keep coming. I drink without the slightest relief of my thirst, to make her happy. Carla hasn't been by the door in a while. Ada holds the streaked cup to my lips.

"Here," she whispers, gazing at me in a transport I can't read. I drink, surreptitiously holding my breath. "Grow strong!"

I'm not strong. My meaty body is like a sandbag dream body, with tidal motion. There's a roll along my arm, the arm rises in the air; there's a rolling back away again, and my arm stays where it is, suspended, just as though it lay on a shelf. Another roll fills it, and when the wave recedes, down my arm goes as before, never limp, never stiff. Ada covers herself in gold. She enters my presence stilled and reverent, holding a brimming golden chalice in both hands, and I receive the unwanted gift. *I'm like a petted houseplant,* I think, and laugh, spraying blood over her, down onto my sheets. She snatches the cup away with an expression of horror, carefully sets it down, and then, apologies streaming nonstop from her mouth, she gathers up the sheets, paws my face to clean it, scurries out the door with the sheets. Chuckling, I wait until I know she's gone downstairs to the laundry room in the basement, then I get up and pour her cup out into the sink, washing with care. I'll make it up to her by pretending to have been a good creeper and drunk the cup to the dregs. She wants me to be as big as a house. All the same, standing up like this is really comfortable, like lying in bed. No matter what, it's as if I'm permanently encased in a cushioned sconce and everything makes me feel pampered. It's the disease. You weaken, and then, who knows why, you fill out again. Perhaps I will wither and swell over and over again.

Weldon, I've just looked in on. Like a pile of branches, smelling. Carla, eyes glazed, wheezing, drawn cheeks, the teeth protruding, a tube of blood draining into a bag. Someone else I don't know, asleep. I pull the tube out of Carla's arm. Blood wells sluggishly from the old wound. I put a wad of cotton there and double her arm up, but she's too far gone to keep her elbow closed, sluggish red stains the cotton, picks up fur on the floor. Eventually I hunt up what I think is a vein and drive the needle in. Not much bleeding. Squeeze the bag to force the blood in, since the suction isn't doing much, end up with a mess. Carla wheezes, coughs, dry eyes fixed. Then Ada.

The power's still out. I can't imagine what's happened. No more nurses' shifts. Ada never leaves. No one comes looking for Ada. No one comes at all. The clinic has slipped into outer space, with windows that continue to show what's going on in the street, or they remember what used to go on out there. The front door is painted on and the windows are movie screens. None of this worries me, none of it concerns me.

I'm bigger now than I've ever been in my life. With aristocratic disdain, I refuse to wear a stitch. Biopsy scars gone without a trace. My supple body smells like fresh butcher's meat. I wash myself fastidiously. There is at least water in outer space. That my new muscular integument possesses virtually no true strength strikes me as a distinction; no vulgar concession to utility.

I hear breathing out in the corridor. Sliding. Ada staggers in to see me, bearing gifts.

"For you," she says tonelessly. "How good you're looking!"

Her eyes are glazed and dim, and she can't raise them to see me. Her mouth hangs open and her lip droops. There's no outward sign of the incredible willpower she must have, because there's no need, as I've told her again and again, absolutely no need for any of it. The clinic's supply is plenty ample enough, especially now that I am the only consumer left.

How some people yearn for a master! I remind her, as she drags herself in what she must be guessing is my direction, "None of this is necessary." I shake my head and open my hands, although I must admit I'm smiling with gratified vanity and the pleasure of taking an interest in a fellow creature.

There was nothing stopping her. She could have walked out long ago and left me to rot. Or I don't, then again, suppose she could have. All I mean is that there was no barrier to prevent her from going, so it was physically possible. So what does that say about physical obstacles? She's the one who wants a master, vampire, and pours out her life and the lives of others into the mirror, my bottomless emptiness, so she can feel herself leashed chastely to her dream.

Falling herself half onto the bed, she pauses to catch her breath, but only for a moment. Now she presses the nearly empty bag into my hand avidly, staring at my hand. She might not be able to lift her trembling head. Glancing down at the top of it, I thank her graciously for her gift. With an effort that's painful to watch, she straightens herself and stands, watching me expectantly, her eyes seeming to glow in her drawn face. I smile, thanking her again, and for her sake, surreptitiously holding my breath I drain the bag into my vacant insides. Ada smiles back at me and I shrink involuntarily, try to pass it off as a sort of spasm. Her eyes suck my body greedily. She sways.

Halfway across the floor she begins to stoop. She leaves on all fours.

I get up and go to the corridor, moving with unreal ease—not lightness, actually heaviness, but heavy and easy at once. Overtaking her, I gather her, with some effort, into my arms and gingerly carry her papier-mâché body into her bedroom, settling her down on her bed. She is sighing and cooing mindlessly. Tears streak her face when I glance at it as I leave again, two glistening tracks curving around the blackness of the open mouth.

Perched atop a lonely platform in the wind the door to your heart-kitchen, the house is alone now where so-and-so used to put in his appearance before he died, and when the bus comes back I can or not. They ride on, on, on trouble now I only want to see it having waved good-bye. The dream won't last, won't go. Let the disease turn me into a brawny, flimsy human bean bag flung down here with my head propped up with a gaping smile and a red-streaked face, while the dust thickens on my eyeballs; that's fine by me. I begin to move.

Is this sleep? The recipe seems to be two hours of nightmares and eight or ten of dreams so banal they're like reliving memories without skipping a single moment. In these dreams I have none of the dreamer's special freedom. I stay put in the blundering of normal events and it's as if I were living an ordinary life disembodied. Life doesn't mean a thing.

It isn't a thing I hang on to with even the gentlest grasp. I prepared myself for death and not for any reason will I leave the brink of it now. I lie on my bed, the sun crashing down on me, and hearken to the cockamamie nerve music it causes, as though I were an enchanted cave opened to the sun, whose stalactites are hollowed-out organ pipes; the cave is me and I am also a cave dweller who sits among the fangs in one of the patches of permanent night the sun missed, listening to the heartbreaking, automatic, earth-computer nerve music playing itself.

The dreams are at an end. They release me, I'm back from hell and I can go over to the French windows and walk out under a red sky into a red garden misted with the spray of a malevolent ocean I can't see, plunge my hairy head into the white fountain and drink.

MULBERRY BOYS

Margo Lanagan

Margo Lanagan has written four collections of short stories: *White Time, Black Juice, Red Spikes,* and *Yellowcake,* and a dark fantasy novel, *Tender Morsels.* She is a four-time World Fantasy Award winner, for short story, collection, novella, and novel. Her new novel, *Selkies,* will be published in 2012. Lanagan lives in Sydney, Australia, and day-jobs as a contract technical writer. She was an instructor at Clarion South in 2005, 2007, and 2009, and Clarion West in 2011.

So night comes on. I make my own fire, because why would I want to sit at Phillips's, next to that pinned-down mulberry?

Pan-flaps, can you make pan-flaps? Phillips plopped down a bag of fine town flour and gave me a look that said, *Bet you can't. And I'm certainly too important to make them.* So pan-flaps I make in his little pan, and some of them I put hot meat slice on, and some cheese, and some jam, and that will fill us, for a bit. There's been no time to hunt today, just as Ma said, while she packed and packed all sorts of these treats into a sack for me—to impress Phillips, per-haps, more than to show me favor, although that, too. She doesn't mind me being chosen to track and hunt with the fellow, now that I'm past the age where he can choose me for the other thing.

We are stuck out here the night, us and our catch. If I were alone I would go back; I can feel and smell my way, if no stars and moon will show me. But once we spread this mulberry wide on the ground and fixed him, and Phillips lit his fire and started his fid-dling and feeding him leaves, I knew we were to camp. I did not ask; I dislike his sneering manner of replying to me. I only waited and saw.

He's boiled the water I brought up from the torrent, and filled it with clanking, shining things—little tools, it looks like, as far as I can see out of the corner of my eye. I would not gratify him with looking directly. I stare into my own fire, the forest blank black be-yond it and only fire-lit smoke above, no sky though the clouds were clearing last I looked. I get out my flask and have a pull of fire-bug, to settle my discontentments. It's been a long day and a weird, and I wish I was home, instead of out here with a half-man, and the boss of us all watching my every step.

"Here, boy," he says. He calls me *boy* the way you call a dog. He doesn't even look up at me to say it.

I cross from my fire to his. I don't like to look at those creatures, mulberries, so I fix instead on Phillips, his shining hair-waves and his sharp nose, the floret of silk in his pocket that I know is a green-blue bright as a stout-pigeon's throat, but now is just a different orange in the fire's glow. His white, weak hands, long-fingered, big-knuckled—oh, they give me a shudder, just as bad as a mulberry would.

"Do you know what a loblolly boy is?"

He knows I don't. I hate him and his words. "Some kind of insulting thing, no doubt," I say.

"No, no!" He looks up surprised from examining the brace, which is pulled tight to the mulberry's puffed-up belly, just below the navel, when it should dangle on an end of silk. "It's a perfectly legitimate thing. Boy on a ship, usually. Works for the surgeon."

And what is a surgeon? I am not going to ask him. I stare down at him, wanting another pull from my flask.

"Never mind," he says crossly. "Sit." And he waves where: right by the mulberry, opposite himself.

Must I? I have already chased the creature five ways wild today; I've already treed him and climbed that tree and lowered him on a rope. I'm sick of the sight of him, his round stary face, his froggy body, his feeble conversation, trying to be friendly.

But I sit. I wonder sometimes if I'm weak-minded, that even one person makes such a difference to me, what I see, what I do. When I come to the forest alone, I can see the forest clear, and feel it, and everything in it. If I bring Tray or Connar, it becomes the ongoing game of us as big men in this world—with the real men left behind in the village, so they don't show us up. When I come with Frida Birch it is all about the inside of her mysterious mind, what she can be thinking, what has she noticed that I haven't about some person, some question she has that would never occur to me. It's as if I cannot hold to my own self, to my own forest, if another person is with me.

"Feed him some more," says Phillips, and points to the sack beside me. "As many as he can take. We might avoid a breakage yet if we can stuff enough into him."

I untie the sack, and put aside the first layer, dark leaves that have been keeping the lower, paler ones moist. I roll a leaf-pill—the neater I make it, the less I risk being bitten, or having to touch lip or tongue. I wave it under his nose, touch it to his lips, and he opens and takes it in, good mulberry.

Phillips does this and that. Between us the mulberry's stomach grumbles and tinkles with the foreign food he's kept down. Between leaf-rollings, I have another pull. "God, the smell of that!" says Phillips, and spares a hand from his preparations to wave it away from his face.

"It's good," I say. "It's the best. It's Nat Culloden's."

"How old are you anyway?" He cannot read it off me. Perhaps he deals only with other men—I know people like that, impatient of the young. Does he have children? I'd hate to be his son.

"Coming up fifteen," I say.

He mutters something. I can't hear, but I'm sure it is not flattering to me.

Now there's some bustle about him. He pulls on a pair of very thin-stretching gloves, paler even than his skin; now his hands are even more loathsome. "Right," he says. "You will hold him down when I tell you. That is your job."

"He's down." Look at the spread cross of him; he couldn't be any flatter.

"You will hold him *still*," says Phillips. "For the work. When I say."

He pulls the brace gently; the skein comes forth as it should, but— "Hold him," says Phillips, and I hook one leg over the mulberry's thigh and spread a hand on his chest. He makes a kind of warning moan. Phillips pulls on, slowly and steadily like a mother. "*Hold* him," as the moaning rises, buzzes under my hand. "Christ above, if he makes this much of a fuss *now*."

He pulls and pulls, but in a little while no more silk will come. He winds what he has on a spindle and clamps it, tests the skein once more. "No? Well. Now I will cut. Boy, I have nothing for his pain." He looks at me as if *I* forgot to bring it. "And I need him utterly still, so as not to cut the silk or his innards. Here." He hands me a smooth white stick, of some kind of bone. "Put that crosswise between his teeth, give him something to bite on."

I do so; the teeth are all clagged with leaf scraps, black in this light. Mulberries' faces are the worst thing about them, little round old-children's faces, neither man nor woman. And everything they are thinking shows clear as water, and this one is afraid; he doesn't know what's happening, what's about to be done to him. Well, I'm no wiser. I turn back to Phillips.

"Now get a good weight on him, both ends."

Gingerly I arrange myself. He may be neither man nor woman, but still the creature is naked, and clammy as a frog in the night air.

"Come on," says Phillips. He's holding his white hands up, as if the mulberry is too hot to touch. "You're plenty big enough. Spread yourself out there, above and below. You will need to press here, too, with your hand." He points, and points again. "And this foot will have some work to do on this far leg. Whatever is loose will fight against what I'm doing, understand?"

So he says, to a boy who's wrestled tree snakes so long that his father near fainted to see them, who has jumped a shot stag and ridden it and killed it riding. Those are different, though; those are wild, they have some dignity. What's to be gained subduing a mulberry, that is gelded and a fool already? Where's the challenge in that, and the pride upon having done it?

"Shouldn't you be down there?" I nod legs-ward.

"Whatever for, boy?"

"This is to let the food out, no?"

"It is to let the food out, *yes*." He cannot speak without making me lesser.

"Well, down there is where food comes out, yours and mine."

"Pity sake, boy, I am not undoing all *that*. I will take it out through his silk-hole, is the plan."

Now I am curled around the belly, with nowhere else to look but at Phillips's doings. All his tools and preparations are beyond him, next to the fire; from over there he magics up a paper packet. He tears it open, pulls from it a small wet cloth or paper, and paints the belly with that; the smell nips at my nostrils. Then he brings out a bright, light-as-a-feather-looking knife, the blade glinting at the end of a long handle.

"Be ready," he says.

He holds the silk aside, and sinks the blade into the flesh beside it. The mulberry boy turns to rock underneath me; he spits out the stick, and howls to the very treetops.

Mulberry *boys* we call them. I don't know why, for some begin as girls, and they are neither one nor the other once they come out of Phillips's hut by the creek. They all look the same, as chickens look all the same, or goats. *Nonsense*, says Alia the goat woman, *I know my girls each one, by name and nature and her pretty face.* And I guess the mothers, who tend the mulberries, might know them apart. This one is John Barn, or once was called that; none of them truly have names once they've been taken.

Once a year I notice them, when Phillips comes to choose the new ones and to make them useful, from the boys among us who are not yet sprouted toward men, and the girls just beginning to change shape. The rest of the year, the mulberries live in their box, and the leaves go in, and the silk comes out on its spindles, and that is all there is to it.

They grow restless when he comes. Simple as they are, they recognize him. *They can smell their balls in his pocket*, says James Pombo, and we hush him, but something like that is true; they remember.

Some have struggled or wandered before, and these are tied to chairs in the box, but you have to watch the others. Though they have not much equipment for it, they have a lot of time to think, and because their life is much the same each day and month and year, they see the pattern and the holes in it through which they might wangle their way.

Why the John Barn one should take it into his head after all these years, I don't know. He was always mulberry, ever since I knew to know, always just one of the milling amiables in that warm box.

Oh, I remember him, says Pa. *Little straw-haired runabout like all them Barns. Always up a tree. Climbed the top of Great Grandpa when he couldn't have been—what, more than three years, Ma? Because his sister Gale did it, and she told him he was too little. That'll send a boy up a tree.*

Last year when I was about to sprout, it was the first year Phillips came instead of his father. When he walked in among us we were most uneasy at the size of him, for he is delicately made, hardly taller than a mulberry himself, and similar shaped to them except in lacking a paunch. Apart from the shrinkage, though, you would think him the same man as his father. He wore the same fine clothes, as neat on him as if sewn to his body directly, and the fabrics so fine you can hardly see their weave. He had the same wavy hair, but brown instead of silver, and a beard, though not a proper one, trimmed almost back to his chin.

The mothers were all behind us and some of the fathers, too, putting their children forward. He barely looked at me, I remember, but moved straight on to the Thaw children; there are lots of them and they are very much of the mulberry type already, without you sewing a stitch on them. I remember being insulted. The man had not *bothered* with me; how could he know I was not what he wanted, from that quick glance? But also I was ashamed to be so obviously useless, so wrong for his purposes—because whatever those purposes were, he was from the town, and he was powerfuller in his slenderness and his city clothes than was any bulky man among us, and everyone was afraid of him. I wanted a man like that to recognize me as of consequence, and he had not.

But then Ma put her arm over my shoulder and clamped me to her, my back against her front. We both watched Phillips among the Thaws, turning them about, dividing some of them off for closer inspection. The chosen ones—Hinny and Dull Toomy, it was, that time, those twins—stood well apart, Pa Toomy next to them with arms folded and face closed. They looked from one of us to another, not quite sure whether to arrange their faces proudly, or to cry.

Because it is the end of things, if you get chosen. It is the end of your line, of course—all your equipment for making children is taken off you and you are sewn up below. But it is also the end of any food but the leaves—fresh in the spring and summer, sometimes in an oiled mash through autumn if you are still awake then. And it is the end of play, because you become stupid; you forget the rules of all the games, and how to converse in any but a very simple way, observing about the weather and not much more. You just stay in your box, eating your leaves and having your stuff drawn off you, which we sell, through Phillips, in the town.

It is no kind of life, and I was glad, then, that I had not been taken up for it. And Ma was glad, too, breathing relieved above me as we watched him sort and discard and at length choose Arvie Thaw. I could feel Ma's gladness in the back of my head, her heart knocking hard in her chest, even though all she had done was stand there and seem to accept whatever came.

While we tracked John Barn today, I was all taken up impressing Phillips. The forest and paths presented me trace after trace, message after message, to relay to the town man, so's he could see what a good tracker I was. I felt proud of myself for knowing, and scornful of him for not—yet I was afraid, too, that I would put a foot wrong, that he would somehow catch me out, that he would see something I had missed and make me a nobody again, and worthy of his impatience.

So John Barn himself was not much more to me than he'd always been; he was even somewhat less than other animals I hunted, for he had not even the wit to cut off the path at any point, and he left tracks and clues almost as if he wanted us to catch him, things he had chewed, and spat out or brought up from his stomach, little piles of findings—stones, leaves, seed-pods—wet-bright in the light rain. He might as well have lit beacon fires after himself.

Climbing up to him in the tree, I could see his froggy paunch pouching out either side of the branch, and his skinny white legs around it, and then of course his terrible face watching me.

"Which one are you?" he said in that high, curious way they have. They can never remember a name.

"I am George," I said, "of the Treadlaws."

"Evening's coming on, George," he said, watching as I readied the rope. This was why I had been brought, besides for my tracking. Mulberries won't flee or resist anyone smaller than themselves (unless he is Phillips, of course, all-over foreign), but send a grown man after them and they will throw themselves off a cliff or into a torrent, or climb past pursuing up a tree like this. It is something about the smell of a grown man sets them off, which is why men cannot go into the box for the silk, but only mothers.

I busied myself with the practicalities, binding Barn and lowering him to Phillips, which was no small operation, so I distracted myself from my revulsion that way. And then, when I climbed down, Phillips took up all the air in the clearing and in my mind with his presence and purposefulness, which I occupied myself sulking at. Then when I had to press the creature down, to lie with him, lie *on* him, everything in me was squirming away from the touch, but Phillips's will was on me like an iron, pinning me as fast as we'd pinned the mulberry, and I was too angry and unhappy at being made as helpless as John Barn, to think how he himself might be finding it, crushed by the weight of me.

But when he stiffened and howled, it was as if I had been asleep to John Barn and he woke me, as if he had been motionless disguised in the forest's dappled shadows, but then my eye had picked out his frame, distinct and live and sensible in there, never to be unseen again. All that he had said, that we had dismissed as so much noise, came back to me: *I don't like that man, George. Yes, tie me tight, for I will struggle when you put me near him. It's getting dark. It hurts me to stretch flat like this. My stomach hurts. An apple and a radish, I have kept both down. I stole them through a window; there was meat there, too; meat was what I mostly wanted. But I could not reach it. Oh, it hurts, George.* I had done as Phillips did, and not met the mulberry's eye and not answered, doing about him what I needed to do, but now all his mutterings sprang out at me as having been said by a person, a person like me and like Phillips; there were three of us here, not two and a creature, not two and a snared rabbit, or a shot and struggling deer.

And the howl was not animal noise but voice, with person and feeling behind it. It went through me the way the pain had gone through John Barn, freezing me as Phillips's blade in his belly froze him, so that I was locked down there under the realizing, with all my skin a-crawl.

I stare at Phillips's hands, working within their false skins. The fire beyond him lights his work and throws the shadows across the gleaming-painted hill-round of Barn's belly. Phillips cuts him like a cloth or like a cake, with just such swiftness and intent; he does not even do as you do when hunting, and speak to the creature you have snared or caught and are killing, and explain why it must die. The wound runs, and he catches the runnings with his wad of flock and cloth, absentmindedly and out of a long-practiced skill. He bends close and examines what his cutting has revealed to him, in the cleft, in the deeps, of the belly of John Barn.

"Good," he says—to himself, not to me or Barn. "Perfect."

He puts his knife in there, and what he does in there is done in me as well, I feel so strongly the tremor it makes, the fear it plays up out of Barn's frame, plucking him, rubbing him, like a fiddle string. His breath, behind me, halts and hops with the fear.

Phillips pierces something with a pop. Barn yelps, surprised. Phillips sits straighter, and waves his hand over the wound as he waved away the smell of my grog before. I catch a waft of shit-smell and then it's gone, floated up warm away.

He goes to his instruments. "That's probably the worst of it, for the moment," he says to them. "You can sit up if you like. Stay by, though; you never know when he'll panic."

I sit up slowly, a different boy from the one who lay down. I half expect my own insides to come pouring out of me. John Barn's belly gapes open, the wound dark and glistening, filling with blood. Beyond it, his flesh slopes away smooth as a wooden doll between his weakling thighs, which tremble and tremble.

Phillips returns to the wound, another little tool in his hand—I don't know what it is, only that it's not made for cutting. I put my hand on Barn's chest, trying to move as smoothly and bloodlessly as Phillips.

"George, what has he done to me?" John Barn makes to look down himself.

Quick as light, I put my hand to his sweated brow, and press his head to the ground. "He's getting that food out," I say. "If it stays in there, it'll fester and kill you. He's helping you."

"Feed him some more," says Phillips, and bends to his work. "Keep on that."

So I lie, propped up on one elbow, rolling mulberry pills and feeding them to Barn. He chews, dutifully; he weeps, tears running back over his ears into his thin hair. He swallows the mulberry mush down his child-neck. *Hush*, I nearly say to him, but Phillips is there, so I only think it, and attend to the feeding, rolling the leaves, putting them one by one into Barn's obedient mouth.

I can't help but be aware, though, of what the man is doing there, down at the wound. For one thing, besides the two fires it is the only visible activity, the only movement besides my own. For another, for all that the sight of those blood-tipped white hands going about their work repels me, their skill and care, and the life they seem to have of their own, are something to see. It's like watching Pa make damselfly flies in the firelight in the winter, each finger independently knowing where to be and go, and the face above all eyes and no expression, the mind taken up with this small complication.

The apple and the radish, all chewed and reduced and cooked smelly by John Barn's body's heat, are caught in the snarled silk. Phillips must draw them, with the skein, slowly lump by lump from Barn's innards, up into the firelight where they dangle and shine like some unpleasant necklace. Sprawled beside John Barn, in his breathing and his bracing himself I feel the size of every bead of that necklace large and small, before I see it drawn up into the firelight on the shining strands. Phillips frowns above, fire-fuzz at his eyebrow, a long streak of orange light down his nose, his closed lips holding all his thoughts, all his knowledge, in his head—and any feelings he might have about this task. Is he pleased? Is he revolted? Angry? There is no way to tell.

"Do you have something for their pain, then," I say, "when you make them into mulberries?"

"Oh yes," he says to the skein, "they are fully anesthetized then." He hears my ignorance in my silence, or sees it in my stillness. "I put them to sleep."

"Like a chicken," I say, to show him that I know something.

"Not at all like that. With a chemical."

All is quiet but for fire-crackle, and John Barn's breath in his nose, and his teeth crushing the leaves.

"How do you learn that, about the chemicals, and mulberry-making? And mulberry-fixing, like this?"

"Long study," says Phillips, peering into the depths to see how the skein is emerging. "Long observation at my father's elbow. Careful practice under his tutelage. Years," he finishes and looks at me, with something like a challenge, or perhaps already triumph.

"So *could* you unmake one?" I say, just to change that look on him.

"Could I? Why *would* I?"

I make myself ignore the contempt in that. "Supposing you had a reason."

He draws out a slow length of silk, with only two small lumps in it. "Could I, now?" he says less scornfully. "I've never considered it. Let me think." He examines the silk, both sides, several times. "I could perhaps restore their digestive functioning. The females' reproductive system *might* reestablish its cycle, with a normal diet, though I cannot be sure. The males' of course . . ." He shrugs. He has a little furnace in that hut of his by the creek. There he must burn whatever he cuts from the mulberries, and all his blood-soaked cloths and such. Once a year he goes in there with the chosen children, and all we know of what he does is the air wavering over the chimney. The men speak with strenuous cheer to each other; the mothers go about thin-lipped; the mothers of the chosen girls and boys close themselves up in their houses with their grief.

"But what about their . . . Can you undo their thinking, their talking, what you have done to that?"

"Ah, it is coming smoother now, look at that," he says to himself. "What do you mean, boy, 'undo'?" he says louder and more scornfully, as if I made up the word myself out of nothing, though I only repeated it from him.

I find I do not want to call John Barn a fool, not in his hearing as he struggles with his fear and his swallowing leaf after leaf, and with lying there belly open to the sky and Phillips's attentions. "They . . . haven't much to say for themselves," I finally say. "Would they talk among us like ourselves, if you fed them right, and took them out of that box?"

"I don't know what they would do." He shrugs again. He goes on slowly drawing out silk, and I go on hating him.

"Probably not," he says carelessly after a while. "All those years, you know, without social stimulus or education, would probably have impaired their development too greatly. But possibly they would regain something, from moving in society again." He snorts. "Such society as you *have* here. And the diet, as you say. It might perk them up a bit."

Silence again, the skein pulling out slowly, silently, smooth and clean white. Barn chews beside me, his breathing almost normal. Perhaps the talking soothes him.

"But then," says Phillips to the skein, with a smile that I don't like at all, "if you 'undid' them all, you would have no silk, would you? And without silk you would have no tea, or sugar, or tobacco, or wheat flour, or all the goods in tins and jars that I bring you. No cloth for the women, none of their threads and beads and such."

Yes, plenty of people would be distressed at that. I am the wrong boy to threaten with such losses, for I hunt and forage; I like the old ways. I kept myself fed and healthy for a full four months, exploring up the glacier last spring—healthier than were most folk when I arrived home, with their toothaches and their coughs. But others, yes, they rely wholly on those stores that Phillips brings through the year. When he is due, and they have run short of tobacco, they go all grog and temper waiting, or hide at home until he should come. They will not hunt or snare with me and Tray and Pa and the others; take them a haunch of stewed rabbit, and if they will eat it at all they will sauce it well with complaints and wear a sulking face over every bite.

"And no food coming up, for all those extra mouths you'd have to feed," says Phillips softly and still smiling, "that once were kept on mulberry leaves alone. Think of that."

What was I imagining, all my talk of undoing? The man cannot make mulberries back into men, and if he could he would never teach someone like me, that he thought so stupid, and whose folk he despised. And even if he taught us, and worked alongside us in the unmaking, we would never get back the man John Barn was going to be when he was born John Barn, or any of the men and women that the others might have become.

"You were starving and in rags when my father found you," says Phillips, sounding pleased. "Your people. You lived like animals."

"We had some bad years, I heard." *And we* are *animals*, I nearly add, *and so are you. A bear meets you, you are just as much a meal to him as is a berry bush or a fine fat salmon. What are you, if not animal?*

But I have already lost this argument; he has already dismissed me. He draws on, as if I never spoke, as if he were alone. Good silk is coming out now; all the leaves we've been feeding into John Barn are coming out clean, white, strong-stranded; he is restored, apart from the great hole in him. Still I feed him, still he chews on, both of us playing our parts to fill Phillips's hands with silk.

"Very well," says Phillips, "I think we are done here. Time to close him up again."

I'm relieved that he intends to. "Should I lie on him again?"

"In a little," he says. "The inner parts are nerveless, and will not give him much pain. When I sew the dermal layers, perhaps."

It is very much like watching someone wind a fly, the man-hands working such a small area and mysteriously stitching inside the hole. The thread, which is black, and waxed, wags out in the light and then is drawn in to the task, then wags again, the man concentrating above. His fingers work exactly like a spider's legs on its web, stepping delicately as he brings the curved needle out and takes it back in. I can feel from John Barn's chest that there is not pain exactly, but there is sensation where there should not be, and the fear that comes from not understanding makes Phillips's every movement alarming to him.

I didn't quite believe that Phillips would restore John Barn and repair him. I lie across Barn again and watch the stitching-up of the outer skin. With each pull and drag of thread through flesh Barn exclaims in the dark behind me. "Oh. Oh, that is bad. Oh, that feels dreadful." He jerks and cries out at every piercing by the needle.

"He's nearly finished, John," I say. "Maybe six stitches more."

And Phillips works above, ignoring us, as unmoved as if he were sewing up a boot. A wave of his hair droops forward on his brow, and around his eyes is stained with tiredness. It feels as if he has kept us in this small cloud of firelight, helping him do his mad work, all the night. There is no danger of me sleeping; I am beyond exhaustion; Barn's twitches wake me up brighter and brighter, and so does the fact that Phillips can ignore them so thoroughly, piercing and piercing the man. And though a few hours ago I would happily have left Barn to him, now I want to be awake and endure each stitch as well, even if there is no chance of the mulberry ever knowing or caring.

Then it is done. Phillips snips the thread with a pair of bright-gold scissors, inspects his work, draws a little silk out past all the layers of stitching. "Good, that's good," he says.

I lever myself up off Barn, lift my leg from his. "He's done with you," I tell him, and his eyes roll up into his head with relief, straight into sleep.

"We will leave him tied. We may as well," says Phillips, casting his used tools into the pot on the fire. "We don't want him running off again. Or getting infection in that wound." He strips off his horrid gloves and throws them in the fire. They wince and shrivel and give off a few moments' stink.

I feel as if I'm floating a little way off the ground; Phillips looks very small over there, his shining tools far away. "There are others, then?" I say.

"Others?" He is coaxing his fire up to boil the tools again.

"'Careful practice,' you said, by your father's side. Yet we never saw you here. So there are other folk like ours, with their mulberries, that you practiced on? In other places in the mountains, or in the town itself? I have never been there to know."

"Oh," he says, and right at me, his eyes bright at mine. "Yes," he says. "Though there is a lot to be learned from . . . books, you know, and general anatomy and surgical practice." He surveys the body before us, up and down. "But yes," he says earnestly to me. "Many communities. Quite a widespread practice, and trade. Quite solidly established."

I want to keep him talking like this, that he cares what he says to me. For the first time today he seems not to scorn me for what I am. I'm not as clear to him as John Barn has become to me, but I am more than I was this morning when he told Pa, *I'll take your boy, if you can spare him.*

"Do you have a son, then," I say, "that you are teaching in turn?"

"Ah," he says, "not as yet. I've not been so blessed thus far as to achieve the state of matrimony." He shows me his teeth, then sees that I don't understand. Some of his old crossness comes back. "I have no wife. Therefore I have no children. That is the way it is done in the town, at least."

"When you have a son, will you bring him here, to train him?" Even half asleep I am enjoying this, having his attention, unsettling him. He looks as if he thought *me* a mulberry, and now is surprised to find that I can talk back and forth like any person.

"I dare say, I dare say." He shakes his head. "Although I'm sure you understand, it is a great distance to come, much farther than other . . . communities. And a boy—their mothers are terribly attached to them, you know. My wife—my wife *to be*—might not consent to his travelling so far, from her. Until he is quite an age."

He waits on my next word, and so do I, but after a time a yawn takes me instead, and when it is over he is up and crouched by his fire. "Yes, time we got some rest. Excellent work, boy. You've been most useful." He seems quite a different man. Perhaps he is too tired to keep up his contempt of me? Certainly *I* am too tired to care very much. I climb to my feet and walk into the darkness, to relieve myself before sleep.

I wake, not with a start, but suddenly and completely, to the fire almost dead again and the forest all around me, aslant on the ridge. Dawn light is starting to creep up behind the trees, and stars are still snagged in the high branches, but here, close to me, masses of darkness go about their growing, roots fast in the ground around my head, thick trunks seeming to jostle one another, though nothing moves in the windless silence.

I am enormous myself, and wordless like the forest, yet full of burrows and niches and shadows where beasts lie curled—some newly gone to rest, others about to move out into the day—and birds roost with their breast-feathers fluffed over their claws. I am no fool, though that slip of a man with his tiny tools and his sneering took me for one. I see the story he spun me, and his earnest expectation that I would believe it. I see his whole plan and his father's, laid out like paths through the woods, him and his town house and his tailor at one end there, us and our poor mulberries at the other, winding silk and waiting for him. A widespread trade? No, just this little pattern trodden through from below. Many communities? No, just us. Just me and my folk, and our children.

I sit up silently. I wait until the white cross of John Barn glimmers over there on the ground, until the smoke from my fire comes clear, a fine gray vine climbing the darkness without haste. I think through the different ways I can take; there are few enough of them, and all of them end in uncertainty, except for the first and simplest way that came to me as I slept—which is now, which is here, which is me. I spend a long time listening to folk in my head, but whenever I look to Barn, and think of holding him down, and his trembling, and his dutiful chewing of the leaves, they fall silent; they have nothing to say.

A redthroat tests its call against the morning silence. I get up and go to Barn, and take up the coil of leftover cord from beside him.

Phillips is on his side, curled around what is left of his fire. His hands are nicely placed for me. I slip the cord under them and pin his forearms down with my boot. As he wakes, grunts—"What are you at, boy?"—and begins to struggle, I loop and loop, and swiftly tie the cord. "How *dare* you! What do you think—"

"Up." I stand back from him, all the forest behind me, and in me. We have no regard for this man's thin voice, his tiny rage.

Staring, he pushes himself up with his bound hands, is on his knees, then staggers to his feet. He is equal the height of me, but slender, built for spider-work, while I am constructed to chop wood and haul water and bring down a running stag. I can do what I like with him.

"You are just a boy!" he says. "Have you no respect for your elders?"

"You are not my elders," I say. I take his arm, and he tries to flinch away. "This way," I say, and I make him go.

"Boy?" says John Barn from the ground. He has forgotten my name again.

"I'll be back soon, John. Don't you worry."

And that is all the need I have of words. I force Phillips down toward the torrent path; he pours *his* words out, high-pitched, outraged, neat-cut as if he made them with that little knife of his. But I am forest vastness, and the birds in my branches have begun their morning's shouting; I have no ears for him.

I push him down the narrow path; I don't bully him or take any glee when he falls and complains, or scratches his face in the underbrush, but I drag him up and keep him going. The noise of the torrent grows toward us, becomes bigger than all but the closest, loudest birds. His words flow back at me, but they are only a kind of odd music now, carrying no meaning, only fear.

He rounds a bend and quickly turns, and is in my arms, banging my chest with his bound purple hands. "You will not! You will not!" I turn him around, and move him on with all my body and legs. The torrent shows between the trees—that's what set him off, the water fighting white among the boulders.

Now he resists me with all that he has. His boots slip on the stones and he throws himself about. But there is simply not enough of him, and I am patient and determined; I pull him out of the brush again and again, and press him on. If he won't walk, I'm happy for him to crawl. If he won't crawl I'm prepared to push him along with my boot.

The path comes to a high lip over the water before cutting along and down to the flatter place where you can fill your pots, or splash your face. I bring him to the lip and push him straight off, glad to be rid of his flailing, embarrassed by his trying to fight me.

He disappears in the white. He comes up streaming, caught already by the flow, shouting at the cold. It tosses him about, gaping and kicking, for a few rocks, and then he turns to limp cloth, to rubbish, a dab of bright wet silk draggling across his chest. He slides up over a rock and drops the other side. He moves along, is carried away and down, over the little falls there, and across the pool, on his face and with blood running from his head, over again and on down.

I climb back up through the woods. It is very peaceful and straightforward to walk without him, out of the water-noise into the birdsong. The clearing when I reach it is quiet without him, pleased to be rid of his fussing and displeasure and only to stand about, head among the leaves, while the two fires send up their smoke-tendrils and John Barn sleeps on.

I bend down and touch his shoulder. "Come, John," I say, "Time to make for home. Do I need to bind you?"

He wakes. "You?" His eyes reflect my head, surrounded by branches on the sky.

"George. George Treadlaw, remember?"

He looks about as I untie his feet. "That man is gone," he says. "Good. I don't like that man."

I reach across him to loosen his far hand. "Oh, George," he says. "You smell bad this morning. Perhaps you'd better bind me, and walk at a little distance. That's a fearsome smell. It makes me want to run from you."

I sniff at a pinch of my shirt. "I'm no worse than I was last night."

"Yes, last night it started," he says. "But I was tied down then and no trouble to you."

I tether him to a tree-root and cook myself some pan-flaps.

"They smell nice," he says, and eats another mulberry leaf, watching the pan.

"You must eat nothing but leaves today, John," I tell him. "Anything foreign, you will die of it, for I can't go into you like Phillips and fetch it out again."

"You will have to watch me," he says. "Everything is very pretty, and smells so adventurous."

We set off home straight after. All day I lead him on a length of rope, letting him take his time. I am not impatient to get back. No one will be happy with me, that I lost Phillips. Oh, they will be angry, however much I say it was an accident, a slip of the man's boot as he squatted by the torrent washing himself. No one will want to take the spindles down to the town, and find whoever he traded them to, and buy the goods he bought. I will have to do all that, because it was I who lost the man, and I will, though the idea scares me as much as it will scare them. No one will want to hunt again, in years to come as the mulberries die off and no new ones are made; no one will want to gather roots and berries, and make nut flour, just to keep us fed, for people are all spoilt with town goods, the ease of them and the strong tastes and their softness to the tooth. But what can they do, after all, but complain? *Go down to the town yourselves,* I'll tell them. *Take a mulberry with you and some spindles; tell what was done to us. Do you think they will start it again? No, they will come up here and examine everything and talk to us as fools; they might take away all our mulberries; they might take all of us away, and make us live down the town. And they will think we did worse than lose Phillips in the torrent; they will take me off to jail, maybe. I don't know what will happen. I don't know.*

"It is a fine day, George of the Treadlaws," John Barn says behind me. "I like to breathe, out here. I like to see the trees, and the sun, and the birds."

He is following behind obedient, pale and careful, the stitches black in his paunch, the brace hanging off the silk-end. Step, step, step, he goes with his unaccustomed feet, on root and stone and ledge of earth, and he looks about when he can, at everything.

"You're right, John." I move on again so that he won't catch up and be upset by the smell of me. "It's a fine day for walking in the forest."

THE THIRD ALWAYS BESIDE YOU

John Langan

John Langan is the author of the novel *House of Windows* and the collection of stories *Mr. Gaunt and Other Uneasy Encounters*. His stories have appeared in *The Magazine of Fantasy & Science Fiction, Poe,* and in *The Best Horror of the Year*.

He lives in upstate New York with his wife and son.

That there had been another woman in their parents' marriage was an inference that for Weber and Gertrude Schenker had taken on all the trappings of fact. During the most recent of the late-night conversations that had become a Christmas Eve tradition for them, Weber had christened the existence of this figure the Keystone, for *her* and her intersection with their mother and father's marriage were what supported the shape into which that union had bent itself.

Over large-bowled glasses of white wine at the kitchen table, his back against the corner where the two window seats converged, Web met his eleven-months-younger sister's contention that, after all this time, the evidence in favor of *her* remained largely circumstantial by shaking his head vigorously and employing the image of the stone carved to brace an arch. Flailing his hands with the vigor of a conductor urging his orchestra to reach higher, which sent his wine climbing the sides of its glass, Web called to his aid a movie's worth of scenes that had led to their decision—during another Christmas Eve confab a decade earlier—that only the presence of another woman explained the prolonged silences that descended on the household without warning, the iciness that infused their mother's comments about their father's travels, the half-apologetic, half-resentful air that clung to their father after his trips like a faint, unpleasant smell. The other woman—*her*, the name custom had bestowed—

was the stone that placed a quarryful of cryptic comments and half-sentences into recognizable arrangement.

As for why, ten years on, the two of them were no closer to learning *her* real name, much less any additional details concerning *her* appearance or the history of *her* involvement with their father, when you thought about it, that wasn't so surprising. While both their parents had insisted that there was nothing their children could not tell them, a declaration borne out over thirty-one and thirty years' discussion of topics including Web's fear that his college girlfriend was pregnant (which, as it turned out, she wasn't) and Gert's first inkling that she might be gay (which, as it turned out, she was), neither their mother nor their father had asked the same openness of their children. Just the opposite: their parents scrupulously refrained from discussing anything of significance to their interior lives. Met with a direct question, their father became vague, evasive, from which Web and Gert had arrived at their secret nickname for him, the Prince, as in, the Prince of Evasion. Their mother's response to the same question was simple blankness, from which her nickname, the Wall, as in, the Wall of Silence. With the Prince and the Wall for parents, was it any wonder the two of them knew as little as they did?

Web built his case deliberately, forcefully—not for the first time, Gert thought that he would have made a better attorney than documentary filmmaker. (They could have gone into practice together: Schenker and Schenker, Siblings In Law.) Or perhaps it was that he was right, from the necessity of the other woman's existence to their parents' closed-mouthedness. Yet if the other woman was the Keystone, her presence raised at least as many questions as it answered, chief among them, why were their mother and father still together? A majority of their parents' friends—hell, of their parents' siblings—were on their second, third, and in one case, fourth marriages. If their mother and father were concerned about standing out in the crowd, their continued union brought them more sustained attention than a divorce, however rancorous, could have. Both their parents were traversed by deep veins of self-righteousness that lent some weight to the idea of them remaining married to prove a point—especially to that assortment of siblings moving into the next of their serial monogamies. However, each parent's self-righteousness was alloyed with another tendency—self-consciousness in their mother's case, inconstancy in their father's—that, upon reflection, rendered it insufficient as an explanation. Indeed, it seemed far more likely that their mother's almost pathological concern for how she was perceived, combined with their father's proven inability to follow through on most of his grandiloquent pledges, had congealed into a torpor that caught them fast as flies in amber.

It was a sobering and even depressing note on which to conclude their annual conversation, but the clock's hands were nearing 3 A.M., the second bottle of wine was empty, and while there was no compulsion for them to rise with the crack of dawn to inspect Santa's bounty, neither of them judged it fair to leave their significant others alone with their parents for very long. They rinsed out their glasses and the emptied bottles, dried the glasses and returned them to the cupboard, left the bottles upended in the dishrack, and, before switching off the lights, went through their old ritual of checking all the locks on the downstairs windows and doors. Something of a joke between them when their family first had moved from Westchester to Ellenville, the process had assumed increased seriousness with an increase of home invasions over the last several years. When they were done, Web turned to Gert and, his face a mask of terror, repeated the line that concluded the process, cadged from some horror movie of his youth: "But what if they're already inside?" Gert, who had yet to arrive at a satisfactory response, this year chose, "Well, I guess it's too late, then."

The fatality of her answer appeared to please Web; he bent to kiss her cheek, then wound his way across the darkened living room to the hallway at whose end lay the guest room for which he and Sharon had opted—the location, Gert had reflected, the farthest possible distance from their parents' room but still in the house. This had left her and Dana the upstairs room, her old one, separated from her mother and father's bedroom by the upstairs bathroom. Gert could not decide whether Web's choice owed itself to a desire to maintain the maximum remove from their parents for his new wife and himself, or was due to an urge to force the closest proximity between her and Dana and her parents, who, seven years after Gert's coming out, and three years since she'd moved in with

Dana, were still not as reconciled to their daughter's sexuality as they claimed to be. Of course, Web being Web, both explanations might have been true. Since some time in his mid-to-late teens, the closeness with which he had showered their mother and father, the hugs and kisses, had been replaced with an almost compulsive need for distance—if either parent drew too near for too long, tried to prolong an embrace, he practically vibrated with tension. At the same time, he had inherited their parents' self-righteousness, and given an opportunity to confront them with what he viewed as their shortcomings, was only too happy to do so. If Gert was uncomfortable, it wasn't in the plastic pleasantness that her mother and father put on whenever she and Dana visited, to which she'd more or less resigned herself as the lesser of many evils—it was in being fixed to the point of the spear with which Web wanted to jab their parents.

As she mounted the stairs to the second floor, she wondered if Web was anxious about his marriage going the way of their mother and father's, if his need for the downstairs room was rooted in anxiety about him and Sharon being contaminated by whatever had stricken their parents. It wasn't only their behavior that displayed the souring of their union. Physically, each appeared to be carrying an extra decade's weight. Their father's hair had fallen back to the tops of his ears, the back of his head, while their mother's had been a snow-white that she refused to dye for as long as either of their memories stretched. Their parents' faces had been scored across the forehead, to either side of the mouth, and though they kept in reasonable shape, their mother with jogging, their father racquetball, the flesh hung from their arms and legs in that loose way that comes with old age, the skin and muscle easing their grip on the bones that have supported them for so long, as if rehearsing their final relaxation. The formality with which their parents treated hers and Web's friends buttressed the impression that her brother and her were a pair of last-minute miracles, or accidents. Without exception, Gert's friends had been shocked to learn that her mother and father were, if not the same age as their parents, then younger. She thought Web had received the same response from his classmates and girlfriends.

Although she swung it open gently, the hinges of the door to her and Dana's room shrieked. *No sneaking around here.* In the pale wash of streetlight over the window, she saw Dana fast asleep on her side of the bed, cocooned in the quilt that had covered it. Leaving the door open behind her, Gert crossed to the hope chest at the foot of the bed and unlatched it. The odor of freshly laundered cotton rose to meet her, and along with it came the groan of the floorboards outside the door.

"Mom?" She stood. "Dad?" The hall sounded with whichever of them it was hurrying to their room. Gert waited for the hinges on their door to scream, wondering why they hadn't when whoever it was had opened it. After ten years of promising to do so, had her father finally oiled them? She listened for the softer snick of their door unlatching. She could feel someone standing there, one hand over the doorknob, their eyes watching her doorway for movement. "For God's sake . . ." Five steps carried her out into the hall, her face composed in an expression of mock exasperation.

The space in front of the door to her parents' bedroom was empty, as was the rest of the hallway. For a moment, Gert had the sensation that she was *not* seeing something, some figure in the darkness—the feeling was akin to that she had experienced looking directly at the keys for which she was tearing up the apartment and not registering them—and then the impression ceased. The skin along her arms, her neck, stood. *Don't be ridiculous*, she told herself; nonetheless, she made certain that the door to her room was shut tight. Later on, she did not hear footsteps passing up and down the hallway.

II

Gert's decision to pursue the question of the other woman, to ascertain her identity, was prompted not so much by that most recent Christmas Eve conversation as it was by a chance meeting with an old family friend in the din of Grand Central the week after New Year's. While waiting in line to purchase a round-trip ticket to Rye (where lived an obscenely wealthy client of her firm's who insisted on conducting all her legal affairs in the comfort of her tennis court of a living room), she felt a hand touch her elbow and a voice say, "Gertie?" Before she turned, she recognized the intonations of her

Aunt Victoria—not one of her parents' sisters, or their brothers' wives, but an old friend, perhaps their oldest, at a dinner party at whose house their father first had met their mother. With something of the air of its presiding genius, Aunt Vicky, Auntie V, had floated in and out of their household, always happy to credit herself for its existence and therefore, by extension, for hers and Web's. During Gert's teenage years, Victoria had been a lifesaver, rescuing her from her parents' seemingly deliberate lack of understanding of everything to do with her life and treating her to shopping trips in Manhattan, weekends at the south Jersey shore, even a five-day vacation on Block Island her senior year of high school. In recent years, Victoria's presence in their lives had receded, the consequence of her promotion to vice president of the advertising company for which she worked, but she was still liable to put in an appearance at the odd holiday.

Victoria's standing in the line was due to a speaking engagement with a sorority at Penrose College, in Poughkeepsie, to which she had decided it would be pleasant to ride the train up the east shore of the Hudson. She was dressed with typical elegance, in a black suit whose short skirt showed her legs fit as ever, and although her cheeks and jaw had lost some of their firmness of definition, her personality blazed forth, and Gert once more found herself talking with her as she would have with one of her girlfriends. The result of their brief exchange was a decision to meet for lunch, which consultation with their respective BlackBerrys determined would occur a week from that Saturday; there was, Victoria said, a new place in NoHo she was dying to try, and this would provide the perfect opportunity. Gert left their meeting feeling as she always did after any time with Victoria—refreshed, recharged.

Not until the other side of her visit with Miss Bruce (ten minutes of business wrapped inside two hours of formalities), as she was watching the rough cut of Web's latest film on her laptop, did the thought bob to the surface of her mind: Maybe Aunt Vicky was the other woman.

The idea was beyond absurd: it was perverse; it was obscene. Victoria Godfrey had been a de facto member of their family, closer to the four of them than a few of their blood relations. She had been present during the proverbial thick, and she had been there through the proverbial thin. To suggest that she and Gert's father had carried on—were carrying on—an affair, was too much, was over the top.

Try as she might, though, Gert could not banish the possibility from her thoughts. The same talents for analysis and narration that had placed her near the top of her class at NYU seized on the prospect of Auntie V being *her* and found that it made a good deal of sense. While both her parents had known Victoria, her father's friendship with her predated her mother's by several years. In fact, Victoria and her father had spoken freely of the marathon phone conversations with which they'd used to pass the nights, the restaurants they'd sought out together, the bands they'd seen in concert. Certainly, the connection between them had endured the decades. And during those years, her father's consulting job had required him to travel frequently and far, as had Aunt Vicky's work first in journalism and then in advertising. That Victoria, despite her declarations that all she wanted was a good man to settle down with, continued to live alone seemed one more piece of evidence thrown on top of what had suddenly become a sizable pile.

But her mother . . . Gert closed her laptop. In the abstract, at least, Gert long had admitted to herself the probability that her father had been unfaithful to her mother, perhaps for years. Restricting her consideration to her father and Aunt Vicky, she supposed she could appreciate how, given the right combination of circumstances, their friendship could have led to something else. (Wasn't that what had brought her and Dana together?) Factor her mother into the equation, however, and the sides failed to balance. Her father's relationship with Victoria might be longer, but her mother's was deeper; all you had to do was sit there quietly as they spoke to know that, while their conversation's focus might be narrow, it was anchored in each woman's core. Gert had no trouble believing her aunt might be involved with a married man if the situation suited her, but she could not credit Auntie V betraying one of her dearest friends.

Nonetheless, the possibility would not quit her mind; after all, how many divorces had she assisted or managed in which the immediate cause of the marriage's disintegration was a friend or even in-law who had gone from close to too close? That the same story might have repeated itself in her parents' marriage nauseated her;

without changing its appearance in the slightest, everything surrounding her looked wrong, as if all of it were manifesting the same fundamental flaw. She shook her head. *All right*, she told herself, *if this is the truth, I won't run from it. I'll meet it head on.* False bravado, perhaps, but what was her alternative?

A week and a half later, pulling open the heavy glass door to Lettuce Eat and stepping into its low roar of voices, Gert repeated to herself the advice that she gave the new lawyers: *Act as if you're in control, and you will be.* She had not been this nervous arguing her first case: her heart was thwacking against her chest; her palms were wet; her legs were trembling. In moments scattered across the last ten days, she had auditioned dozens of opening lines, from the innocuous *(Hi, Aunt Vic)* to the confrontational *(What do you say we talk about you and my father?)*, and although she hadn't settled on one (she was leaning toward *I'm so glad you came: there's something I'd like to talk to you about)*, she was less concerned about the exact manner in which they would begin than she was with the substance of their talk. What she would do should Auntie V confirm the narrative whose principal points Gert had posited on a legal pad she hadn't shown anyone, she could not predict. Nor did it help matters any that Victoria, in addition to a black turtleneck and jeans, was wearing a pair of dark sunglasses, the necessity of which, she explained as she stood to kiss Gert, arose from an office party that had not ended until 5 A.M. "I'm not dead yet, by God," Victoria said as she resumed her seat and Gert took hers. "I can still give you kids a run for your money."

Gert answered her aunt's assertion with a polite smile that she maintained for the waitress who appeared at her side proffering a menu. In reply to the girl's offer to bring her something to drink, Gert requested a Long Island iced tea and focused her attention on the menu, whose lettuce leaf shape was printed with the names of eight lunch salads. After the waitress had left for her drink, Victoria said, "That's kind of heavy-duty for Saturday brunch, don't you think?"

"Oh?" Gert nodded at Victoria's Bloody Mary.

"Darling, this is practically medicinal. Really: if I thought my HMO would cover it, I'd have my doctor write a prescription."

Despite herself, Gert laughed.

"Now," Victoria continued, "you don't look as if you were sampling new cocktails till dawn, so that drink is for something else, isn't it? Everything okay with Dana? Work?"

"Fine," Gert said, "they're both fine. Couldn't be better."

"All right, then, how about your brother? Or—his wife, what's her name, again? Sharon?"

"Sharon's fine, too. Web is Web. He's working on a new film; it's about this painter, Belvedere, Thomas Belvedere. Actually," Gert continued, "there is something—in fact, it's something I need to talk to you about."

"Sweetie, of course. What is it?"

"It has to do with my parents."

"What is it? Is everything okay? Nobody's sick, are they?"

"Here you go," the waitress said, placing Gert's drink before her. "Do you know what you'd like to order?"

Gert chose the Vietnamese salad, which, Victoria said, sounded much more interesting than what she'd been thinking of, so she ordered one, as well, dressing on the side. Once the waitress had departed, Victoria said, "The last time I saw your mother, I told her she was too skinny."

"Nobody's sick," Gert said.

"You're sure?"

"Reasonably."

"Oh, well, thank God for that." Victoria sipped her Bloody Mary. "Okay, everybody's healthy, everybody's happy: what do you want to discuss?"

The Long Island iced tea bit her tongue; Gert coughed, lowered her glass, then raised it for a second, longer drink. The alcohol poured through her in a warm flood, floating the words up to her lips: "It's my dad. I need to talk to you about the other woman—the one he had the affair with."

At NYU, the professor who had taught Gert and her classmates the finer points of cross-examination had employed a lexicon drawn from fencing to describe the interaction between attorney and witness. Of the dozen or so terms she had elaborated, Gert's favorite had been the *coup droit*, the direct attack. As she had seen and continued to see it, a witness under cross-examination was expecting you to attempt to trick them, trip them up on some minor inconsistency. If the opposing counsel were conscious, they would have prepped the witness for exactly such an effort; thus, in Gert's eyes, it was more effective (unexpected, even) to get right to the point. The strategy didn't always succeed—none did—but the times it worked, a certain look would come over the witness's face, the muscles around their eyes, their mouths responding to the words their higher faculties were not yet done processing, which Gert fancied was the same as the one you would have witnessed on the person whose chest your blade had just slid into. It was a look that mixed surprise, fear, and regret; when she saw it, Gert knew the witness, and probably the case, were hers.

It was this expression that had overcome Victoria's face. For an instant, she seemed as if she might try to force her way past it, pretend that Gert's question hadn't struck her as deeply as it had, but as quickly as it appeared to arise, the impulse faded. Her hands steady, she reached up to her sunglasses and removed them, uncovering eyes that were sunken, red-rimmed with the last night's extravagances. Trading her sunglasses for her drink, Victoria drained the Bloody Mary and held up the empty glass to their waitress, passing near, who nodded to the gesture and veered toward the bar. With a sigh, Victoria replaced the glass on the table and considered Gert, who was helping herself to more of her drink, her mind reeling with triumph and horror. The thrill that sped through her whenever her *coup droit* succeeded carried with it a cargo of anguish so intense that she considered bolting from her chair and running out of the restaurant before the conversation could proceed any further. The next time she and Aunt Vicky saw each other, they could pretend this exchange had never happened.

But of course, it was already too late for that. Victoria was speaking: "How did you find out? Your father didn't tell you, did he? I can't imagine—was it your mother? Did she say something to you?"

"No one said anything," Gert said. "Web and I put it together one night—I guess it was ten years ago. We were up late talking, and the subject turned to Mom and Dad, the way it always does, and all their little . . . quirks. I said something along the lines of, 'It's as if there's another woman involved,' and Web took that idea and ran with it. It was one of those things you wouldn't have dreamed could be true—well, I wouldn't have—but the more we discussed it, the more sense it made, the more questions it answered. Since then, it's something we've pretty much come to take for granted."

"Jesus," Victoria said. "Ten years?"

Gert nodded.

"And this is— Why haven't you asked me about this before?"

"For a while, we were happy to let sleeping dogs lie. Web still is, actually; he doesn't know I'm talking to you. Recently, I've . . . I guess I'm at a point where I want to know, for sure, one way or the other. At least, I think I do."

"No, no," Victoria said, "you're right. You should know. I should've spoken to you—not ten years ago, maybe, but it's past time. You have to understand—"

Whatever was necessary for Gert's understanding was pre-empted by the return of their waitress with Victoria's drink and their salads. Gert stared at the pile of bean sprouts, mango, banana, rice noodles, and peanuts in front of her and thought that never had she felt less like eating. With each breath she took, her internal weather shifted sharply, raw fury falling into deep sadness, from which arose bitter disappointment. That she managed an, "I'm fine, thanks," to the waitress's, "Can I bring you anything else?" was more reflex than actual response.

Before the waitress left, Victoria was sampling her next Bloody Mary. She did not appear any more interested in her salad than Gert was in hers. "All right," Victoria said once she had lowered her glass. "I want . . . you need to remember that your father loves your mother. She loves him, too—despite everything, they love each other as much as any couple I've ever known. Promise me you'll do that."

"I know they love one another," Gert said, although she could think of few facts in which she currently had less confidence.

"They do, honey; I swear they do. But your dad . . ." As if she might find what she wanted to say written there, Victoria's eyes searched the ceiling. "Oh, your father."

"Yes," Gert said.

"Let me . . . when you were, you must have been two, your father spent about three days calling everyone he knew. Anyone he couldn't reach by phone, he wrote to. All those calls, those letters, said the same thing: 'For the past seven years, I have been having an affair.' He had decided to end it, and the only way he was going to be able to follow through on that choice was if he came clean with all his family, all his friends, starting with your mother."

Gert tried to imagine her father being that decisive about any-thing. "How did you feel about this?"

"In a word, shocked. It's one of those times I can remember ex-actly where I was, what I was doing. I was in this sleazy motel out-side D.C., prepping an interview with a guy who claimed he had dirt on the junior senator from New York. There was a single, coin-operated bed in the room that had the most hideous green-and-orange spread on it. The walls were covered in cheap paneling and were too thin: for about an hour, I'd been listening to a couple on one side of me having drunken sex, and a baby on the other side of me wailing. Very nice. It was a little after nine o'clock; I had the TV on in an attempt to drown out the circle of life around me and the theme from *Dallas* was playing. When the phone rang, I thought it was my editor, calling with yet another last-minute question. The senator already had a reputation as a vengeful son of a bitch, and my editor was nervous about any story that wasn't ironclad.

"Anyway, I heard your father's voice, and at first, all I could think was, *How did he get this number?* Then I caught up to what he was saying and—" Victoria shook her head. "If you'd had a feather, you could have knocked me to the floor with it. I consider myself pretty perceptive. There isn't much that happens with my friends that I didn't see coming a mile away. But this . . ."

"What was it that surprised you?" Gert said.

"Are you kidding? Your father was cheating on your mother. He had been all through their relationship, their engagement, their marriage. Who does that? Okay, plenty of people, I know, but your father, he was . . . I guess you could say, he played the part of the devoted husband so convincingly. . . . That isn't fair. He was devoted; it's just, he'd gotten himself into such a mess. I screamed at him: 'What the fuck have you done, you asshole?' I mean, there was your mother with two little kids. What was she supposed to do?"

Was the alcohol slowing her comprehension? Gert said, "What about the other woman?"

"*Her.*" Victoria spat out the word as if it were a piece of spoiled meat. "I know," she said, holding up her hand to forestall the objec-tion Gert wasn't about to make, "that isn't fair. It takes two and all, but . . ." Victoria slapped the table, drawing glances from the diners to either side of them. "She was already married, for Christ's sake! She had been for years."

"Did . . . did you know her?"

"No, which is funny, because she lived three doors down from me. This is back when I had the place on West Seventy-first. Over the years, I must have seen her God knows how many times, but I'd never paid any attention to her. Why should I have? Little did I know she was . . . well, little did I know.

"That changed. Although it was after eleven when I finally hung up with your father, I was back on the phone right away. There was this guy, Phil DiMarco, a private investigator we used at the paper. He specialized in the cheating spouses of the rich and powerful; we turned to him whenever the rumor mill whispered that this politician or that movie star wasn't living up to their marriage vows. He was expensive as all hell, but he and I had this kind of thing, so he said he'd have a look around and get back to me."

"Why?" Gert said. "Why did you call a PI?"

"One of my oldest friends had just admitted that he'd been lying to me for years: not exactly a statement to inspire you with trust. Who knew if this was him coming clean, or some other lie? I was pissed off. I was afraid, the way you are for your friends when they're sliding down into something very bad. I felt sick. I kept thinking about your mom and you and your brother. This was when you were living in the house on Oat Street; I don't know if you remember it, but the front door was this gigantic thing you'd expect on a castle, not a modified Cape. It was ridiculous. Whenever I hauled it open, Web would shout, 'Aunt Wicky!' and run at me on those chubby legs of his. You were much more reserved: you'd hide behind your mom with that bear, Custard, clutched to your chest like a shield, until she stepped aside and urged you forward. And now . . . your father had fucked up your lives royally. The whole situation was so unfair—I figured I could at least find out if he was telling the truth; it seemed like one thing I could do for your mother, for you."

"What did this Phil guy find out?" Gert asked. "Was my father telling the truth?"

"As far as Phil DiMarco was able to determine—he did a more thorough job than I'd expected; although he said he could take things further if I wanted him to, which I decided I didn't—anyway, yes, your dad had been honest with me, with us.

"Which was good," Victoria said. "I mean, it beat the alternative. But there was still the matter of what he'd been so honest about. There's no way you and Web could remember any of what followed, the next year. Not to sound melodramatic, but there are large portions of it I'd like to forget. There wasn't . . . it's difficult to see, to hear people you love in pain. And I did love both of them. Furious as I was with your father, he was still my friend who'd made a terrible mistake he was trying to set right. Your mother was . . . she'd been very happy with your father, with you and Web, with all of you as a family, and then, it was like . . ." Victoria waved her hand, a gesture for chaos, unraveling.

"How is everything?" Their waitress stood beside the table, nodding at their untouched salads.

"Wonderful," Victoria said.

"Are you sure?" the girl asked. "Because—"

"Wonderful," Victoria said. "Thank you."

While Victoria had been speaking, Gert had been aware of restraining her emotions; in the pause created by the waitress's interruption, a flood of feeling rushed through her. Gert could distinguish three currents in it: relief, regret, and dread. The relief, sweet and milky as chai, was that her Auntie V could remain her Auntie V, that Gert would not have to hate her for an error she had made decades prior. The regret, sour as a rotten lime, was that her father had in fact betrayed her mother, that her and Web's elegant theory had been incarnated into sordid fact. The dread, blank as water, was that she had not yet heard the worst of Victoria's story, a groundless anxiety which, the instant she recognized it, she knew was true.

Some of what she was feeling must have been visible on her face, set loose by the alcohol she'd dropped into her empty stomach; it prompted Victoria to say, "Oh honey, I'm so sorry. This is too much, isn't it? Maybe we should change the subject, talk about the rest later."

Gert shook her head. "It's all right. I mean, it is a lot, but . . . go on, keep going. Tell me about the woman, the one my dad was with. What was her name?"

"Elsie Durant. Did I mention she was married? I did, didn't I?

She was a few years older than he was; I can't remember exactly how much, six or seven, something like that. Coming and going from my apartment, I kept an eye out for her, and managed to walk past her a couple of times. She was nothing special to look at: pointy nose, freckles, mousy hair that she wore up. About my height, big in the hips, not much of a chest. When I saw her, she was dressed for work, dark pantsuits that looked as if she'd bought them off the rack at Macy's."

"How did they meet?"

"At a convention out west, in Phoenix, I'm pretty sure. Your dad was looking to drum up clients for his business, which was only a thing on the side back then. She was a sales rep for one of the companies he was hoping to snag. When they met, it was as professionals, and that they both came from the same town was a coincidence to be exploited so he could continue his sales pitch. Their conversation led to drinks, which led to dinner, which led to more drinks, which led to her hotel room." Victoria shrugged. "You've attended these kinds of things, haven't you?"

Gert nodded.

"You know: a certain percentage of the attendees treat the event as an opportunity to hook up. It's like, while the cat's away, she's gonna play. If I were a sociologist, I'd do a study of it, try to work out the exact numbers.

"So your dad and Elsie started out as one more tacky statistic. They could've stayed that way if he hadn't called her the week after they returned from the convention—to follow up on the matters they'd discussed. Fair enough. He had a legitimate interest in securing this contract. It was just about enough to allow him to ditch his day job, and it was the kind of high-profile association that would put him on the map. Obviously, though . . ."

"His motives were ulterior."

Victoria smirked. "You might say that. I'm not sure if he knew that she was married, at first, but if he didn't, then he found out pretty soon. Her husband was a doctor, an endocrinologist at Mount Sinai. He was Polish, had immigrated when he was eighteen. In another instance of six degrees of separation, one of my friends was under his care for her thyroid. She said he was a great physician, but had all the personality of a pizza box."

"Did he know? About them?"

"I don't know. Your father insisted he must have, and it's hard to believe he didn't suspect something. Although, apparently he was a workaholic, out early in the morning, home late at night, busy weekends, so maybe he wasn't paying attention. Or could be, he was carrying on his own affair.

"To be honest," Victoria said, "there's a lot of this part of the story I have only the faintest idea of. The night your father called me, I wasn't especially interested in hearing the detailed history of his relationship with this other woman. Later on—when, I admit it, I was curious—encouraging him to revisit the details of his and Elsie's affair seemed less than a good idea. I have the impression that things were pretty intense, at first, but aren't they always? If you're in the situation, it's . . . its own thing, fresh, new; if you're outside looking in, it's a movie you've seen one too many times. He wanted her to leave her husband. She promised she would, then changed her mind. He threatened to go to her husband. She swore she'd never speak to him again if he did. Eventually, they settled into an unhappy routine. A couple of pleasant weeks would be followed by one or the other of them promising to break things off because of her marriage.

"After your father met your mother, he and Elsie didn't see one another for a while. Apparently, she was pretty pissed at him for becoming involved with somebody else. Hypocritical, yes, but what's that line about contradicting yourself? I don't know why he returned to her, and I cannot understand how he continued the affair once he was engaged, and then married, to your mother. I gather their encounters had slipped from regular to occasional, but even so . . ."

"You must have asked him about it," Gert said.

"Oh, I did. He told me he'd been in love with two women. He had been, but he'd decided to make a choice, and that was your mother."

"Do you . . ."

"Do I what? Think he was still in love with Elsie?"

"Yes."

"Your mother asked the same question," Victoria said. "She was obsessed with it. Of course your father had told her that she was the only woman he loved but really, what else was he going to say and have any chance of her not leaving him? This left it to me to hash out with her whether he was telling the truth."

"You told her he was."

"What else was I going to do? I knew that he loved your mother—that he loved you and your brother. If he and your mom could hang in there, gain some distance from what he'd done, I was sure they would work things out. Which they did," Victoria said, "more or less."

"You still haven't answered the question."

"You noticed that. Sweetie, I don't know what to tell you. I thought he was fixated on her, mostly because he'd been unable to have her . . . completely, I guess you could say. Because she'd remained with her husband. I tend to think that isn't love—it certainly isn't the same as what he felt toward your mother."

"But it could be as strong."

"It could."

"Obviously, Mom decided to stay with him," Gert said.

"She told me your father had chosen her, and that was enough. Maybe she believed it, too—maybe it would have been, if—"

"What? If what?"

Victoria answered by draining the remainder of her Bloody Mary. Her heart suddenly jumping in her throat, Gert brought her own glass to her lips. The alcohol eased her heart back into her chest, allowing her to repeat her, "What?"

"That first year was bad," Victoria said. "Your father spent months alternating between the couch—until your mom couldn't stand having him around, and ordered him out of the house—and a motel room—until your mom freaked out at the prospect of him there by himself and ordered him back to the house. There wasn't much I could do for him: when I phoned, your mom wanted to speak with me, and it wouldn't have worked for me to take him out somewhere. He had done wrong; it was his duty to suffer. Once in a while, I would stop over and find your mother out; then I would have a chance to talk to him. Not that there was much to say. Mostly, I asked him how he was doing and told him to hang in there, your mom still loved him.

"Which was the same thing I said to your mom: 'He loves you; he loves you so much; he's made a terrible mistake but he loves you.' Nights your dad was home to watch you guys, I'd take her out. There was a little bar down the road from the house you were living in, Kennedy's—we'd go there and order girly drinks and she could say whatever she needed to. What didn't help matters any was that your father hadn't stopped traveling. In fact, he was gone more. He'd won that contract with Elsie's company, and their association had had exactly the effect he'd expected. By the time he met your mom, he was worth a couple of million; by the time you arrived, that amount had tripled. But whatever the money his firm brought in, it wasn't enough. (I swear, how he found the *time* to carry on an affair, I'll never know.) For about a month after he came clean on Elsie Durant, your dad put that part of his life on hold, turned the day-to-day running of the firm over to his number-two guy. During that month, though, Number Two was on the phone to him at least three or four times a day, and in the end, he made the decision to return. I wanted him to sell the business, take the money and invest it, live off that, but that was a nonstarter."

Their waitress passing near, Victoria held up her glass.

"So . . . what?" Gert asked. "Was my father meeting this woman on his trips?"

"Not as far as Phil DiMarco could tell. Your dad went where he was supposed to, met with whom he was supposed to, and otherwise kept to himself. No clandestine meetings, phone calls, or postcards. His one indulgence was presents, mainly toys for you and your brother, although he also brought back things for your mom, sometimes. Most of it was jewelry, expensive but generic. Your dad's never had much taste when it comes to stuff like that; all your mom's nice jewelry is stuff I told him to buy for her. There was one thing he brought back for her, a little figure he found on a trip to, I think it was Utah of all places, that was kind of interesting. It was a copy of that statue, the Venus of Willendorf? It's this incredibly old carving of a woman, a goddess or fertility figure, or both, all boobs and hips. The copy had been done in this grainy stone, not sandstone but like it, coarser. It was just the right size to sit in your hand."

"Okay," Gert said, "I'm lost."

"Here you are." Their waitress placed a fresh Bloody Mary beside Victoria and removed the empty glass. "How is everything?"

"Wonderful," Victoria said. This time, the waitress did not pursue the matter, but smiled and departed. Looking over the rim of her drink, Victoria said, "By your third birthday, your parents were . . . I wouldn't say they were back to normal, but they were on the mend. Finally. And then, one afternoon, the phone rings. Your Mom picks it up, and there's a woman on the other end. Not just any woman: her, Elsie Durant."

"No."

"Yes. She said, 'My name is Elsie Durant. I know you know who I am. I'm sorry to call you, but I need to speak to your husband.'"

"What did Mom say?"

"What do you think? 'What the fuck are you doing calling here, you fucking bitch? Haven't you done enough?' She was so angry, she couldn't relax her grip on the phone enough to slam it down— which gave Elsie the time to say, 'Please. I'm dying.'"

"No."

"Yes."

"What kind of . . . ?"

"I know," Victoria said. "Your mother said the same thing, 'How stupid do you think I am?' But the woman was ready for her. She told your mother she'd sent a copy of her latest medical report to your parents' house, along with her most recent X-ray. Your mother would have it tomorrow, after which she could decide what she wanted to do."

"Which was?"

"To start with, she called me and asked me what I thought. I said she should forget she'd ever spoken to the woman and find out what she'd have to do to have her blocked from phoning them. What about the report, the X-ray? 'Don't even open that envelope,' I said. 'Take it out back to the barbecue and burn it.'"

"She didn't."

"She didn't. As I'm pretty sure Elsie Durant must have known, the lure of that plain brown envelope was too much. She tore it open, and learned that the woman who had been the source of so much pain in her marriage was suffering from glioblastoma multiforme. It's the most common type of brain cancer. It's aggressive, and there were fewer options for treating it then than I imagine there are now. The patient history included with the report revealed that Elsie hadn't sought out treatment for her headaches until the tumor was significantly advanced. As of this moment, she was down to somewhere between six weeks and three months, although three months was an extremely optimistic prognosis. When your mother held up the X-ray to the light, she could see the thing, a dark tree sending its branches throughout the brain."

Gert said, "She told him."

"She did. How could she not? That was what she said to me. 'How could I keep this from him? She's dying.' It was too much for her to keep to herself. I would lay money that bitch knew that was exactly how she'd feel."

"What happened? Did my father see her?"

"He spoke with her. Your mother told him everything, and when she was finished, he went to the phone and called her."

"What did he say?"

"I don't know. Your mom walked away—"

"She what?"

"She couldn't be there—that was how she put it to me."

Gert found her drink at her lips. There was less left in it than she'd realized. When the glass was empty, she said, "You must have asked Dad what they talked about."

"He wouldn't tell me."

"Why not?"

Victoria shook her head. "He wouldn't say anything. He just looked away and kept silent until I changed the subject. At first, I thought it might be too soon for him to discuss it, but no matter how much time elapsed, he wouldn't speak about it."

"What about Mom? Did he ever tell her?"

"She refused to ask him. She said if he wanted her to know, he'd tell her. I may be wrong, but I think he was waiting for her to ask him, which he would have taken as a sign that she had truly forgiven him."

"While Mom was waiting for him to come to her as a sign that he had truly repented."

"Exactly."

"Jesus." Gert searched for the waitress, couldn't find her. "How long . . . after she and Dad spoke, how long did Elsie Durant last?"

"Two weeks."

"Not long at all."

"No."

"How did they find out?"

"The obituary page in the *Times*," Victoria said. "I saw it, too, and let me tell you, I breathed a sigh of relief. As long as Elsie Durant was alive—not to mention, local—she was . . . I wouldn't call her a threat, exactly, but she was certainly a distraction. They could have moved, someplace out of state, but your father traveled as much as he ever had. With Elsie permanently out of the picture, I assumed your parents would be able to go forward in a way they couldn't have before—free, I guess you might say, of her presence. I had half a mind to drop in on her funeral, just to make sure she was gone.

"As it turned out, I got my wish."

"You were there?" As soon as the question had left her mouth, its answer was evident: "For my father: you went to find out if he went."

"Your mother was convinced he would attend. To be honest, so was I, especially after his silence about his and Elsie's final conversation. Of course, I didn't say this to your mom; to her, I said there was no way he'd be at the funeral. I mean, if nothing else, the woman's husband would be there, and wouldn't that be awkward? She didn't buy it. It was all I could do to convince her not to go, herself. 'For God's sake,' I said, 'stay home. Hasn't this woman had enough of your life already? Why give her anything more?' That had more of an effect on her, but in the end, I had to promise her that I would attend. If anybody asked, I figured I could pass myself off as a sympathetic neighbor."

"Did my dad—"

"Yes. Elsie Durant's funeral was held upstate, at St. Tristan's, this tiny church about ten minutes from the Connecticut state line. It was a pretty place, all rolling hills and broad plains. I don't know what her connection to it was. The church itself was small, much taller than it was deep, so that it seemed as if you were sitting at the bottom of a well. The windows . . . some of the stained-glass windows were old, original to the church, but others were more recent—replacements, I guess. The newer ones had been done in an angular, almost abstract style, so that it was if they were less saints and more these strange assemblies of shapes.

"Your father and I sat on opposite sides at the back of the church, which still wasn't that far from the altar. The funeral was a much smaller affair than I'd expected: counting the priest and the altar boys, there were maybe ten or eleven people there. The rest of the mourners sat in the front pews. There was an older man with a broad back who appeared to be the husband, a cluster of skinny women who were either sisters or cousins of the deceased, and a couple of nondescript types who might have been family friends. Honestly, I was shocked at how empty the church was. I . . . it sounds silly, but Elsie Durant had been such a . . . she had loomed over your parents' lives, their marriage, over my life, too—she had been such a presence that I had imagined her at the center of all sorts of lives. I had pictured a church packed with mourners— maybe half of them her illicit lovers, but full, nonetheless. I was unprepared for the stillness of . . . you know how churches catch and amplify each sob, each cough, each creak of the pew as you shift to make yourself more comfortable. That was what her funeral was to me, an assortment of random sounds echoing in an almost empty church.

"After the service was over, before they'd wheeled the coffin out, I snuck out and waited in my car. Not only did your dad shake Elsie's husband's hand—and say I can't imagine what to him—he accompanied the rest of the mourners as they followed the hearse on foot across the parking lot and into the cemetery. He stayed through the graveside ceremony, and after that was over, the coffin lowered into the ground, everybody leaving, he remained in place. He watched the workmen use a backhoe to maneuver the lid of the vault into place. He watched them shovel the mound of earth that had been draped with a green cover into the hole. Once the grave was filled, and the workers had heaped the floral arrangements on top of it, he held his position. Finally, I had to go: I hadn't been to the bathroom in hours, not to mention, I was starving. I left with him still standing there."

"He'd seen you—I mean, in the church."

"Oh yes," Victoria said. "We'd made eye contact as soon as I sat down, glanced around, and realized he was directly across from me. I blushed, as if he were the one catching me doing something wrong, which irritated me to no end. I kept my eyes forward for the rest of my time there—when I left, I stared at the floor."

"What did he say to you about it?"

"Nothing. We never discussed it."

"What? Why not?"

"I assumed he would call me; it was what he'd done before. And I was . . . frankly, I was too pissed off to pick up the phone, myself."

"Because he'd done what you thought he would."

"Yes. But—"

"You were afraid of what he might say if you did talk."

"All things considered, wouldn't you have been?"

"What did you tell Mom?"

"Pretty much what I said to you: that he'd been at the back of the church and I'd left before he did."

"Did you mention him standing at the grave?"

"She didn't need to hear that."

"I assume they never talked about it."

Victoria shook her head. "No. She knew, and he knew she knew, but neither wanted to make the first move. Your mother discussed it with me—for years. I would come over and we would sit at the dining room table—this was when you were in the house on Trevor Lane, the one with the tiny living room. However our conversation started, it always ended with her asking me what your father attending Elsie Durant's funeral meant. Needless to say, she was certain she knew what his presence in that back pew had implied. Well, that's not it, exactly: she was afraid she knew its significance. Who am I kidding? So was I. Not that I ever let on to your mom. To her, I said that your father hadn't been doing anything more than paying his respects. If he'd loved Elsie Durant that much, he never would have ended things with her; he wouldn't have elected to stay with your mom. All the while, I was thinking, *What, are you kidding me? Maybe he changed his mind after he called things off. Maybe he wasn't the one who ended the affair: maybe she did, and in a fit of pique, he made his confessions. Maybe—God help me—he was in love with two women at once.* The possibilities were . . . it would be an exaggeration to say that they were endless, or even that they were all that many, but they were enough.

"We would make our way through a bottle of red, repeating what had become a very familiar argument. Your mom would have the little statue—the souvenir your dad had brought her, the Venus of Willendorf—in one hand. While we talked, she'd turn it over in her palm—by the end of the night, her skin would be raw from the stone scraping it. On more than one occasion, that statue's pores were dotted with blood.

"After one of those conversations, I had a nightmare—years later, and I can recite it as clearly as if I'd sat up in my bed this very minute. Your mom and dad were standing in a dim space. It was your house—it was all the houses you'd lived in—but it was also a cave, or a kind of cave. The walls were ribbed, the gray of beef past its sell-by date. Your parents were dressed casually, the way they were sitting around the house on a Sunday. They looked . . . the expressions on their faces were . . . I want to say they were expectant. As I watched, each held out an arm and raked the nails of their other hand down the skin with such force they tore it open. Blood spilled over their arms, streaming down onto the floor. When enough of it had puddled there, they knelt and mixed their blood with the material of the floor, which was this gray dirt. Once they had a thick mud, they started pressing it into a figure. It was the statue, the Venus, and the sight of it sopping with their blood shot me out of sleep.

"You don't need to be much of a psychiatrist to figure out what my dream was about, although, given how your parents have been looking these past few years, I sometimes wonder if it wasn't just a little bit predictive. But I think about them—I have thought about them; I imagine I'll keep thinking about them—alone in that big house with that space between them, that gap they've had all these years to fill with their resentments and recriminations. Visiting them, there have been times I've been sure I could feel . . . I don't know what. A something there in the house with us. Not a presence—a ghost, no, I don't think they're being haunted by the spirit of Elsie Durant, but something else."

Gert thought of standing in the hallway looking at the door to her parents' room and not seeing anything there. She said, "What? What do you mean?"

Victoria said, "I don't know."

Returned at last, the waitress took Gert's empty glass and her request for another with an, "Of course." Once she had left, Gert sat back in her chair. "So that's it," she said. "The outline, anyway. Jesus Christ. If anyone had bothered to talk to anyone else . . . Jesus."

Victoria remained silent until after the waitress had deposited Gert's second drink on the table and Gert had sampled it. Then she said, "I understand, Gertie. When I arrange everything into a story, it seems as if it would have been so easy for the situation to have been settled with a couple of well-timed, honest conversations. But when I remember how it felt at the time—it was like having been dumped in the middle of the ocean. You were trying to keep treading water, to keep your head above the swells. If all of us had been different people, maybe we could have avoided this. . . . It's quite the clusterfuck, isn't it?"

"It's my life," Gert said, "mine and Web's. This . . . what happened . . . what's still happening . . ."

"I understand," Victoria said. "I'm sorry; I'm so, so sorry. I don't know what else to say. I tried—we all tried. But . . ."

"Sometimes that isn't enough," Gert said. "It's just—why? Why did they stay together?"

"I told you, sweetie: your mom and dad love one another. That's . . . I used to think the worst thing in the world was falling out of love with someone. Now, though, I think I was wrong. Sometimes, you can stay in love with them."

III

One week after her lunch with Aunt Victoria, well before she had come to terms with much, if any, of what they'd discussed—well before she'd shared the details of Elsie Durant with Dana—Gert found herself opening the front door to her parents' house. She had spent the day a few miles up the road, surrounded by the luxury of the Mohonk Mountain House, at which she'd been attending a symposium on estate law that seemed principally a tax cover for passing the weekend at Mohonk. While Gert could have stayed at the hotel—which would have allowed her to continue talking to the attractive young law student with whom she'd shared dinner and then an extensive conversation at the hotel bar—she had arranged to stay at her parents', whom she'd felt a need to see in the flesh since Aunt Vicky's revelations. That need, together with a sudden spasm of guilt over having spent so long in the company of another woman so clearly available when Dana was at home, working, sped her to the hotel's front portico, where a valet fetched her Prius without remarking the lateness of the hour. Her reactions slowed by the pair of martinis she'd consumed, Gert had navigated the winding road down from the mountain with her palms sweaty on the wheel; with the exception of a pair of headlights that had followed her for several miles, while she worried that they were attached to a police car, the drive to her parents' had been less exciting.

Now she was pushing the door shut behind her, gently, with the tips of her fingers, as she had when she was a teenager sneaking home well after her curfew's expiration. She half-expected to find her mother sitting on the living room couch, her legs curled under her, the TV remote in one hand as she roamed the wasteland of late-night programming. Of course, the couch was empty, but the memory caused Gert to wonder if her mother hadn't been holding something in her other hand, that weird little statue that seemed to follow her around the house. She wasn't sure: at the time, she had been more concerned with avoiding her mother's wrath, either through copious apologizing or the occasional protest at the unfairness of her having to adhere to a curfew hours earlier than any of her friends'. Had her mother been rolling that small figure in her palm, or was this an image edited in as a consequence of Auntie V's disclosures?

The air inside the house was cool, evidence of her father's continuing obsession with saving money. His micromanagement of the heating had been a continuing source of contention, albeit of a humorous stripe, between him and the rest of the family. Shivering around the kitchen table, Web and she would say, "You know how much you're worth, right?" which would prompt their father to answer, "And how do you suppose that happened?" to which Web would reply, "You took all those pennies you saved on heating oil and used them to call the bank for a loan?" at which he, Gert, and Mom would snort with laughter, Dad shake his head. Gert decided she would keep her coat and gloves on until she was upstairs.

Halfway across the living room, she paused. The last time she had stood in this space, the Christmas tree had filled the far right corner, its branches raising three decades' worth of ornaments, its base bricked with presents. Together, she and Dana, Web and Sharon,

Mom and Dad, had spent a late morning that had turned into early afternoon opening presents, exchanging Christmas anecdotes, and consuming generous amounts of Macallan-enhanced eggnog. It had been a deeply pleasant day, dominated by no single event, but suffused with contentment. *Except*, Gert thought, *that all the time, she was here with us. Elsie Durant. She watched Dana tear the wrapping from the easel Mom and Dad bought her. She sat next to me as I held up the new Scott Turow Web had given me. She hovered behind Sharon at the eggnog.*

Nor was that all. Elsie Durant had been present at the breakfast table while she, Web, and their mother had teased their father about his stinginess. During the family trips they had taken, she had accompanied them, walking the streets of Rome, climbing the Eiffel Tower, staring up at the Great Pyramid of Giza. As Gert had walked down the aisle at her high school graduation, Elsie Durant craned her neck for a better look; when Web's first film had played over at Upstate Films, she stood at the front of the line, one of the special guests. Every house in which they had lived was a house in which Elsie Durant had resided, too, as if all their houses had possessed an extra room, a secret chamber for their family's secret member.

A sound broke Gert's reverie, a voice, raised in a moan. She crossed to the foot of the stairs, at which she heard a second, louder moan, this one in a different voice from the first—a man's, her father's. Her foot was on the first stair before she understood what she was listening to: the noises of her parents, making love. It was not a chorus to which she ever had been privy; although Web claimed to have eavesdropped on their mother and father's intimacy on numerous occasions, Gert had missed the performances (and not-so-secretly, thought Web had, as well). Apparently freed of the inhibitions that had stifled them while their children were under their roof, her parents were uttering a series of groans that were almost scandalously expressive; as they continued, Gert felt her cheeks redden.

The situation was almost comic: she could not imagine remaining in place for the length of her mom and dad's session, which might take who knew how long (was her father using Viagra?), but neither could she see creeping up the stairs as a workable option, since at some point a stray creak would betray her presence, and then how would she explain that? After a moment's reflection, Gert decided her best course would be to play slightly drunker than she was, and parade up the stairs and along the hall to her room as if she'd this minute breezed in and hadn't heard a thing. Whether her parents would accept her pretense was anyone's guess, but at least the act would offer them a way out of an otherwise embarrassing scenario.

To Gert's surprise and consternation, however, the clump of her boots on the stairs did not affect the moans emanating from the second floor in the slightest. Unsure if she were being loud enough, Gert stomped harder as she approached the upstairs landing, only to hear the groans joined by sharp cries. *Oh come on*, she thought as she tromped toward her room. Was this some odd prank her parents were playing on her? They couldn't possibly be this deaf, could they?

She supposed she should be grateful to learn that her mother and father had remained intimate with each other, despite everything, despite Elsie Durant. Yet a flurry of annoyance drove her feet past the door to her bedroom, past the door to the bathroom, to the door to her parents' room, open wide. She had raised her hands, ready to clap, when what she saw on the big bed made her pause, then drop her hands, then turn and run for the front door as fast as her legs would carry her. Later, after a frantic drive home, that she had not tripped down the stairs and broken her neck would strike her as some species of miracle.

Of course, Dana would awaken and ask Gert what she was doing home, wasn't she supposed to be staying at her parents'? The smile with which Gert greeted her, the explanation that she had missed her lover so much she had opted to return that night, were triumphs of acting that brought a sleepy smile to Dana's lips and sent her back to bed, satisfied. *I am my father's daughter.* On top of the tall bookcase in her office, dust clung to a bottle of tequila that had been a gift from a client whose divorce Gert's management had made an extremely profitable decision. She retrieved it, wiped the dust from it, and carried it through to the kitchen, where she poured a generous portion of its contents into a juice glass. She had no illusions about the alcohol's ability to cleanse her memory of what she'd seen: the image was seared into her mind in all its impossibility; however, if she were lucky, its potency would numb the horror that had crouched on her all the drive back. At her first taste of the liquor, she coughed, almost gagged, but the second sip went down more smoothly.

IV

The streetlight that poured through the tall windows in her parents' room reduced its contents to black and white. The king-sized bed at its center was a granite slab, the figures on it statues whose marble limbs enacted a position worthy of the *Kama Sutra*. Startled as Gert was by her mother and father's athletics, she was more shocked by their skin taut against their joints, their ribs, their spines, as if, in the few weeks since last she had seen them, each had shed even more weight. In the pale light, their eyes were blank as those of Greek sculptures.

There seemed to be too many arms and legs for the couple writhing on the bed. Her father stroked her mother's cheek with the back of his hand, and another hand lingered there, brushing her hair behind her ear. Her mother tilted her head to the right, and another head moved to the left. Her parents arched their backs, and in the space between them, a third figure slid out of her father and into her mother with the motion of a swimmer pushing through the water. While her mother braced her hands on the mattress, the figure leaned forward from her and drew its hands down her father's chest, then turned back and cupped her mother's breasts. Her parents responded to the figure's caresses with a quickening of the hips, with louder moans and cries that might have been mistaken for complaints. In the space between her mother and father, Elsie Durant drew herself out of their conjoined flesh, the wedge that braced their marriage, the stone at its heart.

For Fiona

THE SIPHON

Laird Barron

Laird Barron is the author of two collections: *The Imago Sequence* and *Occultation*, both from Night Shade Books. His work has appeared in places such as *The Magazine of Fantasy & Science Fiction, Inferno: New Tales of Terror and the Supernatural, Lovecraft Unbound, Black Wings: New Tales of Lovecraftian Horror, Clockwork Phoenix*, and *The Del Rey Book of Science Fiction and Fantasy*. It has also been reprinted in numerous "year's best" anthologies. He lives in Olympia, Washington.

L ancaster graduated from college in 1973 and landed a position in the sales department of a well-known Wichita company that manufactured camping gear. He hated the outdoors but was naturally manipulative, an expert at affecting sincerity and bright-eyed chumminess of variable intensity. Despite this charm that wowed the socks off clients, he never made much headway with management or coworkers, two species immunized against snake oil and artifice.

Around Halloween of 1989, he accepted a job as a field representative with another Wichita firm called Roache Enterprises. His farewell party was attended by four department associates, a supervisor, and a custodian. The supervisor brought a single-layer white cake and somebody spiked the punch with bourbon. His boss projected an old staff picture on the slide panel—Lancaster isolated in the foreground, his expression a surprised snarl, uncomfortably reminiscent of the candid shot of an infamous serial killer who'd been electrocuted by the state of Florida earlier that year. Lancaster was better looking, much smoother, were such a thing possible.

The conference room was brown and yellow, the tables and chairs yellow, bleached by fluorescent strips. Later that institutional light would seep into Lancaster's dreams. The hum of the lights. The cake, a rib bone scalloped to the marrow. The lights. The hum. He dreamed of the two women he'd loved and left when he was young and reckless, before he'd matured and steadied, before he'd learned to maintain his great control. He dreamed how their pleas and imprecations were abruptly stilled, how their faces became empty as the buzzing moon.

He would awaken from such nightmares and grope for the special wooden box in its secret place in the dresser. The box represented that window into a brief, agonized segment of his early post-college years: the red blur he refused to examine except in moments of dire want. A small lacquered coffer, dead black with a silver clasp. Dead black and cool to the touch, always cool as if stored in refrigerator rather than a drawer. Lancaster needed the box, its contents, needed them with a fevered intensity because they fulfilled the hunger at his core, because the switch that had originally been thrown to motivate and necessitate his acquisition of these trophies clicked off as arbitrarily as it had been clicked on and with it his will to pursue, to physically enact his desires. Thus he'd sift through the box of treasures, move his lips in wordless naming of each precious trinket until his mind quieted. Until the humming of the fly in the mantle of the light ceased. Until the humming of the moon ceased and he could sleep again.

Roache Enterprises was founded in 1963 during the height of the Cold War when it manufactured guidance control systems for cruise missiles. Modern-era Roache retained 170,000 full-time employees around the globe. The company dealt in electronics, plastics, chemical engineering, asphalt, irrigation systems; sugar, rubber, and cotton plantations; data mining, modular housing, and a confounding array of other endeavors. The Roache brothers were five billionaires who'd retreated to South American compounds and the French Riviera. The public hadn't seen them—except for annual state-of-the-corporation recorded video addresses—in twenty years. A board of regents ran the show from headquarters in France, India, Scotland, England, and of course, Kansas.

Lancaster spent months abroad, jetting between continents. He'd married once, a union only a mayfly might've envied, which had resulted in a daughter, Nancy, now an adult living in Topeka whom he saw on Christmas and sometimes Easter. The rest of his family was scattered: father dead, mother living in a trailer park in Tennessee, and two sisters in Washington State whom he'd had no real contact with since college.

Incapable of love, its intricacies and necessities a mystery to him,
he was fortunately content with the life of a gentleman bachelor
and disappeared into the wider world. His job was generally one of
information gathering and occasional diplomacy—a blackmailer or
flatterer, depending upon the assignment. Charlatans were kings in
the corporate culture of Roache, a culture that was the antithesis of
the blue-collar aesthetic of his former company. Lancaster excelled
in this niche and Roache rewarded him accordingly. He possessed
apartments in Delhi and Edinburgh, and standing reservations at
luxury hotels in places such as Copenhagen, Paris, and New York.
He'd come a long way since peddling camp stoves and sleeping bags.

The National Security Agency reached out to Lancaster in 1991
while he vacationed at White Sands Beach, Hawaii. He was invited
aboard a yacht owned by the friend of the friend of a former client
who did business with Roache Enterprises on a piecemeal basis. The
yacht owner was named Harold Hoyte. Hoyte and his wife, Blanche,
a ripe and sensual ex-B-movie actress who'd starred under an assumed name in a couple of Russ Meyer's films, owned an import
business; this provided cover for their activities as senior operatives
of the Agency, the bulk of which revolved around recruitment and
handling.

They had dinner with two other couples on the deck of the
Ramses, followed by wine and pills and hideously affected slow-
dancing to Harold Hoyte's expansive collection of disco. Harold
went ashore, ostensibly to locate a couple of fellow revelers who'd
gotten lost on the way to the party, and Blanche promptly led Lancaster into the master suite and seduced him to KC and the Sunshine Band on a king-sized bed washed in the refracted shimmer of
a glitter ball.

Harold Hoyte made a pitch for Lancaster to join the NSA in the
wee hours of the morning as they shared the last joint and the dregs
of the scotch. Lancaster declined. A double life simply wasn't his
style. He told Hoyte he had a good thing going with Roache, and
who needed a poisoned umbrella tip jammed in one's ass, anyway?

Harold Hoyte smiled and said, no harm no foul. If he changed
his mind . . . And an unlabeled video cassette of Lancaster fucking
Mrs. Hoyte with theatrical flourishes soon arrived at the front desk
of his hotel. That a duplicate might anonymously find its way to the

Roache corporate offices was implicit. Roache was protective of its business associations large and small. They wouldn't take kindly to Lancaster's salacious escapades with the wife of a client, considering the ruin such an affair could bring to a lucrative contract were Mr. Hoyte to muster and bluster mock outrage at being cuckolded by a company representative. The Hoytes had caught him in the old honey trap. He didn't feel too angry—it was their field of expertise. Besides, spying might agree with him.

Three weeks later, he was officially an asset of the NSA. He soon learned that several colleagues at Roache Enterprises moonlighted for the government. The company had eyes everywhere the United States needed them. It added a new and unpredictable wrinkle to Lancaster's routine, although the life of an occasional spy didn't prove particularly thrilling. Certainly it resembled nothing of best-selling potboilers or action flicks. Mostly it came down to taking a few pictures, following strangers for a day or two, and occasionally smuggling a memory stick or something as low-tech as a handwritten code across international borders.

The upside was it motivated him to get into shape and take judo for a while—weren't spies supposed to know judo in case of a scrape? He'd watched the original *Manchurian Candidate* eight times, the version where Sinatra got into a knockdown drag-out fight with a foreign agent. To be on the safe side, he also bought a .38 automatic and got accurate with it at the range. He went unarmed abroad because of travel restrictions, but carried it almost everywhere while in the States. He continued to carry until his enthusiasm cooled and he stuck the gun in a shoe box and forgot it. Around then he also stopped attending judo classes.

The aughts passed.

Following a six-month lull of contact with the NSA, Lancaster received a call from his current handler, Tyrone Clack. Clack took over for the Hoytes when they sailed on toward retirement and their golden years back in 2003. All communications occurred via phone—Lancaster had never even seen a photo of the agent. Clack informed him that the Agency was interested in acquiring intelligence on a naturalized citizen named Dr. Lucas Christou. The good doctor, who'd been born in Athens and transplanted to the United

States during adolescence, was a retired chair of the anthropology department of some tiny school near Kansas City called Ossian University. He'd become reclusive since then, seldom appearing in public, content to withdraw from society to an isolated estate.

Christou emerged from his hermitage and would be hosting a foreign national named Rawat, a minor industrialist entering the United States on business with Roache. All that was required of Lancaster was to take the doctor's measure, get to know him a bit, soften him up for possible future developments. No further explanation for the Agency's interest was forthcoming and Lancaster didn't press. None of it titillated him anymore. He'd do as requested and hear nary a peep afterward. A typical, menial task. A mindless task, in fact.

Considering his superstar status as a professional schmoozer, the scheme didn't prove difficult. He returned to Wichita and manipulated events until a big cheese at Corporate asked him to pretty please entertain a small party that had come to town for a tour of a cluster of empty corporate properties outside the city: strip mall–style office buildings that had been hastily built, then left in quasi-abandonment.

The guests included the potential client, Mr. Rawat and his American companion, Kara, and a bodyguard named Dedrick; the Cooks, a moneyed New York couple who'd previously partnered on land deals with Mr. Rawat; and, of course, Dr. Christou.

All of this was explained by Vicky Diamond, an administrative assistant to the Big Cheese himself. Ms. Diamond was a shark; Lancaster noted this first thing. Youngish, but not really, dark hair, dark eyes, plenty of makeup to confuse the issue, a casual-chic dresser. Lancaster thought she smiled so much because she liked to show her teeth. She handed him dossiers on the principals—Mr. Rawat and the Cooks—and suggested an itinerary. He appreciated how she put her fingerprints on the project without overcommitting. Should things progress smoothly, she'd get much of the credit. If the sales pitch tanked, Lancaster would find himself on the hook. He liked her already.

The group met on Friday morning for breakfast at a French café, followed by a carefully paced tour of downtown landmarks. Lunch was Italian, then onward to the Museum of Treasures and a foray to quaint Cowtown, which delighted the Cooks and, more importantly, Mr. Rawat, and was at least tolerated by the others.

Lancaster had slipped Cowtown into the schedule simply to tweak Ms. Diamond as he suspected she'd fear the excessive display of Midwest provincialism. Judging from the glare he received, his assessment was on the mark. He'd softened the blow by reserving one of six tables at a tiny, hole-in-the-wall restaurant that served authentic Indian cuisine rivaling anything he'd tasted in Delhi or Mumbai. Mr. Rawat was a cool customer in every sense of the word. Elegant in his advancing years, his black hair shone like a helmet, his aged and hardened flesh gleamed like polished wood. His watch was solid gold. Even the goon Dedrick who lurked in the background, ready to intercept any and all threats, was rather classy via proximity with his long, pale hair and black suit and fancy eyeglasses that slotted him as a burly legal professional rather than a bodyguard.

Mr. Rawat raised a glass of Old Monk to Lancaster and tipped him a slight wink of approval. Dining went into the nine o'clock hour, after which they repaired to the historic and luxurious Copperhill Hotel and made for the lounge, a velvet and mirrored affair with double doors open to the grand ballroom.

Everything was going exactly as Lancaster planned until Dr. Christou and Mr. Rawat began discussing world folklore and demonology with a passion that turned heads at nearby tables. This vein was central to Dr. Christou's studies. He'd published numerous works over the course of four decades in academia, the most noteworthy a treatise called *The Feral Heart*, which documented cases of night terrors and the mythology of the living dead in the Balkans and the Greek Isles. Mr. Rawat had come across the book shortly after its publication in 1971 and written a lengthy letter taking the professor to task for his fanciful reportage. This initiated what developed into a lifelong correspondence and apparently adversarial friendship.

Dr. Christou was broad through his shoulders and chest. His large head was bald except for a silvery fringe, and his mustache and beard were white streaked with black. He wore a vintage suit and three rings—two on the left hand, one on the right. He drank copiously:

Canadian Club. *These days a proper Greek drinks scotch, but as a culture-strapped American, a Canadian import will suffice.* Lancaster couldn't help but notice he resembled the bluff and melodramatically distinguished actors who populated Saturday night horror features of yesteryear—a physically imposing relative of Christopher Lee. The doctor said to Mr. Rawat, "I don't pretend to know the truth, my friend. There are cracks in the world. These cracks are inhabited by . . . marvels undreamt of in our philosophies."

"We have known each other for an age," Mr. Rawat said. "and I am still uncertain where the truth ends and the bullshit begins with you."

"I think the subject of night terrors is fascinating," Mrs. Cook said. She and her husband were slightly younger than Mr. Rawat and Dr. Christou, around Lancaster's age, a year or two shy of senior discounts and social security checks. The couple were gray and heavyset, habitual tans as faded as ancient tattoos. Mr. Cook wore a heavy tweed jacket, and his wife a pattern dress and pearls that were slightly behind modern fashion. She'd drunk her share of gin and tonic.

"Francine majored in literature," Mr. Cook said, gesturing with his tumbler of Johnnie Walker Blue. "The classics—Henry James, Wilde, Mencken, Camus, Conrad. *That* lot."

"Actually, I prefer Blackwood and Machen during the proper season. When the leaves are falling and the dark comes early and stays. 'The Horla,' by Maupassant. There's a fine one regarding sleep paralysis and insanity."

"A demon that creeps into the bedchamber and squats upon its victim's chest. That particular legend is prevalent in many cultures," Dr. Christou said.

"An oldie, but a goodie," Lancaster said, beginning to feel the weight of his liquor. Ms. Diamond slashed him with a look.

"And thoroughly debunked," Mr. Rawat said. "Like déjà vu and near-death experiences. Hallucinations, hypnagogic delusions. Nothing sinister. No sign of the numinous, nor the unholy for that matter."

"You were so much more fun as a lad," Dr. Christou said, smiling.

"I come by my skepticism honestly. There was a time I believed supernatural manifestations possible. Lamias, *vorvolakas*, lycanthropes, the Loch Ness Monster—"

"Rakshasa."

"Yes, *rakshasa*. UFOs, spoon bending, levitation, spontaneous combustion—"

"Spontaneous erections!"

"What, you don't believe in *rakshasas*?" A sallow, pinch-faced man in a white jacket at the adjoining table leaned forward and partially across Lancaster so the others could hear him. His tie dipped into Lancaster's mostly empty glass of Redbreast. The man was of indeterminate age and smelled of first-class cigarettes and designer cologne. His skull was oddly pointed and hairless, dull flesh speckled with liver spots. He'd styled his mustache into a Fu Manchu. "Sorry, sorry. How rude of me. I'm Gregor Blaylock. These are my comrades Christine, Rayburn, and Luther. My research team." The trio of graduate students were handsome and smartly dressed—the men in jackets and turtlenecks, the woman in a tunic and skirt. Both men were lean and sinewy; sweat glittered on their cheeks. The woman wore bright red lipstick. Her dark skin was flawless. She stroked Mr. Blaylock's shoulder, a pairing of youth and age that was eerily congruous to that of Mr. Rawat and his escort Kara.

Dr. Christou laughed and stood to shake hands. "Gregor! Good to meet in person at last. What great coincidence has brought us together?"

"Oh, you know there are no coincidences, Lucas."

Ms. Diamond quickly made further introductions as the men pushed the tables together so the newcomers might join the festivities. Lancaster wasn't certain of the new peoples' nationalities. Even listening to Mr. Blaylock speak proved fruitless to solving that riddle. Perhaps Asian heritage and a European education accounted for the man's exotic features and the flattening of his accent. It was odd, very odd. Evidently, Mr. Blaylock was also an anthropology professor, and another of Dr. Christou's legion of fans and correspondents, but details weren't forthcoming, just the gibberish of mutual recollection that left all save its intimates in the fog. He finally gave in and said, "If I may be so bold, where are you from? Originally, that is."

Mr. Blaylock said, "Why, I was born here. We all were born here." He inclined his head to include his companions. Something in the curl of his lip, his archness of tone, indicated *here* didn't necessarily refer to Kansas or the heartland, but rather the continent, if not the world itself. So Mr. Blaylock was that smug species of academic who delighted in double entendre and puns. Asshole. Lancaster drained his whiskey, masking a sneer.

Ms. Diamond pressed against Lancaster as a spouse might and muttered, "What the hell are you doing?" She maintained her pearly shark smile for the audience.

"It's a fair question," Mr. Blaylock said, as if he'd somehow overheard the whisper. "Mr. Lancaster, you've been around the block, yeah?"

"I've heard the owl hoot," Lancaster said. "And the Sri Lankan Frogmouth, too."

"I hear you. You Limeys speak your minds. You're inquisitive. No harm. I approve."

"Not *much* harm," Ms. Diamond said.

"You are exceedingly generous, Mr. Blaylock. But I'm American."

"Oh, yeah? Odd. You must spend loads of time on the Island."

Dr. Christou said, "Our kind patron heard a Frogmouth hoot. Have you seen a *rakshasa*, perhaps?"

"Not in Kansas," Mr. Blaylock said.

"What's a *rakshasa*?" Mr. Cook said.

"It's a flesh-eating monster from Indian mythology, dear," Mrs. Cook said. "There are packs of them roaming about in classical Indian literature, such as the *Mahabharata*."

Dr. Christou said, "I've not encountered one, either, nor do I know anyone with firsthand knowledge. However, in 1968 I visited a village on the Greek island of Aphra and interviewed the locals, including a Catholic priest, who were thoroughly convinced *vorvolakas* stalked them. The priest showed me a set of photographs taken by a herdsman that were rather convincing."

"Ha! The ones in *The Feral Heart* were far from convincing, old friend. Very, very far."

"Certainly the lighting was poor. Sunset, so the contrast of light and darkness was jarring. Of course, shrinking them down to fit the page also compromised the quality."

"Was there a creature in the pictures? How exciting," Mrs. Cook said.

"Eh? You haven't read his *famous* book?" Mr. Rawat said.

"In fact, yes. I read books for the words, not the pictures."

"There were at least four creatures, actually," Dr. Christou said. "The shepherd spied them emerging from a crypt in the hills at dusk. The man was on a bluff and they glared up at him. Horrifying once you realize what you're dealing with, I assure you."

"The goat herder took a picture of *something*," Mr. Rawat said. "To settle the matter, the film should be sent to a laboratory and analyzed."

"Alas, that is impossible," Mr. Christou said. "I returned them to the priest after they were copied into the book. The village was abandoned in 1970, its inhabitants scattered along the mainland. What became of the herdsman or the film remains a mystery."

"Rubbish," Mr. Rawat said. "I've studied the photos a million times. Our nameless shepherd captured images of youthful vagabonds. Perhaps grave robbers at rest, if one is inclined toward drama."

"No mystery about the missing film," Mr. Blaylock said. "When the Greek government repatriated the villagers to the mainland I'm sure such materials were confiscated or lost. You mentioned a priest—perhaps the Church spirited away the evidence for secret study. Too convenient?"

"Too conspiratorial, I'd think," Lancaster said. "Most of the tinfoil hats amongst the clergy were exiled to the fringes by the seventies, were they not?"

"You are familiar with the Eastern Church?" Mr. Rawat said, raising an eyebrow.

"There was this girl I met in Athens who'd gone astray from ecclesiastical upbringing in a big way. She gave me the history lesson. The infighting and intrigue, the conspiracies."

"I bet," Ms. Diamond said.

"Life is full of little conspiracies," Dr. Christou said, and looked at Mr. Blaylock. "Imagine running into *you* here of all places. I thought you lived in British Columbia."

Mr. Cook said, "What were those other critters you mentioned earlier? A *vorvo*-something?" He sounded bored.

"*Vorvolakas*," Mr. Rawat said.

"*Vorvo*-whatsit?"

"Blood-sucking undead monster from Greek mythology, dear,"

Mrs. Cook said. "There are scads of them in the old writings of the Eastern Church."

"There's also that Boris Karloff movie," Mr. Rawat said. He smiled coolly and sipped his rum. "You can watch the whole thing on the Internet. I'm certain my esteemed colleague has done so in the name of research."

Lancaster said, "Val Lewton's film. Scared me pantless when I was a wee lad. What a great old flick."

"I like you more and more. *Yia mas!*" Dr. Christou knocked back yet another Canadian Club.

"Val Lewton," Mr. Cook said, his glazed eyes brightening. "Now you're talking. My dad owned a chain of theaters. Lewton was a hell of an auteur, as the kids say."

"Oh, honey." Mrs. Cook smiled with benign condescension and patted her husband's cheek so it jiggled. "Val Lewton? Really? Goodness."

"Hellenic vampire tradition is quite rich," Mr. Christou said. "The damned rise from their graves—day or night—and creep through villages, rapping on doors, tapping on windows, imitating the cries of animals and children. It is said one must never answer a door after dark on the first knock."

Mrs. Cook said, "As I understand it, Grecian vampires are actually more akin to shape changers. Lycanthropes and what have you."

"Quite right, dear lady! Quite right!" Dr. Christou said. "The Balkan wars led to a minor usurpation by the Slavic vampire myth of the Greek antecedent. Or, I should say, a co-option, though who ultimately co-opted whom is open to debate. Ah, you would've been a much brighter assistant than the clods I was assigned on my expeditions. And lovelier to boot!"

"Oh, hush, Doctor," Mrs. Cook said, casually patting her hair as she cast about for the waiter. "Seriously, although you're the expert, doesn't it seem plausible that these legends—*rakshasa*, the lycanthropes and vampires, the graveyard ghouls, the horrors of Dunsany, Moses, and Lovecraft, are variations on a theme?"

"If by plausible you mean impossible," Mr. Rawat said.

"Certainly," Mr. Blaylock said. "And a hundred other beasties from global mythology. Each iteration tailored to the traditions and prejudices of individual cultures. However, as Mr. Rawat so elegantly declared, it's rubbish." He smiled slyly. "Except for ghosts. The existence of ghosts is a theory I can get behind."

There were more rounds of drinks accompanied by tales of werewolves, vampires, and other things that went bump in the night. An orchestra appeared and began to play classics of the 1930s. The Cooks ventured unsteadily onto the dance floor, and gallant Mr. Rawat escorted Ms. Diamond after them—she, ramrod stiff and protesting to no avail. Mr. Rawat's continental chauvinism doubtless nettled her no end.

Lancaster excused himself to visit the restroom. He pissed in the fancy urinal and washed his hands and dried them on a fancy scented towel. He checked his watch in the lobby, decided to risk a few moments away from the party, and ducked into the stairwell and lighted a cigarette. Moments later Mr. Blaylock and Dr. Christou barged through the door, drinks in hand, Dedrick hot on their heels, a pained expression replacing his customary stoicism. Dr. Christou and Mr. Rawat immediately lighted cigarettes. Both smoked Prima Lux. "Ah, great minds!" the doctor said, grinning at Lancaster, who covered his annoyance with a friendly mock salute.

A few minutes later, cigarettes smoked and drinks drunk, everyone headed back to the table. Lancaster did the gentlemanly deed of holding the door. Dr. Christou hesitated until the others had gone ahead. He said in a low voice, "I confess an abiding fondness for Boris Karloff and Val Lewton. Anyone who holds them dear is first class by my lights." The doctor leaned slightly closer to Lancaster, scorching him with whiskey breath. "In recent years I've become convinced the priest of Aphra was duped by the shepherd. Those cemetery photographs were surely a hoax. Which is a damned shame because I think there truly was an extraordinary event occurring in that village." He laid his very large hand upon Lancaster's shoulder. This drunken earnestness would've been comical except for the glimmer of a tear in the corner of the aged scholar's eye. "Please extend my apologies to our fair company. That last drink was a bridge too far. I'm off to my quarters."

Lancaster wondered if the evening could possibly become more surreal. He watched in bemusement as the big man trundled away and boarded an elevator.

He returned to the ballroom where Ms. Diamond sat alone at

the table. She watched the others dance, her mouth sullen. He sat next to her and, feeling expansive from the booze, said, "I have a bottle of twelve-year-old scotch back at the château." His blue eyes usually had an effect on women. He was also decently muscled from a regimen of racquetball and swimming. He assiduously colored the gray from his expensively styled hair, and all of this combined to smooth the rough edges of advancing age, to create the illusion of a man in his late forties, the urbane, chisel-jawed protagonist of sex-pill commercials rather than a paunchy playboy with stretch marks and pattern baldness sliding into the sunset years. But Ms. Diamond was having none of it.

"I think you also probably have a dozen STDs," she said. "Half of them exotic and likely incurable by fire."

"Well, I don't like to brag," he said.

The group dispersed, shuffling off to their respective rooms, and Lancaster shook the hands of the men and kissed the hands of the ladies—Kara's skin tasted of liquor, and Mrs. Cook's was clammy and scaly and bitter. He glanced at her face, and her eyes were heavy-lidded, her thick mouth upturned with matronly satisfaction at his discomfort.

Lancaster hailed a cab and made it to his town house a few minutes after 2 A.M. Nothing spectacular—two bedrooms, a bathroom with a deep whirlpool tub and granite everything, and a kitchen with wood cabinets and digital appliances. In the living room, lush track lighting, thick carpet, and a selection of authentic-looking Monet and Van Gogh knockoffs, a half dozen small marble sculptures imported from Mediterranean antique shops, a gas fireplace and modest entertainment center, and, of course, a wet bar tucked opposite bay windows with a view of the river.

He wasn't in a steady relationship. His previous girlfriend, a Danish stewardess twenty-five years his junior, had recently married a pilot and retired to "make babies," as she put it in the Dear John e-mail. He dialed the escort service and asked for one of the girls he knew. The receptionist informed him that person was unavailable, so he requested Trina, a moderately attractive brunette who'd stayed over a few months back, and this time he was in luck, his Girl Friday would be along in forty-five minutes. He dropped his coat into an oversized leather chair, hit the remote to dim the lights, a second time to ignite a romantic blaze in the hearth, and once more to summon the ghost of Jeff Healey through speakers concealed behind a pair of African elephant statuettes.

The drink and Ms. Diamond's dragon lady glare had worked him over. That and the bizarre dinner chatter and the raw emotion flowing from ponderous Dr. Christou. Lancaster brought forth the special box, currently hidden upon a shelf inside a teak cabinet that housed his cigars and collection of foreign coins. Tonight he needed to gaze within the box, to drink it with his eyes, to satiate the nameless desire that welled from his deepest primordial self.

He sat for a while in the thrall of conflicting emotions. The ritual calmed him less than usual. He shut the box and returned it to its cubby. His breath was labored.

Cigarette in one hand, a fresh glass of scotch sweating in the other, he sank into the couch and closed his eyes. The doorbell went *ding-dong!* and his eyes popped open. The glass was dry and the cigarette had burned perilously near his knuckle. He set the glass on the coffee table and crushed the cigarette in the ashtray. At the door it occurred to him the bell had only rung once, and it bothered him somehow. He peered through the spy hole and saw nothing but the empty walk, yellow and hazy under the streetlamp light. The doorknob throbbed with a low-voltage current that tingled momentarily and vanished.

He opened the door and Trina the Escort popped up like a jack-in-the-box, still fumbling with a compact that had slipped from her stylish red-lacquer handbag. She wore a slick black dress and had dyed her hair blond since their last encounter. "Hiya," she said, and caught his tie in the crook of her finger as she stepped past him from the dark into the light. As the door swung closed, a breeze ruffled his hair and he shivered, experiencing the unpleasant sensation that he'd forgotten something important, perhaps years and years ago. His brain was fairly pickled and the girl already slid out of her dress, and the strange unease receded.

When they'd finished, Trina kissed his cheek, dragged on their shared cigarette, then briskly toweled herself and ducked into the bathroom. He dialed her a taxi and lay in the shadows listening to the shower, the edge off his drunkenness and succumbing to

exhaustion as he recalled the faces of his dinner guests—Dr. Christou's haunted eyes, Mr. Blaylock's predatory smile, and Mr. Rawat
cool and bland even as he dissected and debated. The others ran
together, and uneasiness crept back in as his damp flesh cooled, as
the red numerals of the alarm clock flickered in a warning. The girl
reappeared, dressed, perfumed, and coifed with a polka-dot kerchief. She said she'd let herself out, call her again any time. He
drifted away, and—

Ding-dong! He sat up fast, skull heavy. Only three or four minutes had passed, yet he was mostly anesthetized from the alcohol
and overwhelming drowsiness. He waited for the next ring, and as
he waited a chill seeped into his guts and he thought strange, disjointed thoughts. Why was he so nervous? The vein in his neck
pulsed. Trina must've forgotten something. He rose and went to the
door. As he turned the deadbolt, he experienced the inexplicable
urge to flee. It was a feeling as powerful and visceral as a bout of ver-
tigo, the irrational sense that he would be snatched into the darkness,
that he would meet one of Dr. Christou's unknowable marvels lurking in the cracks of the earth.

Trina stepped back with a small cry when he flung the door open
and stood before her, sweat dripping from his torso. A taxi idled on
the curb. She regained her composure, although she didn't come
closer. "Forgot my cell," she said. Dazed, he fetched her phone. She
extended her hand as far as possible to snatch the phone. She hus-
tled to the taxi without a good-bye or backward glance.

The canopy of the trees across the street shushed in the breeze,
and fields littered with pockets of light swept into the deeper gloom
like the crown of a moonlit sea. The starry night was vast and chill,
and Lancaster imagined entities concealed within its folds gazing
hungrily upon the lights of the city, the warmth of its inhabitants.

Lancaster was not an introspective man, preferring to live an
inch beneath his own skin, to run hot and cold as circumstances
required. Fear had awakened in him, stirred by God knew what.
Imminent mortality? Cancer cells spreading like fire? The Devil
staring at him from the pit? Momentarily he had the preposterous
fantasy that this primitive terror wasn't a random bubble surfacing
from the nascent tar of his primordial self, but an intrusion, a virus
he'd contracted that now worked to unnerve and unman him.

Whatever the source, he was afraid to stand in the tiny rectangle of light that faced the outer darkness. That darkness followed him into sleep. The gnawing fear was with him, too. The dark. The hum of the stars.

Lancaster arranged for a limousine driver named Ms. Valens to pick the party up in front of the hotel after lunch the next day. He suggested a helicopter for speed, but Dr. Christou had an aversion to flying in light aircraft—a train-and-bus man, was the good doctor. Mr. Rawat and the Cooks were traveling to the airport that evening immediately following the tour of the corporate property, so the chauffeur loaded their luggage, which included Mr. Cook's pair of golf bags and no less than five suitcases for Mrs. Cook. Lancaster chuckled behind his hand at Ms. Valens's barely concealed expression of loathing as she struggled to heft everything into the trunk while Ms. Cook tutted and tsked and the muscular Dedrick stood impassively, watching nothing and everything at once.

The two-hour drive was along a sparsely traveled stretch of secondary highway that lanced through mile upon mile of wheat fields and sunflower plantations. The sky spread black and blue with rolling storm clouds, and crows floated like gnats beneath the belly of a dog. Light distorted as it passed through the tinted windows and filled the passenger compartment with an unearthly haze.

Lancaster and Ms. Diamond poured champagne from the limousine bar: A glass to celebrate surviving their hangovers, Lancaster said. Dr. Christou took his with a couple of antacid tablets, and Kara refused, covering her mouth with exaggerated revulsion. The others finished the magnum of Grand Brut with the diffidence of draining a bottle of spring water. Lancaster had seldom witnessed such a tolerance for booze except when playing blackjack with the alkie barflies in Vegas backwaters during his wild and woolly college days. He checked the stock to estimate whether it would last until he got his charges onto the plane. It was going to be close. Ms. Diamond's eyes widened when she met his, and he felt a smidgen of uncharacteristic pity for her distress.

Mr. Rawat took a sheaf of blueprints and maps from his gold-clasped leather briefcase and spread them across his knees. Mr. Cook and Ms. Diamond sat on either side of him. Their faces shone with the hazy light reflected from the paper. Lancaster's eyeballs ached. The scenery slid past like a ragged stream of photographic frames. He pondered the previous evening's gathering at the hotel. Mrs. Cook winked and knocked his knee under the table. Mr. Blaylock grinned, minus an eyetooth, and Christine, the voluptuous vamp, stroked Blaylock's shoulder, her nails denting the exquisite fabric of his dinner jacket. Luther and Rayburn were a blur, unimportant. Mr. Cook drank with the methodical efficiency of a man who'd rather face the scaffold than another day with his wife, and he smiled with the same superficial cheer as Ms. Diamond did— probably a reflexive counter to deeper, darker impulses. Mr. Rawat debated Dr. Christou with a passion reserved for a lover, while foxsharp Kara looked on with jaded boredom, and Lancaster wondered how close the men might actually be and perhaps, perhaps the NSA thought to use them against each other, to leverage a clandestine affair, and damn, this trip might actually prove interesting. Lancaster snapped out of it. His sunglasses disguised the fact he'd dozed for a few moments, or so he hoped.

They arrived at the property, several acres of single-story, hi-tech buildings fronted by immaculately trimmed lawns and plum trees. The office sectors were divided by access lanes, the whole complex erected in the middle of nowhere, an island on an ocean of grain. A groundskeeping truck inched along about a quarter of a mile down the frontage road. Workers in orange jackets paced it on the sidewalk, blasting away with leaf blowers.

No sooner had her feet touched the pavement, Ms. Diamond launched into a rehearsed spiel, subtly leading Mr. Rawat, Dedrick, and the Cooks by the collective nose toward the nearest wall of glass. She unlocked a set of doors with a key card and they walked inside. Meanwhile, Kara squinted at the changeable sky and fussed with the brim of her hat while Dr. Christou stood in the shadow of the car, rubbing his skull and muttering. Lancaster called the catering company, gained assurances the team would arrive on schedule. Ms. Diamond had reserved tables at a restaurant in a town several miles away. He knew she'd underestimated the softness of this particular group—such people couldn't go five or six hours without food and booze, couldn't go without being waited upon hand and foot; so he'd hired one of the finer outfits in the city to prepare dinner and truck it to the site at approximately the time he figured the tour would be wrapping up.

"Had enough, have you?" Dr. Christou said. "Of our chums, I mean."

"Ms. Diamond has them in hand. I couldn't very well abandon you or the lovely Kara, could I?" Lancaster lighted a cigarette. The "lovely" Kara had retreated into the limousine. He suspected she was raiding the olives. Poor dear was emaciated.

"I'd say you are more preoccupied keeping tabs on me than helping your colleague net that big-fish pal of mine."

"You're happy, Mr. Rawat is happy. Or am I wrong?" Lancaster said, thinking fast, wondering if the doctor was cagier than he appeared. "I'm here to make certain everyone has as nice a trip as possible." He gestured at the surrounding plains. "Got my work cut out for me. This is the kind of land only a farmer or Bible salesman could love."

"I have a theory. It's the land that makes people crazy, not their superstitions. Consider fundamentalist Islam and fundamentalist Christianity—then look around. Look at all this emptiness under a baleful fireball. Add a few uneducated peasants to the equation and voilà. Petri dish for lunacy."

"Amber waves of grain far as the eye can see, and me without a drop of milk. . . ."

The big man nodded, still rubbing his skull. "I knew a fellow in Tangier during my callow and malleable youth. French Intelligence, retired. He *claimed* to be retired. A lovely, older man; quite affable, quite accommodating, charmingly effete. He always dressed in a suit and smoked Gauloises Brunes. Kept a little black pistol in his dresser at the hotel—a Walther, as I recall. He spoke of enemies from the old days. You remind me a bit of him."

"Except I don't have enemies. As to the, ahem, French connection, my mother claims we are descended from the Huguenots—but isn't that a socially acceptable variation of the asylum nuts claiming to be Napoléon reincarnate?"

The grounds crew stopped across the way. There were seven of them. They lighted cigarettes and leaned against their truck or sprawled in the grass and drank water from milk jugs. A young Mexican god shaded his eyes with his hand and smiled at Lancaster.

The Mexican's shoulders were broad and dark as burnt copper and his black hair fell in ringlets to his nipples. His chest and stomach rippled with the musculature of a bull. He unsnapped the cap on a jug and poured water over his head, a model pimping it hard in a rock video, and whipped his hair in a circle. Water flew everywhere. His teeth were white, white.

Dr. Christou followed Lancaster's stare. He sighed and lighted a cigarette of his own. "I always enjoyed a cherry pipe. Had to quit— too *de trop* for a professor, chewing on a pipe stem. Damnable shame. You understand the power of perception, of course. I've accrued a fine, long list of enemies. My work is eccentric enough without piling on cliché. Ah, how I loathe those fuckers in admin."

Lancaster laughed, unbalanced by Christou's sortie and disliking the sensation intensely. He said, "An amazing coincidence, running into your colleague last night."

"Indeed. Blaylock wasn't . . . He wasn't as I expected him to be. We've corresponded for years. I thought . . . Well, goes to show, doesn't it? How meager our understanding of the human heart."

"Only the shadow knows."

"What a chestnut! Is that how you get through life, Mr. Lancaster? A sense of detachment and an arsenal of wry witticisms?"

"I'm not the best at small talk."

"Nonsense—that's why they sent you. You are an *expert* at small talk, a maestro at manipulating the inconsequential to your design. I'm hardly offended—fascinated, rather."

The clouds kept rolling and the light changed and changed, darkening from red and orange to purple, and a damp breath moved across the land, but it didn't rain. The air was supercharged and Lancaster tasted a hint of ozone. "Here comes the dinner wagon," he said, as a van with a corporate logo departed the main road and cruised toward them.

"The irony is, my connections are retired or passed on," Dr. Christou said. "We've gotten old. If revolutionaries live long enough they become the establishment. The reef incorporates all discrete elements."

"Honestly, doctor, I don't know what the hell you're talking about."

"Right, then. For the record, you're wasting taxpayer money on me. Any information I've got isn't worth a drachma on the international market. Unless this is about revenge. Perhaps someone simply wishes to discredit me, to ruin my life's work."

Lancaster wasn't certain how to respond. Possibly the man was dangerous; perhaps he possessed contacts within some intelligence agency and had obtained Lancaster's files, maybe he knew the game. He kept his emotions in check, paid out a bit of rope. "Kind of paranoid, yeah? It's late in the day to achieve much by destroying you, isn't it, doc?"

"There are those who can be relied upon in their pettiness. You tell whomever it is, this isn't worth their effort." Dr. Christou drew on his cigarette butt. He knocked on the limousine window glass, coaxing Kara to emerge. Lancaster keyed the caterers into the central office, superintending their deployment and beachhead in the largest conference room he could find. As the team spread tablecloths and arranged the dinnerware, the overhead lights flickered and hummed and Lancaster stood with his cell flipped open, his brain in neutral.

"This place is spooky," Kara said, hipshot against the edge of the nearest table. She popped a cocktail shrimp into her mouth. Her little black magpie eyes blinked, blinked. "I hate empty buildings. This place goes for miles. Just a bunch of endless hallways. Almost all the lights are off. It feels like somebody's going to jump at me from the shadows. I dunno. Silly, huh?"

"Not so much," Lancaster said, marshaling his strength to play the part. He patted her arm, mostly to comfort himself. He suppressed his anxiety and phoned Ms. Diamond and informed her supper awaited. There was a long, chilly silence before she thanked him and said her group would be along shortly.

The meal was passable by elitist standards: overdone beef Wellington and too-bony Alaska king salmon. Lancaster's choice of vintage Italian wines and two chilled bottles of Chopin mollified the party. He stopped after one drink, his stomach knotted, shoulders bunched with rising tension. His guests were more than happy to drain the liquor—even Kara had overcome her squeamishness to hoist a glass of white wine. Mr. Rawat entered the proceedings wearing a dour expression matched only by Ms. Diamond's, but after five or six shots of vodka he melted somewhat and began to joke with Dr. Christou. Meanwhile, the Cooks were inscrutable in their lukewarm affability, nibbling at the finger foods and consuming glasses of wine with impressive efficiency.

One of the caterers approached Lancaster with an apologetic nod and asked if he was expecting more company. Lancaster asked why, and the man said someone had buzzed the intercom at the entrance. He'd assumed a member of the party had gotten locked out, or the limo driver . . . Nobody was at the door. It was getting dark and some of the lights in the parking lot weren't on, so he wasn't able to see much. Lancaster didn't know Ms. Valens's number; he called the home office and got it from a secretary in human resources, then dialed the driver, intending to ask if she'd happened to see anyone on the grounds near the entrance. The call went straight to voice mail.

"A problem?" Ms. Diamond said as she sidled close, knifing him with one of her fake smiles. "And thank you ever so much for cutting me off at the knees by cancelling our reservations at a first-class restaurant in favor of your little picnic stunt."

"They seem to be happily stuffing their faces," he said with his own contrived smile of collegiality. "No problem. The caterer thought someone was at the door. I'm checking with Ms. Valens now." Until that instant he'd toyed with the notion of asking Dedrick to make a parking lot sweep, dissuaded by the fellow's cold-fish demeanor and the suspicion he wasn't the type to run errands for anyone other than his master, Mr. Rawat. Lancaster pushed away from the table and turned his back on Ms. Diamond, went into the deep gloom of the hall, trailing his hand for a light switch. The front office was also murky, ankle-high illumination provided by a recessed panel of track lights in the baseboard paneling. The effect was spooky, as Kara said.

The night air lay cool upon his skin, tickled his nostrils with the scents of dust and chaff. A lone sodium lamp shone in an adjoining lot, illuminating itself and not much else. He approached the limo and noticed the chassis slightly shifting upon its shocks, and as his eyes adjusted he discerned pants and a jacket discarded near the driver-side door, and several empty pocket-sized liquor bottles gleaming in the starlight upon the asphalt. Ms. Valens straddled the young Mexican god as he sprawled across the hood. His giant's hands were on her ass, her fancy cap turned backward on his head.

Lancaster sparked his lighter. They stared at him, drawn by the flame. "Don't mind me," he said, and lighted a cigarette. They didn't.

"What's going on out there!" Ms. Diamond said. Her voice carried from the entrance where she held the door as if afraid to venture forth. She sounded as melodramatic as an actress in a Quaker dress and bonnet, clutching her throat as she scanned the plains for a sneaking Comanche. "Lancaster, where the devil are you?" she said.

"Coming," he said, and chuckled. He tapped his watch at Ms. Valens and walked away.

Ms. Diamond awaited him and they stood for a few moments in the unlighted office, listening to the loud voices and laughter from the conference room. She said, "Good thing it's time to go—the booze is *finito*. Have you seen Kara? The supermodel."

"Oh, that one," he said.

"You haven't been hitting the vodka hard enough to play the drunk asshole card. Got to hand it to you, Lancaster, this has turned into a cock-up. Those bastards aren't buying it. Rawat's not interested in this land. I dunno what the deal is with the Mr. Howell and Lovey. You're supposed to be the sweet-talker, but your head isn't in the game. Now that silly bitch has taken a powder. Anyway, she's mooned over you all day. Sweet little bulimic doe."

"No need to waste charm since you're not trying to sell *her* any swampland. She was binging on hors d'oeuvres, last I saw. Might be a long ride back to the city."

"Where the hell has she gotten to?"

"Likely in the john commencing the purging stage of the operation," he said.

"No, I looked. Would you mind checking down the hall—bet she's somewhere doing a line or having a crying jag or what-the-fuck-ever. I've got to herd my sheep toward the exit before they start bleating in an insane frenzy of DTs."

"Sure," he said, regretting it in the same breath. Kara had uttered a true statement: the halls were dark, dark. She wouldn't have ventured into them alone, not with her apparently sincere apprehension. He located a central bank of dials in an adjoining passage and fiddled with them until a few domes winked on. Mercifully, each door was locked and he satisfied his obligation to search for the woman with a knock and a half-hearted inquiry—yoo-hoo, in there, lady? No? Moving on, moving on, even as the walls tightened like the throat of a cave burrowing into bedrock. His sweaty hand made it increasingly difficult to grasp door handles. He felt liquor in the wires of his brain, but he hadn't drunk enough, Ms. Diamond had noted it rightly, so why this haze, this disorientation?

Inside the employee break room, she lay in a fetal position on a table. A water cooler bubbled in the corner. The refrigerator door was ajar and its white, icicle-chill light shone over her naked legs, white panties, and slip. Her upper body curved away, her face hidden in the sweep of hair. He slapped the wall switch and the overhead light flashed once and went dead. He approached and bent toward her still form.

She shuddered violently and raised herself on one elbow and laughed. Her arm unfolded like a blade. She seized his collar, pulled his face to hers. She kissed him hard with the taste of cold metal and all he could see was the refrigerator shivering in her eye, his own eye shivering in her eye. His eye rolled, rolled. This wasn't Kara. The dimness had tricked him. "Be glad those lights didn't come on," Christine said, sounding different than he'd expected— she hadn't spoken once during cocktails the previous evening at the hotel as she hung on Mr. Blaylock's arm. Her voice was hoarse. "I suppose you're wondering why I've called you here," she said. A certain fluidity suggested multitudes beneath her skin. "The service door was open, by the way. That's how we got in."

"You killed small animals as a child, didn't you?" Mr. Blaylock said. He stood before the gaping refrigerator, backlit so his face was partially hidden. Lancaster recognized the man's voice, his peculiar scent. Mr. Blaylock soothed him. "That's how it begins. Don't be afraid. It's not your turn. Not tonight. Really, you've been dead for years, haven't you?" And to his left, past a door frame that led yet farther into the heart of the complex, more figures crowded. Presumably Mr. Blaylock's acolytes from the dinner party.

Lancaster pulled free from Christine's clutches. She spoke gibberish to him, lips and the sound from her lips moving asynchronously. He wheeled and plunged into the hall, blundered without sight or thought toward the conference chamber and the reassurance of a crowd. His mouth hurt on the inside. The caterers were already gone, leaving the room as antiseptic as they'd found it. The guests milled, awkward and surly in the absence of entertainment.

"Finally you appear!" Ms. Diamond said through her teeth. "Don't believe in answering your phone. Damn it and hellfire, Lancaster! The natives are restless. We need to move on out."

"Yeah, can we just go already?" Kara pressed tight against Mr. Rawat, wheedling in a daddy's-little-girl tone. Her white cheeks were blotched pink. Lancaster's tongue ached and he tried to recall what he'd meant to say, why those two disturbed him. Hadn't he gone searching for her? The possibility seemed more remote by the second. He pressed a napkin to his lips, stemming the blood flow, his short-term memory erasing itself like a tape under a magnet.

He followed at the tail of the procession toward the parking lot. He glanced over his shoulder. A figure watched him from the darkened hallway. It slipped backward and vanished. Then he was letting the door close, a gate shutting on a sepulchre, and a few moments later he couldn't recall why the taste of adrenaline mixed with the mouthful of wet copper.

The limousine and its running lights floated on the black surface of the night road. Farther on, the skyline of the city glowed like a bank of coals. Lancaster thought of his town house, the cold comfort of his large television and well-stocked bar, his firm bed, the expert and clinical charms of his high-dollar call girls. A voice whispered to him that he might not ever again step across the threshold. Blood continued to trickle from his tongue and he swallowed frequently.

Ms. Diamond's knee brushed his own; her hands were primly folded in her lap. She smiled a glassy smile of defeat. Mr. Rawat lolled directly across the way, eyes closed. Kara's cheek rested against the breast of his jacket. The Cooks reclined a few inches over, nodding placidly with the swaying of the car. Dedrick was in front, riding shotgun, hidden by the opaque glass.

Dr. Christou said to Mrs. Cook, "What do you mean, Francine? The land itself can possess sentience? The Great Father of the Native Americans writ in root and rock?"

"Yes," said Mrs. Cook. "Yes, that is exactly what I mean. Vortexes, dolmens, ley lines, sacred monoliths, massive deposits of crystal and other conducting minerals."

Dr. Christou shrugged. "How do you envision these anomalies affecting the larger environment—human society?"

"The natives amplified them with ceremonies and the construction of corresponding devices. Some acolytes yet perform the ancient rituals in the name of . . . various entities. Places of power become more powerful." The dome light was on. Mrs. Cook stared into the mirror of her compact. She patted her nose. "There's an ancient gridwork across this landscape. A scar. You can't feel it? How it plucks at you, siphons a tiny bit of your very life force? No, you can't. My disappointment is . . . Well, it's profound, Doctor. Profound indeed."

"But *you* can feel it," Dr. Christou said. He averted his gaze, grimacing, a man who'd gotten the scent of something rancid and might vomit.

"Yes. Yes! Why else would I let hubby-kins drag me to Kansas of all benighted places?"

Mr. Cook sneered. "I don't give a tinker's damn for office property, only that its foundation lies upon the rim of a vast, primordial wheel. We, this speck of a vehicle, travel across it like a flea on the back of an elephant."

"You see, my good doctor, we've done our homework. The old races made a number of heroic excavations." Mrs. Cook had applied a lot of powder. Her face was ghastly pale, except her lips, which resembled red earthworms. "Those excavations are hidden beneath the shifting stones and the sunflowers and the wheat. Yet they endure and exert significant force. A million bones ground to dust, a lake of blood leeched down, down into the earth, coagulated as amber. This good earth buzzes with a black radiation. Honey and milk to certain individuals."

"Right on," Mr. Cook said, idly adjusting his silvery ascot. He licked his lips at Mrs. Cook as she snapped shut the compact.

"Besides the Serpent Intaglio, I'm unaware of any geoglyphs in this region. Even if these geoglyphs of yours exist . . . Comanche, Arapahoe, Kickapoo, Kaw . . . None of them were terraformers on the scale you suggest." Dr. Christou was rubbing his skull again. A red splotch grew livid on his brow.

"Not the new tribes," Mrs. Cook said. "Rather the civilizations that ruled here when this continent was still fused to Asia."

"Back, back, back," Mr. Cook said. "Only two continents in those days. Plus the polar caps. A wee bit before our time, admittedly."

Lancaster surfaced from his own disjointed thoughts and began to process the exchange. Cold bright recollection smashed through his mind, a dousing of ice water, although he only experienced the visceral epiphany in the abstract, unable to comprehend the nature of its import. He said with practiced and patently false calmness, "Mr. Rawat, how did you come to learn of the Roache property? Someone brought it to your attention. Your investors, or someone in your employ? You have a department devoted to mergers and acquisitions."

Ms. Diamond casually dug an elbow into Lancaster's ribs. Mr. Rawat opened one eye. "Byron and Francine. They prepared a prospectus."

"Byron and I were vacationing in Portugal," Mrs. Cook said. "The three of us happened to stay at the same hotel. One thing led to another, and another . . ."

"We became fast friends," Mr. Rawat said.

"Bosom buddies," Mr. Cook said, staring directly and unblinkingly at Lancaster. What had Ms. Diamond called him? Mr. Howell from *Gilligan's Island*. Yeah, there was an uncanny resemblance here in the shifty gloom.

Lancaster glanced from the Cooks to Dr. Christou. "Last night, who started that conversation about monsters?" He knew even before anyone answered that his assumption Mr. Rawat or Dr. Christou chose the topic was in error. They'd merely carried it along. He remembered kissing Mrs. Cook's hand the previous evening, its repellent flavor of sweet, rotting fruit and underlying acridness. She'd been inside his mind before that, though, been inside all of their heads, that was her power. Even now her likeness floated in his waking mind, whispering to him how it was, how it would be. A river of blood, the sucking of living marrow—

Mrs. Cook's bright smile widened. "*Monsters* fascinate me to no end." She leaned forward and grasped Dr. Christou's thigh as if propositioning a would-be lover. "We've read all of your books, Doctor."

"We've come a long way for this," Mr. Cook said. "There are some friends we'd like to introduce to you."

Dr. Christou's face slackened. He made an inarticulate sound from the back of his throat. Finally, he mastered himself and said to Lancaster, "Do you understand what's happening? My God, Lancaster. Tell me you understand."

Lancaster hesitated and Mrs. Cook cackled, head thrown back, throat muscles bunching.

Mr. Cook glanced out the window, then at his watch. "Oh, my. They're waiting. I almost dared not hope . . . On with the show." He loosened his tie.

The limo slowed and halted at a lonely four-way crossroads overseen by a traffic light dangling from a wire. The light burned red. A sedan was parked at an odd angle in the approaching right-hand lane, hazards flashing. A man and a woman dressed in evening clothes stood nearby, blank and stolid, awaiting rescue, perhaps. Lancaster squinted; the couple seemed familiar. As the limo began to roll forward through the intersection, Ms. Diamond said, "My God." She pressed the intercom button and ordered Ms. Valens to pull over.

"Wait, don't do it," Dr. Christou said with the affect of a man heavily medicated, a man who'd chosen to give warning in afterthought when it was far too late.

"It's them." Ms. Diamond was already on her way out of the car and briskly walking toward the other motorists. Her heels clacked on the asphalt.

"What's going on?" Mr. Rawat said, annoyed.

"Who are those people?" Kara said. Her face was sleepy and swollen.

Mr. Cook reached up and killed the dome light. From the shadows he said, "Victoria's parents. They burned alive in a car crash. 1985. She has lived alone for so long."

"Uh-uh," Kara said. "That's Casey Jean Laufenburg and her brother Lloyd. I went to high school with those guys."

"Did they burn in a car accident, too?" Dr. Christou said.

"Worse. Casey Jean's in retail. It's awful." She gazed at Mr. Rawat imploringly. "Can we please keep going? Why do we have to stop?" She sounded fully awake and afraid.

"Don't you want to say hello to your chums?" Mr. Cook said. "And you, doctor. Aren't you just positively consumed with fascination? This is how it happens. A lonely road at night. You come across someone familiar . . . an old friend, a brother, a sister, the priest from the neighborhood."

Mrs. Cook said, "It could be anyone, whomever is flitting around your brain. Here's the darkness, the haunted byway. Here in your twilight, you get to be part of the legend."

"That's enough booze for you, ma'am," Lancaster said with forced cheer. Mrs. Cook released Dr. Christou and grasped Lancaster's forearm in a soft, almost effortless fashion that nonetheless reduced his resistance to that of a bug with a leg stuck on a fly strip. She opened herself and let him see. He was bodiless, weightless, sucked like smoke through a pipe stem toward a massive New England–style house. He was drawn inside the house—marble tiles, sweeping staircases, bookcases, paintings—and into the master bedroom, the wardrobe, so cavernous and dim. An older couple were bound together in barbed wire. They dangled from a ceiling hook, their corpses liver-gray and bloodless, unspun hair dragging against the carpet. Eyes glazed, jaws slack. The real Cooks had never even made it out of their home.

The image collapsed and disintegrated and Lancaster reconstituted in the present, Mrs. Cook's fingers clamped on his arm. He wrenched free and flopped back into his seat, strength drained. He said to Dr. Christou, "I think we've been poisoned." Someone had spiked the liquor, dosed the food with hallucinogens to soften the group, to break them down. Lancaster had read about this, the government experiments on Vietnam soldiers, the spritzing of subways with LSD in the 1970s. Mind control was the name of the game. "Doctor, this may be . . ." Lancaster shook his head to clear it, trying to decide exactly *why* an oppositional force would want to drug them. "It's a kidnapping." The motive seemed shockingly obvious—ransom. This carload of rich people tooling along the countryside could represent a payday for a suitably prepared criminal. He pressed the intercom and said, "There's a situation. Something's happening."

The glass whisked down and Dedrick swiveled in his seat. "Yes?"

"I believe we're under attack. Please get Ms. Diamond. Drag her if necessary. Ms. Valens, the minute they're in the vehicle get us the hell out of here."

"Excuse me," Mr. Rawat said, his reserve cracked, a raw nerve of terror exposed in his rapid blinking. Doubtless he'd seen his share of violence back in the homeland and was acutely aware of his vulnerability. "Mr. Lancaster, what do you mean we're under attack? Dedrick?"

Dedrick's stony countenance didn't alter. "Sir, please wait." He made no further comment while exiting the limo and striding toward Ms. Diamond and friends. His right hand was thrust inside his jacket. Mr. Rawat appeared shocked and Kara retrieved a baggie from her purse. She dry-swallowed a handful of parti-colored pills. Surprisingly, in the face of fear she kept quiet.

Lancaster squirmed around until he managed to get a view from the rear window of what was happening outside. He simultaneously opened his cell phone and dialed the Roache security department and requested a detail be dispatched to the location at once. He considered alerting his handler Clack of the situation, except in his experience communication with the NSA office was routed through multiple filters and ultimately reached an answering machine instead of a human being 90 percent of the time. It seemed a bad sign that the Cooks were unconcerned that he'd summoned the cavalry. Something great and terrible was descending upon this merry company of travelers. He said, "Who are you working for?"

"The Russians," Mr. Cook said.

"The Bulgarians," Mrs. Cook said. "The Scythians, the Picts, the Ostrogoths, the wicker-crowned God Kings of Ultima Thule. The Martians."

"Mrs. Cook and I serve the whims of marvelous entities, foolish man," Mr. Cook said. "The ones inhabiting the cracks in the earth as the doctor is so fond of opining."

That sounded like some kind of terrorist group to Lancaster. "Why here? Why not at the office where there'd be privacy?"

The Cooks exchanged blandly malevolent glances.

Dr. Christou mumbled, "Because we are near a place of power. A blood sacrifice requires a sacred foundation."

"Or a profane foundation," Mrs. Cook said.

"Like sex magic, the journey is half the fun." Mr. Cook's grin shone in the gloom.

"Really, you don't want to know the who, how, and why," Mrs. Cook said. "Alas, you will, and soon. We procure and thus persist."

"Yes, we persist. Until the heat death of the universe."

"Procure," Dr. Christou said in a monotone. His flesh seemed to be in the process of deliquescing. Blood beaded on his forehead, squeezed in fattening droplets from the pores and rolled down his cheeks. Blood leaked from the corners of his eyes. Blood trickled from his sleeve cuffs and dripped in his lap. "Procure, what do you procure?"

Lancaster recoiled from the doctor. He had visions of anthrax, a vial of the Ebola virus, or one of a million other plagues synthesized in military labs the world over, and one of those plagues secreted in a handbag, a golf bag, wherever, now dosed into the food, the water, the wine, this virulent nastiness eating Dr. Christou alive. On a more fundamental level, he understood Christou's affliction wasn't any plague, manmade or otherwise, but the manifestation of something far worse.

"My goodness, doctor, they *are* eager for your humor to draw it at this distance," Mr. Cook said, gleeful as a child who'd won a prize. He pretended to pout. "I was promised a taste. Gluttons!"

"Go on, sweetie," Mrs. Cook said. "There is more than enough to spare."

Mr. Rawat said, "My friend, my friend, you're hurt!" He extended his hand, hesitated upon thinking better of the gesture.

The Cooks laughed, synchronized. A quantity of Dr. Christou's blood was drawn in gravity-defying rivulets from where it pooled on the seat, first to the floorboard, then vertically against the window where it formed globules and rotated as if suspended in zero gravity. Mr. Cook craned his neck and sucked the globules into the corner of his mouth. "If ambrosia tastes so sweet upon a mortal tongue, how our patrons must crave it as that which sustains them!"

There was a thunderclap outside and a flash of fire. Ms. Diamond ran toward them. Her left high heel sheared and she did a swan dive onto the road. Dedrick also sprinted for the limo, moving with the grace and agility of a linebacker. He hurdled the fallen woman and blasted another round by twisting and aiming from under his armpit. Lancaster couldn't see the gun, but it had an impressive muzzle flash.

The mystery couple pursued on hands and knees, clothes shredded to reveal slick, cancerous flesh illuminated in the red glare of the traffic light. Their true forms unfolded and extended. The pair approached in a segmented, wormlike motion, and the reason why was due to their joining at hip and shoulder. Their faces had collapsed into seething pits; blowtorch nozzles seen front on, except spouting jets of pure black flame. In that moment Lancaster realized what had been leeching Dr. Christou from afar.

As this disfigured conglomeration encroached upon Ms. Diamond, she convulsed in a pantomime of making a snow angel against the pavement. A heavy, wine-dark vapor trail boiled from her, and was siphoned into the funnel maws of the monstrous couple. She withered and charred. The others crawled atop and covered her completely.

The passenger compartment filled with the sour odor of feces. Mr. Rawat screamed and when Kara realized what was happening outside, she screamed, too. The gun cracked twice more, then Dedrick was in the front seat and bellowing for Ms. Valens to drive, drive, drive! and the chauffeur floored it while Dedrick's door was still open.

Lancaster didn't have the wits to react to the knife that appeared in Mr. Cook's hand. He gaped dumfounded while Mr. Cook nonchalantly reached out over his seat back and grasped Ms. Valens's hair and sliced her throat neat as could be. However, Dedrick continued to prove quite the man of action. He reached across Ms. Valens's soon-to-be corpse and took the wheel and kept the vehicle pointed down the centerline as he poked his large-bore magnum pistol through the partition and fired. The bullet entered Mr. Cook's temple and punched a papier-mâché hole out the opposite side of his head. The report stunned and deafened Lancaster, who raised his arms defensively against the splash. A chunk of bone and hair caromed from the ceiling, splatted against Dr. Christou's jacket breast, and clung like a displaced toupee. Now blood was everywhere—fizzing from Dr. Christou, misting the window in gruesome condensation, spurting from the chauffeur's carotid artery, gushing from Mr. Cook's dashed skull, filling Lancaster's mouth, his nostrils, everywhere, everywhere.

Mrs. Cook ended Dedrick's heroics. She grasped the barrel and jerked and the gun exploded again, shattering the rear window. She made her other hand into a claw and gently raked drab, blue-painted nails across his face. One of his eyes burst and deflated, and the meat of his cheeks and jaw came unstitched as if kissed by a serrated saw blade, and his face more or less peeled away like a decal. The man dropped the gun and pitched backward and out of view.

More blood. More blood. More screaming. It was chaos. The limousine left the road, bounced into the ditch, and plowed a ragged line through a wheat field. The occupants were violently tossed about, except for Mrs. Cook, who sat serene as a *padishah* on her palanquin.

The car ground to a halt. The passenger door opposite Lancaster opened and Mr. Blaylock stood there in an evening suit. He said to Mrs. Cook, "Chop chop, my dear. Dark is wasting." He bowed and was gone.

Mr. Cook's dagger had flown from his hand and lodged in the plush fabric of the seat between Lancaster and Dr. Christou. Lancaster caught his balance and snatched the knife, and it was heavy and cruelly curved and fit his hand most murderously. He stabbed it like an ice pick just beneath Mrs. Cook's breast. The blade crunched through muscle and bone and slid in to the hilt where it stuck tight. He tried to climb through the broken rear window. She cackled and clutched his ankle and yanked him to her as a mother retrieving her belligerent child. She kissed him and life drained from his limbs and he was paralyzed, yet completely aware. Completely aware for the hours that followed in the dark and desolate wheat field.

When it was over.

It would never be over. Lancaster knew that most intimately.

But when it was over for the moment, he walked to the lights on the road, pushed through the rough stalks, occasionally staggering as his shoe caught on a furrow. Police car lights. Fire truck lights. The blue-white spotlights of low-cruising helicopters. The swinging and crisscrossing flashlight beams of the cops trolling the ditches. Roache had pulled out the stops.

He walked deep into the dragnet before somebody noticed that a civilian, pale as death in a blood-soaked suit, wandered amongst them.

The police whisked him directly to a hospital. Physically he was adequate—bumps and bruises and missing the tip of his tongue. Rather hale, all considered. The shrink who interviewed him wasn't convinced of Lancaster's mental stability and prescribed pills and a return visit. The police questioning didn't prove particularly grueling; nothing like the cop shows. Even Roache was eerily sympathetic. Company reps debriefed him regarding the car accident and promptly deposited a merit bonus in his bank account and arranged a vacation in the Bahamas. He didn't protest, didn't say much beyond responses to direct questions, and these were flat, unaffected and ambiguous. He shuffled off to the islands, blank.

Following an afternoon that was one long stream of poolside martinis and blazing sun, Lancaster stumbled back to his hotel room and saw a man lounging in the overstuffed armchair by the bed.

"Hi, I'm Agent Clack, National Security Agency. We've chatted a few times on the phone." Agent Clack propped his feet on the coffee table. He smoked a cigarette. Gauloises.

The irony wasn't lost on Lancaster. "What are you, a college sophomore?" He walked to the bar and poured a vodka, pausing to gesture if his guest wanted one.

Agent Clack waved him off. Indeed, a young man—thirty, tops. Pretty enough to model for a men's catalog, he styled his wiry black hair into an impressive Afro. He dressed the part of a tourist: a flower print shirt, cheap camera slung around his neck, khaki shorts and open toe sandals. Lithe and well-built as a dancer, danger oozed from him, "aw, shucks" demeanor notwithstanding. "They like 'em young at HQ. But I assure you, my qualifications are impeccable. Had to snuff three dudes to get the job, kinda like James Bond. Jack Bauer is a pussy compared to yours truly. You're in good hands. Enough about me. How you holding up?"

"Am I being charged?"

"You responsible for the massacre? My bosses don't think so. Neither do I. We're looking for answers, is all."

Lancaster shrugged and drank his vodka. "Did you find them?" He looked through the window when he asked, staring past the brilliant canopy of umbrella-shaded tables in the courtyard to the blue water that went on and on. "I told the cops where. The best I could remember. It was dark."

"Yeah, we found the victims. Still hunting the murderers. They seem to have evaporated." Agent Clack took a computer memory stick from his shirt pocket. "There are hundreds of pics on here. Satellite, aerial, plenty of close-ups of the action, well, the aftermath, in the field. It's classified, but . . . Wanna see?"

"I was there."

"Right, right. Still, things look a lot different from space. It's kinda weird, though, that you were taken from the isolated Roache property. I mean, the remote offices were an ideal setup for a prolonged torture-murder gig."

Lancaster thought of the disc of blackened earth he and the rest had been dragged to, a clearing the diameter of a small baseball diamond in the heart of the farmland, thought of what lay some yards beneath the topsoil, the subsoil, and the bedrock; an ossified ridge that curled in a grand arc, the spine of a baby ouroboros, a gap between jaws and tail. He still smelled the blood and piss, the electric tang of pitiless starlight, the nauseating stench of his own terror. He said, "That dead ground, nothing has ever grown there. I imagine the Indians avoided it during their hunts, that the white farmers tilled around it and called it cursed. It's older than old, agent. A ground for bloodletting. Places like it are everywhere."

"I don't give a shit about Stone Age crop circles. Who was behind the kidnapping. What was the motive. I'll let you in on a secret—we got nothing, man. No claims or demands from terrorist groups, no chatter, nada. That isn't how this goes. We *always* hear something."

"Motive? There's no motive. The ineffable simply *is*."

"The ineffable," Agent Clack said.

"The Cooks are in league with . . ."

"With who?" Agent Clack raised a brow.

"Evil."

"Get outta here."

"Abominations that creep along the byways of the world."

"The big E, huh? Er, yeah, sure thing. I'm more into the concept lowercase e, the kind that lurks in the hearts of men. Anyhow, it wasn't the Cooks you were entertaining. The real Cooks were murdered in their home several days before the incident in Kansas. But you knew that."

"Yes. I was shown."

Agent Clack blew a smoke ring. "And these other individuals. Gregor Blaylock and his entourage. The grad students . . ."

"Let me guess. Victims of a gruesome demise, identities stolen to perpetrate an elaborate charade." Lancaster smiled, a brittle twitch.

"Not quite that dramatic. Guy's nonexistent. So are his assistants. Our records show he, *someone*, corresponded with Christou over the years, but it's a sham. There's a real live prof named Greg Blaylock and my guess is whoever this other guy is, he simply assumed that identity as needed. It's a popular con, black market brokers fixing illegals up with American citizens' social security cards. Could be a dozen people using the same serial number, sharing parallel identities. Not too hard. Blaylock and Christou hadn't actually met in person before that night. So."

"Blaylock's a cultist, a servitor. He was on the killing ground as a master of ceremonies. He . . . Blaylock coupled with Mrs. Cook while the nightmares fed on my companions, one by one." Lancaster poured again, swallowed it quickly. Poured another, contemplated the glass as if it were a crystal ball. "Everybody was after Christou. The monsters liked his books. What about you and your cronies? Was he a revolutionary? Bomb an embassy back in the sixties?"

"That's eyes-only spy stuff, grandpa. I'll tell you this: the geezer mixed with politically active people during his career. The kind of dudes on no-fly lists. He was once a consultant for the intelligence services of our competitors. Quid pro quo. Those bodies we examined . . . That was beyond, man. Way, way beyond. All the blood and organs removed. Mutilation. Looked like the victims were burned, but the autopsies said no. A brutal, sadistic, and apparently well-plotted crime. Yet the hostiles let you walk. There's a mystery my superiors are eager to get solved. Help me, man. Would ya, could ya shed some light on the subject?"

A sort of hysterical joy bubbled into Lancaster's throat. Yes, yes! To solve the ineffable mystery would be quite the trick. Certainly, Agent Clack despite his innocent face and schoolboy charm was cold and brutal, had surely seen and done the worst. Yet Lancaster easily imagined the younger man's horrified comprehension as the most vile and forbidden knowledge entered his bloodstream, began to corrode his shrieking brain with its acid. His lips curled. "Mrs. Cook called, a horrible sound unlike anything I'd ever heard, and three of the . . . *things* that attacked Ms. Diamond in the road shambled from the darkness and dragged us away, far from the limo and into the fields. Mr. Rawat, Kara, and their bodyguard were alive when they were dumped into the center of the clearing. The bodyguard, Dedrick . . . despite his horrible wounds. All of them were alive, Agent Clack. Very much alive. Dr. Christou, too, although I could hardly recognize him beneath the mask of blood he wore. The blood was caked an inch thick and the fresh stuff oozed around the edges."

"I'm sorry you had to go through that. I still don't understand how we missed you out there. The wheat is only four feet tall." Agent Clack sounded more fascinated than sorry.

"I don't know how it was done. But it was. Black magic, worse."

"So, what happened? Exactly."

Lancaster hesitated for a long moment. "Eyes only, agent. My eyes only."

"Now, now, codger. You don't wanna fuck with the man with the shiny laminated picture I.D."

"The others were drained. Drained, Agent Clack."

Agent Clack dropped his cigarette butt on the carpet and ground it to bits under his heel. He lighted another and smoked it, expression obscured by the blue haze. Finally, he said, "Alrighty, then. The investigation is ongoing. You'll talk, sooner or later. I've got time to kill."

"There are unspeakable truths." Lancaster closed his eyes for a long moment. "It pleased them to spare me in the name of a venerable cliché. Clichés contain all truth, of course. The purpose of my survival was to bear witness, to carry the tale. The thrill of spreading terror, of lurking in the night as bogeymen of legend, titillates them. They are beasts, horrid undreamt-of marvels."

"Gotta love those undreamt-of marvels."

"You couldn't understand. After their masters fed, Blaylock and Mrs. Cook made Christou and the others join bloody hands and dance. The corpses danced. In a circle, jostling like marionettes. And Blaylock and Mrs. Cook laughed and plucked the strings."

Agent Clack nodded and dragged on his cigarette, then rose and regarded Lancaster with a kindly expression. "Sure. You take care. My people will be in touch with your people and all that jazz."

"Oh, we won't meet again, Agent Clack. Christou is dead, ending that particular game. Gregor Blaylock and the rest are vanished into the woodwork. I've told the story and am thus expendable. Very soon. Very soon I'll be reclaimed."

"Don't worry, we're watching you. Anybody comes sniffing around, we'll nab 'em."

"I suppose I'm comforted."

"By the way," Agent Clack said. "Is anyone else staying here with you? When I came in to wait, I swore someone was in the bedroom, watching from the door. Thought it was you . . . Couldn't find anybody. Maybe they slipped away through the window, eh? Call me paranoid. We spooks are always worried about the baddies getting the drop on us."

"It wasn't me," Lancaster said. He turned and glanced at the bedroom doorway, the dimness within.

"Hah, didn't really think so. More oddness at the end of an odd day."

"Well, agent, whatever it was, I hope you don't see it again. Especially one of these nights when you're alone."

Agent Clack continued to gaze at the older man for several beats. He slipped the memory stick into his pocket and walked out. He didn't bother to close the door. The gap filled with white light that slowly downshifted to black.

He finished his vacation and returned to the States and cashed in his chips at Roache. No hassle, not even an exit interview. Despite the suddenness of Lancaster's departure, some of his colleagues scrambled to throw together an impromptu retirement party. He almost escaped before one of the secretaries lassoed him as he was sneaking out the back door.

He was ushered into a digital-age conference room with a huge table and comfortable chairs and a bay window overlooking downtown. The room shone in the streaming sunlight, every surface glowed and bloomed. His coworkers bore cheap gifts and there was a white layer cake and a bowl of punch. The dozen or so of them sang "For He's a Jolly Good Fellow" off-key. What dominated Lancaster's mind was the burble and boil of the water cooler, the drone of the inset lights. How the white frosting gleamed like an incisor. He caught his reflection in the shiny brass of a wall plate and beheld himself shrunken, emaciated, a leering devil. He averted his gaze, stared instead into the glare of the lowering sun. After the punch went dry and the songs were sung and the handshakes and empty pleasantries done with, he fled without looking back.

No one called, no one rang, and eventually Lancaster grew content in his final isolation. He allowed his apartment lease to lapse and went into the country and rented a room in a chintzy motel on the side of a less-traveled road. He stocked his closet with crates of liquor and cartons of cigarettes, and by day drank more or less continually in the yard of the motel beneath the gloomy shade of a big tree. By night he drank alone in the tavern and listened to an endless loop of rockabilly from the jukebox, the mutter and hum of provincial conversation among the locals. Cigarette smoke lay as heavy as that belched from a crematory stack. The bathroom reeked of piss. He always wore one of the seven nicer suits he'd kept from his collection. A suit for each day of the week. He thought of the lacquered black box stashed beneath his flimsy motel bed. His killing jar of the mind. So far he'd resisted the pleasure, the comfort, of handling its contents. Cold turkey was best, he thought.

He waited. Waited, lulled by the buzz of the neon advertisement in the taproom glass. Waited, idly observing barflies—gin-blossom noses, broken teeth, haggard and wasted flesh. A few women patronized the tavern, mostly soft, mostly ruined. Soft bellies, breasts, necks, bad mascara. Soft and sliding. Their soft necks stirred ancient feelings, but these subsided as *he*, in all meaningful ways, subsided.

Inevitably, one of the more vital female denizens joined him at his table in the murkiest corner of the room. They talked of inconsequentialities and danced the verbal dance. Her makeup could've been worse. Despite his weeks of self-imposed silence the old charm came readily. The deep-seated switch clicked on and sprang the lock of the cage of the sleeping beast.

Lancaster allowed her to lead him into the cool evening and

toward the rear of the building. He pressed her against the wall, empty parking lot at his back, empty fields, empty sky, and he took her, breathed in the tint of her frazzled peroxide-brittle hair, her boozy sweat, listened to the faint chime of her jewelry as he fucked her. She didn't make much noise, seemed to lose interest in him as their coupling progressed. He placed his hand on her throat, thumb lightly slotted between the joints of her windpipe. Her pulse beat, beat. Her face was pale, washed in the buzzing glow of a single security light at the corner of the eve. A moth battened against the mesh and cast raccoon shadows around the woman's eyes, masked her, dehumanized her, which suited his purpose. Except as his grip tightened his stomach rolled over, his insides realigning with the lateral pull of an intensifying gravitational force, as if he'd swallowed a hook and someone were reeling it in, toying with him.

They separated and Lancaster hesitated, slack and spent, pants unzipped. The woman smoothed her skirt, lighted a cigarette. She walked away as he stood hand to mouth, guts straining against their belt of muscle and suet. The pull receded, faded. He shook himself and retreated to the motel, his squalid burrow. The thermostat was damaged, its needle stuck too far to the right, and the room was sauna-hot, dim as a pit. He sat naked but for his briefs.

He picked up the phone on the second ring. Mr. Blaylock spoke through miles and miles of static. "You are a wild, strange fellow, Mr. Lancaster. Leave the world as a perfect mystery. Confound your watchdogs, your friends, the lovers who never knew you. All that's left is to disappear." Mr. Blaylock broke the connection.

The muted television drifted in and out of focus. Ice cracked as it melted in Lancaster's glass. The cherry glow of his cigarette flickered against the ceiling like firelight upon the ceiling of a cave. His cigarette slipped from his fingers and burned yet another hole in the carpet. He slept.

A single knock woke him. He waited for another until it became apparent none was forthcoming. He retrieved the box and placed it on the table, arrayed each item with a final reverent caress. Photographs, newspaper clippings, an earring, a charm bracelet. Something for those investigators to marvel at, to be amazed and horrified by what they'd never known regarding his secret nature. Then he went to the door, passed through, and stood on the concrete steps.

The tavern across the way was closed and black and the night's own blackness was interrupted by a scatter of stars, a veil of muddy light streaming from the manager's office.

The universe dilated within him, above him. Something like joy stirred in Lancaster's being, a sublime ecstasy born of terror. His heart felt as if it might burst, might leap from his chest. His cheeks were wet. Drops of blood glittered on his bare arms, the backs of his hands, his thighs, his feet. Black as the blackest pearls come undone from a string, the droplets lifted from him, drifted from him like a slow-motion comet tail, and floated toward the road, the fields. For the first time in an age he heard nothing but the night sounds of crickets, his own breath. His skull was quiet.

First at a trot, then an ungainly lope, Lancaster followed his blood into the great, hungry darkness.

About the Editor

Ellen Datlow has been editing science fiction, fantasy, and horror short fiction for more than twenty-five years. She was fiction editor of *OMNI* magazine and *Sci Fiction* and has edited more than seventy anthologies, including the horror half of the long-running *The Year's Best Fantasy and Horror,* the current *Best Horror of the Year, Inferno, Poe: 19 New Tales Inspired by Edgar Allan Poe, Darkness: Two Decades of Modern Horror, Tails of Wonder and Imagination: Cat Stories, Digital Domains: A Decade of Science Fiction & Fantasy, Naked City: Tales of Urban Fantasy, Supernatural Noir, The Beastly Bride: Tales of the Animal People, Teeth: Vampire Tales* (the latter two with Terri Windling), and *Haunted Legends* (with Nick Mamatas).

Forthcoming is *After* (with Terri Windling).

She's won multiple Locus, Hugo, Stoker, International Horror Guild, and World Fantasy Awards, as well as the Shirley Jackson Award, for her editing. She was named recipient of the 2007 Karl Edward Wagner Award, given at the British Fantasy Convention for "outstanding contribution to the genre." In 2010 she was given the Life Achievement Award by the Horror Writers Association.

She lives in New York City. More information can be found at www.datlow.com or at her blog: www.ellen-datlow.livejournal.com.